BEFORE VERSAILLES

Before the History You Know...
A Novel of Louis XIV

KARLEEN KOEN

sourcebooks
landmark

Copyright © 2012 by Karleen Koen
Cover and internal design © 2012 by Sourcebooks, Inc.
Cover image © Bridgeman Art Library

Sourcebooks and the colophon are registered trademarks of Sourcebooks, Inc.

Published by Sourcebooks Landmark, an imprint of Sourcebooks, Inc.
P.O. Box 4410, Naperville, Illinois 60567-4410
(630) 961-3900
Fax: (630) 961-2168
www.sourcebooks.com

Published by arrangement with Crown Publishers, an imprint of the Crown
Publishing Group, a division of Random House, Inc.

Originally published in 2011 by Crown Publishers, an imprint of the Crown
Publishing Group, a division of Random House, Inc.

Library of Congress Cataloging-in-Publication Data

Koen, Karleen.
  Before Versailles : a novel of Louis XIV / Karleen Koen.
    p. cm.
  (pbk. : alk. paper) 1. Louis XIV, King of France, 1638-1715--Fiction.
2. France--Kings and rulers--Fiction. 3. France--History--Louis XIV,
1643-1715--Fiction. I. Title.
  PS3561.O334B44 2012
  813'.54--dc23
                          2012021543

Printed and bound in the United States of America.
                 BG 10 9 8 7 6 5 4 3 2 1

For X
and
for Louise de la Vallière

Purge me with hyssop, and I shall be clean; wash me,
and I shall be whiter than snow.
Make me to hear joy and gladness; that the bones which thou hast
broken may rejoice.
Hide thy face from my sins, and blot out all mine iniquities.
Create in me a clean heart, O God…

—Psalms 51:7–10

CHARACTERS

$\mathcal{T}$HE ROYAL HOUSEHOLDS

Louis XIV: king of France from 1643 to 1715

Maria Teresa: queen of France; infanta or princess of Spain

Philippe: younger brother of Louis XIV, first prince of France; formerly Duke d'Anjou, now Duke d'Orléans; known as Monsieur at court

Henriette: Duchess d'Orléans, first princess of France; married to Prince Philippe; sister of Charles II, king of England; known as Madame at court

Guy-Armand de Gramont: Count de Guiche; friend of Prince Philippe; brother of Catherine; cousin of Péguilin

Catherine: Princess de Monaco, married to crown prince of Monaco; lady-in-waiting to Madame; sister of Guy-Armand de Gramont; cousin of Péguilin

Olympe: Countess de Soissons; superintendent of the queen's household; niece of Cardinal Mazarin

Athénaïs de Tonnay-Charente: maid of honor to the queen

*La Porte: valet to Louis XIV

Péguilin: friend and captain of the guards to Louis XIV; cousin of Catherine and Guy

Louise de la Baume le Blanc: maid of honor to Madame; cousin of François-Timoléon de Choisy; formerly in the household of the late Duke d'Orléans

*Fanny de Montalais: best friend of Louise de la Baume le Blanc; maid of honor to Madame

Anne: Queen Mother of France; former regent of France; mother of Louis XIV and Philippe; a princess of Spain

Madame de Motteville: lady-in-waiting to the Queen Mother

GOVERNMENT OFFICIALS

Cardinal Jules Mazarin: former first minister; deceased
Cardinal Richelieu: minister to Louis XIII; deceased
Viscount Nicolas: superintendent of finance
Jean-Baptiste Colbert: official in Louis XIV's government
Charles D'Artagnan: lieutenant of Louis XIV's musketeers
Marshall de Gramont: one of the officers of the crown; father of Guy-Armand and Catherine
Prince de Monaco: prince of a small nearby kingdom; ally of Louis XIV; his son, the crown prince, is married to Catherine

CHARACTERS IN COURT
AND AROUND PARIS

Madame de Choisy: noblewoman at court
François-Timoléon de Choisy: youngest son of Madame de Choisy; cousin of Louise de la Baume le Blanc
Marie, Duchess de Chevreuse: former lady-in-waiting to Queen Anne
La Grande Mademoiselle: an Orléans, one of the princesses of France; first cousin of Louis XIV
Molière: one of France's great playwrights and actors
La Voisin: a witch
Queen Henrietta Maria: widow of Charles I of England; mother of Henriette of France known as Madame and also of Charles II of England; daughter of Henri IV; aunt of Louis XIV

*fictional characters

PROLOGUE

Intelligent, virile, handsome, a man who made himself master of all he surveyed, Louis XIV was the foremost figure of his age. He was its prize, its comet, its star. His drive, cunning, and absolute determination to forge France into the premier kingdom of its time awed and frightened his fellow kings. None of them could match him. He supported the arts and literature so thoroughly that France became a cultural beacon that shines to this day, and by the time he died, every court in Europe copied the manners and fashion of his. The language of France became the language of art, of culture, of commerce, and of diplomacy for several hundred years. His palace at Versailles is a national monument and was one of the wonders of the world in its time.

From birth, war was his backdrop, and the nobility surrounding him as he grew to manhood was as proud as Lucifer and as trustworthy. The ambitions of others were always faintly in the distance or up close, naked, fangs gleaming. Louis possessed a consummate skill in turning those ambitions to his own advantage, and before he was thirty, he had become the hard, graceful, prowling lion of all of Europe.

There was a moment in his young life when he deliberately chose to grasp power. It was a moment when tenderness was still his—before time and pride closed him—a moment when his heart, like many a man's, yearned for something true. It happened in his forest palace of Fontainebleau. Perhaps it went something like this…

MARCH 1661,
FRANCE

A young woman galloped headlong and recklessly down half-wild trails in the immense forest of Fontainebleau. Her fair hair had come loose from its pins, and she leaned low against her horse's neck and whispered the filly onward, as if she were being chased by murderers. It was said she possessed magic with horses, and the groom attempting to follow behind her believed it. She was like a picture he'd seen once—of a centaur, a creature of mythology, half man, half horse. The only souls to hear the sound of thudding hooves were birds, rabbits, foxes, in burrows or hollow logs or nests of green moss and twigs, all of which stayed hidden, out of sight and harm. The forest around them was wild, huge, one of France's glories. For centuries, kings had hunted under its majestic and ancient trees. It was said to be filled still with forest spirits, shy, sly, summer-like sylphs who blended into the leaves that would unfurl soon and blessed or cursed the humans impinging on their malachite- and emerald-hued domain.

The horses galloped into a clearing in which a tree lay fallen. The young blond leaned forward in her sidesaddle and told her horse that the beast could do it, and the filly responded, sailing over the tree effortlessly. Afraid to take the dangerous jump, tired from their long gallop this day, the groom pulled hard on his reins, and the horse under him snorted and jerked its head and turned in circles, while the blond trotted her horse back to him. Her face was lovely, flushed, incandescent—the way it could be when she was this happy and carefree. Her name was Louise de la Baume le Blanc, and she was just on the cusp of ten and six, and she had no idea of it, but her life was about to change forever as certain stars finished their alignment.

"You ride better than a man, miss," said the groom.

"What a day we've had. So wonderful." She dropped the reins and put her hands to her hair, fallen from its many pins onto her shoulders.

"Ow-w-w," came a long, low yowl from the woods around them.

Startled, both Louise and the groom turned in their saddles. From between trees whose trunks were the size of Egyptian obelisks, a boy appeared. Waving his arms, breath growling rasps in his lungs, he howled like some demon in a church passion play.

The howls took their breath away, but so did what was upon the boy's face: an iron mask, its visage grim and terrible, with holes for sight and a raised impression for the nose. Dark hair fell through leather straps to cascade down the sides of the child's head. Only his mouth, where a string of slobber hung, was visible, and his continuing cries sent shivers down the spines of both Louise and the groom. He ran straight toward Louise, and her horse laid back its ears, reared, danced backward, and she fell.

From atop the other horse, the groom began to hit at the boy with a riding crop, lashing at thin arms and shoulders, and the boy staggered, holding up his hands to protect himself.

"Get away from here! Brigand! Thief! Murderer!" Circling around the boy, the groom hit him everywhere: soft neck, thin shoulders, long arms, bare hands. The boy howled louder and ran toward trees behind them. The groom jumped down from his saddle to Louise, who hadn't moved since her body hit the ground.

"Miss! Oh please, miss!" he cried.

Now others ran into the clearing. The groom cursed himself for letting her ride so far from the château. Were they in danger? What was happening? Who was this now? A band of thieves? Decent people pursuing a mad, nearly grown boy? What? Then he saw that one was a soldier, a musketeer, wearing the colors of the great and powerful Cardinal Mazarin, first minister to the king, dying now—all France knew it—power and wealth unable to stop that grimmest of cutthroats and thieves: death.

The musketeer, gaunt and fierce-faced, made a signal, and every man halted where he stood. The musketeer walked forward, his glance taking in both groom and the immobile young woman on the ground.

"Have you seen someone on foot? A boy, nearly grown?" he asked.

"Yes, he ran at our horses." The groom pointed toward the thick trees behind them. "He ran that way." And then in a pleading tone, "This young lady needs help. Is there a farmhouse near?"

The musketeer shouted orders, and at once the others ran off in the direction in which the groom had pointed.

"Who is he? What is his crime?" the groom asked.

The musketeer didn't answer, asked instead, "Did you come from the palace?" The royal palace of Fontainebleau was some miles distant.

The groom shook his head. "From Madame de Choisy's."

"You're not to speak of this to anyone." The musketeer's face had been beaten by weather and life to a flint-hard grimness. "I command it in the name of the cardinal. Do you know who he is?"

Who did not? Cardinal Mazarin had been virtual ruler of France for years.

The musketeer strode away, picking up his gait into a trot, already halfway across the clearing before the groom dared to open his mouth again. "Sir! Wait! I beg you. My lady is in distress—"

But the man was lost to the thickness of the woods. The groom looked down at Louise, and to his immense relief, her eyes were open.

"Can you sit up, miss?" he asked. "Your horse is gone. You'll have to ride mine. Move slowly and see if anything is broken. Is this the first time you've fallen from a horse, my lady?"

"No. Who was that soldier?"

"He did not say, my lady." The groom helped Louise to rise, brushed at leaves and dirt on her skirt. "He did say we were not to speak of this." Her conduct was, of course, not his concern. He could still see the musketeer's cold eyes. His own mouth was sealed. He was no fool.

"Obscene," said Louise, "that thing on his head, as if he were a monster instead of a man. Not even a man. A boy. What can he have done to deserve such a fate?" In her eyes were tears of distress and pity.

The groom held his hands so she could hoist herself into the saddle. Her legs were slim and colored blue by the stockings she wore. The sight of them—she had to ride astride now, as men did, rather than on a sidesaddle—softened him for a moment, as did the tears and her fresh prettiness. He decided to warn her again.

"The musketeer commanded silence, and his master is master of us all, the great cardinal," he repeated.

Reviled, feared, obeyed, Cardinal Mazarin was the most powerful man in the kingdom of France, first minister to the young king and lover, it was said, to the Queen Mother.

Louise didn't answer. She was a tenderhearted girl, too gentle really for the court she was about to join. But in her was an untested streak of sword's steel. One day, it would move her from the glamorous, wicked salons of court to an isolated nun's cell. It would keep her from going mad with grief at all that was no longer hers and bring her to a solace deeper than she could imagine, but that was years ahead, ten or more, a world away from this moment. This moment, this day, she was just a girl who—like all wellborn girls of the time—would blaze brightly a moment or two before she married, except that only the blazing was in Louise's stars. And it was just as well she didn't know it.

The half-wild, lanky boy in his iron mask was all she could think about on the ride back to the château where she was visiting. She couldn't wait to find her cousin, Choisy, to tell him what she'd seen. Leaving the groom in the château's stable, she walked through ornate halls and antechambers looking for her cousin, but he was not to be found. His mother was busy with guests in the grand salon.

"Women's virtue is man's greatest invention," she heard Madame de Choisy say to a burst of laughter. Madame de Choisy was one of those women who knew everyone and thrived on the whispers and webs of intrigue that were court life. The only way she had consented to leave Paris was to make certain a steady stream of visitors would journey out into the forest—in the middle of nowhere, she'd lamented, but my suppers will be worth it—to visit her. The Choisys were an important family in France, swirling around the throne like bees, and Louise felt fortunate that Madame de Choisy had taken such a liking to her. She peeped into the salon and saw guests gathered around their hostess, as always, enthralled and amused by whatever it was that she was saying—and she was always saying.

She had an opinion about everything and everyone, her family having been near kings and queens for generations. But she was so good-natured and so genuinely amused by life and its variables that no one minded. Certainly not Louise. There was a kind vibrancy about her that Louise found irresistible. Madame de Choisy's humor and laughing eyes were like balm, especially when contrasted to Louise's mother's tight, thin smile and tight, thin heart. Your mother's a merchant. As she had said those words, Madame de Choisy had held up a hand to stop any argument that might come from Louise. I hate to say it, she had continued, but it's true. Blue blood does not guarantee a noble heart. For her, all is transaction. Truth had shown its face then in such a blinding-flash-of-light kind of way that Louise hadn't been able to respond. She was wordless at this older woman's succinct summation of her mother's character. So that's what it's been, she'd thought to herself, transactions between us all this time. Of course.

In her bedchamber, Louise sat down on the stool in front of her dressing table, thinking about the boy. There were worse sights in Paris on any given day, weren't there? So she'd seen a mad, nearly grown boy escaped from his captors. It didn't have to affect her the way it had, as if someone had hit her on the heart. You're too touchy by far, my girl, she could just hear her mother say. Don't take your softness to court, her mother had warned. It won't do there. I certainly hope you are on your knees thanking the saints every night that you attracted Madame de Choisy's eye. She has launched you, my girl, in a way I could never have done.

It was true. At the end of this month, she would join the new Madame's household as a maid of honor, something so amazing she couldn't quite yet imagine it.

This new Madame—well, the fact was she wasn't Madame yet because she wasn't officially married—but anyway, she was a princess and would soon be the second most important woman in the kingdom because she was marrying the only brother of the king. Everyone was talking about it. That's what they'd been speaking of in the salon when Louise glanced in. Talking about how happy Monsieur—which is what the king's brother had to be called and thus his wife must be called Madame—was, saying how much in love he seemed.

It was as if some delightful spell has been cast over the court, said Madame de Choisy. Never has there been so much fun. An enchanting world is just ahead on the horizon, beckoning, smiling, promising things unnamed, things delightful and beguiling. And you, my Louise, shall be right in the middle of it, she'd said. Everyone must see your charming eyes, and Madame de Choisy had taken Louise's chin in one hand. Rings all over her fingers—she always wore all her rings; one must exhibit one's jewelry, she said; our jewels are our medals of valor; the tales I could tell— she had smiled at Louise, as excited as if she herself were going to court for the first time.

I should call my servant, thought Louise, the small mirror propped on the table before her showing her the tangle her hair was in, but she didn't want the company of another just now. So even though a lady wasn't supposed to do her own hair, so said Madame de Choisy, scandalized at Louise's self-reliant—and truth be told, rather shabby—upbringing, she began to search for any pins that might be left among her curls, concentrating as she did so on counting her blessings, as she'd been taught when troubled, so that the echo of the boy's yowls would still inside her.

Blessing one: She might have been stuck forever serving the whining Orléans princesses if not for dear Cousin Choisy. No more ennui. No more complaint. No more endless prayers and pulled-down faces and long days of nothing to do.

Blessing two: She was going to meet Monsieur, the younger brother of the king, great fun, promised Cousin Choisy, there is no one like him. A prince, a worthy child of France.

Blessing three: Cousin Choisy was fairly certain that the new Madame-to-be was nice. What would that be like? Kindness had not been a feature of the bitter household she'd left. Then, there again in her mind was a thought of the boy. It wasn't kind to put a boy in an iron mask. Why would anyone do so?

She brushed out her hair until it was vibrant with life and springing like a blond mane all around her head. He had howled like a wolf, like a ghost, like a banshee, sorrow and fear in the sound. She had had the sense that he was near her age. As she began to tame curls around her fingers, to bunch them so they would hang properly, she mulled over what she'd seen. Gangly. Perhaps in that awkward spurt of growth that came to boys somewhere around ten and four—

"Let me do that."

She leapt off the stool.

Her cousin, Choisy, closed the bedchamber door behind him.

She frowned. "You startled me."

He motioned for her to sit back down, selected a comb to his liking, and began to create the required long bunched ringlets for the other side of her face. "Your hair is so biddable. Mine always requires a curling iron," he complained.

It was the style for men to wear their hair long and flowing, but her cousin had his own style, to say the least. The truth was, it was his habit to dress as a woman. Right now, for example, he wore his mother's dressing gown and diamond earrings and rouge and beauty spots, those little bits of shaped velvet one pasted to the face. During Carnival—when everyone masked and wore costumes and went to party after party as a matter of course—Louise had watched him flirt with other men, none of them aware that the pretty young thing dressed in a low-cut gown and batting eyes behind a fan was a man. It's a game, he had told her, my particular game. A game his brother despised, which was why they were in the country for a while. There had been an escapade in Paris, something that had enraged his older brother, now head of the family, and his mother, who cosseted Choisy, had whisked him out of sight and reprimand, and had brought Louise along to keep him company. Besides, she'd said, I need to train you for court, my dear.

"You were gone a long time," he said, pouting at her. He was as pretty as she was. They'd compared faces in the mirror and agreed on that.

"I fell from my horse." And then the story spilled from her pell-mell: the wild gallop, the jump over the tree, the boy in the mask, its terrible simplicity hiding his face, his heartrending howls, the fall, her opening her eyes to see a musketeer, his strange command. A tear rolled down one of her cheeks as she finished.

Intrigued, Choisy pulled a chair forward, sat down so that they were knee to knee. "Describe the thing on his face again."

She did so.

"Like a disguise," Choisy said, "a mask made by demons. An iron mask. I love it, the boy in the iron mask. Are you sure he was a boy? Might he not have been a small man, like me? Look how slight I am. The man in the iron mask. Yes. That sounds better. More dashing. And the musketeer was wearing the cardinal's colors, you say?"

"Yes."

"Well then, my sweet, you really had best keep silent. It's a wonderful story, but I'd hate to see something happen to you just when you're on the threshold of your grand new life because you've been foolish enough to repeat it."

"What could happen?"

"You could disappear like that!" Choisy snapped his fingers. "Do you know what a *lettre de cachet* is?"

She didn't know. "A love letter?"

"It is a letter signed by the king that places a person in prison with no record of the arrest. A carriage appears outside your door. Musketeers drag you off, and it's over. You're never heard from again. Trust me, the cardinal has used it more than once."

Choisy would know things like this, thought Louise. His family had been up to its neck in all the intrigue and warfare between the king's mother and uncle. Not pretty on anybody's part, as Choisy liked to say, dismissing disloyalty with a shrug.

"And if you do disappear, don't you dare tell them you said a thing to me, or they'll take me away, too, and I'd die in prison like a flower plucked before its time."

He stood up and pantomimed being dragged off by guards, standing in his lonely cell, weeping silently, then he folded forward. "I was meant for the stage. Unfortunate that actors are cursed by the church." Still folded, he spoke to his knees, his long, dark hair sweeping the stone floor.

"I asked the fairies to bless him."

He straightened. "Who?"

"The boy in the iron mask."

"A word to the wise, country mouse. I wouldn't mention forest fairies when you join the new Madame's household."

Louise wished she hadn't mentioned them to him. "Because they'll laugh at me?"

"Far worse. They'll scorn you."

"Do you scorn me?"

"My darling cousin, I adore you." He stood in front of her, put his hands on her shoulders, and kissed the top of her head.

Louise felt confused. There was nothing feminine in the grip of his hands on her shoulders. Usually, he was soft and purring, but she didn't have that impression now.

"Your hair smells sweet," said Choisy, "as if it has been washed in clear spring water. You're so pure, so sweet and clean-hearted. I'm half in love with you—"

The door swung open.

"There you two are." Madame de Choisy walked in and didn't bat an eye at the sight of her son standing a little too close to Louise, still in his nightgown with her own embroidered and heavily laced dressing robe atop it, as well as her best earrings in his ears.

"Cardinal Mazarin is dead," she announced. "The Duchess d'Orléans has sent a letter by special messenger. We return to Paris tomorrow. You, my precious, are riding out this afternoon so that you can present our regards to the viscount tonight. Yes, I know your brother will do it, but he'll wait until everyone in Paris has been there before him, and he'll say the wrong thing." She rolled her eyes at Louise as if everyone knew what a fool the head of the family was. "I should never have left Paris, but I truly thought the cardinal would last longer. You are to present our regards with all the grace and polish imaginable. It is to be your finest performance. Change your clothes, my boy. At once."

She clapped her hands together, the way one would summon dogs or servants, and obediently, her favorite child left the bedchamber. She turned to Louise.

"We thought he'd live forever," she said. "Such changes ahead. And here you are about to join the new Madame's court where you'll be in the midst of everything. If I were your age, I would be half dead with excitement." She spoke affectionately.

"Will Monsieur's marriage be delayed because of the cardinal's death?" The thought of returning to serve in the household of the Orléans family again was too awful. She couldn't go back to being a piece of furniture, taken for granted and ignored, after the fun and liveliness and kindness of the Choisys.

"I very much doubt it. Monsieur's marriage is important for many reasons." Madame de Choisy reached out to caress Louise's cheek. "So," she said, "it's true."

"What is?"

"That your cheek has the texture of a rose petal, or so my Choisy says. Has my son told you he loves you yet?"

The question was casual, no heat or accusation in it, but almost cheerful.

"N-no." Unused to such directness, not wanting to make trouble for Choisy, yet not liking to lie, Louise stammered.

"You really must learn to lie more gracefully, my sweet. He is always falling in and out of love, so don't take what he says to heart." Madame de Choisy spoke as if they were discussing the weather or the merits of a horse rather than her adored and spoiled child. "And, of course, you must wait until you've been to court before you settle on anyone. And when you do, as all girls must, find someone with more fortune than my Choisy. He is the youngest son, you know."

Louise could think of nothing to say to this worldly, kind, amusing woman. No one older had talked to her in this manner before with such unarmed frankness, laughter in its corners.

"What lovely eyes you have, child! A man could fall into them. Those naughty boys at court will do so, bad things that they are. What fun. I do so like bad boys. Now come here and give me a hug so I know I'm forgiven for my lecturing. It's the cardinal's death that's made me so dreary. We all knew it would come, and yet, now that it's here, it is unimaginable."

Absently, she stroked the curve of Louise's arm, not bothering to tell her what the kingdom owed the man now gone. The young never cared about the past, did they? she thought, looking past Louise to a window, not to its view, but to all that had been. The young saw only this moment, she thought. The cardinal's presence had been controversial, wars fought more than once because of it, but he'd kept the kingdom cobbled together for France's young king. And now he was vanquished. All his diamonds, all his tapestries, all his statues from Rome, his palaces and musketeers and affectations, couldn't keep the dark angel away. So it was now and forever, amen. How grieved the royal family must be.

❦

Choisy, whose full name was François-Timoléon de Choisy, ran upstairs, Louise's tale of boys and iron masks forgotten. Born to privilege, he belonged to the cream of the nobility and was as attuned in his own way to the nuances of court as his mother was.

The world as we know it is ending, he thought, initial excitement and surprise turning to elation as possibilities unfolded one after another in his mind. The cardinal was dead. Amazing. For Choisy's entire life, the cardinal had been alive and in power either directly or indirectly. But there was more than that in his jubilance. For the first time in years, France was in the hands of the young. Did anyone but Choisy comprehend that? The king was only twenty and two. Monsieur, the king's brother, was twenty. They were young and mettlesome and high-spirited, as he was. He'd ask Monsieur for a place on one of the king's councils. Why not drop a young man who liked to wear earrings among the old graybeards? It would liven things up. Off with the old, on with the new.

Once he was on horseback, gown gone, diamonds glittering sedately— for him—here and there among his clothing, he told his mother and Louise his intention, and his mother nearly snapped his head off.

"Ask the viscount, my Choisy, not Monsieur! Have you lost your senses? Now, be your most silver-tongued, my angel, your most charming. Even if you have to wait in an antechamber for hours, see the viscount tonight if possible. And call upon the Queen Mother and tell her I return tomorrow and that I send her my deepest condolences."

As the sight of Choisy and his horse faded into the distance, Louise and Madame de Choisy turned to walk back, their heels crunching in the gravel of garden paths, birds filling the country silence with a sunset song, the château looming large and grand before them, forest just beyond its gates.

"Does he call upon the Viscount Nicolas?" asked Louise.

"Who else? There is none other who matters!" Madame de Choisy sounded scandalized, and Louise lowered her head in embarrassment as Madame de Choisy stopped right where she was and looked Louise over. "Mother of God, tell me you're not completely ignorant. Did the Orléans never talk of court?"

The family her stepfather served, this princely house of Orléans, talked of how they'd been wronged over and over again. "I didn't pay much attention, I'm afraid."

"The Orléans's great stalk of a princess could have been the queen of France, you know, only she fired a cannon at His Majesty during one of the misunderstandings. I'm appalled that your mother has not prepared you for the court you will grace."

Misunderstandings? Louise was shocked in her turn by Madame de Choisy's blithe description of what had been civil wars. This stalk, as Madame de Choisy called her, was the king's first cousin who had taken up arms against him. So many of the king's family had done so. It's the history of our kingdom, her mother said, but it was a history of disloyalty that Louise didn't understand.

"Was the exile hard for you?" No longer scolding, Madame de Choisy's expression had shifted from dismay to soft pity, both of which were uncomfortable to Louise.

"You forget I was born in the country. I knew no other life until we came to Paris," she answered.

"You've been in Paris nearly a year," countered Madame de Choisy. "Surely that's given you some sense of court."

Some sense of court? thought Louise. How? The widowed Duchess d'Orléans must mourn by shutting herself away in the Paris family palace, where she must have endless headaches and need her head bathed in lavender essence and be read to and be irritable if the reader became tired, be angry if there were too much laughter or talk. Louise's life had gone from the freedom of the country, where escape was easy—she might ride wherever she liked, for almost as long as she liked—to a cage bound by the four walls of a Paris palace garden. She knew all the world was just across the river at the palace of the Louvre, where His Majesty lived, from which word came of fêtes and parties and dancing and marriage arrangements. The king and his new queen were all that were talked of. To hear of their comings and goings, to be so close and yet so far, had been hard. If Madame de Choisy—well, really Choisy; it was he who had taken an immediate liking to her—had not lifted her out of the purgatory she endured, she didn't know what she would have done. Strange and very wonderful not to endure anymore, Louise thought, and some of the strain that had played across her face eased. Please, she thought to herself, may my good fortune continue.

"What a dear you are," said Madame de Choisy, who had missed none of the various emotions playing across Louise's face, "not to complain. I find the Duchess d' Orléans quite difficult, and as for those daughters of hers—well! I see you're loyal. Not a word against them has escaped your lips. I commend you upon that; such loyal silence will make you a rarity at court, which I must explain to you—otherwise I will be dropping a lamb among lions, and that will never do."

Talking all the while about past intricacies of the court to which Louise was going: the Queen Mother's widowhood, the cardinal's rise, the fact that he had been the Queen Mother's secret lover, Madame de Choisy swept Louise into a exquisitely appointed little antechamber with bowls of flowers and huge tapestries covering the walls and settled her into a chair as if she were an invalid. Her kind briskness touched Louise to the heart, and she almost couldn't listen to everything Madame de Choisy was attempting to make certain she understood.

"You must upon all occasions be polite to him," Madame de Choisy was saying of the Viscount Nicolas. "Cardinal Mazarin, God rest his soul, was His Majesty's foremost minister, and now it is the viscount's turn. The man is handsome and well enough born and has an eye for art and an ear for music and an ability to conjure funds when there are none, all a first minister should be."

"Does His Majesty desire the viscount as his first minister?"

The sharp precision of that question made Madame de Choisy widen her eyes. "My word, does a mind reside amid all this dewy-eyed beauty I see before me? You surprise me, child. I think he has no choice."

"But he is the king!"

Genuinely amused, Madame de Choisy laughed. "Your innocence is most charming, but such does not thrive at court. His Majesty is not an innocent and is wise enough to do what must be done. I'm certain, therefore, the viscount will be first minister. None of us can get along without him, you know."

Louise sat up very straight, her clear eyes suddenly brilliant. "I saw His Majesty once, when he stopped at Blois." The moody face under its great hat was unforgettable.

"I'd forgotten His Majesty made a visit to the old duke. That was when the world and he traveled to Spain for the royal wedding, wasn't it? So you saw the one and only, did you?"

"Yes." It had been the absolute romance of the kingdom, the royal wedding last summer. All the nobility had traveled to see it, one huge, merry entourage, but of course, that did not include the presence of the king's once rebellious, once very dangerous uncle, the Duke d'Orléans, or his household or, therefore, Louise.

"And?"

Louise began to blush, not some slight flattering coloring of cheeks, but a deep hue that stained her neck and shoulders in splotches, as well as her face. "He's very handsome, very gallant."

"Isn't he though? So, will you flirt with him at court? You'll see him there, you know, quite often."

The terrible staining blush deepened. "He—he is married. It would not be proper."

"Oh...are you going to be proper?"

There was a silence.

Madame de Choisy threw up her hands, the jewels on her rings catching sunlight. "Don't tell me I've selected a secret Huguenot or worse, a devotée—yes, you know them, don't you? Dry, somber, pruned-up Catholics, not an ounce of fun anywhere. And you going to serve in what I predict will be the most exciting household in court!"

"I will try, of course, to be proper, but I am—" Louise didn't know the words, but a lovely smile spread across her face in excitement at all that awaited her. The smile was more than lovely; it was incandescent and glowing.

"Charming? Adorable? Fallible?" Madame de Choisy leaned across and pinched her cheek. "And quite extraordinarily beautiful when you smile that way. You take my breath away. I see why Choisy flirts so. You are going to grace Madame's court and make all the gentlemen swoon, and everyone is going to say to me, where did you find her, my dear? A hidden jewel, that's what she is, they'll say. That's what you've been, haven't you? A shining little diamond hidden under the dreariness of the Orléans. Poor dear. Well, what fun you're going to have now! Ah, to be twenty again. Thirty...Mother of God, I'd take forty! Come, my sweet, let's have an early supper, and I'll tell you all I know about our very handsome king of France."

"I would like that!"

"So would I!" Madame de Choisy's infectious laughter pealed out like the clap of bells into the little antechamber, while the sweet light of a cold spring afternoon spilled in to highlight all the beautiful objects placed here and there, to highlight Madame de Choisy with her rings and fashionable gown and lively gestures and love of life, and Louise thought, I can never go back. Never.

❧

A few hours later, in a handsome château just on the outskirts of Paris, Choisy sat with one or two others in the Viscount Nicolas's antechamber. It was late, and most people had gone away to supper and cards, but Choisy waited, as he'd been ordered by his mother.

"Everyone who is anyone has already been here," said a young nobleman waiting with Choisy. "You should have seen the crowd earlier. Do you know what they're saying?" continued the young man. He and Choisy knew each other well, were members of the king's brother's circle of friends. "They're saying the king summoned his principal ministers today to tell them he would have no more first ministers, that he would oversee the details of the running of his kingdom himself."

He raised an eyebrow in disdain, then laughed. Choisy joined him. It was a ridiculous gesture on the king's part. Overseeing the details of a kingdom was tedious. It was why courtiers were invented, to run the kingdom for a king.

"The Prince de Condé has already sent a message to the viscount, I'm told."

"Well..." said Choisy. What a delicious piece of gossip. Condé was a formidable prince who'd warred against the king and his mother.

One half of a set of huge doors opened, and Choisy's name was called. He stood, shook out his hair and the long lace hanging from his sleeves, and smiled significantly at his friend. Even though the other had been waiting longer, Choisy had been admitted first, a testament to the power and high birth of his family.

He walked into a chamber as beautiful as a king's—thickest velvet draperies, embroidered chairs, armoires of wood patterned with ormolu and filigree, paintings by the finest artists in the world, solid silver candlesticks the size of boys—and bowed to the figure sitting in a chair, awaiting him. The viscount held out his hand, and Choisy knelt, as if the man were a bishop of the church, and made a kissing sound above the slim, white fingers, one of which wore a giant emerald set in a ring.

"I'm not the Holy Father," protested the viscount, but he smiled, and Choisy knew he had pleased.

That was good. This man was the only man with the wealth and connection and verve to step into the enormous space the cardinal's death had just created, and so Choisy began the game of court, making certain one's family was allied with those most influential and powerful, and if that wasn't possible, making war.

MAY 1661

ROYAL PALACE
OF FONTAINEBLEAU...

CHAPTER 1

Rapier blades hissed through the air and made zinging sounds when they met one another. The king of France and his brother were both winded, but neither would admit it. They circled each other, and their dueling master thought to himself, thank the merciful mother of Christ there are buttons on the rapiers, or one of them would be bleeding.

Prince Philippe, the younger of the two, stepped back, and Louis, seeing an opening, lunged forward, but Philippe brought his blade singing in under Louis's arm and into the soft center of the armpit, a deadly accurate gesture that disabled or killed an opponent.

"Done," cried the dueling master. "His Highness Monsieur wins."

Louis jerked his head at the dueling master's decision, and the man closed his eyes and swallowed. His Majesty's temper was even, but that did not mean he didn't possess one.

"I won! I won!" Philippe danced around his older brother, waving his rapier and crowing like a rooster, leaping in and out of intricate dance steps they all loved, making the watching circle of friends break into laughter, making Louis himself laugh.

"Say it." Philippe circled this older brother, this first child of France, this keeper of the faith, this defender of the kingdom, this first of all kings on earth, chosen and appointed by Heaven to extend far and wide the honor and renown of the Lily, this heir to the great Charlemagne, he who had been king of the Franks and first sovereign of the Christian empire of the west. "Let me hear you say it, majesty, I won."

Louis reached out and pulled the long, dark, curling hair that was his brother's glory, as thick and beautiful as any woman's at court.

"Ow!" Philippe yelped, his mocking dance effectively stopped, and those watching laughed louder.

"You won."

"Let go!"

Louis did as commanded, faced his brother, grabbed his shoulders, kissed each of his cheeks hard, and said, "You won this time," making the "this time" both a threat and an insinuation.

Philippe grinned, stepped back to bow, and strutted over to the watching courtiers, all men he and his brother had grown up with—Vardes, Vivonne, Brienne, Guiche, Péguilin, Marsillac, and others, the pride of the kingdom, these young men, some princes in their own right or sons of dukes, counts, marquises, the best France had to offer of her ancient nobility, her warrior class who defended her boundaries and then warred among themselves if bored. Like Philippe and Louis, they all wore their hair long, flowing, thick to their shoulders or past it. It was the fashion. They wore lace and voluminous shirts and wide, short breeches that showed off their calves, calves they encased in stockings of colored silk. A man was judged as much by the shape of his legs and the way he danced as by his valor on the battlefield. Philippe had set the style for a higher-heeled shoe, with a crimson heel, and every one of them wore those, stiff bows at the front. Knots of ribbons set off shoulders or garters or hatbands.

They were peacocks, all of them, their virility on display in a proud show of fashion and bravado. They drank too much wine, were unfaithful whether married or not, gambled as if their pockets had no bottom, and looked for the slightest affront to their pride. They were rowdy, raucous, witty, and dazzling. There wasn't a woman around, young or old, whose heart didn't flutter the minute they came into view. There wasn't a woman around, young or old, who didn't wish to be noticed by them. And at their center was their gallant and grave young king, only two months into his solitary reign without his adviser, the cardinal—a king who'd asked none of them to join his councils yet, and they were waiting. They'd grown up with war, within and without the kingdom. They'd seen parents, uncles, aunts without remorse betray the king's father; then his mother, the queen regent and her chief minister; the cardinal, afterward gracefully bowing to whoever was victorious. Off their leashes, they were as dangerous as wolves, as heedless, as ruthless, as ravenous.

"Another, Your Majesty?"

The dueling master knew his king well enough to know he wouldn't be satisfied until he had won, and sure enough, Louis nodded his head and pointed to the captain of his household guard. The man, short and homely with frizzy hair that stood out from his head like a halo, leapt down several steep steps—they stood in a palace courtyard famous for broad, even exterior steps that led to another level. The man pulled off the tight bolero jacket he wore and threw it to the ground in a dramatic gesture. He bowed to Louis and took a rapier from the dueling master.

"En garde." Louis spoke softly. He was tired, but he knew this man well. An impetuous, impatient duelist who would soon become bored with Louis's steadiness and make a flamboyant gesture that would give Louis the opening he needed. And he needed only one.

They were dueling in what was called the fountain courtyard, bordered on three sides by buildings and on the fourth by a large pond. The palace of Fontainebleau had become a favorite royal residence of French kings in the 1500s, in the time of François I, Louis's ancestor. François had been an avid collector, and so the palace was filled with paintings, sculpture, objets d'art, and books, to which heirs to the throne had made wise and wonderful additions. Various kings and a strong queen or two had built wings and pavilions here and there, even a moat, so that the palace was sprawling and irregular, like a starfish with arms lopped off and new growth meandering off the nubs. But it had been decorated by the finest Italian and then French artists of the Renaissance, who had made it everywhere pleasing and often splendid.

One of its allures was that it sat in the forest. French kings and queens were passionate hunters—Louis was no exception—and forest encircled the palace and could be seen from turrets or second-floor balconies. There was a bit of a village nestled to one side, there to serve the palace and house courtiers, but one good gallop past clearings and outcroppings of rocks and boulders, and a man pulled the reins short to breathe in nature's leafy, verdant, abundant aroma, while his eyes rested on stands of trees as ancient as the kingdom itself. In the summer the sky usually spread azure hues above majestic branches.

This May morning, that sky was clear of clouds and promised yet another beautiful day. Watching His Majesty duel, courtiers who were ranged up and down the famous outside staircase, steep, severe, straight-ramped. They lounged, these friends and members of Louis's household, at their ease, as if it were their birthright—and it was—to observe majesty. Some leaned over the stone balustrade of the staircase; some sat on its dangerous downward angle. They were deliberate and daring, full of jokes and humor, quick to spot and mock any flaw in accepted behavior, equally as quick to compliment and copy exceptional grace. High-spirited, polished, witty, they were dashing and devil-may-care and dangerous.

Philippe walked upstairs to stand beside his best friend and watch the next duel and, as was his habit, to talk.

"Did you see that? Can you believe it? I won. I outlasted him. He didn't think I would. He was counting on my tiring out. Ha. I have you to thank. And I do." It was seldom that Philippe bested Louis at anything.

His friend, the son of a marshall of France—a marshall being one of the great officers of the crown, a distinct and unique honor—had been tutoring him, dueling with him every afternoon, forcing Philippe to sharpen his mind and his body, lecturing him all the while: You give up too easily. You're stronger than you realize. You need to force the issue about the rest of your inheritance. You need to insist you be given a place on his council. It's your right as a prince of France. Yes, lecturing him both about dueling and about the skill required to be a presence at court. Philippe was many things, lively, gregarious, generous, laughing, a raconteur; but he'd been overshadowed by Louis all his life, and this friend was determined he should be honored as befitted the second child of France, heir to the throne until Louis sired a child—which of course, Louis being Louis, he had done, except the child wasn't born yet, and in this year of 1661 many things could happen.

"Let me reward you. What do you wish, my friend?" Philippe was extremely pleased with himself, with having beaten the sacred, the semiholy, the one and only Louis in a duel. "Anything. An orange tree. A silver box. A jade vase—"

"A walk with your wife in tonight's twilight before His Majesty stakes his claim."

"Done. That will irritate him, won't it? I've bested him there, too."

"Indeed you have, Monsieur."

And then his friend, noble and privileged, arrogant and self-sufficient, this son of a duke and marshall of France, bowed and walked down the broad stone steps, weaving in and out of men, leaving without waiting for the king's dismissal, or Philippe's, for that matter.

Several of the young men on the steps watched his exit, half admiring, half scorning his haughtiness. Since the death of the cardinal, His Majesty the king seemed to notice deference, or the lack of it, more than he had previously. Some of the bolder among them grumbled that Louis might as well put his royal seal on their backsides, as if they were cattle. But others said, no, it was His Majesty's due. He was their king. The civil wars in which they'd all grown to manhood had soiled the concept of loyalty.

Philippe's eyes followed his friend until the young man was across the courtyard and walking through an arch, out of sight, and Philippe's intent expression wasn't missed either.

"I thought Monsieur was supposed to be madly in love with his new wife," said one of the young noblemen, a suggestive arch in his eyebrow.

"Some things never change—"

"Be quiet," another interrupted. "You're missing the show. His Majesty is shaving the lace off Péguilin's shirt stitch by stitch. You'd think he'd be too tired."

In a sudden burst of fresh stamina, his blade slashing and hissing and seeming to be everywhere at once, Louis had driven his captain backward into a defensive posture. Péguilin defended himself valiantly, but then he stumbled over an uneven stone in the courtyard and fell, and before he could gather his wits, Louis was standing over him, the rapier's buttoned tip at his heart.

"Sire, I give up!" he shouted, alarmed at the expression on the king's face.

Louis smiled, grimness wiped away as if by magic. He brought the rapier to his forehead in a quick gesture of respect and held out his hand to help his friend from the ground.

"Clumsy idiot, Péguilin!" came a shout from among the watchers. "I had a *louis* on you." A *louis* was a gold coin, named, of course, for the man whose image graced its sides.

"More fool you!" Péguilin shouted back. He dusted himself off. "You'd have had me whether I fell or not," he said to Louis, and their eyes met in that way men display when they've had a good, clean fight, and each honors the other for the valor shown. Louis grinned.

Sacred Christ, I'm an ugly fellow, Péguilin thought. The king, by contrast, was tall and lean, his face a little like a hawk's, same flickering eyes, same slight and hard edge to the mouth.

Louis's early morning exercise ended now. Except for himself and those friends who chose to wake early, and of course servants, the palace was still asleep. It would rise for Mass, closer to the noon hour, when courtiers would run from one royal set of apartments to the next: the king's, Monsieur's, the Queen Mother's, the young queen's. Each household was a nest of servants and ladies or gentlemen in waiting, and courtiers dropped in to be both courteous and practical. Where would that particular household gather in the afternoon? Who had the most interesting plans? Walking at the end of which entourage brought the most advantage?

But now, in this early quiet, a courtier leapt over the balustrade to pick up the king's jacket from the ground, while Philippe took the linen with which his brother would dry his perspiring face and neck. He held out his hand for Louis's jacket. That, too, was his right—to hand it directly to the man who was the king of France and Navarre.

Etiquette was ancient at this court—who might do what was the product of several hundred years and one's birth—and since Cardinal Mazarin had died, it seemed to have sharpened. Courtiers noticed the king's slight frown over those who had the privileges of not showing up to wait upon him. This was the beginning of a reign, so to speak, and there were councils and offices and honors waiting to be plundered, and since there hadn't been a reign in a hundred years that hadn't produced a favorite and the plunder that came with that, word had spread: His Majesty liked tradition upheld. The ambitious packed around him.

"Sire," said one of Louis's gentlemen, "I've been given word that Her Majesty is awake."

"Early bird," chirped Philippe, not noticing the hooding of his brother's eyes, as if a mask had dropped suddenly into place. "Madame never rises before noon." He was proud of his wife, bragging about her, pleased at the impact she was making at court.

"Madame" was the official title of Philippe's new wife; they weren't even married two full months. It had been a very quiet affair because of the cardinal's death, little more than family signing the required documents and a priest saying the proper prayers. With that, she had become the second lady at court after Louis's queen, except the truth was the royal brothers' mother was still a commanding figure, so perhaps Madame was really third. It depended upon the Queen Mother's mood any particular day. At the moment their mother was in deep mourning for the cardinal, clutching her grief to herself like a holy relic.

Of course Madame sleeps until noon, thought Louis, not a shard of what he was thinking showing on his face. She has danced all night, she has laughed and delighted us and kept us up with her, unlike my wife, who is yawning by ten of the evening, who hasn't learned French after nearly a year, and who thinks dressing well is putting on more diamonds. Last night he'd come very close to kissing—

He stopped himself. This was a line of thought that led to no good whatsoever. He rubbed his face vigorously on the linen, took his jacket from his brother, accepted his hat from someone else, climbed the steep outside steps two at a time, going into the door at their end, a door which led to that part of the palace where his bedchamber lay.

As in a beehive, where the most important chamber is the queen bee's, so, in royal palaces, the most important room was the king's bedchamber. It was the pulsing heart of the palace. When the king journeyed to another of his castles, the pulse ceased to beat. Those left behind kept chambers cleaned and gardens weeded and waited for the next royal arrival. Those who had any standing traveled with the heart. For the nobility, there was no life that was real life without the king's presence, or so it had been, once upon a time. The wars, the power of royal advisers, first Cardinal Richelieu and then Cardinal Mazarin after him, had shifted and diluted the sense of importance around a king, but the shape of tradition remained. Whether or not the tradition strengthened would be up to Louis.

As he passed through his guardroom, musketeers who were his personal bodyguard stood up at the sight of him and saluted. Their lieutenant had been leaning against a smooth stone wall in the courtyard during the dueling watching not only Louis, but also the great, arched, open entrances from other pavilions. If there was one thing a king of France could depend upon, it was the loyalty of these musketeers. It was their tradition and a prized one.

As Louis walked through the maze of chambers that made up this part of the palace, servants bowed. There was always someone bowing. One creaking step on the intricate parquet of an antechamber, and the massive doors to his wife's apartments opened as if by magic. Two of her ladies, a sullen brunette and a sunny-faced beauty, stood in his path, their gowns belled around them because of their curtsies.

"Soissons, my dear." Louis nodded to the brunette of the two, an old friend of his, a childhood playmate, and sometimes more, Olympe, the Countess de Soissons. "How is Her Majesty this morning?"

But the sunny beauty answered before Olympe could speak. "She slept very well, sire." The beauty was pert and certain of herself and smiled at Louis.

Surprised, Louis looked directly at her. Her smile widened. He didn't return it. He didn't like her, never mind that his friends considered her the most beautiful woman at court. He'd give her that. But she put him on edge, always smiling that bright smile, always watching. And she was bold, like now, speaking to him before he'd spoken to her, answering for the Countess de Soissons, who was superintendent of his wife's household, which made her first lady of the household and far more important than a maid of honor. He'd known Olympe since they were children, and he had loved the man who'd brought her and her sisters to court as if he were his own father.

The beauty always made him want to stutter. He didn't have a true stutter, just a slight stalling of words that he had conquered during childhood through sheer willpower. It unnerved him when he felt it in his throat, swelling his tongue. Those around him would laugh, as they'd done when he was a child, and the laughter hadn't been kind. A king couldn't afford to be laughed at. It had been part of his father's downfall, his nervous, limping, coughing father, who twitched when he was upset and stammered spit when he was angry and trusted no one and loved only brightly, briefly, and very dangerously. Somehow those whom his father had loved ended up dead—his father had always believed they'd betrayed him in the end.

Had they? What was betrayal and what was simple human error and what was suspicion sickened to insanity, coloring even good with its darkness?

"She's up early," he said to Olympe, ignoring the beaming beauty, who lost some of her shimmer. But the young men following Louis smiled and nodded at her, showing their approval in every way save stomping their feet, so it didn't take long for her to brighten back to full power.

Louis walked with Olympe through several other rooms, high ceilings, huge fireplaces, intricate woodwork and molding and inlay, thick rugs, big tapestries on the walls, until finally they were in the queen's bedchamber, the ornate and curtained bed at one end. It was the fashion to have a series of rooms called antechambers that led to the bedchamber, and even the bedchamber wasn't private. For strict privacy, a person of high birth had to retreat to a room called a closet, where, finally, he or she might be alone. Just as there were layers of chambers between him and his wife, there were layers of people, and, at this moment, he was glad of it.

"So, she slept well?" he asked as they walked through the antechambers, and women fell into curtsies wherever his glance moved. I do care about her, he thought. I do.

"I don't think so, and she woke irritable. However, the Viscount Nicolas's gift cheered her."

"The viscount sent a gift?"

"You know how generous he is, sire."

"Does that mean you received a gift also?" Louis was ironic.

Naughty dimples appeared in Olympe's cheeks. That and her sullenness had kept more than one man awake at night. "Ask me no questions, and I'll tell you no lies."

Louis pinched her arm. "You will. You always have."

Olympe winked at him, and Louis's queen, sitting up in her bed, excited as she always was that Louis was visiting her, gave a little sigh. Some of the radiant happiness faded from her square, rather fleshy face, but no one noticed. All eyes were on the king, on Olympe. There were wicked rumors about the two of them, but the queen didn't know of them. Surrounded by a soft bubble of privilege and royalty and lack of speaking French, she was the last to learn of any scandal. Her jealousy was more instinctive. The king was so lean, so grave, so dark-eyed, so kind, that it was impossible not to see other women's notice of him, and this wasn't Spain, where young noblewomen were kept in strict seclusion until their marriages and where even after their marriages they were kept cloistered with other women. This was France, where women were quite amazingly—to her eyes—quite extraordinarily bold. And no one here seemed to mind it.

Dwarves she'd brought with her from her home saw the hurt that moved over her face before she gathered back all of her smile. The dwarves served as her jesters and soothers. Philippe couldn't stand them, but Louis was more tolerant. His and Philippe's mother was fond of dwarves. They were a reminder of the strange and intricate and still medieval court both women had left behind forever when they married and journeyed to France. Maria Teresa, who had been the foremost princess of the foremost kingdom of Europe and was now queen of France, was lonely for her native Spain, lonely for the majestic and glacial ritual she'd left behind, lonely for the manners and way of life, so different from here. Unlike her mother-in-law, she was having a hard time embracing that which was French.

Louis bent down and kissed her on the mouth. He was strict about who might kiss her, allowing only his mother and brother, and now, his new sister-in-law, to do so. It wasn't from jealousy, but from his sense of pride. This was a princess of Spain, most powerful kingdom in the western world, fat with a hundred years of riches from her colonies across the sea. There was no one higher born than she. She is such an important princess that if she doesn't marry you, she has to marry Christ and take the veil, his dear cardinal had joked with him. You're the only one of her stature. You're the only one worthy. Louis's mother was a Spanish princess, too, aunt to his wife, and she'd planned this marriage when he and Maria Teresa were in their cradles.

France and Spain had been at war for a long time, and this marriage had secured a peace, a peace his dear cardinal had killed himself working toward. For forty-one years, there had been war at some border of France. Take her and defang a faltering Spain. Take her and be the lion of the west. France will supersede Spain. I know it. I feel it. And Mazarin had smiled as he spoke, eyes crinkled in his lively face, a face that was too thin, a face that Louis had seen all his life, literally. One of his first memories was of Mazarin leaning over his baby bed, something loving, something safe radiating from his eyes. He was the handsomest man in the world when he came to court, his mother's favorite lady-in-waiting liked to gossip. When we first saw him, we all swooned, and even your mother noticed.

Louis's kiss opened Maria Teresa the way a knife does a ripe melon. She looked almost pretty, a light flush on her alabaster cheeks.

"I'm so glad to see you, dear heart. I had a bad dream, my husband. I can't remember it now, but I didn't like it. It has made me sad. Cats were in it, I think. Stealing my breath. Was it an omen? About dying in childbed?"

Louis sat down on bed covers whose embroidery was so thick that the color of the fabric upon which it was sewn could barely be seen. He took her hands in his, listening thoughtfully, as she continued on, in Spanish, of course.

"I might, you know. Anyway, I just lay here for a while and I thought about my bedchamber at the Alcázar, the vines that grew there in the summer, covering the iron on the balcony. I always smelled them when I woke up, and their smell made me happy. And their color. 'Cup of gold' they're called because they are shaped like a chalice, like the Lord's chalice at the Last Supper. And then the viscount's little gift arrived. Do look, dear heart. It's a fan."

She spread it open for Louis to see the scene painted across it.

"It's the Alcázar! It's just what I needed. Some reminder of home, and so I've been fanning myself with it and thinking perhaps I might not eat breakfast. I'm not hungry, you know, which is strange for me. A fever, do you think I might be coming down with a summer fever?"

Louis put his hand on her forehead. "No, sweet, there's no fever."

She sighed. Several of the maids of honor sighed too, imagining his touch.

"No fever, dear one," said Louis, "and as for home, this is your home now. You are France's queen, and I must have you by my side, and our son is not going to cause any trouble. He is going to pop out like a bean from a pod and say, 'Mama, Papa, where is my milk?' And we're going to find the strongest, fattest, cleanest wet nurse in France to feed him. Maybe we'll even send for a Spanish one. Would you like that? A fat Spaniard to feed him when our French one tires?"

All the time he was talking, answering her in Spanish because it comforted her, there was a distant part of him observing, thinking, she should be speaking French, she should be attempting more, I need her to try harder. And as he spoke, he opened and closed the fan slowly, taking in the scene of this palace in Spain, taking in at some level he was not yet ready to allow emotion into, that the Viscount Nicolas reached here, even to his wife's household.

"And our little French *dauphin*"—the first son of the king was called the *dauphin* because three hundred years earlier a king of France had purchased huge territories that carried a hereditary title, taken from the dolphin on the coat of arms—"is going to teach you French." Pray let someone do so, he thought.

He went on, nothing of what he was thinking showing on his face. He'd learned that early, not to show what he felt if possible. "You're going to learn it as he does, aren't you, my sweet? How happy I will be when I hear you speak French well."

He stroked her hair, wiry with curl, a light brown. The first time he'd seen her he'd been shocked that the portrait of her sent to him lied. Her face was long, her cheeks fleshy, her nose, well, large. But he'd swallowed a quick flash of dismay and concentrated on duty and honor and the fact that she was the greatest pearl among princesses.

"Our little *dauphin* isn't going to cause his mother a bit of trouble." Louis leaned forward and kissed the embroidered bedcovers under which lay his wife's abdomen and the bud who was their child. "My precious son. This is your father. Grow strong, my boy, my prince, my *dauphin*. Grow strong, and then come out to greet me. I'm waiting for you."

Several hearts in the bedchamber beat faster at the sight of this still very young and oh-so-handsome king talking to his wife's swollen belly with genuine love for the child growing there.

Louis raised his face. "Tell me about the vine. What is its name again?"

"Cup of gold," said Maria Teresa. "The conqueror Cortés gave one to Montezuma."

"Who is Montezuma?"

"He was the king of the new world across the sea, great and powerful, but not great enough, not powerful enough to outwit our gentlemen." She arched her neck in a prideful gesture. Spain owned the new world and much of the old. There was the Spanish Netherlands to the north of France, and to the west, the Hapsburgs, sons of Spanish kings.

"I'll have cup-of-gold vines planted outside this window." Louis stood. "I'll plant them outside the windows of the Louvre and Saint-Germain"— these were other palaces in which they lived during the year—"so that everywhere you go you will wake to their perfume. This is your home, sweet plum. Where I am is your home. What do you do today?"

"I will go with Her Majesty to a nunnery in the next village. The voices of the nuns are said to be exquisite."

The "majesty" Maria Teresa referred to was the Queen Mother, Louis's mother, who had been queen of France for years, twenty and more before Louis was born, as well as regent after his father died, but was now in the background, not that his mother ever really stayed out of sight or mind. But Mazarin's death had taken some of her gusto.

Louis felt impatient. While his wife went off to listen to nuns chant, content to be in the shadow of his mother, neither of them noticing or caring that most of their ladies were bored to tears, Philippe's wife would be on her way with her ladies, huge straw hats on their heads, to the river to swim, gentlemen banished with only their imaginations for company. And then several hours later, the women would return in carriages, and the men would accompany the carriages, leaning down from their horses to talk to enchanting young women whose hair was still wet. And they'd gather near the carp pool by the fountain courtyard for a light picnic in the park with some courtiers playing guitars and others practicing dance steps for the court ballet Madame was presenting in July—her idea, this ballet—and the court poet would walk from group to laughing, talking group as he gathered ideas for the poems about the noble performers that it was his task to write for the ballet. Philippe's wife had become the light of court. Everyone adored her.

Wouldn't it be fun, she had said to Louis in her perfect French, her head tilting to one side, and again he was amazed that he'd ever thought her unattractive, wouldn't it be fun if we gave a ballet, you and me and Monsieur and Her Majesty? Don't you think that would be great fun?

Yes. Yes, he did think that would be great fun. There was almost nothing he liked better than music, listening to music, playing music, composing music, hearing music someone else had composed, singing the words to the music. And dance was the beautiful sister of music, his second favorite thing, to dance. He had an innate ear, an innate talent for both. They fed his soul. He was the best dancer of the court. Everyone knew. And they didn't say it simply to flatter him.

"You're too good to me," said Maria Teresa, and startled, his mind a million miles away, Louis took her hand and raised it to his lips.

"So I hope always to be," he said, his way of speaking gentle and courteous. Courtesy had become his mask to hide a growing dismay with himself, with her. He had vowed to love no others, but others were in his mind all the time now.

Hauteur in her glance, Maria Teresa cut her eyes to Olympe as if to say, he's mine.

Outside in the antechamber, Louis rapped out a quick command to his secretary. "Have a fan made with the Louvre as its subject and one of Saint-Germain, and one of Fontainebleau. The most skilled painter in Paris. For Her Majesty. And have him paint *fleurs-de-lis* on the end sticks." The Louvre was his primary palace, and *fleurs-de-lis* were the lilies of France, an emblem, a symbol of French royalty.

To remind her where her home is, he thought, striding through his throne room and down a set of stairs, his gentlemen and bodyguards following, out into the sun, which he loved. It was kind of the viscount to send her a fan. And clever. Playing upon her homesickness. How had he known of her homesickness? Who in her household is his spy? Louis wondered. The viscount's spies were everywhere. Someone his dear cardinal trusted had told him so, but he hadn't quite believed it at first. Now, he had begun to feel that he couldn't sneeze without the viscount, this powerful minister whom his court treated so deferentially, knowing it and sending an embroidered handkerchief. Or was he on his way to becoming as sick with suspicion as his father had been?

Louis's face showed a certain hawkish sharpness, and the men nearest him fell back a little, wondering if they'd displeased. Odd, they'd say to themselves later, how we didn't used to care so much. Louis had been king for a long time. But the cardinal had also been alive, and in the cardinal, true power had lain.

God, I despise myself, thought Louis, striding across his private courtyard and through the massive arch of a gatehouse, out into open grounds behind the palace to where there was a long landscape canal and he could take a decent walk before he held his morning council meeting. He meant to be good to his wife, meant never to hurt her, but his heart was hungry, like a tiger's. He'd wanted to lay that heart at her feet, wanted to love in the way men loved women in the romances, in the troubadour's ballads. In his mind was a ballad: Off with sleep, love, up from bed, this fair morn, see for our eyes the rose-red, new dawn is born, now that skies are glad and gay in this gracious month of May, love me, sweet, fill my joy in brimming measure, in this world he hath no pleasure that will none of it.

He could have sent her ladies from the chamber and climbed into bed with her, whispering that ballad to her as his hands roamed her body, fill my joy in brimming measure, he could have said as he touched her, but he didn't love her that way. He'd made this marriage out of duty and hoped that love would grow. And now he was beginning to understand it never would, not that he didn't respect her—her nobility was of the highest— not that he didn't like her. She was an obedient, pious wife. But he didn't love her. The thought twisted his gut.

Something drove him. Where? To whom? It seemed to him women were everywhere, following him with their eyes, curtsying to him, the tops of their breasts defined and soft above their tight bodices. Why didn't he just take one of them and satisfy this need the way he had once done with Olympe? What was he longing for? Some spark? Some tenderness? Some depth to answer the depths in his own heart? Where was there a woman whose price for him was above rubies?

"Write to His Majesty the king of Spain and beg him to send young cup-of-gold cuttings. Tell him it would be a favor to me if his gardeners sent cuttings from vines that have grown under the windows Her Majesty once looked out from," he told his secretary, never pausing in his restless stride. "From those vines only."

❧

Briefly sneaking away from the flutter that was the dressing of Her Majesty, the sullen Olympe and the beauty, whose name was Athénaïs, leaned out opened windows in a nearby chamber to watch the king stalk through his courtyard.

"Did you see him ignore me? I might as well not exist. I don't think he likes me." Athénaïs was truly astonished.

"He's ripe," said Olympe. As the queen's superintendent, she was an important figure at court. But her power was deeper than that. She was among those few whom Louis counted as true friends. And once upon a time, before his marriage, she'd been more than friendly with him in bed. "There is going to be a mistress soon. I can feel it. There's something around him I sense, a heat."

"I wish it were me!" Athénaïs brought hands to her mouth as if she'd said something wrong. "Oh, I'm terrible. Not that I would yield; I'm saving myself for marriage, of course. But he is enthralling."

There was no dishonor in becoming a king's mistress. In this, as in other things, the court was clear-eyed and unsentimental. It was long-standing tradition that there be one.

You would yield, thought Olympe, with a sharp glance at the maid of honor, younger, fresher than she, but not by much. You would yield, and me, well, I have nothing to save. When he falls, and fall he will, he's going to be mine.

CHAPTER 2

Louis dismissed his council and whistled for his dogs. His valet said his favorite dog wasn't acting in her usual manner, and he wanted to see for himself.

"Belle," he called and stroked her sleek head when she appeared, ahead of the pack, as always. "That's my good girl. Are you sick, my sweet one, my mighty hunter?" He knelt on one knee to take her handsome head in his hands and examine her face. He could see nothing different.

"Your Majesty, just a word, if I might."

He started. He hadn't realized he'd been followed. He kept his hands on Belle's head a moment or two longer, his mood suddenly irritable. Business for this morning was over. This man who broke into his privacy could just as easily have spoken to him this afternoon, for he met with his council twice a day, in the mornings and in the late afternoon, had done so since the death of Cardinal Mazarin. Now was his time for pleasure; in his mind he was already atop his horse, riding to the river to gaze on the guise pleasure had taken, lily-white skin, chestnut hair, an enchanting laugh. A king's business is never over, he heard his beloved cardinal's voice echo in his mind, so he stood and pretended that he hadn't been caught murmuring to a dog by the one man he most wanted to impress.

That man bowed. It was the Viscount Nicolas, his superintendent of finance, whom the court expected to become Louis's chief minister. The treasury was on the verge of bankruptcy. It was one of the reasons why the viscount was so important. He kept the kingdom from tipping over into the abyss, had done so for years. He was a collector of taxes, a maker of loans, and, also, a maker of men.

"Monsieur does me the honor to ask if I, in my humble way, might make a pleasing argument he be allowed a place at this council. Is there a time when I might make such appealing to you, Your Majesty?" As always, the viscount was suave and as smooth as honey.

"A bribe?" asked Louis. "Are you attempting to buy me?"

Nicolas blinked, then bowed low, his eyes on the floor. "How clumsy I am. I've offended, when all I wished to do was champion a man I think would add much to our governance. His highness, your brother, is your most loyal servant. I'll say no more." The viscount unbent and met Louis's eyes. "Allow me to be of service in another way. I understand you are searching for cup-of-gold vines. It happens that I have some at my estate not far from here. They are yours."

Good God, thought Louis, how can he know that already?

"I become clumsiness entirely," Nicolas said as Louis's silence lengthened. "This is not my morning, is it?"

The viscount referred to an earlier, terse exchange about funds to rebuild the navy.

But Louis laughed. If there was one attribute the viscount possessed—and he possessed many—it was charm. "You surprise me, Viscount, that's all. Can you read my mind? I was speaking of the vines only this morning."

"I assure you I am not omniscient. The Countess de Soissons was kind enough to tell me."

"Send every vine you have, then. I accept them with pleasure."

Nicolas smiled as if he lived only to please his sovereign, and in spite of himself, Louis smiled back. I could like this man, he thought, but can I trust him?

"My only wish is to serve you to the best of my talents," the Viscount Nicolas said as if he had read that thought, too.

Feeling awkward and graceless, Louis turned back to his dogs. He knew he should say something equally fulsome, such as how the viscount's least talent was a treasure, but he just wanted to put distance between himself and this man, who seemed too smooth, too capable, too kind, and—was it simply pique on his part and how he hated that it might be—too certain of himself. It was as if he tolerated Louis's whim to rule without a chief minister, all the while knowing such was impossible, that it was simply a matter of time before Louis realized it, too. That's what the court was whispering behind his back. No one believed he could manage without a Mazarin.

Gesturing that he wished no friends as companions, Louis walked not to his wife's apartments but in another direction altogether, toward a quieter, less-used part of the palace. He passed through halls and unoccupied bedchambers and then through the silent ballroom an ancestor had built. It was a magnificent room, a long chamber with huge, wide, handsome bays on each side to let in light through floor-to-ceiling windowed doors with expensive and rare glass in them. Everywhere were the emblems of its builder-king, his letter "H" embossed and entwined, along with the "C" of his queen, but also the crescent moon of the goddess Diana—Diana, also the name of that king's mistress. The large frescoes at one end were allegories of Diana also, Diana and the hunt, that king's favorite things. Two huge bronze satyrs embellished each side of the enormous fireplace, the satyrs signifying lust, the lust that king had felt for a woman.

Lust. Thou shalt not commit adultery. His heels clicked on the intricately patterned wooden floors. The scratch of his dogs' nails against the floors was a comfort to his ears. He was on his way to an old, neglected chapel just on the other side of this ornate ballroom. No one used it anymore, there being a far grander one his father had built in another wing, but Louis liked this one. He felt hidden from the world in it. It had become too small for the size of the court, but it was right for him, for his need to have some time alone, some time away from others.

A small, private door led directly into the chapel from here. Motioning to the lieutenant of his bodyguard to leave him, he stepped into the soothing dim of this quiet and sacred space, crossed himself and knelt, his eyes not seeing the stained-glass windows in a half-circle before him nor the gold-and-green gilded dome overhead. Why had he acted rudely to the viscount? Not only was it childish and impolite, but it showed his growing mistrust. Never let another know what you think. Was it possible that he could trust the man, if not completely, then more than he dared at the moment? Yes, said his mother. No, said something in him. So luscious Olympe was the spy in his wife's household. Of course she would be. Was she the only one? The viscount's knowledge of his conversation with the queen this morning disturbed him. What else did he know? Did he know that Louis had begun to meet someone in secret every night in an attempt to understand finances? Did he know Louis would never, under any circumstances, give Philippe a place on the council? Thou shalt not covet thy neighbor's wife, nor thy brother's either. But he did, the Blessed Savior help him. He stopped that thought. It led to places wild and uncontrolled, to desires he shouldn't have.

He prayed for strength, but like a jeer to his prayer, the face of his brother's wife came into his mind, along with a verse from a poet: As a rose, she lived as roses do. She'd worn rose-colored ribbons last night. He touched the one that was tied around his own wrist, hidden by lush lace at the end of his shirtsleeve that was the fashion. He'd stolen it like some thief in the night, like some besotted fool.

"Henriette," he whispered, and he repeated her name yet again into the silence around him. He didn't wish to hurt his brother, and yet his brother's happiness cut into him like a sword. Would he? Would she? It seemed she felt as he did. Love and war are the same thing, and stratagems and policy are as allowable in the one as in the other, so said his mother's beloved Spanish writer, Cervantes. Had Cervantes desired his brother's wife? He prayed for the strength to resist temptation.

Prayer finished, calm restored, at least until he should see Henriette again, he stood to leave and as he walked back toward the small door that had let him in, he caught sight of a white square, obviously slipped under the great front doors of the chapel, which opened from a hall.

For a moment, his heart thudded. Had Henriette dared to write him? Did she accept or berate him for his almost kiss of last night? He felt like a boy, ready to leap to joy or plunge to despair. He picked up the letter, its paper heavy, grained, expensive, and tore past a plain seal of red wax.

> *Do you know the difference*
> *between His Eminence*
> *and the late Cardinal Richelieu?*
> *The answer is not moot.*
> *The one led his animal.*
> *The other mounts his brute.*

Shock held him still. It was a Mazarinade, one of the hundreds of verses and street songs and written words full of scandal and hate that had filled pamphlets and letters, had been shouted from street corners in his boyhood, full of malevolence for the man who had been resented and feared and warred against and yet lived to be one of the saviors of France: Mazarin. Its subject was despicable and lurid, implying his mother was whore to a man who had deeply loved her. It was a dishonor to her and a dishonor to him, but worse, it was an all-too-vivid reminder of the uncertain past behind him and the uncertain future ahead. Peace was fragile. This little jibe reminded him too sharply of that. Beware, it said. Enough wrong moves, and the court would turn on him. They'd done it before. They could do it again.

He wrenched open the front doors of the chapel and stepped into the hall. A musketeer, arms crossed, took his ease at the end of the hall's long finger on Louis's right.

"Who came into this hallway?" Louis demanded.

The musketeer stood up straight. "No one, Your Majesty."

Back in the chapel, Louis went to the small side door that led to the ballroom. He saw the lieutenant of his musketeers playing ball with the dogs. The lieutenant kept a ball from the tennis court in a pocket.

"D'Artagnan," Louis shouted, and the dogs turned at the sound of his voice, ran toward him, Belle in the lead.

"There's another. Down!" As the dogs obeyed, Louis held up the paper. D'Artagnan took the note from him and read it as Louis walked back into the dim of the chapel and through the wide doors to the hall. He stepped out. The musketeer had moved from his place far down at one end and waited for him.

"I repeat, who came into this hall?"

There were narrow staircases for servants with iron railings that circled up into the attic floors. There was a staircase in the pavilion at the end of this hall and a public staircase for the ballroom. And there were secret passages. Only he was supposed to know of them, but their existence was old. Many knew of them, more than he could imagine.

"No one, Your Majesty. I swear it."

There was a thin sheen of perspiration on the musketeer's upper lip, just above a small mustache, matching Louis's, who'd made such the fashion.

The note still in his hand, D'Artagnan and the dogs were in the hall now. Louis took the paper. His heart felt like it was going to jump right up his throat and out onto the floor. He felt sick to his stomach. He folded the paper into a small oblong and put it into a secret pocket in his jacket.

"That would be the second, Your Majesty?"

The even tone of D'Artagnan's question calmed. Shutters were open to Fontainebleau's forest-blessed air here in this wide hallway, and he took a deep breath of it. The day outlined in the window's frame was clear, temperate, beautiful. Friends of his, seeing he had skipped Mass, were waiting for him in the courtyard.

"Yes, the second. The first was while we were still at the Louvre."

"Did you leave your position?" D'Artagnan asked the musketeer.

Sweat now rolling from his hair, the musketeer said, without looking at Louis, "I went into the Tiber pavilion for a moment." The Tiber pavilion ended this wing of the palace.

"Because?" D'Artagnan's question was gentle.

"A—a girl. We spoke only for a few moments, sir."

"Leave us," ordered D'Artagnan.

The musketeer walked back down the hall, feeling the weight of two sets of eyes on his back.

"It might have happened then," D'Artagnan said to Louis. Royal palaces were filled with servants, courtiers, priests, officials, visitors. Many chambers were reached only by passing through another chamber, and that included royal chambers. He indicated the plain winding stairs beside them. "Perhaps someone came down the stairs when he wasn't watching, sire."

"This is *my* palace." I sound shrill, thought Louis.

D'Artagnan didn't answer. He walked across to a window, looked out. There were musketeers stationed in this courtyard, the oval courtyard, the king's personal courtyard, and there were Louis's friends, Philippe's, loitering, killing time until Louis joined them. It could have been anyone. The king's grandfather had been killed by a man leaping into his coach. Guards riding near had been unable to prevent it. It was his task to prevent such.

"I don't like this, D'Artagnan."

"Nor do I, sire. But I'll find our little messenger, and I'll put a new man on duty."

Louis looked down toward the musketeer. From where he stood, the musketeer could feel the sear of the king's eyes, and he swallowed and began to sweat again.

"No." Louis spoke softly, reflectively. "We'll give him another chance. If he's a good soldier, and as a musketeer, he is, it won't happen again. I would imagine I'm safer than I was an hour ago."

Lieutenant Charles D'Artagnan of His Majesty's royal musketeers, over twenty years' service of one kind or another, thank you very much, bowed stiffly and then watched the young king of France, all of twenty and two—D'Artagnan was twice the king's age and what he'd seen in his time was a story in itself—take another deep inhale, then blow out its air. He watched his sovereign straighten shoulders and shake his head, as if clearing it. The king snapped his fingers and his dogs rose from their sitting position. He knelt among them, patting their heads, receiving kisses, pulling ears. He said their names and grabbed one or another by the scruff, as they milled all about.

"To me," Louis ordered, and he walked away, dogs a circle around him.

The only creatures he truly trusts—the king's valet had been known to say when too far gone in drink—those dogs. A king's role was a lonely one; he might be betrayed by wife, by councilor, by child, and most certainly, by courtiers. This one's father had been. What memories D'Artagnan had of those old days before his present majesty was born and another cardinal ruled the day and betrayal grew in the bones of everyone. He leaned out the window and called to musketeers that the king was exiting at the Tiber pavilion. Then he took a rare moment away from Louis and stepped into the chapel, where many a king before this one had prayed. For what? Strength? Deliverance? Loyalty? Some glimmer of true love? Bring those he can trust into his life, D'Artagnan prayed. There have to be more than myself.

And then the lieutenant of Louis's musketeers began a methodical search of the chapel. The note might have already been here, just waiting, placed by someone who knew the king's habits, where he liked to pray. There was a secret passage here down into the chamber below. D'Artagnan walked down secret stairs, opened a door set so skillfully into its surrounding wood that a maidservant dusting an armoire shrieked and would have fled if D'Artagnan hadn't stopped her.

"How long have you been here? Was anyone in this chamber when you entered it?"

"Not long, sir. No one was here, sir." She gulped her answers, her eyes big and blinking.

"You're certain of that?"

"Oh, yes, sir." Tears were welling up.

"Be gone with you, now, and not a word of this, any of it, do you understand me, girl?" He was brusque, substantial in the authority he carried, the pride and history of the uniform he wore.

"Yes, sir. Of course, sir."

Now a maidservant knows there is a secret doorway, D'Artagnan thought as he marched into an adjoining chamber and glared at the walls as if they might tell him something. Who left this poisonous little message? And why? To frighten? To annoy? To warn? Many a king had been killed by someone he trusted. There was recent blood on nearby floors of this very palace. A visiting queen had ordered a courtier stabbed to death in one of the galleries here. How would His Majesty respond if the notes continued? Would he become like his father, secretive and suspicious, killing those around him indiscriminately? The beauty of this king was his young and handsome fearlessness, his walking among his people, or among his soldiers on a battlefield, as the incarnation of France, which he was. The Queen Mother had used it, displayed him like an icon to the people in those past, perilous days of treachery and war, hoping the sight of him, his innocence, his young, grave, dignified purity, would rally support. By God, it oughtn't to be tampered with, that innocence, and yet it would be. Time would do that, if nothing else. By God, he, Charles D'Artagnan, part gentleman, part adventurer, all of him loyal soldier, would love to present the name of this latest troublemaker to his most Christian majesty—the beauty of all France in his face—Louis, the fourteenth of that name.

He would bow on one knee and hold the name up like a present, anything to wipe away the memory of the expression on his sovereign, his king, his liege lord's face—looking for one moment every inch the boy his position had never quite allowed him to be—as he stood in the ballroom and demanded to know who had approached too near, too near on too many levels, without his or D'Artagnan's knowledge.

CHAPTER 3

It was evening. All the court prepared itself for dusk's festivities.

Louise de la Baume le Blanc, maid of honor to the court's new goddess, counted under her breath to twenty, then pulled a curling iron from the hair of that goddess, the new Madame. The burnished red curl hung in a satisfactory spiral, and choosing hairpins set with pearls, Louise gathered other carefully crafted tresses to pin over the princess's ears, so that a set of four or five long ringlets hung to each side of Madame's face. Among them, on one side only, was a longer curl, which lay against the angle of Madame's collarbone. The longer curl was Louise's idea, and she wasn't certain how it would be received. This was a court where fashion and appearance were paramount. With a tortoise comb, Louise quickly loosened tendrils around the princess's face, and it became framed by tiny, mismatched curling wisps.

"I love it," cried the young woman who was the object of all admiration these days, described by her admirers as a creature of moonbeams and fairy dust. She was that startling white redheads display, as if all color were saved for the tints in their hair and the blue of their eyes. Impulsively, she selected a ring from the litter of ribbons, combs, feathers, and small gold and silver boxes spilling across her dressing table. "For you."

"No, Madame," said Louise, "there's no need—"

"Take it. I command it."

Finished with Louise, the princess stood, and serving women moved forward to help her with the selection of a gown. They were to assemble shortly in the king's ballroom. They'd dance and flirt, dine and flirt, talk and flirt, and agreeably while the night away until the wee hours. Princess Henriette did not like to go to bed early, and what she didn't like wasn't done these days.

Leaving the princess standing indecisively before two gowns, Louise ran upstairs to the attic chambers in which she and the other maids of honor lived. Unlike the opulent surroundings in Madame's rooms—not a ceiling or wall without its moldings, its tapestries, its gilt ovals holding portraits—these chambers were much plainer, little but beds and trunks and charming, big windows out of which to look or call down to friends walking in the courtyard. Shocked, two of the maids of honor had sent home for thick rugs and handsome chairs, and so now their chambers looked quite respectable.

The others were already gowned for evening and were arranging their curls to copy Madame's. Louise had warned them she was going to create the longer curl, and, after much discussion, the three others had told her they thought it was brilliant. A long curl set against a bare shoulder will take the female portion of the court by storm, Louise's best friend, Fanny, predicted.

Fanny, dressed and ready, paused in her task of arranging hair. "Curl no or yes?"

Three sets of eyes regarded Louise with some anxiety.

"Yes," said Louise.

"I knew it," Fanny said to the two others.

Louise looked down at the ring in her hand, gold with an emerald set in it. She'd have Choisy sell it for her; he was always going back and forth to Paris. She opened the trunk in which her gowns lay carefully folded. All she possessed was here, though Fanny was generous in lending small fripperies that made a difference. The choice this evening, any evening, wasn't difficult; she had only a few gowns. Unlike Princess Henriette—Madame as she must now be called—no overwhelming largess had showered down on Louise when she joined this new household. Her mother hadn't a coin she would spare, and Madame de Choisy had helped Louise arrange to borrow money to purchase another gown or two and frivolous items such as shoes and gloves so that she might not be the plainest flower in Madame's new bower.

Putting the ring down a shoe, Louise selected the gown she'd wear, laid it across the bed, then pulled a wicker box from beneath. Inside were odds and ends, castoffs from the Orléans princesses. There were ribbons and shoe buckles, cloth flowers and scarves, shawls and lace collars, a fan or two, some gloves. Louise was deft with a needle and would snip something, a bunch of ribbons or a cloth flower and baste such to her gown, so that at least a gown worn over and over again might have different trimmings once in a while. It was the fashion here at court to buy what one wished and never mind the payment to a merchant or seamstress. Keep them on a string, Fanny counseled, but Louise hadn't been brought up to regard debt lightly. You really do need to move past that, Fanny advised.

"What's Madame wearing this evening?"

Fanny spoke around the hairpin she had in her mouth as she bunched and pinned curls for the girl sitting in front of her. Louise and Fanny felt like they'd known each other forever because both their families held positions in the Orléans royal household, and they'd become friends as young girls. Louise thought Fanny the cleverest person in the world, other than Choisy, and Fanny thought Louise the dearest, and they considered it a bolt of lightning luck that they'd both been chosen to be Madame's maids of honor.

"Silver or lilac," Louise answered.

"It's a pity we didn't know sooner. We could have matched our gowns," said Claude, whose hair Fanny was arranging. Louise could not have done so, but she didn't say the words. She'd learned long ago that those who were given much in life seldom realized or truly wished to know the travails of those who had to struggle. The next thing she knew, Fanny dashed out the door.

"My hair isn't done!" wailed Claude.

"Let me dress, and I'll finish your hair," Louise soothed, already the peacemaker among them.

Quickly, she stitched a big cloth-of-silver and gauze flower to a gown she'd worn more than once. The stitching done, she stepped out of one gown and into this one, her maid there to tie up the back. The style this decade was for a very tight waist that V'd deep into the skirt, for all of a woman's neck and shoulders and some of her bosom to show, and for sleeves to fall in a voluptuous swell to the elbow from those bared shoulders.

Excited that evening was here, excited because they were part of one of the most splendid courts in the world, excited because they were fifteen and sixteen and seventeen, and there's little that isn't exciting at that age, they took turns helping each other, Louise finishing Claude's hair and Claude, in turn, lending Louise a pretty shawl. The fourth of their quartet paid no attention, simply continued to concentrate on herself, on which pair of her numerous earrings she would wear.

Louise and Fanny weren't certain what they thought of this one, this fourth of their four, this Madeleine. Louise was ready to keep her mind open; the priests said there was good in everyone, but after the first week of living together, Fanny had announced in no uncertain terms that Madeleine was selfish and stupid as well, and that's just all there was to it.

Louise pulled on white stockings, each kept up with a garter, and was stepping into high-heeled shoes her maid held for her—shoes of soft leather dyed sky blue; too expensive, they'd put a big dent into her little borrowed bag of coins, but she hadn't been able to resist purchasing them—when Fanny breezed back into the chamber.

"Look what I have."

As proud as if she brought them gold coins or marriage contracts, Fanny held out wads of silver gauze ribbons. "Let's sit down and make shoulder knots. These match the gown Madame has chosen. We'll be like the musketeers, marked by what we wear as hers. Madame loved the idea."

Fanny is so clever, thought Louise, as she began to cut and knot the ends of ribbons. One had only to look at her to see it. One could literally see thoughts passing through her head, or at least Louise could. She depended on her friend's cleverness. It had gotten them out of more than one scrape in the Orléans household.

Part of the largesse of a maid of honor's position was a small stipend, but more than that, the opportunity to meet all the eligible men of the kingdom, not just the ones parents might deem suitable. To be selected a maid of honor was no small thing. It gave a well-born girl extra cachet, made her interesting even when her dowry for marriage wasn't. Of course, Cousin Choisy had been so helpful, teaching her a more graceful curtsy, he and his mother explaining the intricacies of who at court deserved a deep curtsy and who did not. Now you be on your mettle, he had warned, shaking a finger at her, because the men will attempt to seduce you. He'd tried to kiss her when he said this but he'd been dressed in a woman's gown, so it was hard to take him very seriously. It really was a lot of fun to know that men thought you were pretty and said so. It was delicious, actually. Louise could see why the priests and nuns warned against pleasures of this world. They were—well—pleasant.

She thought about that as they—Madeleine the snob among them ordering her maid to do the task—clustered ribbons into small masses in order to sew them to one shoulder of their gowns, their gowns just cupping the lovely rounds of their shoulders. Of course, there was a long discussion as to which shoulder, and somehow it was settled: the left, that being the one closest to the heart. Romantic.

Ribbons in place, the four of them surveyed one another critically to see that each looked her best. The admiration for Madame, heady and delicious, unexpected and fantastic, had spilled over onto them—more good fortune for us, declared Fanny—and they wanted to make certain they kept it. From the moment of their arriving to serve the newly married Madame at Monsieur's palace in Paris, there had been nothing but play. Monsieur loved festivity, and the princess he'd married had adapted at once as if she'd known it all her life.

That sense of gaiety had traveled with them here to this palace with its grand gardens and nearby forest. There was something in the air at this place, along with the scent of summer's opening roses and jasmine, something giddy and high-spirited, flirtatious and daring. There were balls or fêtes every evening as the May moon sometimes seemed close enough to touch in the night sky. During the day there were hunting and riding, and they went with Madame swimming in the river every day the sun shone. Afterward, there were promenades near the beautiful carp pond at the edge of one of the courtyards, as they waited for the queen to return from a visit to a nunnery or to wake from her nap.

Afternoons were leisurely affairs. Talk was idle. They listened to one or another of the men play guitar. Sometimes the king played. He played wonderfully—wildly—Louise thought. He was beautiful in every way that Louise could see, but all the maids of honor thought that. Madame would sit in the shade on a rug under a tree, chattering to one and all, as courtier after courtier came to call on her. Her popularity was immense; it had swept through court like a storm. Madame was presenting a court ballet in July, and her maids of honor all had parts, and rehearsals were beginning. The head of an acting troupe of which Monsieur was patron was working with them so that they would perform better than anyone else. It was all too exciting. Louise felt as if she'd stepped out of a cramped box into an enchanted, open-ended fairy tale, like the ones an admirer of Madame's told them, about sleeping beauties and maidens sitting in cinders before they wore glass slippers or kissed frogs who became princes.

And so, to honor the enchantment of the moment and how beautiful all the compliments and attention made them feel, as well as to make certain such admiration didn't disappear, Louise redid certain key curls for Fanny, and Claude lent small pearl earrings that heightened the beauty of Louise's lithe, incandescent fairness, and even self-absorbed Madeleine offered to share from among her many bracelets.

Bracelet on an arm, long curl on a shoulder, Fanny opened the chamber door, unfurled a fan, stamped a foot encased in smooth, colored leather, and announced, "Hearts will be broken tonight."

"Ours," Claude said with a laugh.

"Only if we're stupid," answered Fanny.

A girl must keep her wits about her. Choisy had been right about that. Many of the gallants who courted and flirted and plied them with admiration were married. This was where the fairy tale showed its dark side. Louise and Fanny discussed it endlessly. What if one of them should fall in love with a married man in spite of herself? It happened. And while this court seemed to regard fidelity casually, Louise had taken in the priests' strictures with her wet nurse's milk: to stay pure, to save herself for marriage. But already, she could see how easily a girl could slip and fall before the ardent persuasion of a man who said he loved her. She thought of true love as something unalloyed and grand, something larger than the two people it bound. Absolute idiocy, was Fanny's opinion. Look around you, for heaven's sake. Is that what you see? We'll marry whoever our families approve, and we'll be lucky if he has a kind word for us, and I, for one, intend to take my fun where I can find it.

Giggling over nothing, the way women will when they're young and lively and in a cluster together and life is alluring in all its unspoken promise, they hurried downstairs to Madame's apartments and sailed through the door, giggles preceding them, and an arrogant princess, who served as Madame's lady-in-waiting and who they secretly had named the gargoyle, looked down her nose at them.

"Late," she said.

She was in her early twenties, the daughter of a duke and a marshall of France, as well as the wife of the crown prince of the small nearby kingdom of Monaco. She was only four years or so older than they were, but in sophistication and certainty, the span might have been a hundred.

It's clever of Madame to have taken her on, Fanny had announced, because the princess was one of the leaders at court. And of course there did need to be an older woman among them as a kind of duenna or superintendent. Madame was no older than they were. But this princess didn't care to supervise. She only cared about how quickly one or another of them could leap up to perform some small task, and it was never quickly enough.

Beautiful and proud, the gargoyle rose from her chair to touch the knot of ribbons at Louise's shoulder. "And what's this?" she asked, scorn clear in her tone.

Looking like an angel in her gown of silver, the red in her hair made even more pronounced by the shade of her dress, their bright-faced new Madame, the Princess Henriette, answered. "A whim of mine. Does it please you?"

"Most charming, of course," the gargoyle answered.

"But not as charming as those who wear it." This was the gargoyle's brother, Guy-Armand, the Count de Guiche.

If the gargoyle—Catherine was her given name—was lovely, her brother was magnificent. Their sophistication made their place at court gilded and glinting, always. Of an old and honorable family, both brother and sister carried themselves with a haughty certainty that reduced the maids of honor into speechless puddles. The other three thought that Guy was the absolute handsomest man at court. All four of them had stayed up one night not long ago arguing this. No, said Louise, the king is more striking. The truth was Guy and His Majesty looked remarkably alike. They allowed the Viscount Nicolas, old as he was, in the running because he had a tender smile and wonderful laugh lines around his eyes and was still slim when most men his age dragged around bellies the size of tubs. Also, he was very, very rich. And the king's captain of the guards, Péguilin, was so ugly it made him handsome, or this was their snob Madeleine's opinion anyway. And of course, Monsieur himself with his snapping dark eyes and vivid smile was included. And after much giggling discussion, all but Louise selected Guy.

The handsomest man at court walked around the maids of honor as if they were fillies he was considering for purchase before he stopped in front of Louise. He has an eye on you, Fanny kept saying, but Louise thought that maybe it was Fanny who had an eye on him.

"I'll dance with you tonight," Guy said, looking down at her.

No, you won't, thought Louise, but of course, she didn't say it. She didn't like this worldly, certain young man. There was something dangerous and flippant about him that distressed her, and she didn't like the way he always seemed to be watching Madame. She kept her head down until he moved on, sauntering over to stand by his sister.

"Are we late? Tell me we're not late." Prince Philippe burst into the chamber, talking even as he entered the door. "His Majesty will frown. 'Stupid Monsieur,' he'll say, 'you'll be late to your own burial.' Guiche, my friend, my discerning one, my valet couldn't get my collar the way I wanted it. And I look puffy in this doublet. Marriage has made me fat. Tell me. I can bear the truth. Hello, darling." He kissed Henriette on the mouth. Philippe had always been one to wear his heart on his sleeve, and right now his wife was his heart.

"Fair Princess," he said, nodding his head to Catherine, "you look beautiful as always," but his destination was the single and large pier glass in this chamber, and he sighed when he stood before it and turned from side to side. "Horrible. I look horrible. Someone here tell me. Count, you're my dearest friend. Don't be kind. I can bear it."

It was amusing—Fanny and Louise found the king's brother witty and kinder than they'd expected—but it was also deadly serious. Fashion in this age was more flamboyant and beribboned and befrilled for a man than it was for a woman. No one dressed better, every square inch of himself embroidered or belaced, than the king. No one, that is, except Philippe, who often set some style his brother then copied and received the credit for.

Summoned, Guy stood behind his friend. He stared for a long time at Philippe's reflection. No one spoke. The maids of honor were afraid to. Monsieur and the count were great friends. That was what Choisy had told Louise, and it was what she had seen for herself. Even when the count was rude, Monsieur seemed not to mind.

Finally, Guy touched at a single dark velvet patch Philippe wore on his cheek. "This would be—?"

"It's a patch, and you know it. The Chevalier de Choisy came by, and one thing led to another, and it seemed like a good idea." Philippe went over to Henriette, brows drawn together, anxious, and as trusting as he'd been with Guy. "Have I gone too far? Do you hate it, my love?"

Henriette kissed her husband's mouth and then the patch, cut in the shape of a star. "I adore it and you, sir."

How sweet they are together, thought Louise. Here, at least, was an example of the true love she envisioned. The prince idolized his princess. And the princess—Louise sighed to herself at the thought of Madame. It was all rapidly becoming complicated, but she hoped for the best.

"No more is needed," Philippe said to Guy.

"Bring me Madame's patch box," Guy commanded.

The command was addressed to Louise, and she walked to the dressing table and brought back a beautiful box made of silver. It was the duty of a maid of honor to accompany, assist, and amuse. And fetch.

Guy looked through the small black shapes that were all the rage, worn on the face and kept there by mastic, and selected another star. He balanced its velvet side on a finger, then placed it on his cheek in approximately the same place as Philippe's. Then he turned to face Henriette.

"Where's my kiss?" he said.

The maids of honor held their breath. The count was disrespectful and unfortunately also very dashing, but if his dear friend's deliberate flirting bothered him, Philippe didn't show it. Henriette dropped her eyes, as if unable to meet the brash, unabashed admiration flung at her, but Louise could see that she was as flattered as she was flustered.

"I think we should all wear patches, stars for us and hearts for ladies," said Guy.

"Yes," Philippe exclaimed.

Henriette pointed to her maids of honor. "But they aren't married." An unmarried young woman of good family did not rouge or powder or patch until a ring was upon her finger.

"That makes it all the more amusing," said Catherine, a slight smile on her face, as if Henriette were a child.

"I approve," said Philippe, "and that's all that need be said." Then he began to supervise as one after another of them placed patches on their faces. He was in top form, garrulous and joking. He knew that the word among the young courtiers was that the place to be was Monsieur's— where there was lively conversation, witty games, good food, lovely young women, and showy young gentlemen. Philippe had always had an eye for what would prove fashionable and what would excite the court's attention.

When patches were on all faces, he stepped back and considered the group, his expression mock serious, making several of the maids of honor giggle again. "Perfect," he announced. "His Majesty will be highly irritated that once more I've done something diverting and interesting." He held out a hand to Henriette, who put hers atop it. "Just as I did by marrying you, my treasure. I'm sorry, but Her Majesty is dull, and apparently there's nothing that can be done about it."

"If you want to be on the king's council, it's comments like that one that will keep you from it," said Guy.

Philippe frowned at one and all. "You did not hear a word I just said. Is that understood? That would likely be an excellent attribute to strengthen if you intend remaining in this household. You must pay me no mind because I say things I shouldn't, especially when they're true. Hypocrisy makes the world go round. Remember that, my angels."

"Her Majesty is very, very dear, and we love her very, very much," said Henriette, clearly nervous at her husband's lively, teasing indiscretion.

"Yes, she is. Yes, we do," said Philippe, who was delighted that he'd done something that was going to annoy his brother. Someone among them would whisper tonight that Monsieur said Her Majesty was dull, and Philippe would of course deny it when Louis confronted him, but truth would out. Her Majesty was dull, prayers and naps and embroidery, and Philippe and his wife were anything but. "Do you hear that, maidens? Her Majesty is very kind, kinder than I've just been, and she is far, far from home and likely homesick."

"We shock her," said Guy.

Philippe looked over to his friend. "Explain yourself, Count."

"I have it on the best authority that she finds us frivolous."

"Us?"

"Us, this court, the French in general."

"Frivolous." Philippe considered the queen's accusation. "I'm afraid it's true. And I, for one, intend to be as frivolous as possible tonight. I believe I've made a splendid beginning. Count"—he arched an eyebrow at Guy and made a serious face—"I trust you'll sustain me in my attempts."

Guy bowed, and there was a chorus of giggles from the maids of honor, even a low laugh from their dreaded Catherine.

Talk and laughter had traveled up through their windows as courtiers walked across the paving stones of a courtyard to a set of great red doors, open for the night to reveal a grand staircase that led to the ballroom. The evening was beginning.

"Let's stand on baptismal gate and watch the courtiers enter the king's courtyard," suggested Henriette.

A colonnade on this story led to the ornate gatehouse built especially for Philippe's father's christening. Stone faces from ancient Rome spewed water into basins on each side of the outside entrance, and the gatehouse's rooftop offered a lovely space in which to walk and look over all that transpired in the king's courtyard.

Catherine wrinkled her nose. "They'll see us watching. A little common, don't you think?"

"Oh, let them see. What does it matter?" said Henriette. "We're going to be talking and dancing with them in just a few moments."

Louise and Fanny looked at each other. This was the first time they'd seen Madame contradict the gargoyle. Hurrah, thought Louise.

"I'm her slave. Her least wish is my command. Her every wish should certainly be yours," said Philippe to Catherine.

It was a reprimand. Catherine's expression went rigid for a moment, but she swept out onto the colonnade with the three others, all of them imperious and very beautiful in their youth and jewels and shining eyes. The maids of honor followed.

Will my husband defend my place to others? thought Louise. Does Madame appreciate how much she is loved?

"Did you see the way the Count de Guiche looked at Madame?" Fanny whispered.

Below, torches lit the courtyard. Above, there were already a few night stars in the sky. People were looking up, pointing at the new royal couple. There was bowing and laughter and waves. One hand on the iron railing of the colonnade, Henriette waved back.

"I'd die if he looked that way at me," said Fanny.

Louise didn't answer. There was no point in encouraging Fanny, to whom gossip was second nature. And it wasn't his friend, the Count de Guiche, that Monsieur needed to worry about, anyway. Louise had eyes in her head. It was his own brother, the king.

CHAPTER 4

T he ballroom was one of the most beautiful chambers in the palace,
almost one hundred feet long, light-colored wood highlighted with
gilt paint and frescoes, enormous bays, chandeliers whose candles
shone like hundreds of twinkling diamonds hanging down inside each.
The woods were made a lovely golden honey color by the candlelight, and
everywhere were the intricate initials of a former king and his wife and his
mistress; everywhere was a carved crescent moon symbolizing that king's
motto: until the crescent has filled the whole dish, symbolizing majesty
filling the whole world with the glory of his name. The king who would fill
this whole world with the glory of his name hadn't arrived yet. From the
musicians' gallery, the sound of violin and flute and hautbois spilled down
over courtiers like silk ribbons.

Louise had a moment's hesitation as she stood on the door's threshold, a slight pulling back into herself, as always she did at the beginning
of any event, but the entrance of Monsieur and Madame before her had
created such a stir that she really had only to glide along behind it. She
smiled and nodded and kept herself near Fanny, who thrived on events
like this, was never at a loss for words. She herself would be fine in a few
more moments, particularly after she drank a goblet of wine. Glancing
around, she saw her cousin Choisy and waved. He made his way over,
grabbing a goblet for her as he did so. He nodded to Fanny as he handed
Louise her wine.

"That cloth flower doesn't change the fact that I've seen this gown
before, but the pearl earrings are perfect for your complexion. And this"—
Choisy touched the knot of ribbons—"is quite original. The queen's ladies
will be biting the insides of their mouths not to complain. As for this"—he
put a forefinger on the patch beside her mouth—"it's very naughty. The
old cats will disapprove, but I love it." He wore several patches; one in
particular was quite unusual, a coach pulled by horses. It covered most of

his right cheekbone. There were no earrings tonight, and his hair hung to his shoulders like any other man's.

Louise took a drink of wine. "I've been thinking—"

"Thinking?" Choisy interrupted. "Stop that at once. You are here to look beguiling and act vacuous, and don't forget it. Once you've found a husband, you may then find a mind."

Trumpets from the music gallery sounded, and everyone stood back to make way for the king and queen, followed by the king's mother. The Queen Mother wore black and pearls everywhere. In her day, she had been the best-dressed woman at court. She still dressed splendidly, but no one was watching her anymore. Madame had everyone's eyes, and after her, the queen. The young queen displayed diamonds in her fair hair and around her neck and at her ears, and her gown was of a pink summer gauze with more diamonds, but her expression was remote and distant.

"Why doesn't the queen ever smile?" Fanny whispered.

"Perhaps she feels shy," Louise whispered back.

"Shy?"

Both Choisy and Fanny hissed the word. It had no meaning for either of them. They were noticed by those nearby, and Fanny glared at Choisy, and he pinched her arm, which made Fanny squeak, which made the king turn in their direction.

Louise blushed and dropped even lower into the curtsy she was making. If His Majesty were to approach them, she knew she wouldn't be able to think of a single thing to say to him.

"Safe," said Choisy. "Adonis has passed us by."

"Who is Adonis?" asked Louise.

"The king, my ignorant one. I must find you a book of mythology. Didn't they read in the Orléans household?"

Fanny shot up out of her curtsy. "If you've gotten me in trouble, I will never forgive you." She flounced away.

"Remind me to be afraid if she ever becomes important," Choisy said.

"I want to ride out tomorrow." They were riding out nearly every morning while the palace slept. Louise was trying to locate the place where she'd seen the boy in the iron mask.

"We should stop." Knowing she would argue and not wishing to, Choisy began to talk of something else. "The dancing is beginning. You'll be besieged with partners, so save the courante for me." The courante was a lively dance loved by the king.

"So, my flower doesn't change this gown at all?"

"No one will notice. They won't be able to get past your shining eyes."

He blew a kiss to her. Like Fanny, he was in his element. Another in her element was his mother, who waved to Louise with an imperious ringed hand, and Louise walked over to pay her respects.

Madame de Choisy kissed her on both cheeks. "You're looking quite blooming. This," she tapped her fan on Louise's shoulder, touching the golden curl, "is lovely. I'm going to instruct my maid to curl my hair so tomorrow, as will every other woman of taste here. That patch is very improper, but I see you're all wearing them, Monsieur, too. Quite amusing. Anything Madame does must be charming, but perhaps you go too far? Yes? You went swimming today?"

"We did."

"Word is you took your hair down to dry it while sitting in the gardens with gentlemen about."

Louise's mind scattered in a dozen directions. They'd all done it. It had been Madame's idea. She'd been the first to pull pins from her wet hair and shake herself like a cat, but Louise wasn't going to say that. It would be tattling.

"The Queen Mother has gotten word of it, my dear, and she doesn't like it. Now you know I'm the last to lecture, but I wouldn't wish you to get a reputation for being too reckless. You've no proper dower and little or no family to protect you." Madame de Choisy smiled to make her words less stinging. "Now, go away, my beautiful child, and play."

Rebuked, however lightly, and feeling it, Louise slipped from the ballroom, found a jutting, angled balcony open to the night, and sat down in one of the chairs placed there. She rubbed her leg. It had healed shorter than the other one from a long-ago fall. The little wooden wedge she wore inside her shoe to make her legs even sometimes caused a deep ache in her hip. She thought about this afternoon, its loveliness, the river so cool on her body, the sun afterward so warm. All the young men, the king among them, full of talk and laughter and flirting, on their great horses beside the carriages that brought them back to court. The king and his gentlemen were like the stallions they rode, gallant and proud and mettlesome, pawing the ground in impatience, shaking their long manes. It was bold to take their hair down while gentlemen were watching, but it had seemed a sweet boldness, tender, somehow, like the breeze playing through the trees. It was an unfurling, ever so gently, that said, see, see how beautiful we are. Her mind went to the searing glance the king had sent Madame's way, the way his mouth had set so grimly when Monsieur had impetuously kissed her. Danger there. Madame flirted with fire. Perhaps they all did, but it was all so delicious—

"Miss, what are you doing out here alone? Are you ill?"

She started. There, with light from the wide foyer framing him, stood the king's superintendent of finance, he who one day soon, so the world around her whispered, would take the place the late great cardinal had held in the king's council.

"Shall I call a servant?" the Viscount Nicolas asked. He looked very grand in a short, tight doublet and lace so embroidered in gold that it was almost stiff.

"Oh, no, I'm fine, really—" Louise stood, but stumbled a little on the shorter leg, and Nicolas caught her by the arm.

"You're—"

"Stupid and clumsy at times, that's all." She was appalled at herself. Had the wine already gone to her head? "Thank you, sir, and excuse me—"

"At least allow me to escort you back inside." Smiling politely, he held out his hand, and obedient—after all he was a great deal older than she, old enough to be her father—Louise put hers on his.

"You're one of Madame's ladies, aren't you? Miss Louise de la Baume le Blanc de la Vallière."

The precision of hearing her entire name shocked her. How could he know that? She had lived all her life away from Paris. Her father might have been a nobleman, but he had been a country nobleman who'd never made his way at court. Several of the court ladies—particularly, the Countess de Soissons—had been quite rude to her because of it. She could feel the viscount's eyes on her, not in the brash way of the other men at court, but all the same assaying her, considering her. She could feel a flush coming into her face. She hated not being able to control it, which made her flush even more.

"Your father was a soldier, I believe, dying in 1650 or so, and your stepfather serves the Orléans family. You're very silent, miss," he said when she didn't answer.

She met his eyes. She had no words to tell him that her father was her talisman, his memory one of her sacred treasures, and that to hear him spoken of so unexpectedly moved her almost to tears.

The viscount had his head tilted to one side as he waited for an answer. His hair was thick and full, like Choisy's and Monsieur's, except that theirs was not shot through with silver.

"Laurent de la Vallière was a noble and decent man," she heard herself say. "The name is a proud one." Proud. Unlike her stepfather, who abased himself to the Orléans—which keeps you clothed, her mother would say.

"So I've been told. Are you enjoying court, miss?"

Again she didn't answer. He had walked her back into the ballroom, and they stood at the edge of the crowd filling the long, glorious chamber.

"Here we are. Good-bye, sir," she said to him.

"Oh, not good-bye," the viscount said, and suddenly she could see why Claude had insisted he be in the running for handsomest man at court. He might be old, but his eyes were tender. "Just farewell for this moment. Will you honor me later with a dance?"

Something in her shut the way a moonflower closes when dawn touches it. Words were in her head and memories of her father. To the prince, like an altar fire, love undying. It was the motto of her house, of her father. She hadn't thought of it in such a long time. Come, Louise, her father said in her mind, bending down to her from atop a horse, ride here in the saddle in front of me, my pretty girl. Her heart swelled with the thought of him, and his long-ago death was once more brutal and too near.

"A dance? Well, if Madame and the Princess de Monaco allow." The gargoyle wouldn't notice or care, but it was the closest she dared come to saying no. "Good evening, sir." And she left him.

Nicolas watched her disappear among the courtiers. She reminded him of some small creature, a rabbit or fox, gone to hiding. Hiding from the wicked viscount. She had lovely hair and shoulders; there was something clean and unspoiled about her. Fresh, he thought. A young woman who didn't wish to talk to him or charm him or impress him or imply the offer of her body for a favor. A purity to her—that was a rarity at court, like seeing a unicorn step down from the bright threads of a tapestry and make an actual bow. Certain, stringent verses came to mind: Purge me with hyssop, and I shall be clean. Wash me and I shall be whiter than snow. I sound like a Huguenot, glum and Scripture-quoting, he thought.

He glanced around this ballroom, this elegant kingly chamber of golden wood and wide arching bays and tall windows and gilt and paint and bronze, the best of another age. He knew these people well, and she didn't quite fit. Everyone here wanted something. They wished loans, they wished help in revenge, they wished places for lesser relatives in the bureaucratic maze that was the government of this kingdom, they wished stipends, they wished marriages, they wished dispensations. They wished anything, everything. He didn't mind. When a man or woman owed you, even slightly, it was the beginning of obligation. They wished, he wished, she wished, but what was it His Majesty, Louis the fourteenth of that name, wished? From where Nicolas stood, he could see the king far down the other end of the ballroom, flanked by his friends.

I misstepped today, thought Nicolas, seeing again the flickering eyes of the young king of France. Do you attempt to bribe me, Viscount? Who was the man beneath the crown? He didn't know him, really; Mazarin had always stood between them. In the grand bay nearest him was the Countess de Soissons, who stood in His Majesty's regard as high as anyone at court, and Nicolas paid her a pretty penny because of that regard and to be kept informed of both young majesties. He approached her, thinking, connoisseur of beauty that he was, her mouth is a taunt. A man wanted to slap her and then kiss her, hard.

"He wasn't happy about the vines," he told her, smiling as if they discussed something pleasant.

"That's your fault, Viscount. Doubtless, you surprised him. He doesn't like surprises."

"You might have told me that."

"And you might have refrained from overwhelming him with your need to be magnificent and magnanimous on all occasions."

Nicolas laughed and took her hand and kissed the soft side of her wrist. She is like a dark plum, he thought. She might be sweet when you bit into her, but it was just as likely she'd be bitter. He liked not knowing which side he'd taste.

"I want to call on you," she said. "Privately."

She wanted something. He made the proper, polite response, and moved on, his progress majestic, like a king's, people continually circling him for a moment of his time, complimenting him even when they didn't have some need to present. His importance was as shiny as the gold thread woven into his clothing. Finally, he left his crowd of admirers and supplicants and went to the Queen Mother.

There was a touch of gratitude in the smile she accorded him. She was glad, he could see, that he paid court. She and Nicolas were old friends; he had done many favors for her, some of which must never be known. He felt pitying. He'd never known this proud, vain, determined woman to be lost or directionless, but Mazarin's death had made her stumble. Not so long ago she would have been in the thick of things. It was as if she were groping for a sense of what world remained without her lover. There was an old rumor that she and Mazarin had married. Her grief certainly seemed large enough for that, despair, bewilderment in her every gesture and expression, black displayed everywhere from her mantilla to her shoes. He took her hand, a great liberty, which he was allowed. "How are you this evening, Your Majesty?"

"Out of sorts. Out of my element. I don't know where I am anymore. Do stay with me a while." She looked around herself with unhappy eyes. "What is everyone laughing about?"

All around them was furious and fast-paced flirting. The court hadn't been this lively in decades. They laugh because they are young with all their lives ahead of them, he didn't say. Seduction and gallantry and sweet promise were in the air as clearly as perfume. A born courtier could smell it, feel it, taste it.

"And those patches atop other behavior I won't mention," she continued, glaring at a group of young people nearby. "Scandalous! What can

Madame be thinking?" Some of her old fire appeared. "I've let her know I don't approve. I told the Princess de Monaco as well."

And how was that received? thought Nicolas, but all he said was, "Come soon with Her Majesty the queen and visit my estate nearby." He was building what he considered to be the finest château in France a few hours distant. There was to be a grand fête to celebrate it at the end of summer. All the court, all Paris, all France, and even points beyond, were invited. "The chapel is almost finished, and I need your fine eye to find fault with it so I may make it perfect."

"As if it won't be perfect. I talked with him today," she said, as if she read Nicolas's mind on certain dark nights when he couldn't sleep. "He needs you. It's only a matter of time."

There was no question of whom she spoke. There was only one "he" at this court, and he stood in front of the ballroom's fireplace in crimson stockings and gold ribbons and a wide hat with a feather around its brim, looking like the statue of a young god found in a Roman ruin.

Her words were reassuring, but then it would be dangerous not to need him. Ambition might be buried deep inside Nicolas—under the charm, the refinement, the creativity—but it was there, sharp as any gleaming blade.

CHAPTER 5

I t was an hour after midnight. Both queens, the older one and the younger one, had retired for the evening, and Louise waited for Fanny's signal. Sitting on a bench in one of the ballroom's arched bays, she passed the time by examining the paintings framed in the curve of the arch. Was one of these lolling women clothed in little more than a piece of gauze the goddess Choisy had explained to her? A goddess of love, what did that mean? A goddess, what was that exactly? A female god? She shivered, the idea bewildering. All her life she'd been presented with stories of the saints and of course the Blessed Mother Mary, women who had no lives but godly ones, suffering, sacrifice, sometimes a martyr's death. The only romance she knew was a scandalous one she and Fanny and the Orléans princesses had snuck away to read, thrilling over inscrutable, noble characters who met obstacle after obstacle without their love ever failing, the touch of a hand enough to sustain them for pages.

Eyes glowing in excitement, Fanny whirled over to interrupt her reverie. "The queen's ladies looked vexed, didn't they? They can't bear to be going to bed. Ha! Too bad for them. Are you ready?"

This last was said in another tone altogether. Louise stood, her eyes and Fanny's upon Madame. Henriette, surrounded by a group of admirers, suddenly gave a gasp and then made a face.

"I've torn my gown," she said to one and all. "If you'll excuse me a moment." And with Catherine at her side, she walked down the long expanse of the ballroom, Louise and Fanny behind. Once outside the ballroom, Fanny stationed herself at a statue halfway down the hall.

Louise followed Madame and the princess into a bedchamber she hadn't even known was in this part of the palace. It was one of the more beautiful chambers in a palace with many grand rooms, created over a hundred years earlier for a king's mistress. Just above eye level was a series of frescoes framed by magnificent and larger-than-life stucco figures of nude women. Woven in among their beautiful, shapely bodies were other smaller figures: animal heads, bunches of cascading fruit, and lolling putti, or cupids. The genius and grace of mixing fresco paintings with stucco sculpture had been a creation of the artists working in this palace, and it had taken the Renaissance world by storm and made the palace one of the wonders of its time. A hundred years hadn't dimmed the vibrancy of the paint or the magic fluidity of the sculpture. Although branches of candles were lit and sending their light outward, the chamber was pitch-dark in its corners, and the king stepped out of one of the corners of that darkness.

"There you are," he said.

Louise shivered at the sound of his voice, all that was in it. The romance she and the Orléans princesses had thrilled over suddenly seemed pale and timid.

"We have only a moment," Catherine warned.

The candlelight seemed to pick out and highlight the silver in Henriette's gown as she walked toward the king.

"Come and sit," said Louis, and he led Henriette to a long bench at the base of the bed while Louise and the princess stood as guards at the bedchamber's open door. Louise watched as the king reached out and took Henriette's hand, bringing it to his mouth to kiss, then bringing it to his jacket, to the place under which lay his heart.

"You know you fill this more and more," he said.

In the silence, Louise heard the beating of her own heart. It was so loud she felt that the gargoyle of a princess standing just opposite her could surely hear it and would reprimand her for possessing one. Its thump was punctuation to the words the king and Madame spoke, their voices soft, their tone intense, as if everything depended on them understanding one another completely.

"Shall I end this tenderness?" the king asked.

"Can you?"

"For your sake, I would."

"I don't think I wish you to."

This last was breathlessly said, and Louise watched Madame put her arms around the king's neck, and then she looked away, feeling constrained and distant, as if she were watching from a star. Out of the corner of her eye, she could see they kissed. She felt perturbed and aware that decisions were being made that were going to impact everyone.

There was a clatter of heels running on wood.

Fanny burst into the chamber. "The Count de Guiche is coming our way. The musketeers tried to stop him, but he wouldn't allow it. He told them Monsieur had sent him to find Madame—"

"La Baume le Blanc, sit down on the bench with her, now!" Swiftly,

Catherine moved from the door to kneel down before Henriette and grab a handful of fabric, bending over it as if she were sewing.

Filled with dread, Louise sat beside Madame, her hands clasped together, her breath caught in her throat. His Majesty had had the presence of mind to stand the moment Fanny ran into the bedchamber. And now the Count de Guiche was here, his face frowning in the dim light of the wall sconces. Behind him was the king's lieutenant of the musketeers.

"Oh, Majesty," Catherine said. Louise was amazed at how natural the gargoyle sounded; she herself couldn't have spoken if her life had depended on it. "That's too funny for words. I just won't believe it." She threw back her head and laughed.

"The Count de Guiche," announced the lieutenant.

"Excuse me if I interrupt," Guy said, looking hard at Henriette.

"Why do you interrupt, Count?" Louis asked.

How calm His Majesty sounds, thought Louise. She had the sensation that the two men were dogs bristling at each other or hawks winging after the same bird. They had the same hawk's cut to their expressions at this moment, hard mouths, set jaws, determination on each face. She couldn't know that there was a rivalry between these two that had been there since they were boys. But she could sense it.

"Your manners lack a certain grace, Count. You were rude this morning, if memory serves me, and you are rude now."

All the women were silent, frozen into stillness. A muscle worked in Guy's cheek. The lieutenant of the musketeers didn't take his eyes off Louis. Other musketeers had gathered, formed a circle behind Guy.

"Your dress is mended?" Guy asked Henriette, as if Louis hadn't spoken.

Silent, Henriette's eyes flicked from Guy to Louis and back again.

"Not quite yet, I'm afraid," Louise surprised herself by saying.

"Monsieur asks for you." Guy's tone was accusing.

"Odd," answered Louis. "I last saw him at the card table with Madame de Choisy and the Viscount Nicolas. When he plays with those two, there is no thought for anything but the next hand of cards."

"He wishes Madame at his side, for good fortune," Guy snapped.

"And I wish to finish the story I was telling her."

"Most amusing it was, too. We were just laughing at it," said Catherine, but her words died in the air, like small birds hit by hawks.

"Monsieur commands," Guy said.

"Ah," Louis replied very softly, so softly that Louise felt her body straining to hear him, "but I command Monsieur in all things, as well, Count, as you."

Every musketeer in the chamber took a step closer, but the lieutenant held up a hand stopping them.

Louise saw Guy's hand clench on the handle of his small dress sword, a rapier that could kill someone. Men wore swords as casually as they did lace on their sleeves. Would he dare draw it in the presence of the king? She felt like she might faint. Surely, one was beheaded if one threatened the king.

Catherine stood, took a step in the direction of her brother, but the lieutenant of the musketeers had placed himself between the king and Guy, calm and definite in his stance. If Guy was going to run the king through with his blade, he'd have to first cut past this soldier.

"I must ask you to consider what you are doing, Count," the lieutenant said.

"I've delivered my message. Now, I am His Majesty's to command." Guy bowed. The bow was like a slap in the face, disrespectful enough to make Louis's eyes flicker, angry lights coming into the brown of the iris. Guy backed slowly out of the room.

"Shall I follow him, sire?" the lieutenant asked Louis.

"No."

Distress evident, Henriette stood. "We must return to the ballroom, Your Majesty."

Louise could hear how upset she was. He who is afraid of leaves must not come into the woods, echoed a voice—her father's from long ago—in her mind. They shouldn't return to the ballroom like chastened children, she thought. They must act as if all were well. "It's so beautiful outside," she heard herself say.

"What we must do," said Louis, smiling as if he had not just been accosted by a friend, "your ladies and I, is go out into this night that—" He looked in Louise's direction, and it was clear that he didn't know her name.

"Miss de la Baume le Blanc." The words came out in a high-pitched croak, and Louise curtsied to cover embarrassment.

"—that Miss de la Baume le Blanc has reminded us exists and look at my carp."

"He'll be angry." There was a begging tone in Henriette's voice.

"Monsieur?" said Louis. "He doesn't even know you're not in the ballroom. Trust me in this. He hasn't beaten Madame de Choisy in a game of ombre in three years. It's an obsession with him." His voice changed. "Walk with me outside. Please?" Now, begging colored his voice.

There were steps in the hallway again, and then two of the king's friends rushed into the bedchamber.

"Sire," said Vivonne, a plump open-faced man, the son of a duke. "I told Guiche Madame wasn't to be disturbed, but he wouldn't listen."

Words spilling out, hands waving, the other, Péguilin, captain of the guard, as short as Vivonne was tall, said, "Guiche is my cousin, Your Majesty. I could see he was up to no good, but I couldn't stop him. I beg you, don't imprison him. I'll have to be arrested too to keep him company. Family, you know."

"This is a tempest over nothing. I happened upon Madame and her ladies repairing her gown and chose to stay. The count was jealous of my good fortune at being surrounded by no one but lovely ladies. We'll forgive him that. We were just going to walk to the carp pond." Louis glanced toward Henriette, but Péguilin's words, the excitable shortness of him, Vivonne's large earnestness, had already altered the mood, lessened the distress of Guy's entrance.

"It would be my pleasure if you joined us," Louis said to the men, and so it was a laughing group that wound its way toward stairs that would lead them to the fountain courtyard. Vivonne and Péguilin were like court jesters, performing anything, from standing on chairs to making faces to force the maids of honor and Catherine and Madame to laugh.

And then they were outside and all walking down the broad, even steps that led them into the courtyard bordered by the carp pond. Louise inhaled the scent of the jasmine growing in great stone pots set here and there. Everyone seemed calmer, she thought, skipping down stairs, her gown held up, Péguilin at her side, absolutely determined to flirt. Certainly she felt calmer inside. Yes, she thought, the king and Madame don't look so wild, now, so startled and yearning. If Monsieur had seen them in that bedchamber, he would have known they were falling in love. The count knew. Louise had seen the shock of it in his face. Above them was a beautiful night with stars in the sky no less bright than the candles in lanterns. She raised her face to the night, feeling vulnerable and shaken.

"Your eyes are stars." Péguilin went to one knee like an actor. "I adore you. Be mine."

"Hush," said Louise. "His Majesty will hear you."

"I care not who hears me. World," Péguilin bellowed, "I adore this one." But he'd moved to stand before Catherine. "No. It's this one. You have my love. And you know it, fair cousin."

Louis stood at the stone balustrade pointing out carp to Henriette. "Some of the fish in this pond were admired by my great-grandfather. Some are a hundred years old," he told her.

Louis could feel himself begin to steady inside, calm a little. He'd been brittle and unanchored since finding the Mazarinade, and the kiss they'd exchanged moments earlier had ignited a fire in him that he thought would burn his heart to ash. Henriette leaned over the balustrade, and in the leaning, her breast crushed against his hand. She met his eyes for a deliberate moment, and it felt to him as if the world stopped spinning. I love you, her eyes seemed to say. I desire what you desire.

Then Péguilin and Vivonne were there, and Louis moved to one side to allow them their preening and peacocking, his thoughts moving on like a rushing river. Henriette's mouth was as sweet as honey. Sweeter. The initiative had been hers. She'd kissed him. He ached for another kiss from her. His heart felt parched. Henriette and her ladies had dried their hair this afternoon by taking off their hats and sitting with it down around their shoulders. The only time a woman's hair was down and upon her shoulders was when she was in her bed. He'd love to climb into her bed and run his hands through her loosened hair, say to her, Love me, sweet, fill my joy in brimming measure. And then his mind flipped like a carp in the pond. There weren't enough funds in the treasury to build even one ship for the navy; they'd have to beg, borrow, or steal the money. Perhaps in a few years from now, the viscount had told him this morning, a little dismissive, as if Louis had requested a toy.

Courtiers were advancing out of the palace, walking down the straight stairs, drawn by his absence in the ballroom, drawn by their fear to miss something. The courtyard was becoming festive. He'd known many of these people all his life. Was one of them the writer of the Mazarinades? Who was truly trustworthy? There was a moat built around part of this palace, a reminder that treachery was familiar to all kings. His musketeers were around the courtyard, in and out of the torches' light. They'd been with him since he was a child, transferring their loyalty directly and without hesitation from his father's deathbed to him. The king is dead. Long live the king. Were any of them in the viscount's pay? Did one of them spy upon his actions and report them to the viscount?

He is an enemy in our midst. So insisted a man named Colbert. Caw, caw, Colbert. The crow. Such a dreary man, mocked Olympe. And here she was, crossing the courtyard, having snuck away from her duties to the queen, certain she'd receive no reprimand from him. She hadn't gone with the queen today to listen to nuns singing in a nearby village, either. Some of my ladies were unwell today, Maria Teresa had told him tonight. Too unwell to hear chanting and prayers, but well enough to appear in the ballroom and now in this courtyard, all teasing and smiles, talking with this or that man. If only his wife weren't so serious.

Olympe marched up and hung upon his arm, as if he were not the king, but some boy, some swain, some simple man she knew. She began to talk of the hunt tomorrow, of how her arrow was going to be the one to bring down the stag, not his. She'd never been shy with him. Never. He'd always liked her for that. And at this moment he blessed her because his feeling for Henriette left him dazed and almost unable to speak.

Philippe appeared at the top of the stairs.

"I've won!" he called. He ran down the steps and found Henriette among the crowd.

"A kiss for good luck," he told her.

"Where are you going?" Louis asked, for Philippe had kissed his wife and, instead of remaining with them, was bolting back up the staircase two broad steps at a time.

"To win again. Once proves nothing."

Louis laughed. He couldn't help but admire his brother's style and zest for life. "They'll pick your pockets."

"Then you'll have to make me a loan, the way you always do." Philippe flashed his warmest smile, and Louis was reminded of how much his every kindness meant to his brother, always had. And what had he done in return? Kissed his brother's wife. Anguish filled him. There was no dear, wise cardinal whispering advice in his ear any longer, telling him to go away and play. There was no one to command him now but his own conscience. His conscience. His marriage didn't touch his deepest heart, and the heart was its own master.

Carriages were being summoned. It had become the custom to ride around the long landscape pool after midnight. Henriette had wished to do so the very first night she'd come to Fontainebleau as Madame, and now it was what the young court did.

Choisy, rushing around playing footman, opened a carriage door for Olympe. "My dear Countess," he purred, "feeling better from this afternoon, I see. What an amazing recovery. One is so glad. Such excitement, yes? Our new Madame has become the queen of all hearts. Isn't it delightful?"

He deflected her venomous look with a cat-like smile and saw that Athénaïs, the sunny-faced beauty who was one of the queen's maids of honor, had also snuck away to come down here and was standing by herself. Daring. It was one thing for Olympe, who was married and had a high position, to disobey rules, but it was quite another for a maid of honor. But Athénaïs belonged to one of the best families of France, and that nobility had earned her a place in the queen's household last year when there had been huge fuss and great pomp around the king's marriage.

"Aren't you going with them?" he asked her. The last carriage was rolling through the ornate gate that separated the courtyard from the gardens.

"I mustn't," she said. "It was bold of me to leave my chambers. I don't dare stay out all night, too. Someone will tattle."

"Vivonne leaves you here alone?" Vivonne was her brother. He was among the king's household and counted as friend, and he'd been the first to leap into a saddle and escort a carriage out.

"He's one of Madame's admirers. He shouldn't have to miss all the fun just because I must. He says it's the fashion to be in love with her. You know Vivonne; he is never behind fashion."

Nor are you, thought Choisy. It must chafe no end to be part of a household as retired as the queen's was.

He walked Athénaïs into the palace, waved to her as she ran down a hall that would take her to the queen's chambers. He found his mother in a small room off the ballroom before a pier glass. She was repositioning an enormous brooch on the bosom of her gown.

"I just won this back," she said.

"Monsieur is losing?"

"But of course."

"The Countess de Soissons slipped her leash. She's out riding in the carriages with Madame's ladies," he said.

Madame de Choisy laughed. "Yes, our little queen is so very pious. It must be very wearing on the nerves of her ladies. If I were in the queen's household, I should jab my wrist with an embroidery needle and try to bleed to death. Walk me back to the game. I feel it my duty to take as much of Monsieur's coin as I may before the sun comes up."

༼༽

The others were riding in carriages or on horseback enjoying the moonlight, but Louis had slipped away. Belle, his favorite dog, at his feet, he sat, legs sprawled, listening to his night crow Colbert, who always wore black and seldom smiled and perched on Louis's shoulder like a messenger sent to advise from Mazarin. Colbert was helping him make some sense of the kingdom's finances. There had been no register kept for too long, no record of what came in and what went out and to whom. There was no record of loans made or the interest at which they had been negotiated. Louis had reinstated the register with Mazarin's death in March.

Colbert, no excess of anything about him, lace or otherwise, a raven among the peacocks of court, a stone cast in the babbling brook that was court, stood before the opened register book, little notes from inside a velvet pouch, black like everything Colbert wore littered around it. We've borrowed on taxes at least two years ahead, the Viscount Nicolas had explained patiently at council earlier this day. It's what we've done for years, living off anticipation. That borrowing cost much in interest. Too much, said Colbert. Exorbitant.

"Here," said Colbert, and Louis saw the figure the viscount had ordered a clerk to enter in the large book that was now the record of finances. From the pouch Colbert took a very small book, which he opened, its pages making a dry rustle. "This is what the cardinal himself told me the amount of the loan was."

He would know, for Colbert had been in charge of Mazarin's private finances, in charge of Mazarin's private life, and gradually he had become part of Mazarin's public life, a trusted servant. I give you Colbert, his dear Mazarin had said on his deathbed. Forgive me my sins.

"If you will compare," Colbert continued in his flat voice, "you will see the viscount has entered the interest at this figure, when it is actually three times higher. And here you can see the viscount has also entered the loan at a smaller figure. The difference goes directly into the viscount's coffers."

Crush the thieves with public trials and begin again, said Colbert. Thrifty, industrious, he wanted a cleaning of the Augean stables that was finance. In his mind, Nicolas was the chief thief.

"Why would the viscount lie?" Louis asked him. "I told him myself that he was to conceal nothing from me, that the past was gone and forgotten, that I understood that desperate times called for desperate remedies."

"I think his misdeeds are too many, sire. I think he cannot tell all. I think he no longer knows all. It is too great a web. I think—" Colbert stopped and pursed his mouth in a way Louis was coming to know.

"Say it."

"I think he is used to living like a sultan, sire, and cannot now, even if he wished, let it go. I now have some accurate figures on the matter I broached before," Colbert continued. "There are twenty-five armed vessels in the whale fishery the Viscount Nicolas owns. And he has secretly purchased six warships from the United Netherlands."

Louis went still inside. Only this morning he had been informed his treasury had not the money to build or buy ships, yet the viscount could buy ships? Warships? "You're certain?"

"I swear on the heart of my oldest son."

Cold, colorless, not an ounce of emotion in either expression or gesture, Colbert allowed himself a glimpse of the king's face and then contented himself with staring at the scenes woven in the tapestries that hung on the wall, ignoring what was revealed for the moment in his sovereign's expression. "It's late. I've tired you, sire," he said. "Forgive my zealousness. Good night, Your Majesty."

Louis sat where he was for a time. What do I do? he thought. Declaw the tiger I suspect? Was a tiger tamed if he had no claws? There were still teeth. If the Viscount Nicolas rebelled, who might follow? He leaned down and patted his dog's head. Then he heard a soft sound and knew his valet had entered, making just enough noise to remind him that for him the night was not done. Could he defang a tiger without waking other tigers, those who could fund private armies from their wealth and connections and high birth, like his cousin the Prince de Condé? Do I rule with the viscount or without him? thought Louis. His father had ordered those who betrayed killed. What should he, Louis, the fourteenth of that name, do? Gently pulling his dog's ears, he said to the valet, "She's not acting her usual self. I've been watching all day."

"She's strong, sire. Don't fret."

Louis stood, off to join the laughing group at the landscape pool, and his valet straightened draperies, ran a hand over a coverlet that was perfectly smooth as Louis lingered a moment longer with Belle. The valet knew His Majesty well. Once upon a time, the valet had allowed a small royal boy to creep into his narrow servant's bed and sleep beside him, their backs touching. It had comforted the royal boy on too many nights when there were bad dreams, when outside the walls of the bedchamber betrayal tiptapped by on courtiers' feet. His Majesty was troubled. The valet could feel it the way he could feel the rise and fall of his own breath. Would, he thought, as he refolded a handkerchief that needed no folding, would that something so simple could comfort him now.

Henriette's maids of honor stood groaning and yawning, stepping out of high-heeled shoes, undoing laces at the backs of gowns, pulling ribbons and hairpins from their hair, while their maidservants scurried to pick up dropped gowns that lay in pools on the floor, hurrying to find shoes, collect pins and bracelets, hand out nightgowns. The maids would rise in just a few hours to brush out these same gowns, looking for any stain that might need to be cleaned. They'd be washing stockings and hanging them to dry, polishing jewels, placing them carefully back into jewel boxes, listening for the sound of the servant's bell that would summon them to wait upon sleepy mistresses who might as easily wake to a bad mood as one good. The maidservants were young, as young or younger than the women they served.

"Wasn't Péguilin amusing tonight?" Louise whispered from the pillow beside Fanny. She and Fanny shared a bed. The other two maids of honor did likewise. "Pretending to be in love with the Princess de Monaco. I thought I would die laughing when he followed her around on his knees."

"He *is* in love, I'd say."

"How do you know?"

"Watch his face when she's near. Look in his eyes. I think you should flirt with her brother, the count. I certainly would. He's beautiful."

Louise made a face in the dark. The Count de Guiche reminded her of a forest wolf: lone, fierce, independent. She'd seen a wolf break the neck of a deer. "No," she whispered back and closed her eyes. Sometimes Fanny's chattering lulled her right to sleep.

"He needs to be diverted. You must do it for Madame's sake. His Majesty and she kissed again tonight. I saw it. They're in love. This is all very exciting," whispered Fanny. "I'm so glad His Majesty hasn't chosen the Countess de Soissons. I hate her. I saw you with the Viscount Nicolas. I wasn't the only one to notice. Oh, Louise, if you attract his regard, you can go anywhere, do anything."

"He walked me from the hallway out of courtesy. He's very polite."

"You pleased him. I saw it in his expression. He's incredibly rich, and he's kind. If you have the opportunity—"

"Oh, be quiet." Louise turned on her side away from Fanny. "I have to get up early tomorrow."

"Going riding with Choisy again? I was angry at him for making the king look my way when he pinched me and made me squawk like some idiot parrot, but I've forgiven him, for he knows all the gossip. Guess what he told me. His Majesty was in love before he married the queen!"

"With whom!?" Louise was stirred out of drowsiness.

"With Marie Mancini, a younger sister to the Countess de Soissons. The Queen Mother and Monsieur wouldn't have it. They said a king of France must wed a great princess."

"Where is this Marie Mancini?"

"Hidden away somewhere. Choisy says she marries a prince who lives in Rome and goes away forever this month."

"I wonder if His Majesty minds."

"He can have anyone he desires. I doubt he thinks of it now."

But what about her? Louise thought she spoke the words, but she couldn't be certain because without meaning to, she'd fallen asleep; surely these were dreams of green forests and a weeping bride and gleaming wolves' eyes and her father and mother walking hand in hand toward a little girl that must be her, only she was asleep far away from the home of her childhood, and it couldn't be, could it? What big teeth the wolf had.

❧⁂❧

Louis stood before an immense fireplace in another wing of the palace. He'd seen his young court to their bed; all that waited was for him to go to his wife's bedchamber, climb in beside her sleeping form. The chamber in which he stood had been the king's bedchamber, but not for a hundred years. Now it was vacant and mostly empty, used for performances by the acting troupes Louis or his brother patronized. Atop the mantel was a marble statue of his grandfather, Henri IV, riding a charger—both man and horse almost life-size—part of the decor of the fireplace, so distinctive, so grand that everyone in the palace called it the fine fireplace.

Louis's grandfather wore a crown of laurel, and on each side of him, there were the beautiful female figures so beloved of sculptors, one representing clemency, the other peace. His grandfather had been every inch a king, large in life, in war, in love, in rebuilding the kingdom. Reared Protestant, he'd converted to Catholicism to take the crown. Paris is worth a Mass, he'd said. At a famous battle, he'd told his gathered army, if you lose your standard bearers, rally to my white plume: you will find it on the road to victory and honor.

The road to victory and honor. Stirring words. A road Louis wished to travel. He wished to make this grandfather proud, to equal or surpass him. His hand rested against the pocket in which lay the small, folded Mazarinade. There was so much to do. The immensity of the task before him—bringing the kingdom to order, to prosperity, to pride—seemed, now that he had a fuller picture, more than he—Louis, God's annointed, God's given as he'd been styled at his birth, but still he was only a man—could bear. Trade was in ruins. The treasury was in ruins. The innate respect that should be given God's anointed had eroded. There were enemies, always. He felt the outline of the note. Seen and unseen. This grandfather forever captured in marble had been assassinated. But there were many ways to die. His own father had been dead inside his soul years before he breathed his last.

God and the saints, let me accomplish something, he prayed, staring up at this marble figure who had accomplished much, who had lived with a zest that was legend even to this day. Let me live, truly live, in this life I've been given. Prepare a table before me in the presence of mine enemies. Anoint my head with oil, Sacred One. I need Thee. At this moment, his responsibilities, the decisions he must make, seemed enormous. She'd kissed him again. He loved his brother's wife.

CHAPTER 6

Belle's wet nose on his hand woke him. Louis opened his eyes, kissed his wife's cheek, and followed his valet and dogs to his own bedchamber. He slipped into his own bed, the dogs with him, for an hour's sleep, then bed curtains were opened, and his day began. Sitting up, he recited prayers and the rosary, his confessor with him. Servants and other, lesser valets swarmed about as he sat on his close stool. He walked into an antechamber to begin dressing. Courtiers—some gentlemen of his household, some not—bowed, and Louis was pleased to see Guy, even with their confrontation of the night before, there.

"La Grande Mademoiselle comes today," chirped his brother.

This was one of their cousins.

Philippe held the cloth with which Louis would dry himself after rinsing his mouth and washing his face and hands, and he found he couldn't look his brother in the eye, but Philippe, who loved ceremony, who loved the fact that as the king's brother, as heir until a son was born, he took precedence during all ritual, didn't notice, but chattered on about their cousin's arrival from Paris and the day's hunt.

"Will you ride your new horse?" Philippe asked. The horse was a gift from the King of Spain and only recently arrived. So proud were the Spanish of their horses' bloodlines that they did not sell them outside their kingdom. "He's fiery," continued Philippe, without waiting for an answer, looking around at those gathered. "I went to the stables yesterday and saw him. He's going to be a beast to ride."

Horseflesh and Spain's horses, the best in the world, took over the conversation until Louis's chaplain entered, and everyone knelt for more prayers. Beginning to dress afterward, this courtier handing him his shirt, another his breeches, a third his stockings, yet another his boots, he was soon ready. He sat down for his hair to be combed, and Guy approached. Louis nodded in a friendly way.

"You want a navy, I'm told," said Guy. "Will you do me the honor to give me command of one of the first ships?"

That was Guy. Ever direct. And nosing around for what might be happening. Talk about a navy had been only yesterday. "If one is ever built," Louis answered.

"It will be, sir. The Viscount Nicolas has alchemist in him. I swear he can make gold from lead. If it weren't for him, I'd be in rags."

"Gone through your allowance?"

"Two years ago."

"Me too," said Louis, and then they both laughed, boys suddenly, amused and lighthearted, old friends who'd grown up together in bad times and good.

"I've another request, sir."

"Only one?"

"Monsieur. He lives to be of service to you. It's his right as a prince of the blood to have a place on your council."

"I think I have no need to be reminded of the rights of princes of the blood. Or how they have too often abused them."

"He's loyal to you." Guy flung out an arm, taking in the day, the sunshine streaming through a tall window, the courtiers and musketeers around them. "You are king of France, my lord. Your least whisper is our command. Make a place for him, I beg you. It would be the finest thing you've ever done."

His temper snapped. "My finest moment was not arresting you three years ago!" He shook his head, and his valet stepped back. He walked into the bedchamber, where fine hats, feathers curling like nested birds on wide brims, were laid out for him to choose. In the antechamber, courtiers began to disperse. A hardy few would join the king on his early morning's ride, but many of them would go back to bed. That would change one day soon; only fools would be absent. A chance to catch Louis's eyes, to be seen by him, to speak to him, would be worth the price of gold, but not yet. The cardinal's reign, the old way of doing things, still hung over court.

Philippe walked up to Guy. "Well?"

"I made him angry," Guy answered.

"It won't last," answered Philippe.

"He brought up his deathbed. He doesn't forget, and I don't think he forgives us." Visiting his soldiers on a battlefield several years ago, Louis had fallen ill. For two weeks, his life had hung in the balance.

"Oh, dear."

"You did what was proper," said Guy. "It was thought he was dying. Don't be ashamed of acting the king. Your blood is as royal as his. If his child doesn't live or is a girl, you're still heir. Do you ride out with him this morning?"

"Back to bed for me." Philippe smiled, knowing everyone, even Guy, envied him the wife asleep in that bed.

"Fortunate man. I didn't see her beauty before," said Guy.

"And that," Philippe grinned—he was smaller than Guy and Louis, finer boned, but no less handsome—"is why I'm married to her and you are not. I've always had an eye for beauty, hidden or no."

"She would never have married me."

"How quickly you forget her plight. She might have leapt at the chance. Your family is distinguished and honorable enough. Your sister is married to a crown prince."

"But would I have desired her then, when she was desperate?" Guy shook his head. "Probably not. I like what I can't have."

"As do I," Philippe said very softly, but if Guy heard him, he ignored him and walked away, his arrogant, just-this-side-of-insolent surety trailing behind him like a cloak.

In the bedchamber, Louis stared down at a hat. He'd been berating himself for letting Guy see that old actions still rankled. But in among white feathers around the brim of the handsomest hat, the red wax of an unmarked seal shouted out. He put his hand out to grasp the small, folded note. Even before he opened it, he knew what it was: another Mazarinade.

❧❧❧

"I want to go north," said Louise.

"I don't want to go at all. This is fruitless, and I didn't go to bed early, and I cannot believe I allowed myself to be talked into this," answered Choisy.

Dawn had lit the day in cool gold and rose hues some time ago, and other than servants, grooms, and dogs, Louise and Choisy seemed to be the only ones up. In the saddle, a groom following, they turned their horses toward the towering palace gatehouse that led to the village and then the forest beyond. Carts filled with lettuces, cabbages, carrots, beans from outlying farms lined up before the kitchen buildings. Chickens roosted here and there on the carts' sides, not knowing that today was very likely their day to be served before the king. Wrapped securely in a black cloak so that he resembled a dark butterfly or bat, wings folded tight, a man walked past on foot. He raised a broad, pale face to Louise and Choisy as they trotted past him and touched his hat in respect to Louise.

"Who is that?" asked Louise.

"Monsieur Colbert." Choisy was curt.

"Isn't he on the king's council?"

"Hardly. Only the Viscount Nicolas, Monsieur le Tellier, and Monsieur Lionne grace the council. But he was the cardinal's right-hand man, and

I believe His Majesty has placed him on some committee about trade or some such."

"Are you on a council yet?"

"Soon, or so Monsieur tells me. He tells me he has the viscount's support and that all of us who are Monsieur's friends will be part of His Majesty's councils, as is our right."

"How wonderful. I'm very glad for you."

They rode in silence, the forest ahead of them, a cool, green canopy of ancient trees. Birds warbled a morning chant, and as they rode in under trees, Louise could feel her heart expand. She loved the forest, the wild emerald grace of it. Her morning rides, with or without Choisy, taken rain or shine, settled her in some way she had no words for, gave her the calm she needed to go back to Fontainebleau and act maid of honor to a princess, a young woman on the cusp of infidelity. And if Madame was unfaithful, what then? Deceit, for certain, by Louise and Fanny. And if something went wrong—it's not going to, said Fanny, who imagined more power, more riches, more honor than was conceivable, spilling down from Madame to them. We'll marry viscounts at the least, said Fanny.

"Tell me about His Majesty's first love, Marie Mancini," Louise said.

"So, Fanny told you, did she?"

"He gave her up easily?"

"Who knows what he felt—"

Louise thought of the face she'd seen when the king had stopped on the way to his wedding, a face drawn at the edges, too finely honed. He felt grief, she thought.

"—it's said she wouldn't be his mistress. Only queen was good enough for her. Ha. As if a Mazarin niece could be queen." He wiped his brow. "It's going to be hot today. I'm going to ruin my complexion."

"You say that every time. We have to cross the river. Your mother's château is across the river." This was the beginning of his arguing with her to turn around. At least twice a week, she managed to talk him into accompanying her on her search for the boy in the iron mask, and for the first hour he tried to change her mind. Hadn't he learned by now she could be quite single-minded?

She pointed. "Let's ride north, and see what we find. I have at least four hours before anyone is really awake enough to notice I've gone." There must be a map of this area somewhere, she thought.

An hour later, she sat outside a hut, drinking from a tin scoop, her eyes scanning the lean-to where these peasants' cow was kept at night, wondering if her boy in the iron mask was hidden in a dark attic somewhere—not here, but somewhere. People tied their mad relatives to braces in attics or basements or back bedrooms. Near her, in the shade, was a baby in a hand-carved cradle, a toddler tied to one of the cradle's ends, and a small boy sitting in the dust shelling beans carefully and seriously into a wooden bowl. Inside the house, an old man and woman sat up in the only bed, shawls around their shoulders, eyes dull. The woman of the farm, after having drawn water for Louise, was back in her garden, hoeing. Without this garden, the family would not survive. It would last them through the summer, and then there must be vegetables from it dried, something put up, for winter, remorseless in its length and cold.

"Look what I found."

Choisy pushed a child from around the corner of the hut. Dressed in a faded gown that had been washed far too many times, the girl was barefoot.

"She was hiding behind a tree there." Choisy pointed to the tree with his fan. "Watching you."

There were purple bruises on the girl's arms from elbow to hand, one side of her face was swollen to grotesque proportions. Choisy raised an eyebrow at Louise, then walked over to the patch of garden the woman hoed.

"Is this one much trouble?" he asked, pointing his fan toward the girl.

"My oldest," said the woman. She looked up from the dirt and raised tired eyes to Choisy's, pleading naked in them. "She's in the way, too many of us. Take her, my lord."

"You need a second servant, Louise," Choisy said without pausing for a breath, and Louise was too surprised to say anything.

Hoe in hand, the woman walked out of the garden and straight over to Louise, dropped to her knees in the dust, and said, "I beg you, noble lady."

"Done," said Choisy. "Do you know where the king's palace is?"

The woman nodded.

"Send her there tomorrow."

"Today," said the woman. "Take her today. Now."

Choisy looked at the hut, the children in the cradle and out of it, the lean-to, the distant figure of a man following a plow pulled by a single ox. That ox was an important part of the farm's survival, more important than this girl, who...what? Spoke too little? Too much? Moved too fast? Too slowly? Looked too ugly? Or too fair? The past few harvests had been bad. Everyone had his breaking point.

"Her clothing?"

"On her back," said the woman.

Choisy lifted the girl into the groom's saddle. "The horse will hold you both," he told the groom, as he opened a small, embroidered, leather bag that hung from his waist and pulled out a coin.

The woman took the coin, bit it once, then closed her eyes, the coin in a tight fist. A single tear, dredged from some place that had forgotten how to weep, slid down her face.

"Back home for us," Choisy said to Louise, and once she was atop her horse, and they were trotting past the lean-to, "No place here to hide a madman; no madman except the one who works the fields. By the Blessed Savior's fingertips, what we do to one another passes all bounds. I refuse to open the cupboards and doors of every hovel we happen across. Enough, Louise. I'm not aiding you anymore. The sight of this girl, atop that woman's tears, has broken my heart. I'll stay in my perfumed chambers and forget this world exists, thank you very much."

"When we find the place where he is—"

"He'll slit our throats. Madmen do that, you know."

"Boy. He was a boy, Choisy."

They rode on in silence for a while, each lost in thought, Louise wondering how she might learn the countryside more precisely and how she could pay for an extra servant, and Choisy wondering why worlds such as the one the peasant woman lived in existed. It's God's will, said his mother, said the priests, but the harshness of God's will overwhelmed him at the moment.

"Choisy," Louise said, a tone in her voice that made Choisy turn to look directly at her. "I—I can't afford another servant. I'm so sorry, but it's true. What shall we do?"

"We'll take her to the Carmelites."

There was a nunnery in a village near the palace. Nunneries, monasteries, the nuns and priests within them, dotted the countryside, served as accent marks in the towns and cities. Every noble family was linked in some way to the church, an unmarried daughter or a widow who'd become a nun; second and third sons looked on the church as another way to advance through society. Jesuits, Carmelites, Benedictines, Poor Clares, Franciscans, and others served the world in ways as varied as the order and tradition of each individual community. Some took in orphans, some the mad, some lived in silence, some wove themselves into the politics of every court. A disgraced wife, the family drunkard, an illegitimate child, the wayward son, any of them might find themselves locked behind a nunnery's gate, confined within a monk's cell, the rules, the chants, the prayers, the ringing of bells, the chores, the ritual of the day unvarying and constant, there to soothe, to chastise, to placate, to soften, to mold, to serve.

"Are you going to rescue every beaten girl you come across?"

"Most probably."

Louise pulled the reins of her horse short, and when Choisy did likewise, she leaned up out of the sidesaddle and kissed him on the mouth. "That's for your large heart, sir," she said.

He looked off in the distance. "Would you marry me if I asked?"

His question made her laugh. What a jester he was and a gossip and a dear. "Would I have to share my gowns?"

There was a short silence she didn't expect. Then he said, "I should have worn a mask and a large hat like you have on. I think I've burned my complexion."

Louise tapped at her horse with the crop to ride on, thinking, I ought to have asked the woman about madmen roaming the forest. There were always legends that were more than half true among peasants and country folk.

I think I truly love her, thought Choisy. What will I do with that?

❧

It was just noon when they returned from the nunnery. The girl had been dropped off as if she were a pumpkin or basket of apples. The nuns would decide her fate, perhaps teach her a skill, sewing or cooking. Such was the lot of poor girls. Louise wasn't poor, but if her mother hadn't remarried, she might have ended up in a nunnery herself because after her father died, managing the farm was too much for her mother. The palace was alive on every level as she and Choisy dismounted their horses, courtiers up, dressed, running from one royal set of apartments to the next. Many of them also called upon the Viscount Nicolas, who wasn't royal but whose power was.

I'll visit and see how the girl fares, Louise thought, as she hurried into a kitchen to grab some bread and cheese, drink down a gulp of cider, because soon she'd have to stand for several hours if Madame chose to dine in public with the royal family. She ran all the way to Madame's set of rooms. In the first antechamber her friends embroidered on an altar cloth Madame was going to present to the queen. Madame's spaniels ran yapping joyously to her, and she, who liked all animals, bent to pull long dog ears, so that her eyes didn't have to meet the gargoyle's, who stood lovely and impatient by the frame of one of the tall windows.

"There you are." Catherine's voice was ice. "Slept in, did we?"

"I'm sorry." Louise had a soft voice, and under the softness was a sweet, clear pitch that touched most hearts.

But Catherine was impressed with neither soft nor sweet. "Take the dogs out, La Baume le Blanc. At once."

Dismissed like a washerwoman's daughter and glad of it, Louise stuck out her tongue at her three friends left behind to embroider with her difficultness, her haughtiness, her nose-in-the-airness, Catherine, the Princess de Monaco, while she, Miss Louise de Nobody, escaped.

Louise ran, the dogs behind her, down to the queen's garden, and the spaniels, naughty half-wild things because everyone stayed too busy to train them properly, did what they should. Dogs in chase, Louise ran from one bronze statue to another, unaware they were replicas of magnificent statues that had once embellished ancient Rome. It had been the whim of one of the king's ancestors to send architects directly to Rome, where marble statues and temples of the long-ago empire were not yet all rubble or all stolen. Artisans had brought back ancient busts, statues, torsos, and molds of that which they couldn't buy. Right here at Fontainebleau a smelting works had been set up, and bronzes were made from the molds: huge, handsome, overpowering mythical figures that had once gazed down at Roman emperors, Roman legions, and Roman citizens, figures with the names of Hercules, Ariadne, Venus, Apollo.

This garden, which had become completely enclosed over time, a verdant cage smelling of sweet olive and orange blossoms, of jasmine and rose, was completely to Her Majesty's taste. She liked being encased and surrounded. The wilderness of forest beyond upset and frightened her. She didn't understand the furor with which the French court hunted there, distrusting the wild passion and abandon displayed, a passion she suspected spilled over into other aspects of life.

Louise stepped out of her heeled shoes so she could run even faster. There was no one about; the queen and her ladies never went outside until after dining with His Majesty. In spite of her limp, she ran like the girl she still was.

❧❀❧

Staring at the remaining maids of honor as if she were envisioning each of them stripped to the waist and flogged, Catherine had remained where she stood.

"Miss de la Baume le Blanc forgot the leashes, ma'am," Fanny ventured. "Shall I take them—"

Catherine snatched them herself and left the antechamber, her skirts swirling around her.

"Poor Louise," said Fanny to the others.

But Catherine wasn't looking for a maid of honor to thrash; she had someone else in mind, and she found him in the chamber Monsieur had given him, a long, open room, comfortable and beautifully furnished, not in one of the attics, but on the same floor as the royals were housed, a gesture of great favor from the brother of the king.

Catherine opened the door without knocking. Writing, her brother sat at a table, a furrow between his brows, and he lifted his head to see who it was and stood to greet her.

"Your conduct last night was unprecedented!" she burst out. "What on earth is wrong with you? You are so fortunate, so loved, and so perfectly capable of ruining everything for a whim. You stop it right now, or I'm going to Father. I mean it."

To summon up their father's reprimand was something neither ever wanted, not because their father was cruel, but because he was the most honorable man either of them knew.

"Abominable," Catherine continued, "charging in on Madame like that, like a bad actor portraying a betrayed husband. Do you fancy yourself in love with her? Is that it?"

He tilted his head to one side. "Are you of all people going to lecture me on the conduct of betrayed husbands, Catherine? I can only wait with bated breath."

But she wasn't to be sidetracked. "I didn't sleep a wink last night. What kind of fool are you, Guy?"

"I should be on His Majesty's council."

"And so you embarrass him as he talks with Madame? If you want a place on the council, you misstepped three years ago. I thought us blessed that His Majesty didn't imprison you then—"

"For what? We were looking toward what could happen if he did die. There were no plots, no cabals, just an asking and receiving of advice. I'll remind you that Monsieur was in the front row weeping with joy at the thanksgiving service for His Majesty's recovery!"

"You press your luck too far; you always have! You can no longer treat him like some rival you have the right to question. He's changing, right before our eyes. I see it if you don't. You were offensive last night. Dangerously so. If Monsieur doesn't mind what his wife does, neither should you!"

"I mind for Monsieur."

"It is none of your affair who the king admires!"

"It is my affair when it is my prince and my friend's wife!"

"Monsieur will be out of love in another few weeks. You know that better than anyone. We both know who he really loves." She was in dangerous territory, but Guy didn't lose his temper.

"That being so," he said, "His Majesty should have the decency to wait until Monsieur indicates boredom. I see no sign of such."

"What of Madame? What about what she wishes?"

"Her wish should be to satisfy her husband in all ways. It's a wife's only duty."

Catherine made a sound of disgust and threw the dogs' leashes at him. "What a hypocrite you are! I can't bear it!" The leashes hit him in the mouth and dropped to the floor. "Take those to the queen's garden and give them to Miss de la Baume le Blanc, who is there with those damned dogs. Take a walk around the garden and think about what you're doing. I'd hate to see you banished from court. You know how I am. I won't come to visit you in exile!" She slammed the door shut behind her as Guy rubbed the place on his face where the leashes had hit.

Downstairs, he stood in one of the garden gallery's huge open arches, the view spreading out before him, Louise playing among shrubs and statues with the dogs. Her shoes were off, and she was running like a child, but he was thinking about the past, of a moment when it had looked as if the world was going to be placed in his hands. He's dying, that was the word that had come. Louis had journeyed to a battlefield and fallen down with a fever, and the fever didn't lessen. The Queen Mother and Cardinal Mazarin rushed to his bedside. Louis, the miracle birth, the God Given, was wasting away. Priests chanted prayers outside the bedchamber. Last rites were prepared as he burned with fever for fourteen days. Important officials and courtiers began to call upon the heir to the throne. You must receive them, Guy advised. Philippe was torn between grief, amazement that the crown might be his, and terror of the responsibility, for while Louis had been trained in every way, Philippe had been trained in none. And then, Louis recovered, and he was furious, as if his only brother had planned treason. Not true, Guy had defended. There was never a plot to take the crown, Guy said, only, God forbid, to receive it, and God did forbid, Your Majesty. Long live the king.

What Louis didn't forgive was that Guy had known what to do.

The maid of honor had a stick and had clearly taught the spaniels, little beggars, disobedient and spoiled, to fetch. She had a way with animals, he'd noticed. One could see it in the response of any horse she rode. He watched her reward the dogs with bits of food from her pockets. What lady keeps food in her pockets? thought Guy. He stepped out from the shade of the gallery and into the strong sunlight and called to her.

"My sister insisted I bring these to you. Is she as haughty with you as she is with me?" he asked, smiling a little. There was something of an angel about the pure lines of her face.

She bent over to put silken cords around the spaniels' necks and murmured, "Thank you."

Comfortable in his arrogance, Guy considered her. Common, his sister sniffed, but perhaps the correct word was uncommon. Her hair was a pale butter color he liked, thick and shining with life where it had come unfastened from its pins. She wore a slim, fitted jacket for horseback, blue braiding at seams that flared downward to her slim hips. The outdoors look of her, the hoyden style of her hair, her face shining from running, suited her.

My hair, Louise thought. She began to repin it. "My mother always says I can't stay neat for a second." She spoke nervously and felt stupid the minute she opened her mouth. This Count de Guiche made her feel wary.

"You've been riding?" Guy asked.

"Yes."

"And where did you go?"

"Oh, here and there."

She isn't about to tell me, thought Guy. She doesn't like me. He felt amused, but also, suddenly, angry. He'd had enough of headstrong women for one day. "How long have you had a limp? Is your leg healing from something?"

Louise felt the onset of her terrible, staining blush heat her neck. "I fell from a horse when I was young."

"I've embarrassed you. Forgive me, I would never have known if I hadn't seen you running like a peasant in stockinged feet." He picked up one of her shoes to examine it, pulled out the special little wooden block that evened Louise's legs, examined it coolly before putting it back in place.

Louise snatched the shoe and put it on her foot. "No shoes on," she heard herself saying. "My mother would be so ashamed. I take you from Amboise, she says, but you keep the dirt of it under your fingernails."

Guy took one of her hands, examined it. "Quite clean. Your fingernails, I mean."

"Yours aren't."

Startled, Guy looked at his hands.

"Is that ink? Writing love letters, Count?"

"Dozens."

"Don't send one to me." She and the dogs ran toward the gallery.

Little adder, thought Guy. Well, he liked that, too. Did she think she couldn't be seduced? If he wished, he could wrap her, and any maiden like her, around his finger. The only question was, did he wish? Do you love Madame? his sister had asked. If to feel a certain, wrenching ache every time he looked at her was love, then yes. He wanted her. Was that love?

❦❦❦

The palace of Fontainebleau was huge, its center an ancient keep that had since multiplied and sprawled and spread out various branching arms that splayed in all directions and were connected by the length of expansive galleries or the vast width of courtyards or the tall stateliness of ornate gatehouses. It was the custom to build townhouses along the back walls of courtyards or at their corners or on the outskirts of the royal gardens, and in these lived courtiers who held high positions in the court or were greatly favored or ministers who carried the threads of the kingdom's policy in their hands and memories. One townhouse, built in the reign of the previous king, had housed a great innovator and visionary of the state, one Cardinal Richelieu, who had served the kingdom until the day of his death. Now it housed another man considered important to the kingdom.

The Viscount Nicolas stood before a long pier glass in a chamber on an upper floor. Turning this way and that, he surveyed himself wearing a new jacket, his quicksilver mind upon the conversation he was holding but also playing upon other things. Pier glass was expensive; only the Venetians made this surface whose silvering showed a man precisely what he looked like, and they extracted a pretty penny for their expertise. We should make it, Colbert had said earlier today. Colbert was an old enemy who had, unfortunately, not been entombed alongside Cardinal Mazarin. The man was obsessed with manufacture. And how would we do that? Nicolas had asked him, feeling irritated and wary, but also interested. Steal their secret, was Colbert's reply. Well. Colbert might have the liveliness of a block of winter river ice, but there was certainly a clever brain frozen inside, but then the cardinal wouldn't have amassed the fortune he had with an idiot managing the figures in his ledgers, would he?

Nicolas ran his eyes over the cut of his short, tight jacket and drew his brows together, but it wasn't the jacket which displeased. His Majesty insisted that a ledger now be kept again, but Nicolas made no attempt to enter correct figures. He couldn't have if he'd tried. One didn't finance war and more war and then a wedding between princes by meticulous addition and subtraction. Cardinal Mazarin had understood such. He had never asked how Nicolas had amassed funds; he had just held out his hand for them. Hopefully, once His Majesty was past this first heady rush of ruling, he'd do the same.

Nicolas slapped his abdomen. With the death of Mazarin, forty had become old compared to the age of the king and his set of friends, but he looked well for an old man. He nodded at the image in the mirror, and the man sitting in a chair in a corner took Nicolas's nod for dismissal and stood.

"A moment more," said Nicolas. "No detail is too small. Is he still his mother's boy? What does he say in private about the cardinal? Does he gamble? How much? What's his favorite dish? Does he water his wine? Who are his favorite friends? His most trusted servants? Who has he loved? For how long? Does he take laudanum to sleep? Has he a favorite color? A favorite hunting dog? A favorite mount? There is no detail too small to be of interest. Do you understand?" He had spies in the king's household, but not enough, he had decided.

A knock on the door interrupted. Nicolas indicated the man could go and waited to see who his secretary would announce next. The whispered name surprised him, but only for a moment. After all, she'd warned him she'd call.

Olympe pulled back the hood of her cloak and untied her mask. A lady who didn't wish to be recognized always wore a small, dark, silk mask over her eyes. Nicolas considered her carefully. She was one of the stars in the sky of court, and as far as he could ascertain, she had no conscience of any kind.

"Will you have some refreshment?" he asked.

She shook her head. Little niceties weren't her style.

"How, then, may I be of service to you, my dear Countess?"

"I want to be moved from Her Majesty's household. His Majesty would never forgive me if I asked it, so you must arrange it for me."

He was astonished. "But, Countess, your position is the highest there is! You won't earn the sinecure you do now anywhere else. Nor have the importance you possess and, if I may say so, deserve." There had been near slaughter for positions in the new queen's household. Had she forgotten?

"His Majesty has stopped asking me to plan entertainments for the court, hasn't asked since they came to Fontainebleau. She's doing it for him now." The "she" was said with a sneer.

Of course, thought Nicolas. This was about the new Madame. "She is the second lady of the kingdom."

"But she isn't the queen! It's the queen's duty to plan entertainments! And if not hers, mine! I ought to have seen it at Easter. That's when he first began to honor her. And I can't join in now when they go to swim in the river—everybody's going, you know. I can't go unless Her Majesty does, and there is no chance of that happening. Oh, trust a Spaniard to make getting out of bed in the morning a religious ritual! Her Majesty doesn't even mind that her sister-in-law takes her place. She's glad to be relieved of the responsibility. She is glad to leave the entertainment of court to someone else. What a fool! Move me to Madame's! Say you'll do it!" Olympe turned obsidian-colored eyes directly to his in appeal. "I'll be ever so grateful. There's nothing I have, nothing that I wouldn't give you."

She left no doubt about what generosity entailed, even leaning forward a little so that he would see her breasts, not that one could miss breasts in the fashion of this day.

"Let me see if I understand," Nicolas said because he was so surprised by her request. "You wish to resign your most high, most important position, the premier position among ladies-in-waiting, and take something in the household of the wife of the king's brother?"

"Thank you, Viscount. I'm in your debt, as always." Olympe put her hand to the mask she'd taken off. "When I'm mistress, I'll see you rewarded a hundred times over for your kindness to me."

Mistress? thought Nicolas. What's this? "A moment more, my dear Countess. He still visits the queen every night, doesn't he? I rely upon you to tell me such things. Or have we misunderstood each other?"

She had tied her mask back upon her face and now stared at him through the eyeholes. "I tell you everything of interest," she answered.

"A mistress is of immense interest to me, my dear. Has his majesty"—he paused to find a delicate way to express his question—"invited you?"

"Her Majesty doesn't satisfy him. Any fool can see it. He's ripe to fall into someone's hands, and he is going to fall into mine, and if I am at Madame's, it will be easier to win him."

"But if he's still visiting Her Majesty every evening—"

"Later and later. He's out until all hours with Monsieur and Madame and their group. It's diverting, you see. He likes to laugh and talk and walk among us as if he hadn't a care in the world. Who wouldn't? Her Majesty, that's who. We pray, we embroider, we go to hear chanting in the monasteries and nunneries, we go to visit the Queen Mother and her ancient coven of witches, we nap. Yesterday, Madame's ladies let down their hair in the park in front of everyone to dry it. Do you know how beautiful, how thick my hair is? He wouldn't have been able to stop thinking of me if I'd been sitting among them."

Nicolas remained in the doorway to watch her walk down his back hall. She was a niece of Cardinal Mazarin, who had brought his sisters' children under his wing, so that His Majesty had known them all since they were children, had lived and played among them as if they were related. Each child had made or would make a grand marriage into the highest families of the land or among the kingdom's neighboring kingdoms, first because Cardinal Mazarin had seen to it, and now, because His Majesty had taken on that task. No one gossiped any longer that the cardinal had begun as nobody because he'd ended as more than somebody. It was a story Nicolas liked, the way a man of exceptional ability could ease himself into a majesty's life, become indispensable, and then he and his children were guaranteed a place in the firmament of court forever and ever, amen.

He was caught off guard at what she'd just told him, surprised at himself, that he hadn't sensed it, seen it, guessed it. The king had been married a year, and, as far as anyone knew, had been faithful. The queen was less than stimulating. Of course he would begin to look elsewhere. He showed restraint not to have leapt from the marriage bed sooner. A mistress was an extremely important piece on the chessboard that was court, more important than the queen, if the queen was weak. A mistress became, in fact, the queen. Strength in a queen or a mistress turned women from delightful companions and playthings into dangerous people who must be pleased, who took sides in official business, who demanded favors, who changed kings' minds. What a secretive young man this king was, this king who didn't like surprises. Well, neither did Nicolas, but the thing was, he paid handsomely so that there should be none, and in that, he became a cat, always knowing where to leap.

CHAPTER 7

L ouis met with his council that afternoon. They talked of Charles II, the king of England, only upon his throne a year, and unmarried. They had manipulated a bride-to-be for him from among the princesses of Europe. The choice was to the advantage of the kingdom of France and certain long-term priorities Mazarin had set in place. The years the three members of this highest of councils had worked together showed in the adroitness with which they had maneuvered a Catholic princess for a Protestant king.

"Who on the English council do we have in our pocket?" asked Nicolas, as skilled in diplomacy as he was in finding funds. Much of the credit for the coming English royal marriage belonged to him, but there were delays in the wedding that they were attempting to hurry with bribes.

"Having just signed orders for payments, I say, all of them." Louis's wry answer surprised everyone, and there was a burst of laughter, as Louis made a motion for the secretary to allow someone else into the meeting.

The man who entered was dressed all in black and carried a large velvet pouch under one arm. He did not attempt to sit down with the others but kept his eyes lowered, as if he were well aware that he was not in the same league as these men, who had been secretary of state, secretary of war, and superintendent of finance for years.

"I'll request Madame write to her brother, to ask him specifically about his marriage negotiations. He and she are very close," said Louis. He kept himself from smiling at his own guile. This gave him an excuse to spend even more time with Henriette.

Nicolas, who was on alert now, didn't miss the gleam that came into Louis's eyes when he said the word "Madame." At once he began to draw conclusions that were slightly different from Olympe's.

"We are all agreed on the importance of commerce to the kingdom. I wish to speak again of a commercial fleet," said Louis, "and so I have summoned Monsieur Colbert."

Known to them all, since Mazarin's death he sat on a lesser council that concentrated upon trade. With a dry cough, Colbert opened his velvet pouch—as black as the coat he wore—and pulled out papers upon which could be seen figures drawn in a tiny, cramped hand. He began to reel off numbers for the building of a merchant fleet, even though Nicolas had explained only yesterday that there was no money in the treasury for ships.

"It is therefore my suggestion that we import Dutch shipbuilders," finished Colbert, as the others sat in silence, a little stunned with his facts and figures.

"I can always find funds if this is what His Majesty truly desires," Nicolas finally said. He threw out the names of several financiers and gold merchants in Paris, eloquent and smooth in his knowledge of them. "My credit is good with them, and if need be, Your Majesty, I'll put my own funds into shipbuilding."

"I don't wish your credit to be good with them, Viscount." Louis was sharp. "I wish my kingdom's credit to be good with them."

"But of course, Your Majesty, such goes without saying." Nicolas bit his tongue on the words that they were already two years in arrears. He'd said it yesterday.

"Excellent. Monsieur Colbert will assist you in finding funds somewhere, so that we can begin."

"I look forward to working with him," said Nicolas.

Colbert had moved back toward the tapestried walls. He didn't raise his eyes to meet the viscount's, did not make a move to draw any attention to himself. But Nicolas could feel triumph radiating from the man. There was enmity between them, bad blood. Does His Majesty do this deliberately to test me? thought Nicholas, but he doubted Louis knew the old struggles between him and Colbert. Was it fate, then, throwing up a wry twist when all was going his way? Whatever it was, nothing and no one were going to keep him from his destiny. Time and finances were on his side, no one else's.

The lieutenant of His Majesty's musketeers, Charles D'Artagnan, wandered through the huge square that was the kitchen and entrance courtyard. It was a habit of his to keep watch on the pulses of the palace. This was where servants and soldiers lived and worked. This was where any coach from the outside must enter and discharge its occupants. The bustle here reminded him of a Paris marketplace, farmers in with baskets of tiny lettuces or potatoes, the Italian troupe practicing its acrobatics and pratfalls by jumping in and out of a ground-floor window, women's voices rising among the men's, to quarrel or order someone about or call a child, girls with bare arms washing clothes in big tubs of water, musketeers off duty enjoying a pipe of tobacco and a peep at anything female. A dog chased one of the royal peacocks that had somehow wandered out of the queen's garden. Cats sat on the ledge of the wall by the moat sunning themselves or seeing what mischief they'd find next. Merchants, sellers of fans and gloves and fabric, sat on leather trunks of inventory awaiting some noblewoman or nobleman's pleasure to view their wares.

One of His Majesty's cousins had arrived with her carriage and her servants' carriages and her guard. Once she, her family, had been His Majesty's enemies. Were they still? He'd go down to the stable later, talk with her chief groom, find out what was the princess's latest whim, who she was seeing in Paris, ask what servants and companions she'd brought with her. In a far corner was a new acting troupe, squatting like gypsies around their wagon. This particular set of vagabonds—that's what actors were; the Holy Church would not even allow them the sacraments—had made His Majesty laugh like a boy last spring with a play that made fun of what had been fashionable for years, women and the men who admired them setting themselves as too refined to have natural urges and emotions and using an absurd, affected language to describe the world at large.

D'Artagnan had seen the king throw back his head and yelp at certain lines in the play. What was the line that had amused His Majesty so much? Oh, yes, an actress, over-powdered and purse-mouthed, looking just like more than one older countess at court, waving her fan like a windmill, announcing, marriage is awful—how can one endure the thought of lying by a man who's really naked?

D'Artagnan had thought His Majesty was going to fall out of his chair laughing. That and the actors calling a looking glass a "counselor of the graces" and a chair "a commodity of conversation." Sweet blue heaven, it warmed an old soldier's heart to see a play so plain and so damned funny when the style was for tragedy with actors marching around in togas and declaiming in deep, serious voices. Of course, the court and Paris society, full of people who talked exactly like the over-powdered actresses, hadn't known what to do.

But since the king laughed, they did also. And the fashion of oversensibility was erased overnight by the yelping amusement of a young king who for days afterward had advised his brother to go back at once to his counselor of the graces or offered his wife a commodity of conversation whenever he saw her. And here in the kitchen courtyard of Fontainebleau was the ringleader of the laughter, an actor in the play and the playwright. Word was his father had a shop somewhere in Paris, was a prosperous merchant, but his son had kicked over the traces, choosing another life entirely.

"Molière, how are you?" asked D'Artagnan. "Working on something that pokes fun at my soldiers?"

The actor bowed. "What an excellent idea."

"Don't do it. I'd hate to have to arrest you. What brings you here?"

"We've been asked by His Majesty to perform our little nothing again. And the Viscount Nicolas has expressed interest in my writing a small farce, and we help the incomparable Madame with her upcoming ballet."

"His Majesty? The viscount? Madame? Well, well. You do move in high circles."

"We're the hors d'oeuvres of the theater, not the entrée."

"Keep making His Majesty laugh, and you'll become the entrée. Where's the tall man wrapped in the cloak I saw the other night?"

"Not one of ours," answered Molière. "Just a vagabond who joined us for supper one night."

"One of yours," piped up an actress, a saucy, plump thing. "I saw his uniform."

"What color was it?" asked D'Artagnan.

"Green."

"For true love," said Molière.

Green had been the color the cardinal's musketeers had worn, thought D'Artagnan. "Did you catch his name?"

"He didn't give one."

"You'll let me know if you see him again?" He walked his circuit around the rest of the courtyard, thinking about the man he had half noticed out of the corner of his eye the other day. He'd assumed he was one of Molière's troupe. Who was he? Why was he at Fontainebleau? Doing something he shouldn't for someone who paid well? But then again, it might be the newly arrived princess who had once been their enemy. This morning, without saying a word, His Majesty had handed him another Mazarinade. Same handwriting, same notepaper. It had been placed with stinging mockery in the brim of a hat. A wind from the Fronde is blowing, blowing, blowing, it said.

The Fronde had been the name given to the civil wars.

CHAPTER 8

May began to while its way toward June. The maids of honor's
Mary gardens—created in honor of the Holy Mother—bloomed
with monkshood and our-lady's-fingers and mother's-heart and
Christ's-eyes. Roses on courtyard walls unfurled crimson buds to bask in
warmer, longer days.

Louise rode with a groom to the nearby convent to see Choisy's waif. A
nun led the girl into a cool, dim chamber, where Louise waited.

"Do you remember me?" Louise asked. Bruises were healing, but the
child's hands were red and chapped. The nuns must have her washing
clothes. The Carmelites were known for their vows of poverty and toil.
Not all orders were as strict.

The girl nodded her head.

"What's your name?"

"Julie."

"I came to see how you do."

A tear appeared. "I miss them."

Of course you do, thought Louise. "Come outside and see my horse.
Perhaps you'd like to ride him?"

Later, back at Fontainebleau, as she changed her gown for evening,
Louise thought more about the girl. If there were tears the next time she
visited, she'd take her to see her family. She went to a window, unable to
withstand the lure of the setting sun. Dusk was here, a long May's dusk.
Someone was singing an old ballad:

> *I send you here a wreath of blossoms blown,*
> *and woven flowers at sunset gathered.*
> *Time is flying, be therefore kind, my love,*
> *whilst thou art fair.*

Whoever sang had a tender voice. Summer was almost here, thought Louise. It was one of her favorite seasons. All of nature unfolded and stretched. Each morning, she eagerly rode in the forest, each night she gratefully watched the moon. It was in its waning phase this night, but romance at court, especially between the king and Madame, did not wane, but like a new moon, opened and grew.

❧❦❧

Several hours before the dawn in a bedchamber with blue draperies and bed hangings and solid silver chairs, Catherine brushed out Henriette's hair. Henriette was in her night robe, but Philippe was off somewhere with Guy and wouldn't be calling this night.

"He says he loves me."

Bubbling, as wide awake as if it were noon, Henriette spoke into the looking glass set up for her at her dressing table. Hers was an amazing story: a civil war begun before she was born, a father dead by the time she was five, a mother a beggar at the court in which she'd been reared as a princess, a brother who was offered back his throne by the same people who'd fought him, and as her brother's star had brightened the sky, so had hers. It was intoxicating and heady, like strong wine, to know how much she was admired at the moment when a little more than a year ago, she and her mother hadn't the funds—for horses, for servants, for new gowns, for jewels, for gifts—to journey with the court across France to witness the king's wedding. It was as if she'd unknowingly drunk a magic elixir.

She tossed two priceless rings into a silver dish on her dressing table as if they were baubles. "What have you done to my court? he asks. He says he needs me to begin his day. The rest is shadow, he says. You are my light, he says." She laughed, her face, small and pointed, gamine, a changeable tableau upon which expressions and moods flitted like lightning, part of her charm to her admirers. She was restless and sensitive and very aware of the impression she made upon others. "Once he wouldn't even dance with me. Do you remember it? Oh, I wish we could stay like this forever, adoring one another, living off kisses."

"You can charm the birds from the trees," said Catherine. "They're saying that and a hundred other things."

"What things?" Henriette couldn't get enough of the compliments about herself. All the admiration she'd received had gone to her head, as the young roosters at court continued to preen and screech before her.

"They call you a sprite. They call you a fairy. They call you a nymph, and there is a disagreement about whether you're a moon nymph or a sun one. They say that you've brought a life and vitality to the court that has been missing for years, that even the Queen Mother didn't provide when she was younger. They say he should have married you."

Henriette gasped in pleasure. "They don't—"

"They do. They say you are all that is best of we French, that you are truly one of us, that your charm and liveliness have changed things forever. They say you've changed Monsieur, that before you, women never held him."

Henriette turned in her chair to face Catherine. Her blossoming vanity turned anxious. "I don't want to hurt him, you know. I adore Monsieur. He's been so good to me."

Catherine leaned over to whisper in Henriette's ear. "But you have more, far more than Monsieur. The king is your slave. You have him in the palm of your hand."

Henriette looked down at her hand on the dressing table's top and turned it to gaze at her palm.

"What are you going to do?" asked Catherine. They both knew exactly what she referred to.

"I don't know."

"Has he asked you to—"

"No!" Henriette interrupted, shaking her head, beginning to flush.

"He will." Catherine kissed her cheek. "Don't be uneasy. I'll help you. Did you see the viscount's gift?"

On a table in the antechamber lay a beautiful book with purple velvet for its cover, and inside were pages edged in gold, and Henriette's crest was woven into the velvet cover in silver thread. Monks at the university in Paris had illuminated in colored inks the stories of three old folk tales written down by a courtier and court official gifted at such things. There was a story of the girl whose foot fit in a glass slipper, the story of a girl who was made to sleep by a jealous fairy, and the story of a girl who wore a red riding hood. I found it amusing to ask him to make his knowledge into a book, the viscount had said, and of course, I thought of you. Please count me as one of your many admirers and champions. The viscount patronized many writers and artists. La Fontaine, Corneille, Saint-Évremond were under his wing. Henriette wished to do the same.

"It's very beautiful," answered Catherine. "He wishes you to know his regard for you."

"He has offered me Vaux-le-Vicomte any time I desire," confided Henriette. Vaux-le-Vicomte was a château the viscount was building several hours distant by carriage, fewer on horseback. "For my rest, privacy, and contemplation, he said."

"How thoughtful," answered Catherine, thinking, Vaux-le-Vicomte would be the perfect meeting place for Madame and the king, away from prying eyes.

"I've told His Majesty," said Henriette, her china-blue eyes wide and innocent, as if she hadn't suggested a place where her romance with Louis might become much more serious.

Catherine turned her by the shoulders to face the mirror again and resumed her task of brushing her hair, thinking all the while of what was unfolding. This princess she served danced on a precipice, adoring the admiration thrown at her and playing as yet with being unfaithful. But there came a moment when play turned physical. Wiser in the ways of the world than Henriette, Catherine thought of the summer days stretching out endlessly before them, the long summer nights when the breeze died and the lace-edged sheets were too heavy and perspiration beaded under arms and breast, behind knees, while the heart beat like a drum at the thought of a desired one, and the forest with its cool, mocking green seemed to offer refuge and a hundred bowers.

She remembered her first infidelity, the guilt mixed with unbearable excitement, when passion could be set alight by nothing more open than a meeting of the eyes, simmering until lovers could finally touch each other, explore naked flesh, exploding, made almost violent by the wait. Those thoughts led her to think of the Viscount Nicolas. Discretion, he advised. He'd met with Catherine in a grotto in one of the gardens several days earlier, to assure her of his loyalty to both Madame and His Majesty. Discretion would be wise, he'd said, meeting Catherine's eyes in a way that had made her heart beat faster, something stern and yet tender about him, something appealing and worldly. Assure Madame I am her friend in this, he'd said.

Your implications insult everyone, Catherine had replied, but without anger, playing the court game wherein the truth lay always behind the words. A thousand apologies, the viscount had replied. How may I make up my clumsiness to you? And she'd remembered that word was he was a wonderful lover, and generous, and they had looked in each other's eyes, the attraction between them neither denied nor spoken aloud, better that way.

The viscount was correct to advise discretion, thought Catherine now. She put down the brush. It seemed to her the king was beginning to show the strain of keeping his passion leashed. He wouldn't be able to hold it inside forever. He and Henriette were like two comets blazing in parallel paths. Sparks were beginning to shower out into the surrounding darkness. They must all make certain nothing was destroyed, or, at the very least, Catherine must make certain that she herself wasn't singed.

Choisy was drunk, so that when a tall man loomed suddenly before him just outside the palace walls in the dark, he broke into helpless laughter, the idea of being robbed hilarious. He hadn't a feather to fly with; Monsieur had just plucked them all in a game of cards.

"If you're going to rob me, someone has all my coins," he announced. He bowed and almost fell over but straightened himself with a liquid, drunken grace. Then he found himself being pushed by a strong hand until he staggered against the hard, round rim of a fountain and fell back into the water. Flame in a nearby wall lantern pierced a little of the night around them. He stared up at the man who'd pushed him, trying to collect his wits.

A gaunt, forbidding face looked back at him. Choisy thought, this man doesn't want money. The man held out a hand, and, dripping, Choisy stepped out of the fountain. "Who are you?" he asked.

"The likes of you may call me captain."

Captain of what? A cloak hid whatever uniform might have revealed that. "What do you wish from me?"

"The fair-haired girl, the one in Madame's household—"

Louise? thought Choisy, his mind suddenly sharper.

"Did she talk to you about a certain day in the forest? It would be the day the cardinal"—and at those words the man crossed himself—"died?"

Giddiness left Choisy. He remembered Louise's description of the musketeer she'd seen that day, his face as hewn as if he'd been hacked by an ax, she'd said. Well, if ever he'd seen a face hacked by God's ax, it was this man's. Alarm walked with its prickly cat's feet at the back of his neck and along his arms. This was Louise's musketeer. "I don't know a fair-haired girl—"

"What do I see one day a few weeks ago when I'm out for a ride but you and her cantering along. Then I see you both another day. It doesn't sit well with me being as I'm suspicious by nature. Then I come here and find you're out together many mornings. Remind her she never saw what she saw. And tell her she'll be rewarded." There was a small leather bag in the man's outstretched hand. "You know what I'm talking about. She spoke to you of it, didn't she?"

"Spoke of what?"

"A man like you, who likes to wear ladies' corsets and gowns and ribbons and earrings, you two talked like magpies, didn't you?" The musketeer leaned forward, tall and grim, beaten by training and life into a cold, clear force. "Tell Miss de le Baume le Blanc that her silence is important."

"She saw nothing. Her horse reared and threw her, if you remember—"

The man grimaced what must be a smile. Choisy felt stupid, muddled, furious at himself. The musketeer punched the leather bag into Choisy's middle, hard enough to make him gasp.

"Take what you like from it that will keep you silent, then the rest is hers. You and I have never spoken. And she was never in the forest of Fontainebleau on that cursed day in March, is that clear? And it might be wise to keep your jaunts closer to the palace."

"You have my assurance as a gentleman that she will say nothing. And we'll stop riding, yes, we will."

"I thought you were a woman at first." There was contempt on the musketeer's face. "I saw you dressed like a girl, dancing like one, flirting with Monsieur and those others in that house in Paris you all like to visit when I was tracking you. Shame on you! Shame on you all!"

He spat, and the spittle hit Choisy in the face. And then the musketeer stepped back like a ghost, into the dark that was the lane down which Choisy had walked.

Stunned, Choisy sat on the rim of the bowl of the fountain. After a time, he was able to stand, able to walk to the townhouse in which he stayed.

❧

"I was told you had a plan, Colbert." Though the dawn was ready to open the day in another few hours, the king met with Colbert, who was as crisply dressed as if it were morning.

"A plan, sire?" said Colbert.

"Of financial reform."

"That was scotched several years ago, sire."

"Why?"

"The viscount learned of it and did not care for it. And it was felt that its timing was not right. Negotiations for your marriage were beginning, and there was pressing need of funds, and when there is pressing need of funds, there is pressing need of the viscount."

"How did he learn of it?"

"I shared my plan with our late, great cardinal, but unfortunately I made the mistake of putting it in a letter. The letter was intercepted."

Louis, who had been standing on a small balcony, staring up at the night stars, turned. "Intercepted?"

"The postmaster general, sire."

"The same postmaster general we have now?"

"Yes, sire."

"You're saying he is in the pay of the Viscount Nicolas?"

"Many are in the pay of the viscount, sire."

"Make me a list."

"The names would be uncomfortable, sire."

Relatives, thought Louis. He means my cousins and very likely friends, too, would be on the list. Well, if his relatives weren't at court smiling at him, they were plotting war against him. And as for friends, they followed the sun. The viscount was the court's sun. He offers Vaux-le-Vicomte, said Henriette, for—and here she had looked away, not able to meet his eyes, and Louis's heart beat so hard he thought it would leap out of his chest—for us.

"Put the names down anyway. What was in your plan?"

"A court of justice instituted to look into financial affairs, prosecution of those who have raped our kingdom."

They displayed the rape in satins and laces, in statues and paintings, in warships and merchant vessels, in the use of royal gardeners, royal crafts-men to build palaces. The viscount was using royal workers to finish his château at Vaux-le-Vicomte, had been for four years, Louis had learned just the other day. They'd razed a village, diverted a stream to create the gardens the viscount wished. And the viscount had purchased the office of viceroy of all islands, shores, harbors, coasts, and mainlands of Louis's colonies. That was the reason he purchased ships. But not under his own name. He also owned an island on the western coast, which made something in Louis coil upward and flick out a tongue in warning.

But all he said was, "Cardinal Mazarin spoke of your court of justice in his last days. He told me he regretted that he had not implemented it. I was a coward, he said to me."

"He was never a coward, Your Majesty. He was a wise man who knew how to be pliant when circumstances called for it."

"I could dismiss the postmaster general. But would that be too transparent?"

It took a moment for Colbert to answer, the late hour having exhausted even his indomitable precision. "Excuse me, sire?"

"Yes, too transparent. A warning shot the viscount would notice. Therefore, we'll best him at his own game. Go to this postmaster general and tell him his king desires his utmost loyalty, that old sins are known but will be forgotten if he now understands he is to serve only me. And of course, such loyalty will be rewarded. He may open the mail for the viscount, but he must also do the same for me. I will see all of the viscount's correspondence, and I will know precisely what the viscount has seen. And put a man in place who will watch the postmaster general's every move. Make certain that both men understand I forget the past, reward loyalty, but always, always punish liars. I've kept you up very late this night, haven't I? Good night, Colbert. Remind the postmaster general I am his liege lord."

"I will do so, Your Majesty."

"Pay him more than what the viscount pays."

Colbert put a hand to his heart in obedience.

"Colbert? Tell me the name again of the viscount's island?"

Colbert gestured toward the elder of Louis's dogs. "Belle. Belle Isle, sir."

"Find out everything there is to know—discreetly—about this island. Does he visit it? How often? And what precisely is there?" He'd given Colbert charge of the cardinal's spies. My dear boy, forgive me, but I give you Colbert, said the man he loved in his mind. Was Colbert as trustworthy as Mazarin promised?

Colbert bowed himself out of the chamber. Louis rubbed his eyes in fatigue. Desire for Henriette stretched him to a breaking point. When his beloved violins played, he could feel their high quaver in his bones. What to do about the viscount, who offered his own château for their love? How did he know? And how did he dare? And he was now a viceroy. There must be no more Richelieus keeping their kingly state, he could remember his mother shouting in fury, while the true king, your dear father, sits at his devotions in a badly furnished palace.

And yet she had created Mazarin, who kept a kingly state and twisted the crown's revenues into his own just as the viscount was doing. Beloved Mazarin. Godfather and friend. Mentor and teacher. A wind from the Fronde is blowing, blowing, blowing, and Mazarin is going, going, going. No new Mazarinades to keep him anxious and wary. Yet. If the viscount were arrested, would his arrest rupture existing contracts and agreements? Would he rally the financiers who had been his accomplices, who had done nothing without his consent and for their profit as well as his? Would public credit hold? Would there be war, another Fronde? Was it the viscount who sent these veiled threats? Why? So that Louis should be afraid to make a move against him?

He insinuated himself into Louis's love affair. He insinuated himself into every aspect of court that Louis could see. He was going to have to break the viscount in half and hold the pieces up like trophies to paralyze his court with awe and under the awe, real fear. What do you say to that? he asked Mazarin in his mind, and for just a moment, he thought a morning star whispered, Well done, my boy. But he was tired, and the new day had already begun, and, as always, there was too much to do.

It was past noon the next day before Choisy found Louise with Madame's dogs as her companions in the queen's garden at a bronze statue of the daughter of the king of the ancient gods. Louise sat on stone steps built in a circle—like an ancient amphitheater—around a pedestal that held the goddess's statue.

He sat down beside Louise and began to describe what had happened to him. The musketeer had really frightened him, made him frightened for her. All this he tried to convey to her, the sound of birds twittering and trilling in their aviary, the fragrance from orange blossoms and sweet olives a contrast to his words. Near them, four bronze dogs surrounding the goddess peed four arcs of water to make a fountain.

Near her foot he placed the leather bag and a rose he had picked. "We're neither of us to say a word."

"We haven't said a word, but I can't just forget what I saw."

He began to feel upset. "Louise, my bonbon, this is serious. You've led a sheltered life on your farm and then with the Orléans. If someone is powerful enough to give a bag of gold, powerful enough to command a musketeer, it is best to obey. You could find yourself dismissed, worse."

"Worse?"

For the first time since he'd met her, he found her innocence less than charming. "I've already told you. Don't you remember my lecture? Inconvenient people disappear from court. Just obey me."

"Obey you?"

"I'm your patron, Louise. If it weren't for me, you wouldn't be here. You must listen to what I say."

She laughed, which hurt his feelings. He was serious, and she didn't seem to realize it. He took her arm.

She shook him off, pointed. "There's La Grande Mademoiselle."

A tall, big-boned woman had appeared in the open gallery that ran along one side of the garden. Stalk, Madame de Choisy called her. A first cousin of the king, she was the richest princess in France, had once been traitor to the king, but had been forgiven.

"I don't want to have to talk to her." Like a boy, Louise whistled for the dogs, then, as they clustered at her feet, she said, "Does this mean you won't go exploring with me anymore?"

Furious, Choisy stood. "Have you not understood a word I've said? No, I won't go exploring! And neither will you! This isn't a game, Louise. Forget the boy."

"What if I can't? What if I won't?" She ran off toward the orangery, the dogs right beside her. He saw that she took neither the bag of gold nor the rose with her.

"Whoo-hoo," called La Grande, waving a long scarf and carrying one of her pet dogs. She was past her first youth, still unmarried, but that was her choice. I can't bear to leave France, she told one and all. Those who knew her best said she couldn't bear to have a master, but since the existence of a married princess very much depended upon the kindness of her husband, perhaps she was more wise than headstrong.

Cursing silently, Choisy turned, bowed low. He could not ignore this princess whose family was intertwined with his. He walked toward her, to play courtier, to pretend to be interested in what she said, to pretend she was a fount of wisdom or goddess of beauty or however it was she wished to be perceived today.

"Where did La Baume le Blanc run off to?" she asked him. Her scarf had fallen from her hands, and she ignored it, waiting for Choisy to pick it up, which he did.

"She had to return at once to Madame's," he said. "She sends you her respect and greetings."

"Tell her to come and examine my dog. My precious hasn't been pid-dling the way she should. Look at the way they pee." She pointed to the bronze dogs. Sunlight played on the water arcs made.

Choisy coughed not to laugh. "Forgive me, but those are male dogs."

"I know how a dog ought to pee, male or female." La Grande took a deep breath of garden air. "Ah, it's good to be here. Now, walk with me around the garden and tell me all the gossip."

Choisy bowed obediently, amused now rather than irritated. This statue with its dogs was his favorite, for the impudence of it if nothing else. The ancient Romans had wrapped their art in the sacred and the profane. For them, the borders blurred. Choisy liked that blurring. It mirrored his own. As for Louise, he'd find her in the evening and insist she do as he said.

JUNE 1661

CHAPTER 9

Louise and Choisy weren't speaking.

He paid elaborate court to La Grande Mademoiselle, but if he expected upset from Louise, he was mistaken. Choisy was the last thing on her mind. She was determined to find a map, and she asked innocuously pointed questions of ladies-in-waiting and footmen and His Majesty's flirtatious entourage until she had her answer.

It was an evening in early June, the day having been devoted to the feast of Corpus Christi. The royal family had led a procession of monks, nuns, courtiers, and villagers to the chapel while bells rang endlessly and candles shone like beacons in the chapel dark. Afterward, the palace was silent, courtiers snatching a bit of rest from a morning spent on their knees in long prayer and contemplation. Those more worldly met a lover at some prearranged place, which is what Madame was doing. Her household thought she was asleep, but Louise knew she'd crept from her bedchamber and had gone to meet the king.

Louise was exploring the oldest part of the palace, the medieval keep that King François I had made the center of the palace's rebuilding in the 1500s. He'd added a gallery to link the palace with a monastery that had once stood nearby, and on the ground floor of that gallery were the king's tile-and-marble bath and steam rooms, such as the Romans had created. She was told that in other chambers were kept treasures: paintings, engravings, medals, coins that kings and queens of France had collected for more than a century. But that wasn't what she searched for.

One of the footmen who thought she was pretty had assured her this corridor held a room of royal books. Where there was a chamber of books, there would be maps, she reasoned.

Musketeers stood here and there along the corridor, and as Louise walked on, one of them stepped in front of her. Stocky, the way men become as the middle of their life settles in, he stared at her with intent,

twinkling eyes. Louise recognized him as the lieutenant of the king's musketeers. Was the king in his bath? She would die if she had ventured onto
this floor when he was in his bath. But he wouldn't be in his bath, would
he? He was meeting Madame.

"Are you lost, miss?" the musketeer asked.

Louise hesitated, bashfulness taking her by the throat. "No, sir. I was
searching for a room of books."

"You wish to read, miss?"

"I, well, I wish to find maps of the surrounding countryside. I'm from
the country, you see." You're talking too much, she told herself, but she
couldn't seem to stop. "And I knew every hill and dale and farm for miles.
My father and I rode them together. And I still like to ride, oh, I ride all the
time if I can, but I don't have a sense of where I am, and I wanted to know
the country around the palace." Her voice trailed off. She felt tired from her
lying. He won't believe me, she thought. She didn't even dare look at him.

But D'Artagnan was already thawed. Louise had no idea of it, but she
was one of the favorites among the musketeers because she was as polite as
she was quietly beguiling. D'Artagnan found her humility most charming,
just what he'd want if he had a daughter at court. "And who is your father,
miss, if you'll forgive my asking?"

"My father was Laurent de la Baume le Blanc de la Vallière."

"I knew him. He was a fine soldier, and now that I look at you, I see you
have his eyes. He was a most gallant warrior."

Touched, she smiled, and D'Artagnan blinked. Well, now. Her smile was
something else again. What an enchanting young woman. He touched at
his moustache, pulled in his stomach, the automatic gestures of an old flirt.

"Allow me to introduce myself formally," he said, feeling fatherly
with a pinch of palest lust thrown in. "I am Charles de Batz-Castelmore
D'Artagnan, lieutenant of His Majesty's musketeers and proud of it. You're
in Madame's household, are you not?"

"Yes, sir."

"Well, come along, there is indeed a room of books, and I can well
imagine in it there are maps of the countryside. You like to ride, miss?"

"More than anything."

He opened enormous double doors to a chamber lined floor to ceiling
with books. Low cabinets sat in the middle of the room and atop them
onyx vases with gold or silver handles as well as bronzes of heads, the
hair on them short and combed forward, reflecting another time, another
empire. D'Artagnan strode at once to the low cabinets, pulled open one of
the narrow, long drawers.

"If there are maps, miss, they will be in here. Now, I must go, but I wish
you happy hunting."

Left alone, Louise stood still a moment. So many books together in one place were a rarity. There was also the luxury of a thick rug on the floor, draperies falling in folds at the windows, embroidery in silver and gilt thread picking out patterns on pillows fat and tasseled, lying in piles before the shelved books. There were tall, figured candle stands and even a clock.

She was drawn to the sight of the elaborate gold clock, its pendulum moving back and forth. Clocks with a pendulum and a hand that measured off minutes were quite new. She'd never seen one before, but she'd heard of them. At the Orléans palace in Paris there was the usual sundial in the garden and also a water clock, which someone had told her the ancient Greeks had invented.

The water clock measured the passing hours by means of water flowing from one container to another. To be able to know the time at night hadn't been possible when she was a child, and she and her friends had gone outside in the evenings with lanterns or candlesticks to observe the water clock and see just how late they were staying up. The precise ticking sound of this clock in this chamber transfixed her, and she stood watching, as one of its long golden hands moved a fraction, and then another. But finally, she shook herself. Time was passing, and she had a task to accomplish.

She began with the drawer the lieutenant had opened, carefully sifting through the papers there, maps, as he'd said, the paper heavy in her hands, the ink and paint long dried. She opened a second drawer, sifting quickly but carefully through the papers. When she'd gone through the fifth drawer, she sat back on her heels. There were five of these low cabinets in this chamber. How long had she been, half of an hour, more? Had she time to look through one more cabinet before hurrying back to change for the evening?

Irritated, she walked over to the clock. Nearly three quarters of an hour gone. She bit her lip, trying to decide what to do next. Then she saw what she'd come for. Mounted on the wall, in an ornate frame, was a map. It showed a coastline with drawings of ships sailing in a sea. There were the requisite dragons painted along the ocean's edge. A river labeled *Seine* ran downward from the coast. Castles on either side were painted in. *Louvre*, she read, *Saint-Germain-en-Laye, Vincennes, Versailles.* She found the word *Fontainebleau.* His Majesty's palaces. She had heard talk of the court traveling to Saint-Germain. Versailles was a small hunting lodge, rather close to here; sometimes they rode there with His Majesty during the course of their hunts. Attempting to imprint it in her own mind, she stared hard at the map, but something else caught her eye.

To her right was an ornate standing cabinet, every inch of its wood carved into a display of swags and fruit, with caryatids, those draped female figures craftsmen loved, disguising its solid legs. A tassel dangled from the key that transformed the cabinet into a writing desk. Unable to stop herself, Louise turned the key and a great square in the cabinet's front popped down. It was a writing desk. She found the side slats that would hold the weight of the square and then considered what was inside. Many little shelves filled with odds and ends, seashells, bowls of rock crystal, a small mother-of-pearl casket, figures carved in ivory, an inkwell of silver, quill pens, paper in an ivory box. She pulled out a piece. A *fleur-de-lis* was embossed in gold.

It was the king's paper. She crossed herself and said a quick prayer to the Holy Mother, imagining His Majesty, with his frowning, serious eyes, writing something important. Would he mind if she borrowed just one piece? The inkwell's top was set with rubies. Dipping a pen in, she quickly traced the river, wrote the names of the castles. Geography was considered unimportant for a girl. Girls who had gone to convents for schooling might have learned some, but she'd been schooled at home with the Orléans's princesses, whose tutor had soon tired of trying to teach anyone anything. She could read and write French, paint, sing in Italian without knowing what any of the words meant, add and subtract sums, and she did possess an excellent sense of direction. Her father had taught her when she was barely talking, just as he'd taught her to ride. Sometimes, she dreamed of sitting before him in his saddle, his arm strong around her waist. Look at the sun, he'd told her. Look at the moss. This map was already making her explorations form a more sensible whole in her mind.

She replaced the stopper, looked at the quill pen. How would she clean the ink from it? The ticks from the clock seemed loud now. At any moment, someone was going to come in and accost her. What are you doing? the footman or major domo or someone important would say. And what would she answer? She tried to clean the pen upon the paper and managed a little, but now she had ink on her fingers. Then she accidentally touched the soft, padded leather of the writing surface and to her horror left a faint fingerprint.

She heard voices, the sound of footsteps. Sweet Mary, she thought, was His Majesty's council meeting without him? Had they come down to look at the books, to find some answer to some important question raised? Would they enter and find her here? She dropped the half-cleaned pen among its brothers, wiped her fingers on the back of the paper, waved it back and forth frantically to dry, then pushed up the great square front of the cabinet. She pushed in the slats, turned its key. Folding the paper, she slipped it into the pocket sewn in her skirt that usually held food for the dogs or horses. Looking once more around the chamber, she saw she'd left a drawer in a low cabinet opened. She pushed it closed with her foot.

"What are you doing?" a voice said.

She froze.

"I repeat, what are you doing?"

Louise turned. Dressed in black from head to foot except for an enormous collar edged in lace, a somber, square-faced man frowned at her. Mister Colbert.

"Well?" Colbert's voice was frosty.

"I—I was looking for maps. Lieutenant D'Artagnan assured me it was all right. Forgive me. I had no intent to disturb—"

"Maps? Of what?" Cold, very dark eyes added her up and found her sum lacking.

"Of-of the countryside. I like to ride, you see, and I don't know where I am or where I'm going, and I thought, that is, I was told by a, er, a servant, there was this chamber of books, and I thought…" Floundering, Louise stopped, exhausted with her explanation atop her actions of the last hour.

"Did you find what you wished?"

Louise pointed toward the framed map. "I found a map there."

Colbert looked from her to the map on the wall and back again.

"Why is there ink on your fingers? What have you been writing?" His voice was very sharp.

Let the ground open up and swallow me, thought Louise. She took a deep breath, said, "I—I tried to draw the map. I was afraid I would-would forget it."

"You brought paper and ink with you?"

Turning her terrible deep red, she had passed the point of being able to summon up one more lie. She pointed toward the ornate cabinet. Colbert walked to it, turned the key, pulled down the square, and looked for a long time at its insides. Please let him not see the fingerprint, Louise prayed to herself, please, please, please.

Colbert turned. "Give me what you wrote." He held out his hand imperiously.

"I know I took a piece of His Majesty's paper." Confessing, babbling, holding the paper out, Louise couldn't stop a single word that fell out of her mouth. "I meant no harm. I was just afraid that I wouldn't remember the names. I can be stupid that way. Please don't tell His Majesty. Please. I'll pay for the paper. I have some coins saved. I meant no harm."

Every line of his body stiff, Colbert unfolded the paper, looked it over, turned it to its other side, went to the window, and held it to what light the evening still held. The door opened, and Louise shrank back. If it were His Majesty, she would die, just curl up and die right here on the rug.

"I thought to light the candles," a footman said, but Colbert sent him on his way with a curt, "No." He held the paper out to Louise with two fingers as if it were offensive, and Louise took it, backed away, stumbled into one of the pile of pillows, found her balance, and left the chamber in a whish of skirts and panic.

Colbert remained at the window, looking out at the courtyard, where servants scurried to set up a supper given by the Duke de Beaufort tonight. The duke, an elderly illegitimate son of the king's grandfather, had rebelled against the Queen Mother and the cardinal once upon a time but was tamed now, one hoped. Would that all were. Colbert watched footmen hang lanterns from iron stands, his mind moving over and about the young woman he'd discovered in this chamber. Lucky for him he'd come in to borrow a book. He hadn't the education, the finesse, of those of noble birth, and he spent spare moments reading so that he might at least equal those around him in knowledge. She played the part of timid dolt well, well enough to be believable. She came from the Orléans's princesses, her stepfather having been chamberlain to now-deceased Prince Gaston d'Orléans, brother of the king's father, Louis XIII. Prince Gaston, believing he should be king, had been a double-dealing dog if ever there was one, in constant rebellion or constant plotting against and sometimes with the Queen Mother. His daughter, La Grande Mademoiselle, had once fired a cannon at royal troops, but banishment to her estate had soon tamed her, and these days, she pranced around court like a tame pony.

If memory served him, this maid of honor had a brother who was not at court who lived back on their country estate, which meant the family had little or no money to spare, else he would be at court also. No money to spare made people vulnerable to the desires of others. Madame de Choisy had been her advocate, Madame de Choisy, who excelled in intrigue and double-dealing herself and was among those—was there anyone who was not?—the Viscount Nicolas called friend. Was the girl a spy for the viscount? Sent to peek and pry or even catch the king's eye? There was a lovely glow about her that would make a man look twice. Lying, or the innocent she seemed to be? One never knew at court. Never.

He opened the door. There stood Lieutenant D'Artagnan giving evening orders to musketeers. Colbert called him in, and a few questions verified the girl's story.

"She could very well be a messenger for this writer of the Mazarinades," said Colbert. "A pretty girl is allowed much leeway." There was a pause as the two men eyed each other. The king trusted each of them, but neither was yet completely certain of the other.

"I'll have her watched," said Colbert.

"I'll make certain she's followed," said D'Artagnan.

They spoke at the same time, and their words fell over one another.

We sound like the chorus of a damned Greek tragedy, thought D'Artagnan. That sweet little wildflower an intriguer, I won't believe it. If it's true, I'll eat the feathers in my hat and leave court, because, by God, its treachery is too much for me.

⁘

The next day, sunrise barely an hour old, Louise walked down the road that ran along one side of the carp pond to the stables. The morning mist hung suspended over the pond, and in the distance, beyond the stables, the mist blanketed the meadows and moors. There would be vapor on the forest floor wetting the ferns and priest's-heart, and the birds would be singing chansons as they darted from tree to tree. She could hardly wait.

Seeing her, grooms smiled and bowed their heads. They liked her. She knew a good horse when she saw one, and she could ride the most unruly. An elderly groom, sitting down because a horse had kicked him in the back and he'd healed crooked, drank a morning cup of warmed, watered wine.

"Miss de le Baume le Blanc," he said, bowing his head. "Off again this morning, I see."

"Yes. Most of your grooms are from around here?"

"All of us."

"Well, then." Louise tipped over an empty bucket with her shoe, sat down on its upturned bottom, took the map from a pocket. The groom squinted at it, unable to read, while Louise explained the marks.

"Here's Paris, and here's Fontainebleau. Is there more I should know about, other estates, other castles?"

"There's a château about there," said the groom, pointing with a gnarled finger. "The Duke de Choisy owns it now."

Louise took a tiny piece of broken coal from her pocket and marked where he touched. So, she thought, that's where I begin. "Anything else?"

He tapped at a point above the Choisy château. "The Viscount Nicolas be building something here."

Louise made another mark.

His finger moved to the east. "There's a small monastery hidden by forest near the viscount, makes honey sweet as your young eyes and good wine. Vow of silence, the fathers don't speak."

Louise made another mark. "What else?"

"Farms here and there. Forest all the rest."

To his delight, Louise drew some small trees. He took the handkerchief from around his neck and handed it to her to clean her hands of coal dust and called for his son.

"My youngest," he said to Louise. "You will accompany Miss de le

Baume le Blanc on her ride this morning," he ordered importantly. "Saddle Violet for her."

"I love Violet," said Louise.

"It's done, Father," said the youth. "I brought down the saddle when I saw my lady walking up the road."

"How did you know to saddle Violet?" asked his father.

The young man smiled.

"In spite of his impudence, he's a good boy," said the elderly groom.

"I know I'm in safe hands. Thank you." Louise walked over to the open stable doors to wait outside for the youth to bring the horse.

The old groom allowed himself to watch her. There was nothing like a pretty girl to make a man's morning. And this one had a smile as pure as an angel's. His son walked by leading the horses for her and himself. He grinned at his father, and even though the old groom frowned, inside he laughed. What young man wouldn't want to spend the morning gallivanting through the woods following a beautiful young woman instead of mucking out stalls or helping overly plump countesses into their sidesaddles?

An hour or so past noon, Choisy chatted idly with a friend in a palace garden that was famous across Europe. It was suspended in the water of the carp pond, close enough to be an extension of the courtyard it faced, but approachable, except for one footbridge, only by boat. The whim of a Medici queen, whose Renaissance background made her tastes fanciful, it lay several yards on a stone and brick bastion separate from the outermost edge of the fountain courtyard and was literally in the pond, surrounded on all sides by water. This suspended garden—four large parterres, closely cropped shrubs or massed flowers outlining the swirls and arabesques so loved by the previous generation and still admired by this one—rose several feet out of the water. The court liked nothing better than to walk down the dividing paths in the dusk, delighting in the flowers, enjoying the breeze, leaning over the garden's brick wall to admire their image in the water below or throw food to the carp, as the water around them captured and cooled the summer's heat.

Choisy saw Louise hurrying up the road from the stables and stopped his conversation mid-sentence. He ran through the garden, across the footbridge, and into the fountain courtyard and looked her up and down when she, out of breath and panting, stopped in front of him. He was so angry he almost couldn't speak.

"Need I ask where you have been?" he demanded.

"No."

"You're continuing your search, aren't you?"

"I'm late. I don't want to argue."

She went into the pavilion rising tall behind them, and Choisy walked back to his friend, who had come in from Paris with La Grande Mademoiselle and was as vain and proud as any peacock in the queen's garden.

"That looked like a lovers' quarrel. This new fashion for loving women is more than I can understand," the friend said. His name was the Chevalier de Lorraine; he belonged to a distinguished family and was a particular friend of Monsieur's. "Surely you know the old saying: True love is like ghosts—something everyone talks of but scarcely anyone has seen. Am I witnessing true love? Do be still, my own beating heart."

"Be quiet," said Choisy.

❧❧❧

It was cool in the vestibule, unlike outside where June's early afternoon heat was high. Louise walked up wide stone steps that led to an upper floor, feeling some of the blush that had rushed into her face recede. She owed Choisy no explanations, but she hated that he remained angry with her. I don't know why I feel compelled to search, she would have answered if she'd stopped long enough to formulate the words. Your stubborn streak will bring you no good, her mother always said. You're like your father. Worse things to be, Louise thought now, hearing the king's violins singing their lovely song. She stood a moment to fully catch her breath, to smooth her hair, pull ringlets tighter in their pins.

It was an age-old tradition to watch the royal family dine in public, but the courtiers also liked that royal forks were lifted to the sound of violins. Wildly fond of music, the king was growing his orchestra to a size not seen before and insisted that they play at every meal. Choisy had nattered to her about someone named Lully, apparently a musician of great skill among the king's musicians, who sat among the violinists now, sawing away, his face full of the emotion the music engendered in him.

At one end of the antechamber sat the royal family, the king in the exact middle of the table, the queen and Madame on either side of him, his cousin La Grande Mademoiselle on the other side of Madame, Monsieur and the Queen Mother on the ends. Footmen were everywhere, behind each chair, moving back and forth in a line from the distant kitchen courtyard. Louise had passed several of them on the stairs.

After tasting for poison, a favorite method of disposal for at least a century—folklore blaming the Italians for having brought that art along with others—a gentleman of the king's household took each platter from a footman and served the king himself on bended knee. Louise had been told that in Paris anyone might see the king dine, if properly dressed, and walk in and out of chambers in the palace to gawk at will. Choisy said the Parisians adored their young king's large appetite. They consider it a sign of virility, he'd said. Slowly, unobtrusively, she made her way toward her friend Fanny, but someone blocked her path.

"Miss de le Baume le Blanc," said the Viscount Nicolas, smiling down at her. "How do you do this day?"

"Very well, thank you, Viscount."

"I'm told you ride in the morning, early."

How did he know that? Who noticed what a maid of honor like herself did? She didn't answer, just stared up at him, looking like a village idiot, she was certain, remembering some snippet of talk from somewhere, from someone, Fanny, probably. Spies. He was said to have spies everywhere, knowing all things there were to know about the court and its inhabitants.

"I offer my presence should you ever wish company. I, too, sometimes like to ride in the mornings. I go several times a week to see my château."

"Thank you. You're very kind." She moved away, weaving in and out of people until she was standing behind Fanny. She didn't want his attention, his notice. She didn't want anyone's. But that wasn't true. It was complicated, something she didn't understand herself—all she didn't want, and all she did.

Nicolas remained where he was. It was clear this rebuff was not as alluring as the first one she'd made.

Olympe, her perennial pout in place, detached herself from the queen's cluster of ladies and made her way to Nicolas. "You've been avoiding me," she accused.

"Your happiness is foremost on my mind."

They both turned to watch the royal family dine for a time. The king was eating pheasant now. He'd just finished a stew. From her own plate, the queen fed her dwarves, who stood a little behind her. One could just see their hats and foreheads.

Olympe shuddered. "When I'm mistress, I'll have those dwarves sent back to Spain. Look at them. She feeds them as if they were dogs."

"Their Majesties seem on good terms." The queen looked placid to Nicolas, like the surface of a lake undisturbed, no sign that, just on the other side of her husband, danger sat eating with the appetite of a small bird. For His Majesty to pursue this love affair with his sister-in-law was going to shock the Christian world. It was considered by church law to be incest. He was going to have enormous need of his superintendent of finance, who would become his superintendent of finesse.

"He still visits every night, if that is what you're asking. What does Madame say? Is she agreeable to my serving her?"

"I haven't asked yet," he replied, and at her furious intake of breath, "I've been singing your praises and talking about what a blessing you are to the queen. Your presence must be desired by Madame, pined for, as a pearl above price. That will give you more influence."

"It's the Princess de Monaco, isn't it? She doesn't like me."

Ah, the divine Catherine, thought Nicolas. His eyes found her standing with her cousin Péguilin, and she caught Nicolas's look and answered with a small smile and a lift of her chin. What a handsome creature she was: statuesque, dark-eyed, certain of herself. She'd ridden out to Vaux-le-Vicomte, and he'd shown her its chambers, both of them aware she made a reconnoiter for Madame. He'd taken her to his own bedchamber on a top floor, even though he'd had a chamber built specifically for His Majesty, and she'd stood with her back to him as she'd inspected the bed, its magnificent embroidered hangings, and he remained behind her, his eyes on her neck rising out of her gown, the soft swell of her bare shoulders. The primitive desire he suddenly felt had startled him. He could have pushed her to the floor and taken her with the brutality of a ravaging soldier.

She had turned at the precise moment such thoughts were in his mind and met his eyes in a long, heart-stopping moment in which they'd both known they would make love sooner or later. Then she had moved past him to the doorway, and they had continued on as if such a moment had never occurred. But it had. I will visit again soon, she'd told him as she'd extended a delectable arm through the carriage window to allow him to kiss above her glove. How ironic and sensual that he and she would very likely christen the bed His Majesty and Madame would lie in.

Feeling a tug on the elbow of his very tight, very well-fitted jacket, he looked impatiently into another pair of dark eyes, eyes that didn't move him in the least.

"I know it's the princess who's against me," Olympe repeated.

"Not at all," said Nicolas. "She has the highest regard for you and your family."

"She thinks we're parvenus."

Well, and so you are, thought Nicolas. The princess's family had served kings for a number of generations, while Olympe's family's rise began in the previous reign, when the son of a simple notary had moved from nobody to cardinal.

He wished Olympe a hundred miles away so that he could concentrate on Madame, who sat there at the great table at her ease, laughing and chatting to the royal family as if a crowd did not watch her every move. No wonder the king was entranced. How charming she was. How civilized and chic. If she was going to become the king's mistress, he, Nicolas, was going to be a part of that equation. If she was going to become the king's mistress, Monsieur must have a place on the council, a consolation prize, so to speak. That would put Monsieur firmly into Nicolas's pocket and make yet another ally in the royal family.

"I'll show her a parvenu. Colbert, for instance, my uncle's minion. It's said His Majesty and Colbert meet late at night before His Majesty visits the queen."

Nicolas's heart stopped. There was a literal stop in all his body, but Olympe didn't notice.

"Maybe he prefers men like his brother. Maybe Colbert does to His Majesty what the prince's pretty boys do to him so he can rise higher in His Majesty's regard—"

"Who told you that His Majesty and Colbert meet in the evenings?"

"A footman complained to one of the dwarves, who told Her Majesty because she was upset at how late the king comes to her bed, and I overheard."

He excused himself, trying not to show the jolt of what she'd so casually—like a cat with its kill—laid at his feet. If Colbert were meeting with the king, it meant only one thing. They were looking at the register of finance. Nicolas touched at the slight perspiration that had beaded across his lip. Colbert was a bloodhound, never moved off course. He'd tried to ruin Nicolas before and failed. Had he begun another attempt?

The wildest notions took hold, notions of going to His Majesty and confessing all and seeing if the forgiveness the king had promised in the first days of his rule was truly meant. Of fleeing in the middle of the night, holing up at his island to watch as the kingdom staggered to its knees in bankruptcy. Of stockpiling gold in the hold of one of his ships and sailing away, of letting everything go, just like that, stopping it all, the tightrope of financial tricks and games he played, so many he no longer knew them all.

One of the other ministers on the king's council tapped him on the arm.

"Come and meet my nephew," the man said. "He's just in from England with some delicious gossip about King Charles and Lady Palmer."

Nicolas allowed himself to be pulled away to listen to the latest salacious gossip about the knight's wife who had the king of England following her like a dog in heat, but his mind was in another place altogether, thinking taxes have to be collected, which could not be done without him, and if taxes weren't collected, there were no funds at all.

A dozen other financial matters imperative to the kingdom came to his mind, and he calmed. Whatever Colbert might be implying, the presence of the Viscount Nicolas was so necessary for the financial well-being of the kingdom that any fool knew it. And he was tied to the Paris Parlement, that stiff, proper, ambitious body of men who formed a high court of justice, in a way that made his disgrace dangerous. And he was linked to everyone inside and outside this chamber in a dozen ways, all of them paved with gold. His Majesty was young, eager, but finance was a morass. He would tire of it. All monarchs did. Nicolas couldn't keep himself from looking toward the dining table, and he saw that the king was watching him.

Deeply, reverently, Nicolas bowed. Louis smiled. People noticed, and Nicolas felt their admiring glances. I can outwit Colbert, he thought. His Majesty was about to commit behavior that would have other courts gossiping the way they did now of England, but France was far more important in the scope of the world than England. His Majesty was about to commit behavior that would call down the wrath of the Holy Father in Rome, and relations with the Holy Father were not at their best. His Majesty was about to commit behavior that might force the prince his brother into rebellion. Nicolas's presence was, in fact, imperative, more imperative than this young king could possibly imagine.

How many people pay their respects to the Viscount Nicolas, Louis thought, the smile on his face but not in his heart. He walks through my dining chamber like a king.

Not everyone was watching the king dine. In that part of the palace where the king's ministers and officials had their offices, the oldest groom in the stable shifted awkwardly, uneasy to be where he was. His life was the stables and the public courtyard where for years before his injury he'd brought horses for the courtiers to ride. His life was the smell of dung and fresh straw and the sounds of jingling harness or a horse's whinny. It was an open life of sun and rain and moor and forest. He was uncomfortable standing in his crooked way in a small chamber with fine, polished wood for its floor and velvet draperies at the windows.

The dour man dressed in black questioning him assured him he had done nothing wrong, but he already knew that. His caution was instinctive.

Colbert cleared his throat, and the old groom brought his eyes from the open window to this man, making notes about what was said, seated behind a table. The making of letters at every word spoken also disturbed the groom.

"So she asked about the countryside. You're certain that's all?"

"Yes. And then she went riding. My son accompanied her."

"Your son." Colbert looked down at his notes and said the groom's son's name.

For some reason, hearing his son's name, knowing it was written down on paper right there between them, made the old groom even more cautious. He'd seen a hare go perfectly still, hoping to blend in with its surroundings, when a predator was near, and at this moment, he felt like the hare.

"You're to let me know whenever she goes out riding."

The old groom raised his hand in a gesture of obedience. There was another long silence as Colbert's eyes drilled into him, but it was no crime to saddle a lady's horse or for her to go out riding, and they both knew it.

"You may go."

The old groom nodded his head and limped to the door, but Colbert stopped him. "This is king's business. Don't speak of this to anyone, or the consequences will be severe."

"Has the young lady done something wrong? She is such a kind young lady."

"Likely not."

"She rode out this morning." Head lowered, eyes gleaming like a wise old boar hiding in the forest, the groom gave Colbert the information reluctantly and only because he said it was king's business, and the groom loved his young king, had put him upon his first horse, in fact. "She's back now."

"Where did she go?"

"Rode an hour or more northeast of here."

"Did she meet anyone?"

The old groom shook his head.

"You may go now," said Colbert, and the old groom glanced back once to see the man, the crow he was called behind his back, staring down intently at all the words that were written on the paper before him.

CHAPTER 10

I t was Madame's birthday; she was midsummer's princess in all ways. Everyone knew the king would acquiesce to no entertainment without her presence or approval, though few yet suspected what lay behind their intense friendship. And now her husband gave her a birthday fête. The fountain courtyard and suspended garden were filled with courtiers, many of whom had driven from Paris in their carriages to pay their respects to her.

In the famed suspended garden, lantern after lantern had been lit for night's strolling. The courtyard was a fairyland with light spilling in soft patches everywhere from candles and torches. In the carp pond around the garden, gondolas floated, footmen at the oar to row courtiers to the small open-air summer pavilion built on a little man-made island at the pond's southern end. It was late dusk, when dragonflies made a final flurry of flight, and their wings caught the tints of the setting sun, while all along the pond's edge frogs chirped.

Henriette looked wonderful, dressed in white but with a flame-colored sash pinned with a huge diamond cross at her shoulder. The sash splashed across her gown in a burst of drama. White feathers were pinned in her hair and trailed down into her curls. And there was one patch, a single patch, at her mouth. Her ladies all wore the same dramatic white feathers in their hair fastened with little pearl dragonflies she'd given them as gifts, and tonight, once more, they all wore a single, forbidden patch upon their faces.

"We're so lucky," Fanny said as they walked among the crowd. "Do you remember six months ago when I was crying out of boredom?"

"You're up to something. I know that expression, Fanny. What mischief are you plotting?"

"Hello! Hello! You there, La Baume le Blanc!" Waving a large scarf shot through with silver thread, one of her tiny, badly behaved, growling dogs tucked in her arm, La Grande Mademoiselle advanced across the courtyard. The princess, towering over nearly everyone around her, called greetings, nodded approvingly or ignored as if she were deaf, and accepted the bows and curtsies around her as her due as she approached.

"Pretend you don't see her. Follow me," hissed Fanny, and she immediately thrust herself into a group of chattering courtiers and vanished from sight. But Louise wasn't quick enough. The next thing she knew La Grande was at her side.

"Are your ears filled with wax?" said the princess. "Come with me at once. We've a mission." Raising heavy skirts and marching up the broad, wide, outside steps, she left the fête behind her, and Louise suppressed a sigh and followed obediently.

She trailed the princess down halls and through antechambers, La Grande never looking back to see that she was there or addressing a word to her. In the princess's mind, Louise was simply one of the legions of lesser nobility who were hers to order about. Musketeers stationed along various walls saluted her, and Louise realized with a start that they were in the king's chambers.

"Here we are," La Grande sniffed once they were inside a bedchamber, everything about it magnificent, from the thick, intricately embroidered hangings on the bed to the gilt in the woodwork to the size of the surround of a fireplace large enough for Louise to stand in. La Grande's little dog began to yap. She put it down, and it ran in circles until it stopped and, to Louise's horror, urinated on the floor. I should never have cured her, thought Louise. All of a sudden, dogs came leaping over the *ruelle*, the low railing that separated His Majesty's bed from the rest of the chamber. Barking and growling, they surrounded La Grande's dog.

"Silence!" commanded La Grande. "Sit! Come here, my precious Odalisque, come to Mama." La Grande opened the gate of the *ruelle* and stalked to the bed.

"Come here," La Grande commanded, and realizing she, not the dogs, was being summoned, and in spite of the fact that she didn't wish to obey, Louise walked into the sacred space that only a king and those he allowed might enter. She saw that another dog lay in the center of the king's bed. The dog was large and tawny with a handsome head. Everyone knew her. She was His Majesty's favorite, Belle, his best hunter.

"My father gave her to His Majesty," said La Grande, "and the king tells me she's sick and that though his physicians have given her an emetic, she seems no better. I told him I knew someone who had a way with animals, that you'd made my little Odalisque all better. What do you think, La Baume le Blanc?"

Louise sat on the bed, put her hand out, and felt the dog's muzzle. "She feels warm, a fever, perhaps." She lightly caressed the dog's back and haunches, pulled her front paws. "Where does it hurt, Miss Belle?" she whispered, and Belle turned over, exposing her belly, and when Louise caressed that, a low growl was the response. At once the three other dogs were on the bed, barking furiously at Louise.

La Grande batted at them with a pillow. "Get down! Down, I say! They won't hurt you."

"I think it's her stomach," said Louise. "Run your hand just here, Princess, but be careful. I think it hurts her for us to touch it."

La Grande did as Louise suggested.

"A hint of swelling, don't you think?" asked Louise.

"I don't feel it, but I haven't your touch. La Porte!" The princess walked away from the bed bellowing the name. Her little dog went scurrying away to the fireplace, where it hid behind one of the elaborate silver fronts of the andirons. The other dogs leapt back upon the bed and walked around Louise, who held out her hands so that they could smell them. She knew them from the hunts, but she'd never been this close before, and she was an invader in their territory. Her smell would reassure them; she knew that. It always did.

A boy entered the chamber, clapped his hands, and all the dogs but Belle bounded off the bed and to him. Belle's tail whipped back and forth. "You'd go to him if you felt better, wouldn't you?" Louise said to the dog. "He's a friend, isn't he?"

"There you are, La Porte," said La Grande. "I've brought La Baume le Blanc to see the dog, at His Majesty's request. My little Odalisque wouldn't be with me today if it weren't for her. I need to wash my hands. Tell His Majesty that Belle has a swelling on her stomach. A poultice should do the trick, I think. And tell him she has a fever. I'd give her whatever he takes for fever. Odalisque! Where are you, darling sweetness?"

La Grande remained exactly where she was until he brought a basin of water. Then she dipped her hands in it, waiting, those same hands out-stretched and dripping, until the valet brought a cloth to dry them. The dogs growled and pawed at a fireplace andiron. The boy, Louise realized, wasn't a boy at all, but a very small, very trim man, hair pulled back into a neat tail.

He clapped his hands again, and the three big dogs went swirling out of the bedchamber as Belle whined. He reached down and pulled La Grande's dog from one of the silver andiron pillars. It tried to bite him.

"Odalisque, my jasmine blossom," La Grande said, folding the dog into the crook of her arm.

"It will be too much to give her the same amount of fever water His Majesty might take."

Both La Grande and the valet looked over to Louise, who had moved outside the *ruelle*.

"Yes," said La Grande. "Half—"

Louise shook her head.

"A quarter, I would say. Yes, that should help." La Grande marched out of the bedchamber, leaving Louise behind her like a discarded ragdoll.

The valet considered Louise, then nodded, a small, neat movement matching his small, neat presence. "Would miss care to wash her hands?"

"Oh, yes, please. Thank you so much." Louise hurriedly splashed her hands in the basin of water, dried them on the cloth. "I think Belle would like to be wherever the others are."

She fled, not daring to tell him about the mess La Grande's dog had left on the other side of the *ruelle*. She just didn't dare.

❦

At midnight, Philippe's birthday gift came rumbling up the road from the stables. It passed along the length of the carp pond, and linkboys ran before it lighting the way with the torches they carried. The gift, a carriage, pulled up to the ornate doors of what was called the golden entrance, the king's personal entrance into the palace, a beautiful pavilion built to resemble a gatehouse. Courtiers crowded around the vehicle, lacquered black with Philippe's crest picked out in gold and blue paint on the doors. Six white horses—matched in size and color, no easy task to find—were in harness. The inside was blue velvet and blue leather, and Philippe played footman, opening the door for Henriette, while Louis walked around the carriage inspecting it.

"Do you ride inside or with us?" Philippe asked his brother. He pointed to Guy, who sat in the coachman's place. One nimble movement, and Philippe was up beside Guy in the groom's seat. Louis climbed up to join them as courtiers looked on enviously.

"Stand aside. We take Madame for a drive," Guy shouted.

"Don't be disappointed not to join them." Anne, the Queen Mother, patted the hand of Louis's queen as they watched the carriage being turned around. "His Majesty would do nothing to harm the child you carry, and with that scamp driving"—she pointed toward Guy with her fan—"anything could happen."

"Élan," Molière said to one of his fellow actors as they stood among the crowd watching the carriage depart. Part of the kitchen staff this evening, the two carried heavy trays to the courtyard laden with food from the kitchens—duck floating in orange sauce, flan with lemon, a swan stuffed with pigeon breasts and apricots—to tempt Madame's capricious appetite. "His Majesty has tremendous élan. Take that and exaggerate it, and you have a hero."

Guy maneuvered the horses toward the grand canal that anchored one end of the gardens. Built by the king's grandfather, the canal stretched nearly four thousand feet in length; it was this same canal the young court drove around in the wee hours of the morning.

"Where did you find six white horses?" Louis asked his brother.

"I found three, and the viscount, when he learned of my dilemma, offered the other three."

The wheels of the carriage came too near the wall of the canal, and Philippe gripped the wooden coachman's seat they sat upon with both hands, as Guy laughed.

"Afraid?" asked Guy.

"Let me have the reins," snapped Louis.

"I've practiced for weeks, Your Majesty. You're safe."

"It's not my safety I'm fretted about but Madame's."

"She'll survive a jostle, won't she, Monsieur?"

Louis spoke evenly. "I don't wish her jostled—"

Philippe put his hand on Louis's arm. "It's all right; really, it is. Slow down, Count. Back to the palace in one piece, I beg you."

"He's too unskilled to do this," insisted Louis.

"He did practice for weeks," Philippe said. "And it's his gift to her tonight, to be her coachman. Please, my brother."

When the carriage had safely returned to the golden entrance, Philippe hopped down to play servant to his wife one more time.

"Does my gift please?" he asked her as she descended.

"You're too kind to me," Henriette exclaimed.

Philippe brought her hand to his lips. "You make it easy to be kind, my dear love."

Guy, still in the coachman's seat, scowled.

Once she was in the fountain courtyard, ensconced in a chair between the yawning queen and the Queen Mother, Henriette began to open her gift from their majesties.

"The Mazarins?" said Anne, the Queen Mother, looking at diamond pendant earrings Henriette held up for all to see. The diamonds were famous, a legacy from their dear cardinal.

"Like mine, Majesty." Maria Teresa pulled back her ringlets, so that Anne could see a duplicate pair hanging from her ears. "His Majesty, he have made. For me. Then, for Madame." Maria Teresa leaned over to touch Henriette's hand affectionately. "I am glad you have. Happy day of birth to you."

Henriette stared down at the magnificent earrings, then turned to her mother-in-law. "Thank you for sharing these, Majesty. These are so lovely."

"I had nothing to do with it." Anne spoke testily.

Louis held out a matching crimson box to his mother. "You have everything to do with it."

Anne opened the box to reveal earrings that matched those Henriette had just received.

"How lovely." From the front row of courtiers, where she had stationed herself, determined to see and be seen, to miss nothing, the queen's maid of honor, Athénaïs, spoke. She smiled brilliantly at the royal family. "The queens of our court sparkle like stars."

"There are only two queens here." Anne's tone was sharp, her look toward the dazzling maid of honor, whom she normally favored, a razor's cut.

Louis knelt on one knee before his mother. He smiled, his smile tender, beautiful really. It made his whole face suddenly remarkable. One saw humor and passion and bright intelligence.

"With your permission, Your Majesty." He was very formal, like an ambassador come to call, as he put his hands to his mother's ears and unscrewed the earrings she was wearing. "I could not bear to have no earrings for you." And then, low enough so that only she could hear, "Our dear cardinal would not like it." And when the new pendants were in her ears, he said, "I claim a kiss." And he kissed her.

"With your permission," he repeated, kneeling now before Henriette, moving her hair, unscrewing her earrings.

Standing where he could see both their faces, Guy's expression turned stern.

"A birthday salute." Louis dropped his mouth on Henriette's, the briefest of touches, as Guy made a sound and looked around to see where Philippe might be.

"And witness how to play the hero," Molière whispered to a fellow actor who helped him refill great silver platters with food, "seriously, as if all your heart were in it, no mockery of any kind. One must also be handsome."

Happy that his friends from Paris had journeyed to Fontainebleau for this fête and for his sake, happy that his gift of the carriage had impressed, Philippe had abandoned his brother's gift-giving and stood with friends near the outside staircase. They were playing a guessing game.

"Tiberius," said the Chevalier de Lorraine.

"Caligula," argued Philippe.

"Cleopatra set the fire," insisted Choisy.

"It was Nero, you imbeciles," said La Grande Mademoiselle. "Here's the Count de Guiche. He will tell you I know of what I speak. Guiche, tell them it was Nero."

"I could care less who fiddled while Rome burned. We have our own fire." Guy advanced directly toward Philippe, but a palace page reached Philippe first to announce, "His Majesty asks for you, Your Highness."

"What, now?" Philippe rolled his eyes, but it was clear he was pleased to be summoned.

"You'd better go, hadn't you? Your master is calling. Do you bark and slobber when he pats your head?" Guy was mocking.

"Someone seems miffed," said the Chevalier de Lorraine.

"Miffed," answered Guy. "What a petty little word. I think I'll throw you in the carp pond."

"I don't like your tone, Count," said La Grande. She was as tall as Guy, taller because the feathers she wore pinned in her hair stood straight up behind her head in a style that had made the Chevalier de Lorraine laugh aloud when he saw it. "There are ladies present."

"There certainly are, half of them right here—"

Choisy put himself in front of the Chevalier de Lorraine. "We've done nothing to deserve your insults, Count. You may not treat us so."

Head lowered, looking a little like a bull on the verge of charging, Guy turned away and walked back toward the king and queens, toward Henriette.

"'You may not treat us so,'" mimicked the Chevalier de Lorraine.

"I'll throw you in the carp pond myself," threatened Choisy.

"Oh, you'll tear a lace, and that will be the end of that."

"Must we bicker, my pretty ones?" asked La Grande, and the other two gazed up at her as if she'd lost her mind. Of course they must.

❦

Philippe stood before his brother. The wonderful evening, his gift, which had been more showy than Louis's, his friends' assurances that he was very much missed in Paris, the fact that his parties were better than his brother's and this one proved it, shone on his face.

"Will you escort the queen to her bedchamber?" Louis asked him.

"The honor is too great to bear," Philippe said in Spanish and placed Maria Teresa's small hand on his arm to lead her away, as the women of her household detached themselves from partners and groups of courtiers to follow their queen like bright, gowned, reluctant butterflies.

Louis's eyes didn't leave his brother, who was asking the queen if she had enjoyed the fête, if she'd tried the duck, if she'd seen the relic the Viscount Nicolas's brother had sent from Rome, a saint's finger bone, he was saying, Saint Peter's, we believe. Philippe was at his best: kind, genial, gallant, lively. The pain that was Louis's betrayal of him began its ache.

"Where's my wife?" Philippe demanded an hour or two later. Wine and the largesse of the evening glowed in him.

Guy pointed to the pond. Louis and Henriette, Catherine and two maids of honor sat in a small galley, a replica of an actual galley that had been given by Cardinal Richelieu to Louis's father. They were being rowed to the summer pavilion at the far end. Other courtiers were also out on the water in gondolas imported from Venice, the lantern lights on the gondolas like enormous fireflies hovering above water.

"I wanted to tell her again how wonderful she looks," said Philippe, just on the edge of slurring his words. "Jump in the pond with me. We can swim to the galley."

"You're drunk."

"I'm happy, happier than I've been in my life."

"You're a blind fool," said Guy. "It's time you saw what is happening right under your nose."

Feeling safe, feeling unseen aboard the small galley, Louis and Henriette held hands.

"Thank you for the earrings," Henriette whispered.

Louis put a hand to her neck, caressing the flesh there, touching the pendant of the earring. "I went through a great deal of trouble just so I could kneel before you and put them in your ears."

They looked at each other, and even in the dark, even standing on the other side of the galley, Louise felt herself tremble inside at the sight of their expressions. They gave themselves away. To be loved that way, she thought, and then, too much wine, I've drunk too much wine tonight, gone from practical to maudlin, as Fanny says. The memory of the sight of the king kneeling before the women of his family, unscrewing earrings as carefully as a servant, twisted her heart. It was so courteous and grand, so flamboyant and yet dignified. He'd been like an actor no one could take his eyes from.

The galley bumped into the small island, and servants jumped out to help the king and Henriette disembark. Catherine went with them, but Louise and Fanny stayed on board.

"I think we warn the gargoyle," said Louise, wine-bold. She leaned over the side looking down into the water. I could take off my clothes, jump in this water, and swim like a fish, she thought. How lovely to be a fish. "I think people are beginning to notice."

"That can't be our concern, Louise. We're of little or no importance in this."

"We are important. We're their messengers. Did I see you kiss the Count de Guiche tonight?"

"No. You saw him kiss me."

Louise turned on her side to look on her friend. "Be careful, Fanny."

"Pooh."

Inside the summer pavilion, a charming folly of sandstone and marble with arched openings on all sides, Louis pushed Henriette against the farthermost wall.

"I want to make love to you," he said. "It's all I think about." He kissed her neck and shoulders, pressing her against the wall, his hands urgent, roaming up and down her dress, rumpling it.

"My dress—"

He didn't hear. "I can't imagine life without you, Henriette." He kissed her mouth, biting her lips, putting his mouth on the swell of her breast just where her gown covered it, but Catherine stepped into the pavilion.

"We have to go. We can't linger any longer! Monsieur and my brother are in a gondola drifting our way!"

At the anxiety in her voice, Louis lifted his head, but he couldn't help shivering. Henriette laughed, her voice shrill. Color came into Louis's face, but that was lost in the three of them straightening Henriette's gown and sash before they returned to the galley, Louis unable to stop himself from taking another kiss or two just before they stepped into the open.

As servants began to row them back, he could feel the powerful pulse of his heart. A refuge, he thought, my kingdom for a refuge. I am weary and lonesome. When would Henriette allow him to make her his? To take what he desired so much that he couldn't help shivering like someone with a fever? And where? At Vaux-le-Vicomte, urged the Princess de Monaco, but he would not take his beloved naked and trembling as he also would be in the house of the man he must destroy. Why had Henriette laughed? He couldn't get the sound of it from his mind, that shrill, coquettish, little sound she'd made.

My heart hurts, thought Louise, as the galley moved through the water, an oversized swan, toward the suspended garden, and she looked up into the sky, to the stars there, sparkling bright everywhere, to the moon, mist around it. Choisy courted her again, told her stories of the old gods who turned themselves into showers of gold to make love to women they desired, of men who were part bull and lived at the center of a labyrinth or who fell in love with their own reflections, of women who saved the hero with their wit and passion but were left behind as he sailed away. She was dreaming the stories at night. Their symbols were everywhere, painted in the ballroom frescoes, turned to statues in the queen's garden or the stag's gallery, woven into the figures in the wall tapestries. Seeing the king and Madame and their desperate love this night made something in her feel languorous and tender, opening. She'd allowed Choisy to kiss her the other day. The kiss had not been chaste, but a mingling of mouth and tongue and desire from him that had surprised her. She didn't love him, kissed him only because he begged, and hadn't let him kiss again. But it felt like a door in her was becoming unsealed, that there was something deep and mysterious on its other side, another layer, which would leave the girl in her behind. She'd taken another girl, the little Julie, to see her family. The child had wept and begged to stay, but her mother had caught Louise's eye and given a sharp shake of the head, and so Louise had brought the crying child back to the nuns. She understood the child's loneliness. She'd often been lonely in the midst of the Orléans ragged splendor. The child didn't yet understand that another world beckoned to her, a better life. She preferred the poverty of the farm and the brutality of her father to loneliness, preferred that which was known to what was yet unknown. I must do what I can to ease her sorrow, thought Louise, for that, too, she knew, that sorrow carved a deep path in one's heart.

I've made the king of France shake in his shoes with desire for me, thought Henriette. What triumph.

Still later that night, the fête finally over as dawn showed a hint of light over the horizon, Henriette's maids of honor tossed words back and forth from their beds.

"She danced with him three times in a row, and when she went off in the galley, people noticed. The Count de Guiche's face was a storm cloud. Madame's face when you came back from the pavilion, it looked, well, it looked kissed," said Madeleine.

"I didn't see any kisses, and I was right there with them," said Fanny. "Did you, Louise?"

"It's a sin to be unfaithful," said Claude.

"But it is not a sin to flirt," answered Fanny.

"Nothing would make me flirt if I were married," claimed Madeleine.

Fanny laughed. "If the king began to smile at you, Miss Madeleine, if the king asked for your hand to partner his favorite dances, looked pensive until you appeared on the scene, gave you diamond earrings, and knelt at your feet to put them in your ears, are you telling me that you wouldn't entertain the thought of making him happy? Her very presence makes him happy. That's all there is to it."

There was silence in the chamber. Then Fanny spoke again, driving home her point.

"I'm speaking of His Majesty, that serious man with the thick curling brown hair I have to make myself not reach out and touch, that man who takes off his hat to talk to any one of us and seems to listen, too. So that man, who happens to be master of us all, smiles at you, wants to listen to what you say, wants to escort you hither and yon just to be beside you. And you'd be cold as snow? Nothing tingling? Nothing sparking? Nothing in you urging you to accede to his wishes? The only thing Madame is guilty of is enjoying His Majesty's very high regard. I would, too. And so would you, any one of you, and you know it!"

No one answered.

It's not a good sign, Louise thought, as she tried to settle under the covers, that we're talking of this. If we are, others are, too. Her most recent canter had taken her to a farmhouse near Vaux-le-Vicomte. Beware on your way back, said the farmer, leaning against a rake. There was a were-wolf seen. My cousin saw it. Wolves and legends about wolves were part and parcel of country lore. When? Louise had asked. In the spring, he'd answered. A werewolf, she'd thought, riding out of his farmyard, might just be a boy in an iron mask, weeping and howling as he ran through the forest.

❧

Louis stared down at the Mazarinade that had been left in Belle's collar. It had fallen onto the bed as he touched her neck. The words were cruel:

> *Licentious birds of a feather,*
> *she a tool of unnatural passion,*
> *he a tool of unnatural ambition.*

The "she" was his mother; the "he" was Mazarin.

CHAPTER 11

The next day, indolent and sad and yawning, Anne, Queen Mother of France, lay in a special daybed her beloved Cardinal Mazarin had commissioned for her from Italy. The finest artisan in Rome had carved its frame, and soft padding covered with lustrous silky fabric lined its exterior. She could half sit, half lie upon it, and she did so now, facing tall doors opened to the terrace and pond and gardens. Curtains hung down to protect her from the sun pooling into this chamber—she was vain of her white complexion, her equally white hands—but the wind lifted the fabric in graceful arcs that allowed her glimpses of the palace gardens. All about her was the finest of furniture and paintings and tapestries. Above, her initials were handsomely carved in each honeycomb of the coved ceiling. A little brazier sent out the sweet scent of a perfumed lozenge, for she couldn't bear even the hint of an offensive odor. Over in a corner, her favorite musician played the guitar.

She craved sleep. Since Mazarin's death, she slept little. The music lulled; she began to doze as her mind darted lightly here and there among impressions from the previous night…surprising how Henriette had turned out so well…Philippe settled…thank the Holy Mother and all the saints for that…no need to worry anymore…Louis seemed almost a little too appreciative of his new sister's grace…A soft snore wafted toward the honeycombed initials on the ceiling.

Madame de Motteville, her favorite lady-in-waiting, who had been with her forever, in good and bad times, who carried secrets that if ever uttered would send the woman, no matter how favored, to the deepest dungeon of the terrible Bastille prison in Paris, entered the chamber, stepped to the daybed, and said loudly enough to wake, "Your Majesty, he demands to see you."

Anne opened blue and still quite lovely eyes. "Tell His Majesty—"

"It's Monsieur, and he won't be denied."

Oh, bones of Mother Mary, the last thing she wanted to deal with at this moment was her excitable, high-strung, talkative second son. She sat up, a frown on her face. From being pleased at the thought of the way he'd settled down, she moved to feeling extreme annoyance. After the lovely fête only last night, what could he possibly have to complain of?

"He says 'Nero fiddled while Rome burned. Your Majesty naps,'" said Madame de Motteville.

"What on earth does that mean?"

Madame de Motteville made a gesture, and at once a woman of the bedchamber glided forward to hold out a bowl of water. Anne dipped her hands, patted her face, took the crisp, starched, white-as-snow linen, her initials painstakingly embroidered in a corner—she would have no other touch her, never had—to wipe her face. Her tastes were fastidious and had been a hugely civilizing influence on the court. Courtiers no longer spat wherever they pleased or blew their noses on their sleeves. She had become queen of France at ten and four. She'd been vivacious enough to learn French and hate her husband's chief adviser. She'd been strong enough to outlast not bearing an heir for years. That strength served her now, though she was a ghost of the self she'd been before Mazarin's death. She would need her wits about her if Philippe were in a temper.

He was. He marched into her bedchamber in a fury. Anne surveyed him coldly, as if he were an opponent. It was second nature to do so. No one who survived on the throne could do any less. Both her boys were so handsome. This one's hair was darker than his brother's, more magnificent, thicker, but he was slighter than his brother, more like a boy. Sensitive and intelligent, he tried always to please. She didn't love him the way she did Louis, never had.

"He's fallen in love with my wife! He is seducing her right under my nose!"

With one gesture from Anne, the chamber emptied. Only her lady-in-waiting remained, standing silent against one wall. There was no point to hide anything from her. Sooner or later, Anne would have to make use of her.

"I'll kill him! I will, Mother!" ranted Philippe. "First he denies me the governorship of Languedoc, which is mine by precedent and right, then he doesn't appoint me to his council, again my right as a prince of the blood, now this—"

She slapped him.

He was stunned into silence, his eyes wide, his expression hurt, as she selected words to underscore her gesture.

"He is the king of France! You owe him all obedience! I could have you arrested for what you've just said! If I ever hear you say it again, I will order you sent to the deepest dungeon in the kingdom, from which you will never emerge, not while I'm alive!" Always, she had striven to make certain he knew his place in their life, behind Louis, behind he who was king. "Sit down and be silent," she ordered, trusting his respect for her to make him obey. "Now, what in God's name has summoned up this hatred for your brother, a hatred I won't countenance, by the way." She already knew the answer. Last night. The regard between Louis and Henriette.

"He courts my wife in front of my face! And she responds! People are beginning to talk—"

"What people?"

"The Count de Guiche, for one."

"Well, isn't this pretty? We're going to take what an arrogant trouble-maker like Guy-Armand de Gramont, Count de Guiche, says seriously, are we? Doesn't he always stir up trouble between you and His Majesty?"

"Henriette—"

"Is young and high-spirited. I was the same at her age. Men flocked to me like birds to a flower. Was it my fault? No. Did I enjoy it? Yes. Was I unfaithful to your father, bless his sacred memory? Of course not! But that didn't stop people from talking, gossiping, flies making muck. Revel in her success, my darling. It's your success for having had the good sense to marry her. She would never do anything to hurt you, Philippe, I'm certain of it."

"I won't be shamed!"

"The only shame I perceive is in having allowed someone to plant such thoughts in your head. I demand that you go immediately to your confessor and pull this sin of jealousy and suspicion from your heart. Trust Guiche to make trouble between you and His Majesty. I have half a mind to have him sent from court—"

"Don't do that! He's the only one I—"

"Trust? Was that the word you were going to use? He certainly served you no good three years ago."

"I was never treasonous! And neither was he!"

"So you say. When I remember how His Majesty forgave you—we had only to ask, and it was done—your evil suspicions of your brother at this moment break my heart. I want you on your knees repenting before God. Here." She held out the ornate silver cross that hung from the long neck-lace she wore. "Kiss this, swear you will put vile thoughts from your mind for my sake. Swear it! Now. For my sake."

The cross was made from Spanish silver mined in the new world, rough emeralds on its four ends, ground bone from the Montezuma said to be mixed in with the metal.

Reluctantly, Philippe knelt, took the cross, and kissed it. Like her, he was extravagantly religious. The face he raised to her was stunning in its even male beauty, in its desire to believe, in its struggle for humility and obedience to his brother.

"High spirits," she said. "That's all. Diversion. It's the froth of youth, my darling. Don't let a serpent in the garden spoil this. One day you'll be old like me, and these times will seem another world, and you'll regret any waste of them. The king—your brother and my son"—her voice throbbed with sincerity and high drama—"has no desire to do anything but honor the charming young woman you've had the cleverness to choose! It's those with perverted minds who take that honor, that lightheartedness, that gallantry, and twist it! It's innocent."

"But if—"

She put her hand over his mouth. "Do you think I would allow something as foul as that in my court? I'm watching, my darling. Always. Trust me. Take this cross." She pulled the necklace over her head, dropped it into his hands. "Take it as a pledge that all is well, that you must and will purge your heart of these thoughts. Go now to your confessor and empty that heart, your beautiful heart, my prince, my Monsieur, of its dross. Don't trust Guiche. Not again. Surely you realize you cannot."

Tears welling in his eyes, Philippe clutched the cross in his hands. "But—"

"Trust in the Lord, my son, and in me, your mother, and in the purity of your brother's heart."

Chin lifted, demeanor calm, Anne watched her second child bow to her, then walk away. The moment the door closed behind him, doubt flooded her. Louis wasn't a full year married. Maria Teresa carried their firstborn. Could he...would he? His own sister-in-law? Her mind flew to Henriette. Could she...would she? Things she'd done herself in her youth, and even past it, rattled warnings at her. She turned to her lady-in-waiting.

"Can this folly be true? I won't believe a word of it!"

"Best begin."

In another part of the palace, unaware that her little world had suffered its first crack, Henriette scribbled a love note to Louis in her private closet. The walls were lined with portraits of her family. There was one of her father, with his fine and sensitive features, wearing a huge lace collar and the single pearl earring that had been fashionable at the time. Her prayer stand was placed beneath his portrait, but she had no memory of him whatsoever. Her oldest brother had fought beside their father on the battlefield and assured her that their father had been all that was honorable and proper in a man and a king. A portrait of her mother, painted before the civil war in England, showed a beautiful woman, but Henriette had never known her like that. And there were portraits of her brothers and sisters, the large family she'd never known, all gone now except for the three who remained. And their mother. It will take a stake through the heart to kill her, her brother Charles jested.

She raised her head at a tap at the door, and a page entered to tell her the Princess de Monaco asked to see her.

"Of course."

She was surprised to see the princess wasn't alone. Her brother, the Count de Guiche, accompanied her and was frowning, and as he walked toward Henriette, she felt something like foreboding run through her.

"On your knees before her, merciless creature," Catherine said.

Guy dropped on both knees before Henriette.

"Monsieur went this morning to the Queen Mother to complain of your behavior with His Majesty. Here's the troublemaker, kneeling before you. He is the reason Monsieur is upset. He has betrayed you!" Catherine said.

Henriette fell back in her chair. She thought for a moment she was going to faint. "Why?" she asked when she could speak. "Why would you do this to me? I thought you a friend."

"I've never felt friendship for you." Guy grabbed her wrist, and dread opened in her like a terrible, huge, black cloud. It had all been a dream, hadn't it, that she and His Majesty might do as they pleased forever and ever without being seen, caught, lectured, judged. Her head felt light.

"If I'm not a friend," Guy said, pulling her forward, closer to him, "what am I?"

"A fool!" cried Catherine.

"Take your hands off me! I don't know what you are, and I care even less," said Henriette.

But he didn't let go of her wrist. "I love you," he said.

There was silence. Neither Henriette nor Catherine spoke a word.

"If I can't have you, no one will." Fierce, wild-eyed, Guy spoke through clenched teeth. "Certainly not him!" He let go her wrist, flinging it away.

"He's the king," said Catherine, aghast. "Kings must be obeyed!"

"Kings are made and unmade," Guy replied. "History has shown us that."

Catherine hit him on the shoulder, a hard shove, and he stood to face her. "I grew up beside Louis de Bourbon. He is a man, no more, no less. He bleeds just like I do."

"You are not the king! And you're speaking treason—"

"Stop it!" shouted Henriette. "I am the one who is ruined. I am the one who must face Monsieur. How can you say you love me and yet put me into this awful situation?"

Guy turned to her. "Lie," he said. "Tell Monsieur that you love him only and that others are jealous—as they are—that I am jealous, as I am, as I will tell him myself, and that His Majesty has done nothing more than honor a new sister. Have you graced his bed?"

Something in his eyes made her lean back in her chair and put her hands over her ears.

Catherine beat at her brother's back. "You have to stop now, Guy-Armand!"

"You've ruined me," said Henriette. "You say you love me, and you've ruined me! I never want to see you again as long as I live."

Guy's face went white. He made a move to touch her, but she turned her face from him. "Get out!"

Guy bowed, an abrupt, jerking movement, and left the chamber. Henriette collapsed, beginning to sob. "What am I going to do?"

✿

Anne paced her balcony, her mind working with all the vigor that rebellion had once brought to the forefront. Intolerable, she was thinking. It must be headed off, scotched, stopped in its tracks. She'd take Henriette off at once to a dear friend of hers where the child could cool down and reconsider this flirtation. And a note was already written, already on its way by special messenger to Henriette's mother, the queen of England until her son married. If two queens, who between them had faced revolt, betrayal, widowhood, and more than one impossible choice, couldn't snuff this out without anyone being the wiser, they deserved to die quietly right now in their beds. This just proved once and for all that Louis needed her, that he hadn't the maturity yet to manage the throne by himself. Deciding to take care of the state in person and to rely on no one. Ha. They were little more than children, Louis only twenty and two, her confessor reminded her. She'd called for him at once, flung the news at him as if it were his fault. She must not judge until she knew more, he had soothed. Ha. She'd had a warning word with Monsieur's, too. Now she waited for the Viscount Nicolas.

She was ready to tear out the viscount's heart when he was finally ushered into her chamber, but her anger melted slightly at what was held in his outstretched hand, a black pearl, quite large, quite wonderful, quite rare.

"For you," he murmured, smiling at her.

She loved his extravagance. It suited her own. Her jewel boxes were littered with his little gifts. And if there was a need for extra funds, for some discreet favor done, he quietly took care of it. He had been a good friend to her.

"All is well, I trust," said Nicolas. The expression on her face told him otherwise.

Anne made no attempt to be discreet. She and the viscount had known one another too long. "Have you noticed anything untoward in His Majesty's conduct?"

"Other than that he insists on handling all state business himself?"

"That will pass. It's too much for any man, as we both know. He'll weary of it. His father did. I did. I meant unseemliness in his personal life, his private time with friends. Is there talk of his—his flirting in particular with anyone?"

"He's quite taken with Madame, but all are," Nicolas answered smoothly, and as Anne's face stiffened, "perhaps a little more than partiality toward Madame, but they're young, after all."

She told him the story of Philippe's visit this morning, his anger and accusation. "I've already spoken to Monsieur's confessor. And I shall broach His Majesty's also. And you, I plead with you, do what you can to see this—this—dreadful infatuation ended. The right word at the right moment from a man such as you..." She let her words trail off.

"I will do whatever I can." Nicolas allowed some silence to pass, then added ruefully, "You may give me too much credit, however. I sometimes wonder if I've inadvertently offended him. I live to serve him. I am not certain he accepts that."

"He is aware of your loyalty in every way, my dear Viscount, as am I. It's the novelty of ruling by himself. It's been only three months since—" Anne's composure cracked, and tears began a slow course down her cheeks, ruining her carefully applied rouge and powder.

"Majesty," Nicolas said, thinking how swiftly the currents of power move. She who had been the heart of this court no longer was. "If I may." He held out his hand, and she clasped it.

Anne sobbed rage that Mazarin should be gone, rage that she should be forced to make decisions on her own, rage that her children should misbehave when she needed quiet. "I miss him so," she finally said to the gilded wainscoting, the woven tapestries, her initials carved in each honeycomb of her ceiling.

"We all do. He was a great man," said Nicolas. "May I call for your ladies?"

"Send in Motteville. She's the only one who knows what to do with me anymore."

"He was a fortunate man to have your love."

She put a hand on her heart, fresh tears starting. "I remain his until I die."

So, thought Nicolas, they did marry. He'd always thought it.

"By the way," he said, pausing at the door, "I thought you'd wish to know His Majesty appointed a lieutenant governor to the province of Brittany."

In the antechamber, he found Madame de Motteville.

"She asks for you," he told her, and then in a low voice because other of the Queen Mother's ladies were scattered about the chamber, "What precisely did Monsieur say?"

Without looking from the embroidery threads she was tying off, Motteville answered as quietly as he'd asked, "Not here."

"You'll send a note around later?"

"A personal visit would be better."

She didn't wish to put it to paper, thought Nicolas, as he walked down the long gallery that was part of the Queen Mother's apartments. He smiled to himself. Madame and her ladies had become the sirens of court, luring men toward shipwreck. Claw marks from Catherine were still red on his back. They'd made love yesterday, not in the bed, as he'd imagined, but on the floor in a wild, tumbled, frenzied joining. Magnificent and completely satisfying. His Majesty the king of France, Louis the fourteenth of that name, was about to make one very grand misstep, and he, Nicolas, the first viscount of that name, was going to be absolutely necessary to keep the disorder contained.

❦

Searching for the Countess de Soissons, holding up her skirts so that she wouldn't trip, beautiful Athénaïs de Tonnay-Charente ran in high heels through the galleries of Fontainebleau. She had gossip. Shoes skittering on the intricate, inlaid woods of the floors, she ran from one chamber to another. This wasn't an age for privacy, so one chamber opened into another, and she disturbed gatherings everywhere, except for the king's council. She had nerve, but not for that.

Olympe was alone in the queen's gallery, a long, wide, majestic space that faced enclosed gardens. She sat in a window seat, feet drawn up under her skirts, and stared down at those gardens, where the young queen and her ladies were assembled, and where she should be, only she wasn't. And neither was the maid of honor running toward her.

"You'll never guess what's happened," Athénaïs blurted out.

Olympe lifted an eyebrow.

"Monsieur has had a fit in the Queen Mother's chambers this morning over His Majesty and Madame's flirting."

"His Majesty couldn't have serious feelings for that skinny, pale wand."

"He might, I think."

Olympe glared at her, but Athénaïs didn't care.

"It's because I didn't go to the witch," said Olympe.

"What witch? Are you going to see one? I've never met a witch."

Olympe didn't answer.

"When you go, may I go with you? Please, oh please." Athénaïs was charming without trying, but when she tried, she was difficult to resist.

"I suppose so. Where are you off to now?"

"I have to find my brother."

"As the queen's superintendent, it's my duty to tell you not to spread gossip. Not a word of this can be even hinted to Her Majesty, or we'll lose our positions."

"Oh no, I wouldn't do that. My lips are sealed. This was just for you."

As quickly as she'd entered the gallery, Athénaïs was gone again. That damned Vivonne, she was thinking. Her brother, as gentleman of the king's household, had to know what was happening. He never said a word to me of this intrigue, she thought. But it was far worse than that. She'd gotten herself attached to the wrong household. Her family was wild and ambitious, and she possessed the same surety that Guy and Catherine did, except theirs was polished to gleaming arrogance. She'd thought she'd played the ace by being appointed to the new queen's household, but excitement was occurring in Madame's, where Madame's sudden burst of acclamation had carried over to her maids of honor, most of them nobodies, certainly not daughters of dukes like Athénaïs. It just wasn't fair.

CHAPTER 12

I wish to revisit the idea of intendants," Louis told his council.

"An old idea, Your Majesty, from your father's reign, and if I may speak frankly, it failed," said Nicolas.

"That's true, Viscount, but I think the wars, both foreign and civil, caused its failure. Mister Colbert has had the goodness to compose a brief treatise on why my father's chief minister thought the idea a good one. I'm going to beg your indulgence and ask you to read it. It's there among your papers."

Answerable only to the king, intendants were official administrators who collected taxes and watched the politics of a province. The position had been the idea of Cardinal Richelieu, minister to Louis's father, as he labored to turn the fiefs and smaller kingdoms of France toward loyalty to the crown rather than toward their own interests. No one on the council could know that in ten years' time their presence would be a key component in France's march toward an absolute monarchy that was the envy of Europe.

As the council members began to shuffle through the papers Colbert had prepared, a knock sounded, and one of the Queen Mother's pages nervously entered with a note for the king.

Louis ripped past the seal; his mother summoned him. He was to go to her chamber as soon as his council ended. He put the note to one side, but the page still lingered, and Louis turned to the boy. "Well?"

"Would there, is there—" The boy swallowed. It took every ounce of his courage, but he had his orders. "Is there a reply, sire?"

"Tell my mother I am her obedient servant in all ways. Go." He turned back to his council. "Last year we imported corn and sold it cheaply from the royal granaries. The summer is dry so far. If there isn't rain by August, harvests will be poor. I think we should consider it again, and I want to reduce the land tax. I thought to disband some of my infantry and the cavalry to cut expenses. Here are the details."

Louis's minister of war passed out four single sheets of paper upon which specific regiments and amounts and estimated savings were listed. But Nicolas did little more than move the paper from one place to another. He already knew what was written on it. He and the minister of war were firm allies; there were no surprises between them.

"And if we do have need for funds, you'll find them, won't you?" Louis said to Nicolas.

"Of course."

"Colbert has put forth a proposal to build up the kingdom's woolen industry. It is my thought to recruit cloth makers and weavers from Flanders," Louis said. "If we find them places to live and wives, they'll stay."

"Will any woman do for the worthy Colbert, or must she be pretty?" snapped Nicolas. He was tired of hearing Colbert's name.

"All French women are beautiful," said Louis, and there was general laughter as a clock chimed, and Louis pushed back his chair. Council was ended for the day.

"For him to disband some of his army," one minister said to the other, shaking his head. There was no army larger than France's, and Louis had been part of it, on its battlefields, among its soldiers, since he was a boy. He loved his soldiers.

Nicolas followed the king into one of the antechambers. "If I may have a moment more of your time," he said to Louis's back.

Louis turned and regarded him.

"First, know I am your servant in all ways." It was the closest he dared come to the looming scandal.

Louis's eyes flickered a moment. "So I have always assumed."

"There's something I've been wishing to confess," Nicolas went on. "I've not been completely straightforward in my estimation of loans outstanding and taxes collected. There was war for so long and such need for coin that I became careless. When you first asked, I could not summon together all the figures. Now, I have done so." Nicolas lowered his eyes, held out a set of papers bound in blood-red leather. He didn't look up until Louis took the bound papers from him. "I hope this mitigates my carelessness and shows my earnest desire to serve you as best I may."

There was silence. Louis's face was unreadable.

"I hope I am forgiven."

"Honesty can never be punished. This kingdom, and I, cannot do without you." Louis held out his hand, and Nicolas bowed over it. "I, too, have a confession to make. I need one million for my personal purse. Is that possible, Viscount?"

Not by so much as a blink did Nicolas betray the dismay that spread through him. "If I may have a few weeks, sire?"

"You need them?"

A bit of perspiration gleamed just above Nicolas's upper lip. "If that is not inconvenient."

Louis didn't answer, but walked into an adjoining chamber, and Nicolas heard dogs begin to bark. He sat down in a chair. Here it was when he least expected it. His test. It came at a bad time, of course. His personal fortune was overextended, but no matter. His tendrils into the world of money reached deep. His Majesty would have his million given to him as if it were easy to obtain. So this was to be the way, was it? His Majesty would ask for sudden large sums, and Nicolas would supply them. And one day, as reward, he would be first minister. Well, good to know. Now, at least the way in which he would have to satisfy to be all he wished to be was clear.

❦

The great doors to his mother's bedchamber opened. What a bold, skillful scoundrel the viscount was, Louis was thinking. He saw that his mother half sat, half lay on the daybed their beloved cardinal had given her, but his thoughts were elsewhere. The viscount gambled Louis would be bound by his word, given at that first meeting after the cardinal's death, that all old sins committed by ministers were to be forgiven. He felt like slamming his fist into something. Instead, he leaned down and kissed the top of his mother's head. When she didn't immediately turn to look up at him and smile, he noticed how tightly her hands were clenched together. He saw that the bedchamber was empty of everyone; not even his mother's fat dog lay panting in its brocade bed in the corner, not even faithful Motteville was here. He suddenly knew. She had learned of his desire and love for Henriette. He straightened, waited a few moments for her to acknowledge his presence, and when she didn't, he turned on his heel to leave.

"Don't you dare walk away from me!" she said to his back.

The soldier in him took a sword from its scabbard and raised it. Unsmiling, he turned to face her. Inside, his pulse was beating hard, but the sword's blade gleamed bright.

"Is it true?"

"Is what true? Which rumor in this dung heap has caught your ear this morning?"

"Answer me!"

Her eyes were daggers. If he'd been closer, they would have stabbed him a thousand times over. It used to frighten him, that quick fury of hers. But today he felt fierce himself. He owed the viscount a thank-you for having enraged him.

"I've heard the most disgusting, most immoral thing," she said.

Those words stung. They were true—not the disgusting, but certainly the immoral. He fought to keep his face stoic.

"I'm asking you one more time, is it true?"

"And I'm asking you, one more time, is what true?"

"That you and your brother's wife are lovers."

"Good God! You can't be serious!"

"Don't toy with me. Your brother is beside himself. He called on me this morning to tell me that the regard you and Madame share is shaming him. I want to hear from your own lips that it isn't so."

"It isn't so."

It was like watching ships' sails collapse when the wind dies, but she continued to measure his every blink. Silence grew. Neither would be the first to break it. They were matched in stubbornness. She patted at the cushions upon which she sat.

"Come, my son, sit." Heat was gone from her voice.

He fought to keep his face and bearing stoic as he sat down on the end of the daybed. She'd done everything in her power to keep the throne for him, and he knew it.

She took his hand. "I was young once upon a time. I was indiscreet."

The Duke of Buckingham story, he thought. He'd always wondered what the truth was.

"I felt affection for someone other than your father. I was so lonely, so abandoned. He—the man I felt affection for—was ardent, handsome, dashing. I flirted. I loved. But in the end, I remembered my duty as queen of France, and I did nothing I should not have done. You set the tone for court, my dear one. Everyone watches you. You are God's anointed, God's given."

Yes, he'd suckled it in with his breast milk, Louis, the miracle of the kingdom, coming after more than twenty years of marriage between his mother and his father, the last fifteen of those years in estrangement. Quite a miracle.

"Your duty is to your queen—"

"I do my duty to the queen."

"Of course. She adores you. Discretion, my son, discretion is all. If your feelings for our sweet Madame are stronger than they should be, then I plead for you to be the resolute man you have shown yourself to be and walk away from them."

The way I did before, he thought, bitterness at the back of his throat, bitterness at his younger self, at that self's innocence and obedience, even though he knew he'd done what was best for the kingdom. It had been hard.

"In the eyes of the Mother Church, Madame is your sister. Love her as one. She is lively and graceful—"

"And innocent of these lies about her!"

"I am so pleased to hear it. I would hate to think of our court being mocked or scorned in other kingdoms."

He had not gone this far in his imaginings, to what would be said of him and of her in other courts. He felt suddenly foolish, naïve.

"This could never be ignored. You'd be lectured, gently, of course, by the king of Spain for certain, and she, well, she will be an object of ridicule and contempt in all courts."

"Spain wouldn't dare—"

"Spain's princess is your wife! Its king, my brother, would dare."

"I'll go to war—"

"Over a flirtation?" She laughed.

"Over my dignity."

She patted his hand. "Yes, you do possess dignity. And I trust you'll do all that is proper to maintain it. There will also be the Holy Father in Rome with which to contend. You are his most Christian king. Such a title comes with responsibility."

He hadn't thought about the Holy Father, either.

"You appointed a lieutenant governor to the province of Brittany."

Nonplussed, he stared at her. What had that to do with anything? And he'd only just done so. How could she already know? "Yes."

"I am Brittany's governor."

As if he didn't know that. "Then you've decided to give the lieutenant governorship to the man I've selected, Mother."

"No, I haven't."

He would have smiled at her ruthlessness, except that he felt so bitter. "Dearest Mama and dearest majesty, will you allow me to select a lieutenant in Brittany? I'm going to choose someone our dear cardinal would have wanted." She paid him back for not having put her upon the council, where she'd always been before.

She looked out the windows to the gardens and sun, to her past, Louis would imagine, and all that had been. "Yes, then."

She pulled Louis forward, kissed his forehead, his cheeks, as if thinking about Mazarin had softened her. "He served you so well. There is another who wishes to do the same. The Viscount Nicolas thinks only of you."

He told her about the governorship, thought Louis. Who was the first name on the list Colbert had compiled for him of the viscount's probable spies and friends? His mother. "Why do we speak of him, Mama?"

"I was thinking of our dear cardinal, and thoughts of him led to thoughts of the viscount, who, as you know, is a treasured friend to me, now more than ever. May I ask if all is well between you?"

A possibility unfolded itself in his mind. "The viscount is a good man. I'm fortunate in my ministers. How old is our dear Séguier now?"

Séguier was chancellor of France. The position of chancellor was a grand, ancient one, one of the offices of the crown; only death took it away.

"Ancient, my darling. I've heard he's been ill. I must write him a note."

"When he leaves us, my dearest Mama, who do you think should take his place?"

"I hadn't really thought of it."

"Might the viscount consider it?"

"The viscount chancellor of France? You don't mean it!"

"Why not?"

"It's brilliant. It would honor him as he deserves and give you an excellent servant in a most important position."

"It's early days, yet, Mother. Our Séguier may live another twenty years, and let us pray to God that he does."

"Oh, my darling, I'm honored that you've confided in me this way." She pressed at the sudden tears in the corners of her eyes with one of her exquisite linen handkerchiefs.

"I wished to lay no burdens upon you in your time of mourning, Mother." He could see that for this moment she was torn between continuing her grieving and being involved in governance of the kingdom again. He'd made that decision for her, but he was wise enough not to say so.

She settled back against her lustrous, plump cushions and sighed. "My grief is so heavy some days I can barely lift my head. And your brother today—heartbroken."

"His usual drama over little, Mother. His usual jealousies. It was only a matter of time, wasn't it?"

"I hate to see you two at odds over anything, darling. I told him to pluck his suspicion from his heart and sent him to his confessor. And you"—she didn't meet his eyes—"must consider your admiration of Madame and understand more fully the impression it might be making upon others."

"How astute you are, as always." Louis stood, kissed each of her cheeks, let her pat his face and fuss with the lace at his throat.

What a king he's made, thought Anne, watching his exit, admiring his straight back and legs, the graceful way he moved. It was like Philippe to exaggerate. You don't include me, he had always whined. She'd suggest to Maria Teresa that she request Madame's presence in visiting convents. She needs your influence, she'd say to the queen. She'd talk to the Spanish and Venetian ambassadors, ask a few questions, see what they might be writing in their dispatches. Or perhaps she'd have the viscount do it for her. Certainly he already knew through his spies. If he didn't, shame on him. This little tender friendship between Madame and her son was not going to advance a fraction farther, not while she had breath in her body.

Louis strode through his gallery. It was empty of people. Only the king might invite them in, and Louis seldom used this long, echoing chamber, beautiful as it was with its windows on each side and intricate, vivid frescoes with their Renaissance surround of graceful stucco figures. He preferred to hold court in his wife's gallery where all the maids of honor were, where Henriette and her ladies congregated, and as he walked through, his steps made a lonely, echoing sound.

Adultery. That's what they were contemplating. He could bear it, but could she? Had Philippe shouted at her? His temper could be terrible. Was she sobbing in her bed right this moment? Was that why there was no note from her today? He'd strike Philippe if he'd threatened or browbeat her. His grimness made his heart a stone. Good. A king needed a heart of stone.

Catherine stood at one side of the bed Henriette had refused to leave all morning. Louise was stationed near the closed doors.

"You have to get out of bed," Catherine begged. "You have to act as if everything were just as it should be."

A spaniel whined, stood on hind legs, and pawed against the bed.

"Merciful Hands of Jesus Christ the Lord, will someone take these damned dogs out before they soil the rugs?" Catherine shouted.

Louise moved from her place near the doors, walked forward, and bent down to pick up one of the dogs. "It's only natural," she said in her soft voice.

"What's only natural?" snapped Catherine. "That the dogs should make shit on the rug?"

"No. That Madame should be distraught to hysterics. If such lies about me were spoken, I would be hysterical, too. And angry once I was finished crying."

For the first time in hours, Henriette sat up. "She's right. I should be crying. And raging. How dare they pick me to pieces like this?"

Louise whistled, and the other spaniels surrounded her skirt as she led them out of the bedchamber.

"That's it," said Henriette, her voice a croak from sobs, but something like vigor in it again. "I don't need to stop crying. Of course I'm crying. I'm distraught with the horror of this. Now, would I join the festivities tonight or would I lock myself in my rooms?"

"Can you brazen it out?"

"Wouldn't I? Or would I hide away?" Tears had magically dried in the absorbing intricacies of examining her own behavior.

"Can you face the queen?" asked Catherine.

Henriette drooped. That the Spanish infanta would be hurt in all of this was one of those consequences she had refused to consider closely. "She doesn't know, surely. No one would dare tell her. His Majesty would banish them."

"What about the Queen Mother?"

Henriette sniffed. "Old busybody."

"What about Monsieur?"

"I'm innocent, and I'm hurt beyond words. I've done nothing, really." She looked Catherine in the face. "I haven't."

Yet, thought Catherine, thoughts straying to her own adventures. Nicolas had laughed when they were done, as they lay on the floor of his bedchamber like two animals. They'd never made it to the bed. If His Majesty receives half the pleasure I just have, he'd said, kissing her nipple, he is a fortunate man.

"You will fling yourself in his arms, expecting his support. Trusting it." Catherine said.

"We've been married only a few months, and already this court is trying to—"

"Foul your marriage."

"Foul our precious, precious marriage. And it is precious to me. It really is. I love Monsieur. I just can't withstand His Majesty's admiration. And what about your awful brother?" She glared at Catherine.

"I think the sight of your weeping today gave him pause. He can't help his feelings for you."

Henriette sighed and fell back among her pillows in a calmer frame of mind. It really wasn't her fault, was it? She had captured the two most exciting men at court without trying to—well, perhaps a little trying, but only to test her wings, so to speak. She was new at this game of flirtation and its companion, seduction. It was a dangerous, powerful, and exciting mix. She loved it.

But her calmness frayed when Philippe didn't arrive to escort her to the night's festivities.

The maids of honor, gowned and jeweled, clustered restlessly in the antechamber. Every one of them knew something was wrong. It was in the air.

Guy marched into the antechamber and told a footman to announce him.

In her bedchamber, Henriette said, "No!"

"Yes." Catherine spoke over her.

Guy walked in. Chambermaids were whisking away refused gowns, and spaniels were worrying a high-heeled shoe, and the dressing table displayed its feminine welter of ribbons and abandoned jewels and small silver jars.

"Where's Monsieur?" Catherine asked.

"I come in his place to offer Madame my escort." No one who knew Guy would believe him capable of embarrassment, but to Catherine, who knew him better than all others, he looked embarrassed.

"He won't escort her, will he?" Catherine said. "I swear I could strike you a hundred times over. You've ruined us!"

"The viper known as the Chevalier de Lorraine has added his bitterness to the brew," said Guy.

"What does that mean?" Henriette spoke for the first time since Guy had entered her bedchamber.

"The chevalier is a mincing, vicious fool," answered Catherine.

"A very dangerous, very acute fool," corrected Guy.

"I'm not going." Henriette looked around blindly for a chair to fall into.

"You must," said Guy.

"He's right," agreed Catherine.

Henriette looked from one handsome face to the other. These were the sophisticates of court. If she didn't trust them, whom did she trust? Guy held out his arm. Henriette put one gloved hand on it.

"I could weep," she said.

"I am desolated that I have caused this—"

"Don't speak to me!"

Hating himself, the ache in his chest for her even deeper, Guy made a small, imperceptible movement of despair before he led Henriette and his sister into the antechamber.

The maids of honor whispered among themselves as they followed behind.

"There's been a quarrel. It's her behavior," said Claude.

"Nonsense," Fanny hissed with all the authority she could summon.

"If there's disgrace, no one will dance with us," said Madeleine.

"Everyone will dance with us," said Fanny. "And what's more, they won't know anything is wrong unless we tell them. No one is to breathe a word that they've quarreled. Is that clear?"

"Who crowned her the queen?" Claude whispered, but not loud enough for Fanny to hear. Louise, however, did.

"It's about loyalty," she told Claude.

In the ballroom, Philippe, his expressive face grim, stood with his cousin, La Grande Mademoiselle, his mother, and his friend the Chevalier de Lorraine. When he saw Guy walk in with Henriette, he flinched.

Anne opened her fan with a snapping sound. "I've always thought the Count de Guiche had the most divine manners when he wished to display them. He does what you ought to have done."

"What ought you to have done?" asked La Grande, significant in diamonds that rivaled the Queen Mother's, obtuse to the private drama unfolding around her.

Anne motioned, and Guy made his way toward her, dragging Henriette along with him.

"I can't," she said.

"You can, and you will."

Anne kissed Henriette resoundingly on both cheeks, and said, a pleased smile on her face, "Do sit down here by me, my dear. I don't see enough of you. Monsieur and I were just discussing how lovely you look these days. You know, my dear, I think I will accompany you tomorrow if you choose to go swimming with your ladies. I've been hiding away too long. Some hours at the river, the water, the sun, they'll do me good."

"How-how very kind," said Henriette.

"My dear Grande Mademoiselle will join our party. She was just complaining she's not had time to know you better. We must remedy that. I predict you are going to be fast friends as well as the dear cousins you already are."

Fifteen years on and off at the same court weren't enough time? thought Henriette. She met the eyes of her overbearing, enormously wealthy giant of a cousin and knew that La Grande cared as little about a friendship as Henriette did. The Queen Mother was erecting a cage for her bar by bar, surrounding her with tattletales. Henriette clenched her jaw in rebellion.

"May I speak with you privately, Monsieur?" Guy nodded in the direction of an empty ballroom bay. Dripping in lace and ribbons and angel-faced curiosity, the Chevalier de Lorraine followed, but Guy spat the word "alone" at him.

When they were in the bay, Philippe said, "How dare you!"

"How dare you! She is your wife; the honor of your house rests with her, and you act like a cad."

"You're the one who—"

Trumpets interrupted to herald the king's entrance.

Maria Teresa's hand on his arm, her ladies displayed behind her like a peacock's tail, Louis looked around the ballroom, seeking and finding his brother, whose expression he understood instantly. Philippe was furious, rage stirred to burning no doubt by the Count de Guiche or that pest from

Paris, the Chevalier de Lorraine. Louis found his mother. She had a smile pasted on her face, but she clutched her fan convulsively. Watch your mother's hands, Mazarin had always said. They give away everything.

Louis went to his mother, Maria Teresa at his side. Henriette didn't meet his eyes but held out her hand to him. He kissed the air just above it and then leaned forward and kissed each of her cheeks.

"Don't shrink from me," he whispered.

Before Henriette was even certain she'd heard him, he walked to the bay holding his brother and Guy, his purpose to greet his brother and kiss him also. Any other night, Philippe would have been full of himself to have Louis make such a display; His Majesty kissed no other man, but Philippe's expression remained openly furious. Guy stood behind Philippe, his stalwart defender, thought Louis. Suddenly, though he'd come to soothe the turmoil made by his own behavior, he knew Guy had had a hand in it, and then, his anger was up.

"I demand a place on your council," Philippe said. "I'm a prince of the blood. Precedence and law require my presence on your council. I could be of service, Brother."

"Majesty," Louis corrected. "You must address me as 'Your Majesty.' You want to be of service? The way you were when I almost died?"

"Do you ever forget? Do you ever allow missteps in others? There was nothing traitorous in my actions. You were on your deathbed—"

"You hate that, don't you? That I didn't die?"

"What kind of monster do you suppose I am? You're my liege lord. If it were God's will that I be king, I would be! I believe that with all my heart. May God strike me dead if I have ever done anything to harm you, if I have ever plotted against you, my brother!"

"Majesty," Louis said again. Across one of Philippe's shoulders, he met Guy's eyes.

Guy had never allowed Louis to win at anything simply because he was king. The rivalry between them had a life of its own, and at this moment, it was a stiff-legged, growling presence. You told him this was the moment to ask directly for his place on the council, thought Louis. How clever you are.

From the musicians' loft, violins began their thin, piercing sweetness. Louis left them, walked back across the open space of the ballroom to take his wife's hand for the opening dance. The next couple in rank, Monsieur and Madame, must join the king and queen, and then, after a measure or three, other couples might.

"You did beautifully just now. I was proud. Now take Madame out onto the dance floor." Guy spoke very quietly to Philippe.

"No!"

"If you don't, I will do it, then drag you into the courtyard and beat you senseless."

"You told me—"

"I was mistaken. Do you hear me? I lied!"

Philippe blinked. This was the one man, other than his brother, whom he trusted in a way he did no one else.

"I am jealous of your happiness with her. I'm a little in love with her myself, so I took His Majesty's admiration and exaggerated it. It isn't honorable or kind, but there it is. Go and repair the damage I've done this day by disparaging her. She's done nothing amiss except to be beguiling to one and all. I beg you. On our friendship and our long regard for one another, I beg you, sir."

Philippe walked across the ballroom floor to Henriette and bowed. At a measure when others had finally filled the floor with dancing couples, Henriette said, "I know that certain people are saying the most vile things of me. I wept all day. But to think that you would believe them—I am desolate."

In one of the bays, Louise and Fanny watched Madame and Monsieur.

"It's like a play," Fanny said to Louise.

Louise moved away, went to one of the open windows. A breeze gently breathed on her. I can smell the forest, she thought, closing her eyes for a moment. Under its green canopy, she felt safe, comforted, at home. There was a part of her that flourished here, where there was no glitter, frivolity, no deceit.

She turned around to face the ballroom. And yet I would miss this, she thought. Can there be any world as wonderful as this one? How fortunate I am to be here. The candlelight from the chandeliers made the wood a clear, sweet golden color. The paint in the frescoes seemed as clear as if it had been brushed on yesterday. The gilt covering another king's initials and mottoes sparkled. The sighing sound of the violins, the swirling of skirts as women turned in dance movements, were beautiful. Everything seemed so gracious, so refined, so civilized.

But it wasn't.

Athénaïs found her brother lounging with his friends in a hall near the ballroom's entrance. She stopped a moment as sets of eyes regarded her. There was enough maleness in the small space to frighten another woman. The little queen was terrified of the king's friends. Too bold, she said. But they haven't done anything, someone, usually Olympe, would answer. Their eyes do things, the queen would respond. Her brother kissed

Athénaïs's cheek, walked her near the huge entrance doors, the violins above in the musicians' loft very loud.

"Why didn't you tell me?" she accused.

Vivonne was big and lazy. "What have I done?"

"His Majesty is in love."

His face closed, just like that. Now, he didn't seem so lazy. Athénaïs wanted to slap him.

"Are you in love?" he said, really looking at her face, really trying to understand her. "With him?"

Fool, she thought. Every woman under the age of thirty is in love with the king. She didn't bother to answer, walked back into the ballroom, passing Louise de la Baume le Blanc looking particularly lissome tonight in the gown she wore, standing dreamily, one shoulder against the corner of a bay. Louise didn't seem to see her, was staring out at the dancers, staring at His Majesty. All of us, Vivonne, she wanted to shout. We're every single one of us in love.

CHAPTER 13

By midnight, the atmosphere in the ballroom had become lighthearted again. Madame and Monsieur's quarrel had vanished, taking sourness with it. The court was young. Those who had suspected trouble early in the evening had already forgotten it. Madame and Monsieur had danced together so many times that everyone was talking about it. It was almost scandalous for a husband to be so openly in love with his wife.

"My dance, I believe." Choisy led Louise away from her friends. "How is life in the household of Madame these days?" he asked, and Louise knew at once that he knew more than he should.

"Well and happy."

"His Majesty certainly seems taken with Madame."

"Yes, he is very fond of her."

"Oh, more than fond, wouldn't you say?"

"Well, she's so delightful, I think everyone is in love with her a little." How easily I lie, thought Louise. Perhaps I'm more at home here than I know.

"Might I tempt you with a late supper in my chambers later?" Nicolas stood with Catherine near one of the bronze satyrs that bracketed one end of the ballroom.

"Why not here? Why not now?" Catherine asked without turning around.

Nicolas felt his breath catch.

"Come to the Étampes bedchamber."

The bedchamber was on this floor, down a hall, and had belonged to a suite of rooms built for a king's mistress, rooms that were seldom used these days.

Knowing better than to follow immediately, Nicolas walked over to

Anne, who hadn't retired, as was her habit, when Maria Teresa had earlier. All around, young people flirted and laughed and talked to everyone but the Queen Mother, who sat like some forgotten relic upon a high altar.

"I have some news for you," he told her very softly. "He goes to the queen's bed later every night, but it seems he meets only with the officious Colbert. What do you know of that, Your Majesty?" He had other information at his disposal. His Majesty was not confessing, had not been for several weeks. But this was not information he would share unless it became necessary.

"It means nothing to me," Anne answered.

"It might mean something to me. Will you be kind enough to honor me by sharing any word that might satisfy my curiosity?"

"Curiosity killed the cat." Anne might be grieving, but she was not toothless.

"Ah, but then a cat in gloves catches no mice." Nicolas smiled his easy smile, but he was suddenly angry inside at all that royalty took for granted. If both he and the king abandoned her, she might as well go to a convent and spend the remainder of her days in fruitless prayer. She wouldn't be the first Queen Mother sent into exile or seclusion.

"I take my upset out on you. Forgive me," Anne said.

"Always." He bowed, the anger hidden.

"Wait." She made certain no one was standing close enough to hear, then said, "Would you like to be chancellor?"

For a moment, he didn't think he'd heard her correctly. It was beyond anything he'd thought of.

"Yes," said Anne. "He spoke of it to me this very afternoon. I think you can rest easy about your situation with him."

Nicolas walked down the hall toward the bedchamber feeling as if a hundred anxieties had fallen from his shoulders. Chancellor of France. It was higher than he'd imagined in his wildest dreams. He stepped into the dark that was the chamber.

"Close and bar the door," he heard Catherine say, but he couldn't see a thing.

"Where are you?" he said, when he'd done as she asked.

"The bed," she answered.

Slowly, he groped his way forward.

"Stop," she said.

He listened to interesting rustles. She was lighting candles, not many, two or three that threw only a little light in the dark all around them. But the shape of the bed was visible, and when he walked closer, he saw a pool of fabric on the rug nearby. It was her gown. He stepped to the edge of the bed. She sat like a queen in its middle, except that she was completely naked.

Louis was dancing with Henriette again. She had been avoiding him all night, nervous and ill at ease when he'd asked her for another.

"Perhaps we shouldn't—" she began.

He interrupted her because he was afraid for her to finish her sentence. "Dance? Why ever not? We enjoy it. We always dance four or five dances."

"People are saying—"

"I know exactly what people are saying. Don't you dare draw back from me, Henriette. You smile at me the way you always have. Even more so. Trust me in this."

She smiled, her wide, engaging smile, but her mouth trembled, and he could see tears at the corners of her eyes. The strain of the day, of the evening, was showing.

"Jewel of my heart," he heard himself say, "if you wish to break with me, you have only to tell me. I would never presume—"

"It's just that everyone seems to be watching."

"And what do they see but a brother who loves his sister? Don't abandon me, abandon our love. I can't bear it. I'll protect you in this. I promise."

She didn't reply, and the dance was finished, and he walked her to her place near his mother and went to find someone else to dance with. But he was in shock. Was she going to end it before it was even begun? How would he endure that?

Anne, who had watched every move Henriette made all through the evening, but particularly when she was with Louis, turned to Henriette and said, "Wonderful news. Word of your acclaim is everywhere. My most dear friend, the Duchess of Chevreuse, has sent a letter saying she just must meet you."

"Must she?"

"I've decided a visit the day after tomorrow would be perfect. We'll be there for a while. A little hint from me. Too much frivolity can hinder conceiving a child. You look as tired as I feel. I'm off to bed. Good night, my dear. Sleep well."

You meddling hag, watching me like a hawk, thought Henriette.

Anne gave her daughter-in-law a long, steady, warning look before she kissed her good night on each cheek and retired with her ladies.

Are you threatening me? thought Henriette. Do you think if I'm out of his sight, I'm out of his mind? I have only to raise my little finger, and he's at my feet. And a new expression appeared on Henriette's face, one that even her most avid admirer could have only described as mulish.

Across the chamber, pretending not to watch, Louis put a hand over his heart covered by his soft shirt and doublet. His chest literally hurt. Why had he brought up his near death to Philippe? Why did that stay in his heart? Had he become so wary that there was no one he trusted? Would not even Henriette's love soften the hardness collecting under his hand? His brother had been a madcap these last hours, delightful and funny in a frenzied way, extravagantly courting his wife, leading the young court out of doors now for who knew what. I owe you an apology, he'd said quickly, softly, to Louis, during some moment in the evening. Louis could have borne outright accusation better than the sight of what was in his brother's eyes, renewed trust, but also hurt somewhere beyond it.

CHAPTER 14

Philippe swallowed past the lump in his throat, concentrated hard on not weeping like a woman and thus causing more talk this night. At least there had been none of the caustic titters that his behavior often summoned. He concentrated on what he'd done well this night: asked Louis for what he wanted, apologized to his brother and to his own wife. Both had been difficult to do, in spite of the fact, as his confessor had warned him, that the gossip had all been lies, exaggerations. Majesty, said Louis in his cool, correcting tone. I hate him, Philippe thought, and the thought made him ill, something else to confess and repent. Under the hate was choking love and an admiration that Louis allowed only in measured amounts. Below him in the courtyard the court assembled. Was his wife unfaithful? No. What was wrong with him? Why couldn't he let this go? The court waited for him to organize their fun. Trying to outwit emotions with their wide, painful swing, their guilt and self-reproach, Philippe ran down the straight, wide outside steps. He ran past Guy.

Guy watched as Philippe clapped his hands to summon courtiers around him, commanded a gondola race among them, watched as Henriette declined to join it. The expression on Philippe's face struck Guy to the heart, and Guy's heart was hard, not easily moved, bent on its own pleasure most of the time.

Where to find a place to talk? thought Guy. There was the summer pavilion at one end of the pond, its lanterns summoning. Gondolas were lining up near the Queen Mother's terrace. In another few moments, he and Philippe had boarded one, and Guy, abandoning the other racers, was poling them toward the little open-air pavilion at the far end of the pond. Several bottles of wine were in the gondola's bottom.

"What are you doing?" asked Philippe. "The race starts from over there."

"I must apologize to you more fully than I have. I was wrong to say the things I did to you, wrong to make you unhappy and suspicious. You know what a devil I can be. Well, I've outdone myself this day. There isn't a penance large enough in the world for me to pay, and I'd give anything to take back my words. Your conduct makes me respect you even more. I was so proud of you tonight, the way you made up with Madame, the way you spoke to His Majesty. I don't know when I've been prouder." Guy didn't look at Philippe as he spoke, just pushed the long pole in and out of the water.

Tears rolled down Philippe's face. The lantern's light was bright enough to reveal too much.

"You are becoming a great prince," Guy said, keeping his eyes away from all that was plain on Philippe's face, keeping his focus on gaining the little island, on isolation, on somehow repairing what he'd destroyed, on bolstering Philippe in this new show of courage against Louis's will. Wine would help. They'd drink wine and talk and plan, like old times. They'd drink wine until Philippe didn't hurt anymore.

"You never touch me now," said Philippe.

"It isn't proper now."

Philippe looked out over the water, to the suspended garden with its majestic surround of water, to the handsome palace lit by lantern light, to the gondolas from which shouts of laughter and jesting insults could be heard. "I don't know if I can give up everything," he said.

They had reached the little island, but Guy pushed the pole against turf, and the gondola slid backward into the water rather than landing. It floated in place. Guy sat down, maneuvered open a bottle of wine, handed it to Philippe, opened one for himself, clinked their bottles together.

"To friendship," he said, and drank a long swallow.

Philippe considered the word, all it meant and all it didn't. The lump in his throat was larger. Would wine move past it?

Silent, they drank and watched the races. Louis lost to Vivonne but won two others. Péguilin fell overboard, swam to shore, and was being petted by tipsy maids of honor. Vivonne jumped into water waist deep and began to shout he was drowning. Guy threw his empty bottle overboard. Philippe did the same.

"Open another for us," Guy said, "while I pole over to the suspended garden. I see La Grande Mademoiselle with your darling Chevalier de Lorraine. What a bore she was tonight, going on and on about her father, as if he had possessed an honorable bone in his body."

"He was brother to a king, and it's a hard life. He did the best he could," Philippe said.

"Let's scale the sides like pirates and threaten her virginity unless she drinks a bottle with us, see if the grape can make her unbend."

"She unbends."

"Does she? Well, I'm going to have to ascertain that for myself. As tall as she is, she must have beautiful legs. You need to reconcile with Madame tonight. Completely." Guy didn't look at Philippe, just pushed the pole up and down in the water as he steered the gondola toward the suspended garden.

"Must I? That will take more wine, my friend."

"We have it."

❧❦❧

Louis dropped a blood-red leather portfolio into Colbert's lap. "He apologized for past sins. He asked for my forgiveness. He says these records will be closer to the truth."

Colbert stared down at the portfolio.

"So I asked him for one million."

"Excuse me, sire?"

"One million. That will keep him occupied for a time. What are you looking so glum about? Because of his new facts and figures? He has maneuvered around us, but only for the moment." Louis rubbed at his eyes. His usual vigor had deserted him. I'm tired, he thought. I won't be able to bear it if she decides against loving me. I'll lie down on the ground like a dog and howl. D'Artagnan thought he'd found the writer of the Mazarinades: his cousin, La Grande. It was possible. She'd fired a cannon at him. Another cousin, Condé, a famed warrior whom Louis had worshiped as a boy, had marched away to the side of the Spanish during that long war. His family was capable of every treason, large and small. He would never have family interconnected with the governing of the kingdom again. He might forgive, but he did not forget. Hold your friends close and your enemies closer, so said his beloved cardinal. I'm watching her, D'Artagnan said.

"Your Majesty is fatigued," Colbert said.

❧❦❧

Henriette couldn't sleep. She made one of her serving women brush her hair, but the brushing didn't help. She sent the woman away and paced up and down her bedchamber, wishing she hadn't allowed her ladies to leave her. Then she saw a note, slipped under her door, and she opened it.

> *I love you. I don't wish to retreat in the face of opposition, but I am yours to command. What is that command? Did you wish me to turn my heart from yours? Impossible. You command obedience of everything but my heart, which remains—always—yours.*

She slipped it into a special, hidden drawer in the table her brother had given her. You may need, Minette—her brother called her Minette, his adoring Minette, and she was—you may need a place of privacy, and her brother's dark eyes had glinted, and he had showed her the small raised griffin, which when touched, made the drawer open. Charles was fourteen years older than her, king of England now, a miracle everyone except her had ceased expecting. Last year had been a year of miracles, hadn't it? Her brother's restoration and hers. Who could have guessed the glorious young king of France would fall in love with her? She picked up a hand mirror to look at the face that had captured a king's heart.

There was a knock, and Catherine came in, walking in that special, long-legged way of hers, the expression on her face pleased.

"Monsieur is on his way," she said, and she went to Henriette's dressing table, rummaging through the silver boxes and jars there. She selected a rouge color, dipped her fingers in it, ran it across Henriette's cheeks in even motions, then pulled the neck of her nightgown down, rouged the nipples of her breasts with quick strokes that tickled and shocked.

"Whatever are you doing?"

Catherine didn't answer, was opening wine she'd brought, wine that she gave to Henriette and which Henriette obediently drank, even as Catherine was at the bed, plumping pillows, making the bed an inviting nest of linen and lace-trimmed coverings, then she was striding toward the door again. "Leave no doubts in his mind," she said.

In the withdrawing chamber, Catherine heard sounds and stepped quickly to hide beside a huge armoire. Leaning against Guy, Philippe staggered in. Guy had to open the bedchamber doors and push Philippe through them. Closing them again, Guy leaned his head against the wood in a weary gesture.

"Are you praying?" Catherine stepped out from the armoire. "What possessed you to betray her?"

"Jealousy. I didn't want His Majesty to have her. I've done what I could. I've told Monsieur I love her and that in my passion I allowed myself to say things of which there was no proof."

"You told him you loved her?"

Guy opened his eyes. "He's proud I should love her. It proves to him that he is right to love her, too."

How handsome my brother is, thought Catherine. And how dangerous.

She put her arm in his, and together they walked out of the withdrawing chamber.

At the sight of Philippe, who was drunker than she'd ever seen him, Henriette began to cry. She sat where she was on her dressing stool and laid her head on her hands on the dressing table and wept.

Philippe found his own eyes filling. Their first quarrel. In all their months together, they'd done nothing but laugh. He lurched forward, stood over her, staring down at her chestnut curls, her white, white neck and shoulders. His hand went out, to touch her head, to comfort her, but he leaned too far forward and fell on the floor. It didn't hurt him, but it did surprise him.

"What vileness there is outside these rooms," Henriette said after he had lain there a while.

She needs to help me up, thought Philippe. I don't think I can manage by myself.

"I was so proud to accept your proposal of marriage, so proud to be allied with you. You were the only one who was kind to me all those long years. I can't bear your anger," Henriette said.

"I could have married anyone. I chose you," he tried to say, but none of the words came out of his mouth coherently.

All his life, his mother and his brother had wished him to be different, to be as they were. So he might be, with this enchanting girl whose face was swollen with tears from his jealousy. Remember your princely duties, his priest had told him. Trust in the Lord thy God. Beware the things of this world. She would bear the sons who would carry on his seed, his lineage, his house. She graced his life. All his friends thought him fortunate. Guy loved her. Louis admired her, perhaps more— Stop, he told himself. Don't allow suspicion. He was not king, but he was brother to a king, for once a fit brother. Guy didn't love him the way he once had, and it broke Philippe's true heart, but this was enough. To be with her was enough. He closed his eyes. In another moment a snore erupted.

Henriette placed a pillow under his head, then covered him with one of her coverlets. She nestled in the bed, blew out the candle, and turned on her side, exhausted. They'd muddled through. There was no open break with Philippe, and she didn't have to acquiesce to him tonight, thank the Holy Mother. Lying was easier than she had imagined. She wasn't quite certain what to make of that.

CHAPTER 15

The Queen Mother was as good as her word. Before two full days had passed, Madame was being swept out of Fontainebleau and off to visit the elderly duchess who was a dear friend to the Queen Mother.

"The carriage is ready," Louise said, then she stood to one side as Henriette, followed by Catherine, moved past her.

"See to the dogs." Henriette tossed the words over her shoulder. She made no secret of her fury at being forced to accompany the Queen Mother. Fanny said she was only going because Monsieur had begged her. Fanny had overheard the begging.

Louise held out a folded note. "You forget this," she whispered. It was yet another secret missive from His Majesty. There'd been no time for a private meeting between Louis and Madame, but Fanny and Louise had taken notes back and forth. Louise and the other maids of honor followed Madame downstairs to the golden entrance, the king's entrance. They weren't going. At the last moment, Henriette had decided to leave her maids of honor behind, but Louise didn't mind. This gave her an opportunity to expand her exploring. She was continuing to ignore Choisy's warnings.

On the ground floor was a great, hulking carriage, and also, Louise saw, the king's favorite troupe of musketeers, called the Grays because they rode horses of that color. Louis was waiting by the door of the carriage, his dashing hat pulled from his head, in his hands.

"I plan to accompany you part of the way," he spoke to Henriette.

Louise watched the sullen look leave Henriette's face.

"My brother does us an honor," announced Philippe, but to Louise's eyes his face looked a little haggard. There was quite a crowd gathered to watch the departure, the Viscount Nicolas, other officials, and several from the queen's household. The atmosphere was festive and excited. If

Madame was in disgrace, none of these courtiers realized it yet. Many of them were at the carriage door saying good-bye to her, telling her she'd be missed. The Queen Mother, late, as was her habit, marched through a gatehouse door, her lady-in-waiting following, and narrowed her eyes at the sight of so many people. Once she was in the carriage, Louis mounted his horse, a huge, white stallion trained in Spain. The Spanish were famous for their horses and did not export them; it was a gift from his father-in-law. The horse reared and danced small steps forward on its back legs. Louis sat as easily atop it as if he were sitting in a chair. He shows off for her, thought Louise. She and the others left behind waved. Maids of honor from various households ran out of the palace to watch the carriage roll down the road toward the stables and then out into the world beyond the palace.

"Where's Her Majesty?" Fanny asked Athénaïs, as the carriage and horsemen finally disappeared from sight and there was nothing to do but walk back into the king's courtyard.

Athénaïs rolled her eyes. "Sleeping."

"Well, she has the heir to protect," Fanny answered.

"Now don't forget you promised you'd walk with me in the queen's garden later." Athénaïs smiled in a friendly way at Louise. "Please, you come also."

Louise and Fanny walked up the gatehouse staircase by themselves.

"When did you become friends with her?" Louise asked.

"We both notice things, and we noticed that we notice, and we've decided to compare notes. She's quite nice, not at all with her nose in the air, like others I could name." Fanny shook her head. "Poor queen. Athénaïs says she stayed in bed today. I almost feel sorry for her. It's as if she lives in another world."

"Choisy told me the only man the queen saw until her marriage was her father." The Spanish court, said Choisy, keeps its maidens locked away and guarded close.

Fanny shuddered. "I'm glad I'm not Spanish, then. What are we going to do with ourselves while she's gone?"

Plenty, Louise thought but didn't say.

❧❧❧

Inside the carriage, Anne watched Henriette across the short space separating them. Louis rode beside a window, and Henriette hung out of it, talking to him about this and that, the ballet to be performed in a few weeks, how pleased her brother was with his coming marriage to the Portuguese infanta, and Catherine leaned forward more than once to join the conversation.

Have you always been this delightfully lighthearted? thought Anne, as she considered Henriette. Let me marry her, Philippe had suggested, before her brother was crowned king of England, when it looked as if that prince would roam a vagabond forever. Philippe was eager for his inheritance, for his own household, eager to move out of the shadow of his brother, and even if Henriette was poverty-stricken and without influence, her mother was a princess of France, a daughter of France. And their dearest cardinal agreed. It was best that Philippe not possess a foreign princess with foreign connections, so the engagement was allowed. And then there'd been all the bustle of Louis's splendid wedding, a new queen to be presented to one and all, and her own dearest ill, so ill he could not stand up. There had been his dying to deal with, and so she'd withdrawn her gaze from court, from family, from Philippe's new marriage. Anne put a handsomely gloved hand to her throat, to the knot of grief that lived there. She'd withdrawn her gaze, and look what had happened. Her bereft heart was not allowed its quiet. There was misbehavior and poor judgment.

She brooded on that grievance until, midway on their journey, the carriage stopped. Anne watched as Louis dismounted, opened the carriage door himself.

"I bid you adieu," he said directly to Henriette. His face was somber. "I'll be counting the moments until you return to grace my court again." He turned to Anne. "Majesty, have a care for my dear sister, for I would not wish to see her have anything but the most pleasant of visits."

He warns me, thought Anne. She swelled with anger. Philippe was behind Louis, and Louis moved aside, watching his brother with hooded eyes.

"Madame," said Philippe, grasping Henriette's gloved hands and kissing them. "I await your return with eagerness. Majesty my mother, you'll give the duchess my kindest regards, won't you? You'll like her, my darling. The stories of her are extraordinary. If my mother does not share them, I will, when you return. Well"—he looked from his mother to Henriette, sensing the coldness in the carriage, feeling guilty for his part in it—"enjoy your visit."

Guileless, thought Anne. The victim in all this. My precious waif. She leaned forward, taking his chin in her hands, kissing him on the lips. The occupants of the carriage were silent as men called to one another. They listened for a while to the sound of retreating hooves and then to the silence of the country around them. Philippe's lieutenant of the musketeers appeared at a window and suggested they commence their journey. The carriage made a lurching movement, began to roll forward. Even in this, the best of carriages, the ride was jolting.

"I have a headache," Henriette said to no one in particular.

"Dear Madame, do let me tell you about the Duchess de Chevreuse," said Catherine. "It's most amusing. His Majesty, the late king, hated her, but our dear Majesty here felt only adoration. They were best of friends."

"We are best of friends," corrected Anne.

"In her day, she plotted against Cardinal Richelieu and the oh-so-worthy Cardinal Mazarin, and our gracious majesty is so large-hearted, so full of tenderness and Christian charity—such an example to us all—that she forgave her. I swear it. Perhaps the duchess will instruct us in statecraft, in how to plot, yet never be punished." Catherine's mocking laugh filled the interior of the carriage.

"Is this true, majesty?" asked Henriette. "Not only do you sweep me away like some disobedient child, but I'm to be lectured by a traitoress?"

"Who said anything of lectures? And I will not allow her to be called a traitoress. Those were treacherous times, times you cannot imagine."

"Do you think I can't imagine treachery?" asked Henriette. "I, whose father was beheaded? Let us make no more pretense, if you please." She sat up straight-backed and pale on the carriage seat opposite Anne. "You blame me for His Majesty's affection."

Anne felt Madame de Motteville, sitting beside her, stiffen. "You're overwrought," said Anne, reeling a little at Henriette's defiance. "That's why I take you from court. To divert you. You aren't thinking clearly just now."

"I am here only because Monsieur asked me. I obey him in all ways, even if you don't believe it." With that, Henriette turned her head to look out the window.

Catherine watched Anne with an arrogant glee.

This was off to a bad beginning. Anne looked down at her hands, held tightly together so that she would not put them around Henriette's throat and strangle her—after, of course, she had strangled Catherine.

The others left behind, Louis galloped toward his stables, and when the buildings were in sight, he pulled the reins of his horse, his mind playing, as it always did, over the business of his kingdom. The Dutch had fifteen thousand merchant vessels in their fleet. France had twenty, and that number was both war and merchant ships. How to rebuild? The other thought in his mind was Henriette. What if his mother, his mother's clever friend, should convince her not to love him? How would he endure?

An elderly groom limped out to take the reins of his horse. "Left them in the dust, didn't you, Your Majesty?" he said. Others could be seen in the distance galloping forward. "Well, if I were riding that handsome beast, I'd do the same."

"So, you give tribute to the horse and not to its rider's skill?"

"Now, now, sire, I didn't say naught about skill. Everyone knows you could ride a whirlwind. It's just that's a fine fellow you're on. He keeps the grooms hopping, he does. Likes to kick a man now and then."

"He's Spanish."

"Don't I know? That's why he kicks, I say. We may be at peace, but a Spaniard never stops fighting. They'll lash out in death."

The others were close now. Louis expected a musketeer in the lead, and several were, but alongside them was Guy.

"Sire," called Guy, as he reached Louis and trotted his horse in a circle around him. "I didn't hear the signal for a race to begin."

"I didn't give it."

Guy laughed. "That is one beautiful horse. I might have beaten you if I'd had a better mount."

"Just what I was thinking," said Louis.

Some distance away, Philippe leapt from his horse and threw the reins toward a groom. "You didn't give a signal to begin. That isn't fair," he called.

"Keep him occupied," Louis said to Guy, "as you so well know how to do."

Guy's jaw clenched. Louis was beginning to push at everyone; a space around him was widening into an unseen circle into which no one could step. He was beginning, really, to become king. In all the time Guy had been at court, that role had been a ghost, Louis's father indecisive off a battlefield, and Louis himself deferring to the cardinal and to his mother. He stared after this man, this king, walking away from him toward the palace, this boyhood friend whom all the court said he so favored, to whom he had never yielded an inch. He had yielded to Madame. Did Louis really expect him to yield all?

❧❧❧

The carriage rolled into the gravel courtyard of the duchess's estate, and Marie, the Duchess of Chevreuse—a true legend in her time, married or lover to the most important men in the kingdom, once superintendent of the household of the very queen who now came to visit her—stood waiting on the château's stone steps. At the sight of the carriage, she ran down the steps with the grace of a girl and curtsied and then kissed Anne on her cheeks when the Queen Mother descended from the carriage.

"My dear friend," said Anne. "I have such need of you," she whispered.

Henriette was the last out of the carriage.

Marie ran her eyes over this new Madame's face. "But how wonderful to meet you at last," she said, smiling and gracious and displaying a charm that had initiated many plots and lured many a man into them, "you are even more darling than I have heard. Let me—"

"I have a headache and need to go to my chambers immediately," interrupted Henriette. She moved past the duchess, following the major domo into the house, and Catherine, with a quick curtsy to the duchess, followed behind her.

Anne and Marie walked slowly up the steps.

"So," said Marie, "my task isn't to be an easy one, is it?"

"I'm afraid not."

Marie linked her arm in Anne's, a great breach of etiquette, but etiquette wasn't needed between these two. They had run through the halls of the palace of the Louvre together as girls of fifteen and sixteen; they had, more often than not, been on the same side in the maze of plots that had been the reign of Louis XIII and his Cardinal Richelieu. They knew each other to the bone.

Anne went through the ceremony of greeting family and friends and faithful servants gathered in the hall, but at a signal from Marie, everyone melted away, and Anne followed Marie into her most private of chambers and sat down with a sigh as Marie poured wine. She unpinned her hat. "Is it possible that we've gotten old? I feel quite ancient."

"You're ageless. How does His Majesty?"

"Well." Anne took off her leather gloves, smoothed the fingers of each one. She had asked Louis to allow Marie back at court after her dearest had died, but he'd refused. Marie never mentioned it. For some reason, that made Anne love her all the more.

"One hears he meets with his council twice a day."

"Yes."

"Most enterprising. Most unusual. Will it last, one wonders. You'll forgive me if I say I was surprised you weren't named to the council."

"I didn't want it. All that fuss, all the decisions," Anne lied. "Time to read my prayers and count my grandchildren."

"Ah, yes, my congratulations. And when is the *dauphin* expected?"

"In November."

Marie took a small sip of wine. "And Her Majesty? Does she suspect?"

"The queen is an innocent child." As simply as that, they were at the crux of the reason Anne traveled from Fontainebleau and dragged her reluctant daughter-in-law with her.

"And this one?"

"She is a heartless minx!"

So I would be too, thought Marie, if I held the heart of the king of France in my hands. She looked down at those hands. Once they'd held hearts, and other parts of men, and made them do her bidding. Now all

that heat was cooled in her; sometimes it was hard to remember the passionate woman she had once been, never mind that she had married again.
It was for reasons other than passion. Her husband told her that the natu-
rals of the new world across the sea were advised by their old women as to
when to make war or treaties with other tribes. An old woman's heart was
wise if it wasn't too bitter. The duchess could feel her wisdom now, coiled,
sitting dispassionate, interested in its cool way, waiting to put her mind,
her talents, to this task Anne brought her, first in a hurriedly dashed-off
letter delivered by a musketeer, now in a visit.

"She has His Majesty's regard?"

"I'm certain of it," answered Anne.

"Have they bedded?"

Anne gasped and crossed herself.

You've gotten lazy, thought Marie. Jules Mazarin allowed you to become
lazy so he could gather all the power in his hands. I knew he would. "If
they've bedded, you have no need of me. There is nothing I can do."

"Surely they haven't! It's a sin before God!" Anne cried.

"Did we not sin in our time?"

Anne didn't answer.

"The English ambassador will call in a few days, as you requested,"
Marie said. "I've a confessor who is all that is discreet and will guide her
in the right direction, should she choose to confess. And I must add, he's
quite handsome. I find it easier to confess to a handsome man myself."

"Discretion." Anne laughed without merriment in the sound. "That would
be a blessing. She insults an infanta, not to mention the Mother Church!"

Marie remembered a long ago time when another infanta had allowed a
young and handsome and ardent English duke into her bedchamber. That, too,
had been a scandal. You will like this Mazarin, Cardinal Richelieu was reputed
to have said, when he introduced an upstart Italian wise enough to change his
name from Giulio Mazzarino to Jules Mazarin to Anne, the frustrated queen of
France. He looks like the Duke of Buckingham, purred Richelieu.

"After all we've done," Anne ranted on. "His Eminence died from
laboring too hard to arrange the details of the peace. To marry His Majesty
to the infanta was all his hope."

It was your hope, your ambition, thought Marie, and Jules died of greed.

"For the future, he said, of both kingdoms. All the others must bow
before France and Spain. The infanta is a pearl beyond price, a gentle,
well-bred girl. I won't have her hurt!"

A gentle, well-bred girl content to stay in her chambers all day and snack
on Spanish almonds and play cards. Did that really do for a vital young man
who held the destiny of the kingdom in his hands? "And Monsieur?"

"Monsieur is willing to trust my guidance in this."

So, Philippe had little or no importance in this. Had he ever? "And one had heard he was so in love with his wife—"

"He was! Is!" Anne's mouth tightened. "Monsieur will make no trouble, that I promise."

Broken already, is he? thought Marie. But of course he would be. You above all people know how dangerous a brother to the king can be. She picked up a fan left lying on a table, moved it gently to stir the air. Alliances were so interesting; the way they could break on a whim or cross word. If she'd been younger, this would have been perfect fodder to start another civil war, another Fronde, as they liked to call such skirmishes, where those ennobled kicked against the traces of the king and thus won more privileges, taking their rightful place by his side. A wind from the Fronde is blowing, blowing, blowing, and Monsieur Mazarin will be going, going, going. So they'd sung in the streets and in the court once upon a time. Long live the princes of the blood, they sang, but murder him who knows neither joy nor law nor religion. Murder, murder, murder Mazarin.

"I depend on you to show her the error of her ways," said Anne. "It is not acceptable for her to conduct a love affair with the king of France, and I want her to understand that in no uncertain terms! I will be her enemy if she does so, an implacable enemy!"

"You give me my head in this?"

"I bow to you. No mind is more supple than yours."

"Well, then, leave all to me. You are here as my guest. You must rest and not fret about a single thing during your stay," Marie said. "My cook has a new dish to present for your supper."

"Oh, I can't think of food at a time like this."

"Come and see my chapel," Marie said soothingly. "It's the only thing I've done to this old barn. We'll have vespers there this evening, and perhaps you and I might pray for wisdom and forbearance before I escort you to your chambers."

"I already have wisdom and forbearance!" Anne snapped.

"But I haven't," smiled Marie. "We'll pray for me."

Anne walked beside her to the chapel. "His Eminence always said you were the most intelligent woman he knew."

Then why did he end as adviser and more to you, while I was exiled? thought Marie, but her thoughts weren't angry. She'd seen other lands and other ways; she'd played spy over and over and yet over again, changing sides like a chameleon does color. She'd driven Richelieu to swear and almost brought down his successor, the Italian turned Frenchman, Mazzarino who styled himself Mazarin, and then she had ended on his side. Ah, it had all been great fun. So many men, their lust often larger than their wit. So many men, with their wit larger than their lust. So little time.

Time, the hussy who weakened us all. Even someone who was a hussy to begin with. Was this Henriette a hussy? If she was, Marie could only wish her well. What was the saying? It is extremely useful to die in God's grace, but it is extremely boring to live in it. Would God take a hussy? A woman who had been crafty and faithless and lied as easily as she smiled? Who looked in her mirror now and could no longer find herself? Who longed for something more and had discovered that it could be found not in men or wine or ambition or diamonds but only sometimes in prayer. Ah, she must meet this God whose sense of life, of timing, was so ironic. She had a feeling His smile was as wide as the sky, His love as deep as the ocean, that they would get along, she by amusing Him with her past, and He by bringing her restless heart, a lioness that stalked the plain of her being, peace.

Marie's handsome confessor led vespers. An acolyte with a voice like a silver bell had been borrowed from a nearby nunnery to sing for them.

"What is that prayer?" asked Anne. Its Latin words flew up the vaulted ceiling and cascaded back down into their ears and hearts.

"I have lately become enamored of Saint Hildegard," answered Marie.

"O most radiant Mother, Mary, star of the sea, sweetest of all delights— pray for us…" the acolyte sang in Latin, her voice one of shivering purity, the prayer a repeating chant of drawn-out syllables, her voice rising up and down a scale of notes.

"Charming," said Anne. "I must tell the queen."

"You must take the acolyte to court and have her sing for Her Majesty."

"O most sweet and most loving Mother, authoress of life, you birth light, as God breathes you…" sang the acolyte.

But the one for whom all this soothing loveliness was planned wasn't present. She was in her bedchamber with a vile headache brought about by the trip, Catherine had explained. And Marie had watched Anne twitch with irritation.

Catherine knelt now with them. A handsome thing with a carnal, cool look to her that no man could find unpleasing, thought Marie. It was said her cousin, the captain of the king's guard, was wild for her. The viscount was to be named chancellor, Anne told her, but said nothing of the man named Colbert. He was a rising star, Marie's young husband told her.

Later, as the lovely twilight flirted with its promise of dark, she went to the chambers that held Henriette and found her sitting in a chair staring moodily out at the fading light. Marie curtsied low.

"Have you all you need, Highness? Is there anything I may order for you?"

She saw that bowls of food sat untouched on an enameled tray on a nearby chest. The duchess considered the young woman brought here so that some sense and decorum might be argued into her. Friends wrote that Henriette had brought a lightness and festivity to the court that His Majesty much enjoyed. What an inept, blind fool the queen must be.

Marie pushed the shutter on one side of the window open even more. "Do you smell it?" she asked. "Jasmine. Once I would bathe in nothing but jasmine water, and men who loved me swore they knew when I'd walked through a room by the fragrance of jasmine that lingered behind."

Catherine was drawn, she could see, but it wasn't for her that Marie was setting her lure.

"I've heard you carried on affairs with six men, two of them dukes," said Catherine.

"Oh, hardly that. But I did manage three, and they were all dukes."

Catherine laughed.

Marie stepped back from the window, the soft summer night. She curt-sied again to Henriette. "I am honored that you visit my house. The Queen Mother is an old friend, and you, I hope, will be a new one. I've heard nothing but praises sung about you, and now I see they didn't say enough."

"Not from the Queen Mother, I imagine. I blush to think what she's said of me to you." Henriette was brittle, defiant, chin lifted, eyes sparking, ready to do battle.

"But what can be said, except that you are lovely and so of course the king desires you."

Marie was so matter of fact, so without blame, that some of the stoni-ness left Henriette's posture. She met the old duchess's eyes, worldly wise, smiling, crystalline, clear. "Which she doesn't like."

"She doesn't like mess and bother." These days, thought Marie.

"I can't command someone's heart."

"Of course not." Marie reached out her hand and touched a strand of thread that made up the heavily embroidered draperies of the bed. "You see the blue picked out there in the flower? Your eyes are that same shade. Remarkable. No wonder he's fallen in love. He cannot help himself. Might I sit down just a moment? I'm tired after my walk in my gardens. Now you really must walk them tomorrow. Every ache, every care will be scattered by the sight of them. I have a rose bush said to be a hundred years old, and my jasmine, well. I'll have my servants cut some for you. We'll make a special bath for you. We'll put the tub right here, at the windows, and you can look out on the trees and sky as jasmine-scented water is poured over you. Delightful, no?"

Less sullen, but still wary, Henriette gave a short nod of her head.

Marie smiled to herself. First lure taken. "I so wish you to have the most pleasant of visits in my home. I so wish you to visit me often, to bring your young, fresh face and ways for my old eyes to feast upon, but I wouldn't be a friend to Her Majesty if I didn't speak plainly. I ask you, in the quiet that is my garden at its best, in the beauty, which will only be heightened if you grace it, that is my chapel, if you will think about the kingdom, the king, if it, if he, can bear this scandal, for the scandal will be large. You are, after all, a princess of France, and you must consider your position."

"I've done nothing wrong!"

"Of course you haven't." Marie agreed, warmth in the smile that accompanied her words. "You've simply been your charming self. Do we blame the rose for its beauty or alluring fragrance?"

"Are you going to lecture me about sinning? I know the Queen Mother told you to!"

"Sin. What a distasteful word. Let he who is without sin cast the first stone. If loving you makes His Majesty a better king, then whatever sins are committed are mitigated by circumstance, no? Perhaps His Majesty needs your love to be all that he must be. Perhaps your duty is to love him. I do not know that. Such is between you and His Majesty. But not for the world's eyes. Never for the world's eyes. That is foolish and ill bred and will bring down a wrath that might break you into pieces. You're far too charming to be smashed to pieces." She touched Henriette's arm, lightly, with one cool fingertip. "You'll be the one blamed, not His Majesty. I hope you understand this."

"So you tell me to deny his love?"

"I've never been one for denial of love. I will tell you a secret." She was silent a moment, and both Henriette and Catherine leaned forward in anticipation, and again, Marie smiled inside. "I was not always discreet, nor, as you know, faithful. There are ways to do what we will or what we must, and the rest of the world knows little."

"What are you saying?" asked Catherine.

"I'm saying that my hidden loves were the most alluring of the many I enjoyed. I am saying that Madame is foolish to believe she may openly enjoy the love of the king of France. It is a slap in the face to all that is proper. What she does, however, in secret, is quite another matter." Marie stood up. "It takes a great deal of wisdom to be discreet, to pretend one thing while feeling another. Perhaps, for all Madame's beauty and charm, she hasn't wisdom, which would really be too bad."

Marie looked around the chamber, as if ascertaining that it was as welcoming as possible. Both Henriette and Catherine were silent. She could see that her words were burrowing inside them, and she felt a caressing delight at her skill.

"Well, now." She walked to an enormous arrangement of flowers and pulled from it one small, drooping, almost invisible leaf. "That's that. We'll speak no more of such dull matters as sin and duty. You are simply my most welcome guest. I leave you to this sweet night, Highness. My château, my gardens, my chapel, my flowers are all yours. I so hope you enjoy your stay with me. I am honored to have your presence in my home, honored to meet the woman who has taken the court by storm."

"I don't feel well." Henriette blurted the words out, like a child talking to its nursemaid.

"Yes, a headache, you said."

"And the smell of the food. It made me ill."

"Did it? How unconscionable of my cook. He will be most distraught to know he did not please you. He will fall on a kitchen knife, but he's so fat it won't hurt him."

The thought of a distraught, fat, suicidal cook made Henriette smile.

"What a lovely smile," said Marie. "No wonder all adore you. I'll have some barley water sent. It might soothe your stomach, and if there is a child growing, it will nourish him."

"A child?" Henriette said the words blankly.

"At your age, the ills of a stomach are usually traced directly to the beginning of an heir." She paused at the door. "There is one more thing. At some point during the visit, it might be wise—it would certainly be discreet—to hint to Her Majesty that your behavior has been perhaps too exuberant and that there is regret. Whether one does regret or not is quite another thing. Good evening, my lovely ones. Sleep well. You must come to chapel tomorrow and hear the prayers sung. There's an acolyte whose voice is sheer heaven."

"If she thinks I will apologize to Queen Anne, she's wrong," Henriette said once she was alone with Catherine.

"An heir," said Catherine. "That would be wonderful. Monsieur so wants an heir. And when one is pregnant, making love with another is made safer."

Henriette shook her head, and Catherine was silent. After Henriette had rinsed her mouth and her servant had loosened her tight top and placed her in a nightgown and she lay on the bed, she stared down at her body. Was she carrying a child? She felt triumph at that. A princess's primary duty was to bear children to inherit. She'd done her duty and quickly, even more quickly than the queen. Where else did duty lie? Was it to Monsieur or was it to the king? She truly wanted to please them both. How amazing the Duchess de Chevreuse was. She'd never been spoken to in such a frank way before, as if she were an experienced woman, as if her mind might be sharp and nimble, her choices complex and subtle, not easily made. If there were no scandal, that did not mean there was no love. It simply meant there was discretion. She lay upon her pillow and thought about that word for a long time, the scent of the gardens' jasmine lulling her.

CHAPTER 16

Athénaïs had never seen a face as wrinkled as this woman's, La Voisin she was called. The eyes were black stones, no light in them; the hands were dirty, the nails long arcs of yellow that grew over the ends of shriveled fingers. Wishing with all her heart that she'd not begged to come along, she made certain her cloak was fastened all the way to her feet, that the small silk mask she wore over her eyes was secure, that the cloak's hood was pulled over her head so that her face was in shadow.

Behind her was the carriage that had brought them out of the palace and onto the road to the outskirts of Paris. Inside the carriage waited the Viscount Nicolas, who had decided at the last moment to join them. She and Olympe had been rushing through a courtyard, and there he was. Do you still see your witch today? he had asked Olympe, and she'd nodded, and the next thing Athénaïs knew they were in his carriage, and he was part of the adventure. She'd much rather he had not been. She didn't want anyone to know she was doing this, but there was nothing she could do about his presence.

Taut and attentive, masked also, Olympe sat in an elegant embroidered chair placed in an overgrown garden as if it belonged there. Casting bones inside a circle, the witch knelt on the ground. Olympe watched her every move. The witch sighed.

"No?" exclaimed Olympe. "I won't believe it!"

"It's not your fate."

"I'll give you more gold. Try again," ordered Olympe.

The witch threw the bones three more times. She stood and walked in a larger circle that included Olympe and Athénaïs, too, and Athénaïs saw the witch's stone eyes on her. She shivered. The witch went back to her bones and threw them once more.

"No," she announced to Olympe, "no matter what you do. Love potions, spells, nothing will bring his love the way you wish."

"Can I hurt she whom he loves?"

The witch barked a laugh. "Always."

"How?"

"Come down on your knees beside me."

Olympe obeyed. Athénaïs was both repelled and fascinated. The witch took a little clay figure from a pocket in her gown and set it down in the dirt of the circle.

"That's her," said the witch. "I'll need something of hers—a hair, a ribbon she's worn, a glove. Send it soon. Tell the spirits what you want."

"Curse this one His Majesty loves. Make her womb barren, her woman's place dry and unpleasing to him. Make her life a sorrow. If she bears a child despite my curse, let it die or at best, be a girl," said Olympe.

"I beg in the name of..." and then the witch said names Athénaïs had never heard before, names of ancient and dark spirits, and Olympe repeated each one of them.

"Curse the name of Christ Jesus and spit six times," the witch instructed.

Athénaïs felt another shiver go up and down her back. Was she going to be asked to curse the name of the Christ? Well, she wouldn't do it.

"Does the golden-haired one desire anything?" the witch asked, without looking toward Athénaïs.

Athénaïs's heart began to beat. The cloak covered her hair. There was no way the witch could know its color. "A husband."

"I'll speak alone with her."

Olympe was displeased.

The witch made a gesture outward as if to include invisible presences all around them. "The spirits speak to La Voisin. I've something for him in the coach. You'll give it to him with La Voisin's compliments? And tell him to go to his island. Tell him La Voisin sees trouble if he does not."

The flesh on Athénaïs's arms prickled. No one had spoken of the viscount, who had remained in the carriage. She turned to look at it. His crest was painted on the door. Athénaïs felt better. The witch wasn't all-seeing, after all, just observant.

Olympe held out her hand, and the witch put a glass vial in it. It was filled with what looked like white dust.

"Tell him it will lessen the melancholy humors that haunt him at night. Tell him it comes from the new world, to inhale a few pinches...no more." As Olympe walked to the carriage, the witch looked inquiringly at Athénaïs. "A husband, is it?"

"Yes, please."

"Did you bring La Voisin coin?"

"Of course." She opened her gloved hand, and there were two. The house behind the garden looked abandoned; its window shutters were missing slats of wood, and some of them hung at crazy, odd angles, as if a storm had torn them from their hinges. Did the creature live there?

La Voisin's dirty hand hovered like a bird of prey, snatched, and the coins were gone. "There'll be one for you."

Athénaïs was disappointed. "Aren't you even going to cast the bones?"

"I don't have to. You were almost all they'd talk of. Don't be telling her in the carriage now. She won't like it. She'll curse you, and her curses are strong."

"What do they say?"

"That you'll have a husband, a fine, handsome one, but he won't be the first that offers for you. There is more than a husband in your fate. You're going high, girl, like the falcons in the sky, but there's a price."

I knew it, thought Athénaïs. "What price? I don't have any more coins."

"You have to do as she did." La Voisin pointed toward the carriage. "You have to curse the one who has his heart now; send me something of hers separate from she in the carriage, something from your own hand a-stealing."

La Voisin held another clay figure. Athénaïs stared at it. Could she do this? Curse Madame? And even as she was asking herself the questions, she was stepping into the circle.

"May his love for her wither. May he look on others, not her." She didn't dare name her own name. Besides, the witch had spoken her destiny. She repeated words the witch told her to say, old and evil names. She was cursing Christ and spitting. She stepped out of the circle, the clay figure held tightly in her hand. "When will I have my good fortune?"

"Someday."

Athénaïs turned on her heel, angry at the answer and guilty for what she'd just done.

"The husband will be jealous," La Voisin called to her. "You'll have to watch that."

The coachman opened the carriage door and Athénaïs stepped up the little step into the carriage, into the middle of a tirade from Olympe.

"…stupid old hag!" Olympe was saying.

"Perhaps she's wrong," Nicolas soothed.

"She's never wrong! What did she tell you?" Olympe asked, but Athénaïs shook her head, not wanting to speak about it in front of the viscount.

The carriage gave a lurch forward. Nicolas shook out the white powder on the back of his hand and brought it to his nose and inhaled it. "Ah," he said after a moment. He leaned back against the leather of the seat, closed his eyes, and smiled. Eyes closed, he licked his lips.

"Do you like it?" Olympe asked.

"Very much. Tell your hag I'll send her a bag of gold."

"What does it do?"

"It reminds me I can't fail." He opened his eyes, head still leaned lazily back against the carriage seat. "And it makes me want to kiss beautiful women."

"She said beware. She said there was trouble for you. You ought to go and ask her yourself," Olympe told him.

"Another time, perhaps."

"It isn't fair!" Olympe continued. "Her Majesty must know." She shook her fists in exasperation. "I forgot to curse the Princess de Monaco!"

Nicolas stopped looking so sleepy. "And why would you do that?"

"She's the one that kept me from Madame's household. And now His Majesty is in love with Madame."

"There are three things I must say to you. First, Her Majesty must never know your suspicions. It would be unkind to Her Majesty and very, very unwise, I think, to stir His Majesty's wrath. Do you think he would allow upset to his queen and not punish the one who caused it?" He reached across the carriage and took the balled-up fists of her hands and smoothed them out as he continued. "Second, there's nothing yet but speculation. I don't think Madame has him captured as completely as you imagine. Three, it wasn't the Princess de Monaco who kept you from Madame's. It was me. You are too important to me where you are, and no other position reflects your grandeur. To go from superintendent to lady-in-waiting is ridiculous." He pulled her from the seat across the space to him, made her sit close, holding her hands tightly in his. "There's no one like you. You can capture his heart. Don't despair."

"I don't despair. I hate."

Nicolas shuddered. So did Athénaïs. Nicolas pulled Olympe into his arms, ran his hands up and down arms covered by the cloak, as if to soothe the savagery evoked. "You're the most desirable woman at court," he assured her. "His Majesty can't help but see that. Make him jealous. Find a lover."

Once at Fontainebleau, they descended from his carriage.

Athénaïs felt the weight of the clay figure in the pocket in her cloak. Ahead loomed the entrance to the king's courtyard. Two enormous square columns, the massive head of a Roman god upon each, marked a small bridge she must cross. Under the bridge was a moat. The king's grandmother had built the moat to protect from invaders. But envy, deceit, jealousy, and malice could never be repelled. If she were very, very good and gave extra to the poor and said her prayers with fervor and blessed

Madame at Mass every day, the curse she'd summoned would somehow work but hurt no one, and all would be well. Yes. She shook her shoulders and summoned a smile and walked forward, conscience quieted.

❧

Louise pulled her horse up short before a walled compound as a bell in its church tower pealed, filling her ears, vibrating out into the summer's air with a toll of the day's hours.

This, thought Louise, must be the monastery on the map. Roses had been planted in neat lines along the outside of the high brick wall, and they'd grown long arms, espaliered with fastidious precision to the wall behind them, dotted now with heavy blossoms. The groom accompanying her pointed, and she saw a vineyard some distance from the compound, monks and servants toiling in it, walking among trellised grapevines.

Louise pulled a mask from a silk bag attached to the saddle and tied it around her eyes.

"Remember," she told the groom, "we're fretted that perhaps my horse had thrown a shoe. Take your time with it, so I have a chance to look around. There's a gold *louis* for this."

The groom rode up to the wooden gate, pulled on the bell there, and after a moment, a face peered out of the grate in the gate, took in the sight of him and behind him, a masked Louise, her gown cascading down the sidesaddle.

"I think my lady's horse has thrown a shoe," the groom called. "Have you a smithy where I might repair it?"

The face disappeared. After a time, Louise and the groom heard the sound of wooden slats being pulled back. The gate opened on one side, and they trotted their horses through it. There was a large garden to the left, and a number of boys working in it. They wore simple, short robes that showed their bare legs and feet. I wonder if they're initiates, Louise was thinking, when they caught sight of her, and the next thing she knew, her horse was surrounded by the boys, all of whom were saying words she couldn't quite understand, pointing at her and pulling at any piece of her skirt they could grasp. Something was wrong with them. Everywhere she looked was a young boy's face that was not quite as expected. Some of them jumped up and down, shrieked at her. The groom leapt from his horse and tried to push as many of them as he could away from her. Louise was so frightened she couldn't breathe. Her horse began to snort and twist its head.

"They're idiots," cried the groom, pulling one after another away from her, but there were too many others crowding around. A boy had Louise gripped by the boot. She could feel herself slipping out of the saddle. She lashed out with her riding crop, and then she was pulled off the horse to the ground, and they crowded around her, jabbering in words she couldn't understand, pointing and pulling, and she fainted.

She woke choking and light-headed. She lay in someone's arms, and someone else was attempting to make her drink something. Her arms flailed, and she struggled to sit up, crying out, "Stop!"

"My humblest apologies, my lady."

A white-robed monk knelt before her. "My children have frightened you, and I am so sorry for that. Our dear boys aren't used to seeing a woman. They aren't used to seeing anyone. We live in seclusion, you see."

The boys had been herded back into the garden, but they weren't hoeing or weeding. They stood staring at Louise, still pointing, still making those sounds she didn't understand.

"They miss mothers and sisters," the monk said. "You'll forgive my gracelessness of words. I am so seldom in company."

But he spoke like a courtier, fluidly if simply, a slight accent to his French that Louise could not identify but which seemed familiar.

"Will you take another sip of our brandy? We're famous for it, I'm told."

She sat up straighter, looked around. There was a chapel with wings on each side. Of brick and marble and sandstone, the chapel was extraordinarily beautiful, rivaling anything in Paris or built by the great families for their estates. Figures of saints decorated its roofline, its small cupola was covered in gold, and the Holy Mother spread her arms wide above gilded double doors. Sets of stained-glass windows glinted their magical colors. Nearby was a house of brick and marble as handsome as the chapel. Other buildings near the chapel had long arbors built to shade their fronts, ivy and columbine twining up to form leafy shelter. A kitchen building, an outside oven, a well, and several barns and sheds stood within the walls. And there were old trees everywhere, their thick canopy reaching upward and outward like the benevolent arms of green angels.

"I think her horse has thrown a shoe," the groom repeated. "Might my lady rest somewhere while I see to it?"

"Of course," the monk answered, but it seemed to Louise that there was something reluctant in his answer. He stood and whistled. When several monks appeared, he pointed to Louise's horse, making a series of gestures with his hands. She remembered the old groom at the stables had said that they were an order of silence.

"I forget my manners. I am Monsignor de Reyes, abbot of this community." He held out his hand to help Louise from the ground. "If you will follow Father Edoardo, he will take you to a chamber where you may refresh yourself. Because we are an order of silence, only I may speak, and I speak now to bid you farewell."

She followed the younger monk into the shade of the porch of the building near the house, then into a broad hallway with stairs leading to another floor. The hallway's furniture, chairs and a chest, was hand-carved and simple, its walls whitewashed, a cross with the crucified Christ dominating all. There was nothing here of the majesty and baroque decoration of the outside of the chapel and house. At the stairs, he motioned for her to precede him.

Upstairs, she stood in a long hallway into which a series of doors opened. The monk opened the closest door for her. She stepped into a pleasant room, chairs covered with embroidered cushions, a rug on the floor, a harpsichord in a corner, a fiddle nearby. He made a motion indicating the chamber was hers, and she nodded her head as, bowing, he left her.

She went at once to the window and looked out. From this height, she could see the vineyard and the monks working there. It wasn't servants working with them, as she'd thought, but the larger children of this place, this monastery of broken boys. She opened the door. No one was in the long hallway. Doors lined its length like sentinels. Did she dare open them? Were there monks behind each one? Or more of the boys?

You're being foolish, she thought. All the monks would be working. That was the way of a monastery, everyone with his duties. There was no stopping until prayers and supper and dark.

She crossed the hall and eased open the first door. A simple chamber, with a bed and a table holding a basin, hooks on the wall to hold clothing, a crucifix, no more. She opened all five of the doors on that side of the hall, her heart beating like a drum in her ears each time the door creaked open. Inside were monks' cells, one after another. She was at the end of the hall now. She stood at its opened window, and for a moment, she couldn't believe her eyes. There in a horse corral were the musketeer and the boy with the iron mask on his face. The two were fencing, rapiers zinging as the blades met.

Her mind raced. She'd never thought past this point. What on earth did she do now? The musketeer hit the boy's blade and sent the rapier flying through the air. The boy stood a moment, his head lowered. Then he ran straight at the musketeer, hitting the older man hard enough to send him sprawling backward. Louise watched the boy begin to pummel the musketeer, who, with one quick motion, pushed the boy to the ground and sat on his chest.

"Stop!" the musketeer said. "Stop it now, Highness! I command it. Your mother commands it."

The boy stilled. Carefully, the musketeer stood. The boy sat up, began to howl. Then he leaned over to hit his head against the ground and howl as he did so.

"Father Gabriel! Father Umberto!" Shouting, the musketeer ran to the edge of the corral, just as Louise heard steps on the stairs and turned in panic. Had she time to run back to the first chamber?

No.

She walked forward down the hall, pulling at the fan that was tied by a silk ribbon to her waist. Her heart was beating so hard that for a moment she literally couldn't hear over it. A monk appeared with a tray holding a goblet and two pitchers, but with him was the abbot who'd rescued her from her faint, Monsignor de Reyes. She walked forward, fanning herself in what she hoped were confident strokes. The memory of Choisy's warnings told her it wasn't a good thing she'd seen the musketeer and the boy and that it wouldn't be a good thing to tell this abbot so. Pretend you're the gargoyle, she told herself. What would she do?

"It's stifling hot," she heard herself say. "I thought the hall would be cooler. Whatever are those howls? One of the boys?" Silence, she told herself. Don't say another word. Be as proud and cool as the princess.

"Yes," the abbot said, his eyes searching her face. "Those we nurture sometimes have fits, as you may imagine—"

Spanish, thought Louise, he has a Spanish accent, like the Queen Mother's.

"—and I fear you're hearing such a fit now. Alas, as you see, our humble monastery is difficult on its visitors."

She followed him into the chamber where the harpsichord and fiddle were. Did music soothe the boys? she wondered, as she watched him pour wine into a goblet and then indicate the other pitcher, which held water.

"We train our boys to grow and tend grapes. No one has such gentle hands as our children. I think the grapes thrive on their touch. How did you stumble upon our little monastery, my lady?" he asked.

My mask, thought Louise. She'd just realized that it was no longer on her face. It must have come loose when she fainted. It was all she could do not to fall to her knees and confess everything to him. The Princess de Monaco, Louise repeated to herself. Act like the gargoyle.

"I did not think to see you again, monsignor," she said, haughty and bored.

"I was afraid the noise would disturb and frighten you, and since I am the only one who may speak…" He shrugged and held out the goblet of wine to her, and Louise drank it almost empty.

Now perhaps her hands would stop trembling, and her heart would quit trying to leap out of her chest. The howling had ceased.

"So how did you find us, if I may again so inquire? Did you come to buy brandy?" he asked.

"Find you?" She laughed without mirth, the way the gargoyle did. "By not attempting to, I must suppose, else why visit this"—she searched for words, a brow lifted—"place of sorrow. I scarcely know where I am and must depend on you to point us toward..." at the last moment she said "Paris" instead of "Fontainebleau."

"What a long way you've ridden."

She shrugged. Great ladies never bothered to explain themselves.

"If I may, who have I the honor of addressing?"

She gave her mother's name, put down the goblet, and walked to the door. "I'm going downstairs to summon my groom," she said. "We've a long journey back."

"Indeed you do."

She stood at the door waiting the way the gargoyle would have done, and after what seemed forever, the abbot opened the door for her. In his open hand was her mask. She snatched it from him, was over the threshold and down the stairs in the blink of an eye. She was out the open door, into the shade of the porch, and walking as fast as she dared toward the barns and sheds. Inside one, her groom stood with the horses.

"Did you hear that howling?" he asked her, his eyes wide.

"We have to leave at once," answered Louise, tying the mask in place.

He held his hands cupped, and she stepped into them and then onto the sidesaddle.

"They're watered and rested a little. They'll get us back," he told her.

"Just let them get us out of here."

She could hear the edge to her voice, and so did the groom. Blessed Mother, she prayed, let me leave here without being seen by the musketeer. Please, Blessed Mother, I beg you.

Outside, she saw that the gates through which they'd entered were closed. The boys in the garden looked up from their tilling.

"Give me the reins of your horse," she ordered. "Run and open the gate."

He obeyed, her voice making him swift. The boys in the garden stared. Louise looked around. The abbot had followed her outside, was crossing the front of the house, but she didn't slow the gait of the horses.

"How will you find your way back, my lady?" the abbot called to her.

She kicked harder at her horse's sides. "I'll trust in the Lord."

The groom had the long wooden slats that barred the gate pulled back, and one side of the gate gaped open. She tossed his horse's reins to the groom as she trotted her horse through, and she looked behind once to see that the groom was astride his own horse, and seeing that he was, she whipped at her horse's haunches with her riding crop hard enough to make the horse leap into a gallop. She intended to gallop all the way back to Fontainebleau if that were possible, but then she remembered that there was a hill that they'd come across earlier, and that from its top, it was possible to see the monastery compound. She wanted another look.

"What frightened you? The addled children?" asked the groom as he rode up beside her.

"Yes."

"They mean no harm. My brother is such a one, sweet as a lamb."

The musketeer had called the boy "Highness." A royal lamb. The musketeer didn't see me, Louise thought. Thank you, Holy Mother.

The horses slowly climbed the hill, and at its top Louise could see again the vineyards and the monastery chapel's cupola amid the trees. Forget, the musketeer had ordered Choisy. Noblewomen abandoned unwanted children to all kinds of fates. If the boy was an idiot, this was best, wasn't it? Why did something in her say otherwise? She was so intent on her thoughts that she didn't hear the sound of other horses approaching until it was too late, until her horse neighed, and she and the groom were surrounded.

✣

"Sir?"

Nicolas looked up from a letter he was reading. One of his private guards stood outlined by sunlight and by the lovely columns of Nicolas's open-air rotunda in this château he was building.

"We found trespassers, sir," the guard said.

Nicolas stood and saw two people still on horseback in the courtyard on the other side of his moat. He walked out into the sunlight, down the steps of his great porch. There were hundreds of workmen everywhere, around the house, on the roofs, in the gardens. The house must be finished as soon as possible for his fête, for his special guests, the king and queen and royal family. He was throwing the grandest fête ever seen, a fête worthy of a future chancellor. Everyone in Paris was coming. Everyone who was anyone in the kingdom was coming. Nicolas saw that one of the trespassers was a masked woman, and he was at once intrigued. Her groom had dismounted, was standing in front of her horse as if he would fight everyone for her sake. Smiling, he stepped forward and offered his hand.

"Forgive my guards' zeal, miss. Won't you dismount and allow me to offer you a cup of wine?"

Louise dismounted, said something to her groom, and Nicolas realized at once that it was Miss de la Baume le Blanc. Had she gotten lost? Surely this wasn't a deliberate visit. And why the mask?

"If you will follow me, miss." And he led the way back up the steps, across the terrace, into the beautiful rotunda, and then through a series of chambers on the right, until they were in a small chamber with very high ceilings, its walls elaborately gilded and painted and festooned. There was a huge impressive mirror and, under it, a long sofa with legs of gilt. Tall candlesticks the size of boys stood in the four corners. He gestured toward the sofa, covered in cut velvet, just delivered, in fact. The wagon that had brought it had only just rolled away. He stood near the window, enjoying both the breeze and Louise's clear discomfort.

A servant brought wine, but she refused it. Was she not going to reveal who she was? Did she think he did not know? What a silly child she was. "Miss, I must ask why you trespass upon my land."

"We were lost."

Lost? This little horsewoman who rode out with a groom nearly every morning, who rode like an Amazon during the king's hunts? Word was His Majesty had commented on her skills just the other day. She must know the countryside by heart by now. He didn't believe her. "Won't you take off your mask, Miss de la Baume le Blanc? It feels so unfriendly."

Louise sagged against the upright back of the sofa, untied her mask, and dropped it in her lap. She knew she needed to say something, to be light and playful, but she couldn't summon up a single word. Her playacting at the monastery had taken all her wits.

"Well," he said, when it was clear she wasn't going to speak. "What a delight for me. I have the honor to show you my wonderful château. It's the penance you pay for trespass. Allow me to escort you around the grounds and boast a bit, the way a man must when he has something new of which he is very proud. Then I will bundle you back in your cloak and send you and your groom on your way to Fontainebleau with one of my guard as escort."

"All right, then."

Her response wasn't enthusiastic, but Nicolas ignored that. She was his guest; it was a beautiful day, and there was nothing he liked better than showing off his château.

One hand on his arm, Louise allowed herself to be led back into the rotunda. All around her, in a perfect circle, were immense arches, some leading outside, some to other chambers in the château. The symmetry was beautiful, and it was continued upward, on the next level, where even sets of windows, spaced perfectly above the arches below, made their own circle. And then above them was a dome.

"Do you know of Le Brun?" he asked, and she shook her head and listened to him explain that Le Brun was a great artist and that he had not yet completed the painting that would be inside the dome. Louise didn't yet understand that the men and women of this age measured themselves not only by their bravery, but by the beauty they created. The man who was destined to love her would set the standard for his century, but before him, creating that standard, was this man beside her. All of this was in the future, years from now when she would have been taken to the heights of her century and known all that was fashionable and exquisite and beautifully done. But now, this day at the viscount's château, she was just an exhausted girl aware that everywhere she looked were beautiful things, from polished wood to onyx-topped tables to huge golden candlesticks to dozens of busts sitting atop marble columns in between the arches. On one of the tables in one of the chambers they'd passed through was a tumble of crystal decanters and goblets, of silver trays and épergnes, all piled together like pirates' booty.

She stood on the terrace with him and looked out at his gardens. They were magnificent. Even the gardens in Paris, at the Luxembourg Palace, where the Orléans and her mother lived, were not this beautiful. Everywhere she looked, there was order and beauty. She saw a landscape canal, alleys of young trees, statues and fountains, gravel paths, sets of steps, patterned parterres in which gardeners were still planting lilies and carnations and in which stood graceful statues or fountains. She caught her breath at the splendid, grand symmetry of it, and hearing the sound, Nicolas was pleased.

Yes, he thought, looking out at a vista before him, I leave a legacy for generations. They will be talking of me, of the beauty of this, a hundred years from now. Too bad the fountains aren't playing, but she'd see them soon enough.

"Do you know Le Nôtre?" he asked, and Louise shook her head, no.

"Well, he is one of the king's gardeners, and he has designed all of this for me. For five long years, he's been designing this." He told her of the many fountains that sprayed water upward and pointed out a long waterfall a mile or so in the distance. We diverted a river, he told her, and she listened and looked around her and thought that she'd never seen anything so magnificently ordered, but she was so very tired now.

"I really must go now, sir," she said. "I have a long ride ahead."

He leaned against the terrace balustrade. "Ought I to send you back in my carriage?"

She shook her head.

"It's said that you were born in the saddle."

She laughed, and he was reminded again of her youth and freshness.

"My father taught me to ride when I was very small. He took me all through the woods around our home, used to tell me there were fairies everywhere, watching. If one was very quiet and sat under an old tree, one would see them, he said."

"And did you discover any fairies on my land?"

"They must exist in this beautiful place."

"I am so glad you find it to your taste."

"I find it exquisite beyond words. Thank you for your hospitality, and forgive my intrusion."

He followed her back into the rotunda, stood watching as a servant brought her cloak and she retied it. He felt curious again as to how she had ended up on his doorstep. "You were near the monastery, I'm told. Did you go in?"

She hesitated. He watched her struggle about whether to lie to him or not. Not, please, he thought.

"My horse stumbled, and we went in to see if she'd thrown a shoe."

"What do you know of the order?"

"Very little. They care for addled, idiot boys." In spite of herself, she shuddered.

"Yes, the sight of them is disturbing, isn't it?" One visit had been enough to cure him of any further curiosity. He walked her outside, helped her into the sidesaddle, looked up at her as she settled in it. The sun framed her thick hair, casting light through it like the halo of a young Our Lady. She must be the age Mary was when the angel loved her, he thought. What a divine visit for the angel. He watched her ride away, thinking about the monastery. It was on the edge of his land, but he never rode there. He'd visited it once. Seeing boys born without wits, some of them half-wild, had been more than he could bear. If he remembered correctly, it had been founded by the Queen Mother years earlier. Or was it the cardinal who'd founded it? Unlike the cardinal to found an order and then ignore it. Mazarin would have led yearly pilgrimages with all the court along to applaud his piety for the less fortunate and abandoned, so it must have been the Queen Mother.

Perhaps when he was chancellor, he'd order a large yearly stipend to the monks who cared for such troublesome children. A tragedy, to bear a son without a mind, but not his tragedy. He wanted to walk all the way to the waterfall and admire the enormous statue of Hercules that his brother had sent from Italy only a few months ago. One stood at the statue and looked back to the house and knew that magnificence and subtle grandeur had been summoned and shaped, and that he, the Viscount Nicolas, was the sorcerer who had conjured it into being.

※

The musketeer Cinq Mars stood in the frame of the doorway of the house in which he and the boy lived. Like its outside, the interior of this house was fit for a king, or at the very least, a prince of the blood. His charge was inside, being fed the drugged wine that always quieted him. We'll bathe him, he had been thinking, and cut his hair and nails while he's quiet. He'd allowed the hair to become too long, hadn't he? The boy hated having his hair cut. In his heart, Cinq Mars was devoted to his charge, having been with him since he was a babe. He walked out to smoke a pipe of tobacco, which explorers to that vast new world across the sea had brought back to the kingdoms of Europe. Cinq Mars found that smoking a pipe soothed him. He always hated it when the boy had to be held down and force-fed. The child was growing strong. He was ten and six, a young man, really, not a boy. What were they going to do with him? Was he going to languish forever in this netherworld? Should he risk angering the Queen Mother by asking her such? He was thinking those thoughts, grieving and bitter for this boy who would never take his rightful place, when he realized he was watching the gate swing shut, and he thought he caught a glimpse of a horse's tail. He saw the abbot standing in the chapel yard, saw the boys in the gardens with their hoes suspended. Had visitors come to the monastery? When? And what had they seen? Damn their eyes if it was the boy.

CHAPTER 17

There was a certain listlessness to the evenings with Madame still absent. On this particular one, ladies were spread out near the queen on rugs and cushions, and the queen was content to sit in the suspended garden while her dwarves irritated courtiers by stealing fans or other trifles and dropping them into the water of the carp pond. Louis and his friends were on the water racing gondolas again.

"I shouldn't say so, but I find I'm glad she's gone. Aren't you, Majesty?" Olympe's voice was a silk ribbon falling from the sky. Reclining on her cushion, she looked like a sultan's favorite, all creamy arms and shoulders, dark hair, sullen mouth.

"Who?" Maria Teresa asked, watching one of her dwarves who had just taken La Grande Mademoiselle's shoe and dropped it in the pond.

"Madame. When she's around, His Majesty doesn't pay as much attention to you, I've noticed."

Maria Teresa stared at her superintendent of the household as if she didn't quite understand, and since Olympe spoke in French, such might be true. La Grande, however, stopped scolding the thieving dwarf and was unable to keep herself from glancing toward the water, toward the gondola that Louis commanded. His Majesty would be furious at this conversation.

"Majesty." La Grande was imperious and not to be trifled with. "I think we ought to walk a while."

"She's a flirt. I don't trust her." Olympe was not intimidated by La Grande.

La Grande frowned down at Olympe. "A nice walk will do us good."

Olympe smiled. "But you're lacking a shoe."

"Trust? What is this word 'trust'?" Maria Teresa looked from one of her ladies to the next.

"Was that a raindrop I felt? You mustn't get wet." La Grande shivered dramatically. "We mustn't have you rained upon, Majesty. The *dauphin*, you know."

But one of Maria Teresa's dwarves translated the word into Spanish for her, and it hung there in the air like something threatening.

Athénaïs watched the queen absorb Olympe's venom-filled words, and once they were understood, watched Her Majesty's face change from careless and laughing to something somber. Athénaïs could literally see the queen cast her mind back over the past weeks, where, if she tried, she could find a hundred examples of Madame's favor over hers.

So. As easily as that, poison pierced, and the little queen of France stopped being quite so maddeningly innocent and blind. Interesting, thought Athénaïs, as intrigued as if she were witnessing the quarrel that led to a fatal duel. A single sentence could sow doubt. Useful to know.

Obedient to the suggestion that the *dauphin* could be harmed by a raindrop, tingling with emotions she didn't understand, Maria Teresa began to walk toward the stone stairway.

"She doesn't like anyone." It was one of her dwarves, the female one, speaking quickly in the language of their home.

"Who?" asked Maria Teresa. She trusted this little being, a link with her beloved Spain, with her court there, her past, where all was simple and rule-bound.

"The one with the dark heart."

Servants marched across the courtyard with lighted lanterns for the gondolas; twilight was here. The queen and her ladies walked toward the outside stairway, their heels clacking on the stones. Louise curtsied in the queen's direction, returned Athénaïs's wave.

Choisy and Lorraine made vague bows but returned at once to their gambling. They were throwing the dice at the stones under their feet, and Louise watched, her mind elsewhere, a dog with a bone, the bone being the day's events. Who was the boy in the iron mask?

"By all that's holy, you must be cheating." Choisy picked up an offending die and threw it into the water of the carp pond.

"Pay your forfeit," drawled the Chevalier de Lorraine.

Louise watched as Choisy leaned forward and dropped a quick kiss on Lorraine's mouth. Until she'd come to court, she hadn't known men could kiss one another the way a man and a woman did, hadn't known they could love one another in that way, too. She didn't mind it. It was just she hadn't known.

Lorraine put his arms around Choisy, but Choisy pushed Lorraine back. "You'll make Monsieur jealous."

Lorraine pointed toward the pond, the gondolas gliding in it, the laughing, jesting men. "Guiche has been rowing him around the pond all evening as if Monsieur were a lady he courted. I assure you I can't make him jealous, though I don't give up trying. I never knew affection could be so painful."

Choisy bowed to Louise. "Do me the honor of rowing with me to the summer pavilion and back."

At the Queen Mother's terrace, a few rowboats waited to be taken out and floated on the pond. Choisy rowed as Louise leaned back on her arms and looked skyward. How pleasant it was here on the water with a breeze as cooling as a fan. She touched her cheeks. She'd felt hot all day long. What was she going to do about what she'd seen today? Who was he? A bastard child of one of the families of the blood? With a deformed face? She didn't notice that they were now floating quietly in a part of the pond where there were no rowboats and no gondolas, no strolling courtiers on the shore, only willow trees whose limbs bent to touch the water.

"I'm sorry I kissed him. I saw it upset you, but I had to pay the forfeit." Choisy had let go the oars, leaned toward her, earnest, appealing, curling hair framing his eager, beautiful face. "It's you I want to kiss." And when Louise didn't answer, "You were gone a long time today."

"I rode to the convent of the Carmelites in nearby Avon to hear the nuns sing and to visit with little Julie. And I stayed to pray." How much I've lied today, thought Louise, looking up at early stars to avoid the expression on Choisy's face. June was nearly ended. She had begun the month looking for a map. She ended it with finding the boy.

"I think you're still looking for your boy in the iron mask."

Did he read her mind? "I've quite given up on that. But I must have my gallop, or I'm irritable all day."

"I want to kiss you, Louise."

"I don't understand."

"What don't you understand?" He leaned forward and put his mouth on hers.

It was gently done, no tongue intruding as before or as one of His Majesty's friends had done after catching her alone in a hallway not too many days ago. That man had touched her breast, too. She pulled her face away.

"I'm thinking of running away. Of going to the provinces and acting. Molière says I have talent," he told her, his hand still on her neck.

"Would you go as a man or a woman?" She regretted the words the moment they left her mouth.

"In bed, I am fully a man, Louise." He grabbed her hand to force her to touch him between his legs, but she snatched her hand back.

"I don't want to!"

"You owe me an apology! If you were a man, I'd call you out."

"I'm sorry, Choisy."

"Words aren't enough. You have to kiss me."

Oh, let's get this done with, thought Louise. She pursed her lips as

Choisy's mouth fell on hers. What if I hate kissing my husband? she thought. Her marriage would be arranged. She might never know the feeling that Fanny said the Count de Guiche gave her when they kissed. No telling who her mother and Madame de Choisy would drag out of a box for her to marry: some down-at-the-heels cousin, some toadying troll desperate for office at court. In a way it was too bad that she'd been set in such a rarified atmosphere, set among the sun and moon and stars of court, the handsomest, most dashing of men, with laughing eyes, white teeth, smooth manners, their youth and birth and brio like magic talismans spilling light over those who watched. And yet she wouldn't have missed it for anything. When she was old, she would tell her grandchildren about the dazzling men of this court. He noticed you, he noticed you, Fanny had danced the words around her today. Yes, apparently for a few, brief seconds the young sun of their court had placed brilliant eyes upon her and complimented her riding. It was the stuff of dreams.

"No," she said, as Choisy tried to kiss her again. "No!"

CHAPTER 18

His fingers drumming against the velvet pouch, Colbert waited. Without Madame to distract him, His Majesty was keeping earlier hours, so there was a possibility Colbert's head would touch his pillow before too much longer, and sure enough, within three quarters of an hour, in walked the king.

Restless, prowling the chamber, touching this or that objet d'art, he was curt. "What do you have for me?"

Colbert took a deep breath. This was a moment he'd been waiting for. "I've had word about his island. It isn't good."

Louis stilled.

"He forbids all access to this island. No one may leave. No one may visit."

"But someone you trust has done so."

Colbert allowed himself the smallest possible smile. Another man would have been beating his chest in triumph. "Yes."

From his pouch, he pulled out a sheet of paper. "Here is a map of the island, procured under most difficult circumstances, if I may say so. A full report of my spy's difficulties awaits your pleasure."

He spread the map open on a nearby table at which earlier, envisioning this moment, he'd taken a quiet and very deliberate pleasure in slowly lighting every candle of a large branch of candelabra whose rock crystal drops reflected back the flames.

Louis stared down at the map. The island was located just off the coast in the bay that separated Spain and France. It was along a main shipping route. His fingers traced various squares and lines. "A fort? Your man is certain it's a fort? How large? What are these? Ditches? For what? To repel whom?"

"There is already a garrison of two hundred men."

Colbert read the figures out in dry tones, letting not a single inflection betray emotion. He might have been giving the king numbers about the harvest. "There are four hundred cannon in the fort, as well as bombs and explosives, enough weapons and munitions for six hundred men. There are three hundred casks of wine, as well as wheat for bread. The weapons have come from our neighbors to the north." This was the hated republic of the Dutch. "The locals stand guard on the island and welcome no strangers. I would assume the nobility and governor of the province are in his pocket. I have furnished a list of their names. There are some one thousand men working to finish the fort and trenches, and they work day and night and are forbidden to leave."

"My God…" breathed Louis.

The king's incredulousness was all that Colbert could have desired. He folded into himself like a bat and waited.

"The man who obtained this information…he's trustworthy?"

"My first cousin. He would lay down his life for you."

"How did he gather this?"

"Materials are always needed. A mason must have stone, a carpenter wood. And weapons must be delivered by someone. My cousin was that someone."

"Remind me how many ships the viscount possesses."

"Thirty-one."

"How many copies are there of this?" Louis touched the map with one finger.

"You look upon the only one, Majesty."

"What work you've done, Colbert. This is astounding—the depth of his—" Louis stopped himself. He put his hand on Colbert's shoulder. "I have no words to thank you, but you and yours shall remain forever in my high regard. That is my solemn oath." He gave Colbert a quick, shy smile.

"There is one more thing, sire." The whole of Louis's attention was back upon Colbert. He could literally feel it. "It seems that the commander of your navy bankrupted himself—"

"Fighting the Turks," Louis finished for him. Yes, commanders often had to spend their own coins on military campaigns, and they were seldom paid back.

"I have it on the best authority that the Viscount Nicolas has been most kind in opening his own coffers and paying the commander's debts."

"Thank you. You may go now."

Once Louis heard the door shut, he closed his eyes a moment, then opened them to look back down upon the crude map showing the location and fortification of the viscount's island once more. The viscount would need a place to provision the colonies he now administered, but there was no excuse for two hundred men, for rations for four hundred more. No excuse for cannon and trenches. No excuse for such secrecy. Why did he not brag of it in council, showing Louis all he did from his own pocket? Because he didn't wish Louis to know, that's why. And it seemed the commander of the royal navy, such as it was, now lived in the viscount's pocket. If there were a war, the viscount would have the Atlantic seas. What have I? thought Louis, marshalling what assets he possessed. His minister of war was a friend to the viscount, owed him, according to Colbert, much money, so if there were a war, if Louis had to summon generals, there was a great likelihood that the viscount would know as much in the beginning moments as Louis. And then, if he went to his island and blockaded the coast and summoned the nobility of his home province to his side, the court would split asunder. Then, and only then, would Louis know who was on his side, who was not. Was it the viscount who placed the Mazarinades to remind Louis of the destruction of civil war, a snake eating its own tail? He needed no reminding. He'd grown up in it. Ah, my cardinal, you've left me quite a viper to step upon, haven't you? Even you were afraid of him, weren't you? Have I the cunning for this? Louis thought. The wit? I must have it, mustn't I? There is no other choice.

JULY 1661

CHAPTER 19

The Countess de Soissons strode into the antechamber of Madame's rooms where Fanny and Louise sat. They rose from their chairs and curtsied.

"Madame is not here?" Olympe asked.

What a strange question, thought Louise. Of course she wasn't. The whole palace was waiting with bated breath for her return at any moment.

"No," answered Fanny politely, and when the countess didn't say anything else, just stared at them as if they weren't supposed to be there, "We're embroidering pillow covers for our trousseaus."

"I had no idea anyone was interested in you. Who are the fortunate men?"

They were saved from answering by the arrival of a court page, who put his head through the door's opening and said, "Her carriage has been sighted."

"If you'll excuse us, Countess," Fanny said, and she and Louise rushed out to join the throng that would gather in the courtyard.

Olympe went into the empty bedchamber. There on the dressing table among ribbons and combs was a small rouge brush, a lovely one with a silver handle. This, thought Olympe, and she picked it up and walked back out to the withdrawing chamber and then into the hall, at last a smile on her face.

❧❧❧

A discreet knock sounded on the door of the chamber in which Louis held his council meetings, and one of his pages entered and whispered in his master's ear.

"Madame has arrived," Louis told his council. Not one of the men around the table, nor Colbert, who had been summoned to make a report on trade, missed the sudden smile that spread across Louis's face.

"I suggest we adjourn for the day," said Nicolas.

"Yes," replied Louis, and then he was gone, bounding out the door like a boy.

Nicolas caught Colbert's eye. "A moment."

Colbert bowed coldly.

"This place is a rumor mill. One hears a thousand tales. Have you heard the one that His Majesty has selected a candidate for chancellor when the august Séguier dies?"

"I have not, but I think we both know his choice," Colbert answered.

"You flatter me."

"Let me flatter you further, Viscount, and say that I might agree with His Majesty's choice, except for one small thing."

"And that would be?"

"You hold the office of attorney general of the Parlement of Paris, do you not?" The *parlement* was a high court of justice. All the kingdom's large cities had them, but none was as powerful as Paris.

"That honor has been mine for a number of years."

"To my thinking, it is incompatible with the office of chancellor."

"May one ask why?"

"The chancellor must be above specific loyalties."

"I was never part of the *parlement's* disloyalties!" The *parlement* of Paris had warred against the king and Queen Mother and cardinal, and Nicolas had, in fact, worked to aid Her Majesty. Colbert gave a small shrug that caused Nicolas to grind his teeth and say, "Nonetheless, I take it you've expressed this opinion to His Majesty?"

"He has not asked, but if he does, it is my duty to tell him the truth."

Each examined the face of the other. You starched, dried, joyless eater of numbers, thought Nicolas. One of Nicolas's spies had told him that Colbert studied Latin when he was journeying from one place to another. All gentlemen knew Latin, but Colbert was a merchant's son. You study Latin like a schoolboy in your carriage to make yourself fully one of us, thought Nicolas. "*Contra felicem vix deus vires habet,*" he said.

Color came into Colbert's expressionless face. You traitorous, ambitious, flamboyant fool, squandering your talents and the kingdom's coin, he thought. I'll see you hanged. "You have the advantage of me," he said.

In all things, thought Nicolas, but he replied, "Evil to him who evil thinks." It wasn't what he'd said, but it amused him to tell Colbert so. "You'll have supper with me one evening?" He had no intention of suppering with Colbert.

"Of course." Colbert bowed, the viscount's equal in polite mendacity.

Outside in the courtyard, the throng parted for Louis, whose face was alight with pleasure.

"Majesty." Henriette, already out of the carriage, standing by Philippe, dropped into a curtsy.

Louis pulled her up and out of it. Louise, clustered around Madame with all the maids of honor, thought, oh, dear, his face is an open book. Anyone could see he was in love, and Monsieur stood right there. Her eyes flew to Guy's face, taut and narrow-eyed.

"You've been missed," Louis said.

Philippe took Henriette's hand from Louis's, placed it on his own arm. "So I've been telling her." He led Henriette away, toward the elaborate portico of this courtyard, as Louis watched their exit. Philippe didn't allow a moment of silence between himself and Henriette.

"Benersade had a quarrel with Lully." Benersade was the court poet. He created the verses that were spoken or given out in small books at the court ballets. And Lully was the musician who displayed the most talent. Both had enormous tempers and opinions of themselves.

"He said he wouldn't write another word until you returned. Not even I could console him. And the viscount insists we go to Vaux-le-Vicomte as soon as possible. I depend on your excellent taste, he says. He has the fountains flowing. He wants us to see them before the fête in August. Rumor has it he is going to be named chancellor when Séguier dies. And I'm to have a place on the council. He promises it. He and I had a long talk yesterday, and he understands and sympathizes with my every concern. Oh. By the way, your mother's here. She arrived yesterday."

She stopped where she was. "My mother?"

"She wrote to say she misses you and she wishes to see you as a married woman."

"But I didn't invite her."

"I did," said Philippe. "Ought I not to have done so?"

"You know how she is. She'll pick me to death."

"I'll protect you."

In the bedchamber, dogs began to bark and jump for Henriette's attention. Henriette made a gesture that had Catherine ordering everyone out, as Henriette sat down on the floor and gave herself to their yelps and licks.

What is happening between us? thought Philippe, and he sat down among the dogs and, feeling Henriette's distance like a pain in his heart, he pretended he was a dog, too. He barked, but Henriette didn't seem to find him funny.

"It's possible we're going to have a child," she said.

His eyes blazed suddenly.

"Don't tell anyone yet," Henriette said quickly. "It's so early."

"A child! I'm head over heels." He took her hands in his, kissed them passionately. "When did you know?"

"I've only just suspected it."

He touched one of the saint's medals at his neck. "I'll pray to the Holy Mother." He swept aside dogs and took her into his arms, kissing her forehead, her neck, the soft hollow there. You have given me everything, he thought, my own household with its independence, your enchanting self, the admiration of the court, and now, this. I have fathered an heir. He felt strong and masculine, straightforward and clean, the way he imagined Louis always felt.

"Stop—oh, stop. I just feel—I don't feel myself," said Henriette. "I feel odd and mixed up and cranky, Philippe."

"Are you ill?"

"Yes."

"My poor darling. And here I am all over you like a beast." He stood, held out his hand, helped her to her feet.

"Tonight," she said, "after I've rested."

He pulled her to him, held her tight a moment. When he was gone, she sat back down on the floor among the dogs. She did feel odd, confused, irritable. And she did not want to make love to her husband. And then real bile rose in her throat, and she rushed to the close stool with its velvet cover, as the dogs followed and nearly made her fall. Afterward, she went to a window and leaned out, breathing in gulps of air. There was a soft knock on the door.

"It's La Baume le Blanc," said Catherine and allowed Louise inside.

"Your mother sends a message that she desires to see you, Madame," said Louise.

"Will you tell her that you found me napping?"

There was mischief in Louise's sudden smile. "Are you perhaps ill, also? A headache from travel, I would guess. Is there anything you need before I go?"

Henriette shook her head.

Louise held up a sealed note and waved it back and forth. "Are you absolutely certain you need nothing?"

Henriette snatched the note. It was from Louis. She opened it to read how much she was missed and profoundly adored.

Philippe went to his mother's wing of the palace. Her chambers were busy. Ladies scurried here and there, arms filled with gowns and shawls and linens—Anne could not bear to sleep on anything other than linen woven and embroidered by Spanish nuns. She always traveled with too many things. Philippe did the same.

In her closet, alone, Anne stared out at her view of gardens and water as Philippe entered.

"I trust you found the duchess well," he said. When he'd been a boy, the duchess would feed him sweetmeats and ask him question after question. Was his mother very fond of the cardinal? Who came to his mother's chambers? Had his mother seemed happy or unhappy lately? She had used him the way she used everyone, to keep track of the shifting policies, but he had liked her. She had advised him: Don't wear your heart so openly on your sleeve, little prince. This is a court that swallows soft hearts as if they were oysters. "The visit was a good one?"

"Madame was all that she should be."

Anne touched his face, as if to reassure him, and he felt his heart beat harder at the gesture. It was dangerous to love his mother too much, but he could not help it at this moment when he felt so blessed. In spite of himself, words came out of his mouth. "She's with child."

The expression on her face was for a moment so aghast that Philippe exclaimed, "What is it? Mother! Shall I call for your ladies?" He went to a table, poured her the Roman wine their cardinal had taught them to love.

Anne drank it down. "I've been in the carriage too long this day and feel faint from the heat. I offer you congratulations, but darling, please, if you will listen to your mother who is both a woman and a queen, it's too soon to tell the world. In another month, we shall celebrate."

"I know. She said the same, that it is far too early to speak of yet, but I had to tell you."

"Thank you from the bottom of my heart for sharing this with me. Now, I'm going to send you on your way, my dear. I'm tired and need to rest before whatever it is your brother will have planned for tonight. Some celebration, I'm sure, now that our precious Madame is returned."

And when he was gone from the room, Anne sat down feeling every year of her life weighing on her like heavy stones. Is the child Louis's? she thought.

❧❦❧

Catherine couldn't keep the news to herself either. She'd already sent Nicolas a note about it and waited impatiently to hear from him. He'd been among the throng of courtiers greeting their return. Now she walked with her brother outside the palace, in distant gardens, down the long length of the landscape canal. The sun danced here and there in the water.

"She's with child," she told him

"Whose?"

His question was like a blow. "How ungallant of you, Guy. I thought you'd be happy the lineage of your precious prince is assured."

She lifted her skirts as if she'd stepped in mud and walked back toward the palace. A mistake to tell him, she thought. How odd, her Guy, as cold-hearted as she—they used to have such fun mocking their admirers—and here he was, acting like some hero in a Corneille tragedy. It was too boring, really, all this emotion. Was this what love was? She wouldn't know. But she did know desire, and she'd surprised herself by missing Nicolas, and the carriage ride home had been one long fantasy of all the delicious ways to make that evident to him.

❧❦❧

The young groom who always accompanied Louise sat uncomfortably in the chamber of Monsieur Colbert. "No, sir, we didn't see anything unusual," the groom answered. I'll say nothing to bring her trouble, he thought to himself, his thoughts resolute, nothing.

"Why did you go to the monastery?"

"We just happened on it, and we was afraid her horse was about to throw a shoe—she knows everything there is to know about horses, sir."

"Does she?"

"Oh yes. We had her in last week to look at El Cid. He wasn't eating, sir. No matter what we gave him. And he'd started to bite us."

El Cid was Louis's Spanish stallion, specially trained in the art of prancing on hind legs and other arts going all the way back to the ancient Greeks. "And what did Miss de la Baume le Blanc do?"

"Well, sir, she sat by his stall for a long time, then she went inside—that upset us—he's been so bad-tempered lately. And she ran her hands all over his body. Then she put her hands on his fetlock for a time, and then she told us we was to sing Spanish songs to him."

"Excuse me," said Colbert, as if he hadn't heard properly.

"It's the truth. We laughed, but my father went to one of the queen's musicians and asked him if he wouldn't come and play the guitar and sing those wild howls the Spanish like, and he did, and I tell you what, El Cid is eating again."

"Miraculous." Colbert was sarcastic.

"Well, it makes sense, don't it, sir, him being so far from his home and all. His other grooms might have sung—"

"The monastery. You were telling me about the monastery."

"Well, we went in and my lady went into a room to rest, and I checked on the horse's shoe, and we got that all to rights, and we left, sir."

"Where is this monastery?"

"To the northeast, sir."

"Near the Viscount Nicolas's château?" Colbert was abrupt. "You saw the viscount, didn't you?"

"Well, his guards took us to his house, and he and my lady talked for a time." The groom was uncomfortable. "We'd strayed onto his land. It was a mistake, sir. She's a good lady, sir, has a kind heart, likes to ride is all, likes the forest and the sun and the wind in her hair. That's all. No harm in it."

"When do you ride again?"

The groom shook his head.

"Thank you. That's all." Colbert watched the groom leave the chamber with his eyes narrowed. So, she'd seen the viscount. Something was up. He could smell it. And Miss de la Baume le Blanc was involved, he'd bet money on it, and he wasn't a betting man, to say the least. Did she make a regular report to the viscount on the blossoming feeling between His Majesty and Madame? Or something else? Did she leave Mazarinades that the viscount composed?

He sent for Lieutenant D'Artagnan, and when the lieutenant appeared before him, Colbert said, "Did you know there was a monastery near the viscount's estate?"

"Yes. They make excellent wine and an even better brandy. I'm surprised the viscount didn't order it moved. He has leveled more than one hamlet, I hear, for his estate, but then, he probably likes their wine."

"Anything of note to tell me about Miss de la Baume le Blanc?"

"She visited the monastery a few days ago. Saw the viscount, too. Apparently his guards found her on the property and took her to him, poor thing, though I'm certain he was suitably polite."

Colbert sat unmoved, and D'Artagnan felt challenged. "She is little more than an innocent child. She wondered onto his property by mistake."

"There are no innocents at court, lieutenant."

"She's a good girl."

"She moves among the highest in the land, goes to see after His Majesty's ailing dogs, his horses, visits with his most personal servant. I think she's a spy for the viscount." Colbert was cold, like the ice people said was in the place of his heart.

"She's a good, kind girl. I'll bet my first child it isn't her leaving the Mazarinades. It's La Grande Mademoiselle."

"Who you have yet to catch in the act. I smell a rat. Make certain you know where Miss de la Baume le Blanc is at all times," said Colbert.

D'Artagnan puffed out. "As I already do, do you mean?"

"Where is she right now?"

"Walking Madame's dogs and avoiding the Count de Guiche."

"What has the Count de Guiche to do with anything?"

"He flirts with her, but she won't have much of it. That is unusual for the count, who has at least one of the maids of honor misbehaving." D'Artagnan enjoyed court gossip, enjoyed the romantic adventures of the young. He and his friends had had many an adventure, romantic and otherwise, in their day. "Miss de Montalais isn't behaving as she ought."

"Miss de Montalais is the dark-eyed one who is always with Miss de la Baume le Blanc, isn't she?"

D'Artagnan watched Colbert write something on one of those papers of his. He heard himself say, as if he were driven to defend, "They're very good friends. They both come from the Orléans household."

"Nest of snakes, those Orléans."

Colbert waved him away, but D'Artagnan didn't mind. A man like Colbert loved very little, his wife and family likely, his God for certain, and the king. D'Artagnan had no doubts of that anymore. Every ounce of Colbert's incisive, aloof, and broad mind was in service of his sovereign. His Majesty had found another Mazarinade last night, pinned to his pillow, an ugly little piece of filth.

"The Cardinal," and here the first initial of an extremely graphic word was used, its meaning clear, "f---- the Regent, and what's worse, the bugger boasts about it; to make the offense less grave, he only f---- her in the ass," it said.

Who continued to bring up again those turbulent times when the kingdom howled that a Spaniard queen and an Italian lackey ruled badly? Had pretty little Miss de la Baume le Blanc a part? She didn't compose them, D'Artagnan would bet on that, but she might be one of the means by which La Grande Mademoiselle, an Orléans to her fingertips, aimed such perfect, poisonous darts at His Majesty's peace of mind. Colbert thought it was the Viscount Nicolas, but D'Artagnan put his money on the royal cousin.

Louise delivered Madame's excuse to an attendant and then hurried away, down broad stone steps, and then she was out of the palace buildings, into the bright sunlight of the courtyard to take a moment for herself. She sat down on a bench to watch the officials and clerks that worked in this part of the palace. What would happen now that Madame had returned? She felt fretful and worried for everyone, Madame, Monsieur, His Majesty. But she couldn't linger all day thinking about that. She must return to her duties.

She ran through a ground-floor arch of the staircase called the horseshoe because of its shape, her mind on the play Molière and his actors had performed upon it before Madame had left. Tell me with your eyes, don't explain, the actress had said. His Majesty's eyes had told their tale today, she was thinking, when suddenly a man hidden in the shadows stepped in front of her. Louise took an instinctive step backward and almost screamed. It was the musketeer from that day she'd been in the woods. The shock of seeing him nearly paralyzed her. I don't know him, she told herself. I've never seen him before, she thought, as he caught her arm in a bold and rude gesture.

"Sir! Unhand me!"

He didn't reply.

"I am a lady of Madame's, and you may not treat me so!" Valiantly, she strove for arrogance, disdain, playing the Princess de Monaco, the way she had at the monastery, but her teeth were chattering. "I—I'll call a guard and have you arrested."

"But there's no one about, is there? And I have only to do this." With one insulting yank, she was pulled inside the shady overhang of the stairs, pushed against its harsh stones, a calloused hand over her mouth. "Must I continue?"

Her strength broke, and she shook her head. He dropped his hand. She began to shake so badly that she thought she'd fall.

"You're a sly one, giving your mother's name. I went to Paris. Your mother thought I was a madman, nearly had me thrown out on the street. But for the right amount of coin, servants always talk, and when I learned she had a daughter, I knew it was you. I thought you understood that I wished you to forget that day in the woods. Your friend, the oh-so-changeable Choisy, delivered my message, didn't he? And coins?"

She didn't answer. She couldn't have if she'd tried. Standing so close to him, Louise could see the puffiness under his eyes, the way the sun had dried his face to leather. She began to cry very quietly. She knew it would do her no good, but she couldn't help herself.

"Miss de la Baume le Blanc, your curiosity is dangerous. How do I make that clear to you?"

"I won't say anything! I promise!"

"It would be best for us both if I believe you. So I will, for now. This"—his voice was soft, as menacing as if a river snake were slithering around her body—"is your last warning. I knew your father. I give you a last warning for his sake, for the honor due a fellow soldier, nothing more."

He stepped out into the sunlight, which made every angle on his face as rough as the stone on the staircase around them, but fortunately Louise didn't see that. She was weeping too hard. She listened to his retreating footsteps. She had to sit down on the bench that was pushed back into the underside curve of the staircase. She had to cry for a long time before she could compose herself enough to simply find the wits to stand up and walk away.

That night, Henriette swept into the ballroom to see her mother sitting at one end on the raised dais between the huge bronze satyrs there, an irony considering how pious Henriette's mother was. Radiant in midnight blue and matching dyed feathers and wonderful dark pearls Philippe had given her, Henriette moved forward smilingly and people watched, as always they did, but it seemed to her their eyes were upon her in a new way. You'll be blamed, said the duchess, not he. Well, why wouldn't they stare after Louis's impulsive behavior this afternoon?

"Finally, I see you," her mother said to her.

Her mother was the daughter of France's renowned King Henri IV, was sister of King Louis XIII, was widow of England's King Charles I, queen of England until her son married. Once a beauty, bitterness had eroded into age. She turned her cheek to be kissed, and Henriette did so.

"I have duties too, now, Mother," Henriette said. "And I wasn't feeling well. The journey didn't agree with me."

"It didn't? Only His Majesty's regard pleases you these days?"

It begins, thought Henriette. She ground her teeth and sat down on a stool at her mother's feet in a liquid rush of satin skirts and petticoats.

"As it must all of us. We all are his loyal subjects."

"Who knew when I bore you," her mother lamented, "that God would leave me only you and your two eldest brothers? Who knew the heartache I would suffer? Not that I complain. I bear all things as the will of God. Not my will but His. Always."

Henriette saw Guy looking her way and made a signal with her fan. He was standing before her in moments, frowning down at her, but she didn't care as long as he rescued her from her mother.

"I have a private message for you from the Duchess de Chevreuse," she said to him.

"Do I interrupt?" Guy asked, looking from mother to daughter.

"You do," said Henriette's mother.

"Nonsense," said Henriette, speaking over her mother.

"You will call on me tomorrow, my dear. Early." Her mother's voice was icy.

"Of course, Mother."

Henriette dragged Guy across the ballroom and out its doors and through a corridor until they were at the private balcony. "I am going to scream at the moon, and you are going to watch me silently," she told him.

In spite of himself, Guy smiled. "I wish I didn't find you adorable," he said.

"I do too." She lifted her face to the stars, the half-circle of moon there. It was that bewitching hour before complete darkness. What am I going to do? she thought. I can't bear all these people picking at me. Can Louis command them away? Can he command their silence? I am already a scandal. I can see it in Guy's silence, in my mother's face, in Louis's mother's face. Can I bear it? Do I wish to? Can love bear all things? On her visit to England the previous year, a young duke, flirting to woo her, had read to her from the English Bible, translating into French as he read each verse about charity, about love, which beareth all things, believeth all things, hopeth all things, endureth all things. Could it be true? She heard trumpets sounding. Louis had arrived. He'd be looking for her. And where was she? Off on a balcony with the wild Count de Guiche. And then an idea occurred to her.

"You're with child," said Guy.

"If I am, it is no concern of yours."

"I beg to disagree. Whatever you do is my concern. I love you."

The second man this day to say those words. When Louis said them later, that would be three. Oh, she didn't wish to deal with Philippe in bed tonight. How late could she encourage the court to stay up? Forever?

"Let's go for a ride." She felt impulsive, wild, trapped.

"What? Now?"

"As soon as we can. Go and ask His Majesty if he will bear with Madame's wishing a twilight ride under the rising stars."

"You'll ride in a carriage, not on horseback."

"I will?"

"For the child's sake. Monsieur must have his son and heir."

"I will if you go away and do as I say."

"Kiss me."

"No."

He laughed again.

"Make certain Monsieur drinks too much tonight." She faced him squarely.

Knowing they were bargaining, that someday he'd demand a payment—there was a part of her that liked that in him—they met each other's eyes; then he went away to do as she asked.

Men ready to do whatever I command, she thought over a restless nervousness that threatened to send her into fits. I do like that. When am I old enough not to be lectured? she asked the stars. Now, they answered, just the way they had at the duchess's estate. You are Madame.

CHAPTER 20

Late that night, Louis waited for Henriette in front of the palace's
garden grotto, tucked away at one end of the Queen Mother's wing.
Everyone else was on the pond, in boats and gondolas, masked, at
his order, to make this tryst easier. When he heard her hurrying steps on
the path, his heart began to beat in his ears. He felt like a starved animal
scenting sustenance. He would die if he didn't kiss her. He stepped back
into the dark of the grotto itself, a wonderful Renaissance fantasy of a cave
with hundreds of pieces of tile and shell overhead marking out dogs and
fish and other beasts. What stonework there was had not been smoothed
to an even surface as it was everywhere else in the palace. Here, it showed
its harsh birth from larger stone. The stonework, the beasts, the tumble of
rocks outlining ovals in the ceiling were in a style called "primitive," and
that's how he felt this night, urgent and desperate to take her. A candle or
two burned in the niches of the walls and on the edges of the opening so
she wouldn't stumble over her long skirts.

She came into view, stepped hesitantly into the grotto, looking all
around her, not seeing him. He reached out a hand and dragged her into
the dark where he kissed her like a savage, letting his mouth travel to her
ears, to the long sides of her throat. He fell on his knees, pressed his face
into her stomach, groaning. Henriette ran her fingers over his face, over
the mask there and then his mouth. He bit her fingers.

"I feel like a deer being chased by hounds, Louis. Your mother was cold to
me the entire visit, and the English ambassador called at her insistence—"

Louis raised his head. "He didn't—"

"He did, and the Duchess de Chevreuse's priest invited me to confess,
and when I replied I had nothing to confess, he said pride might be foremost and spoke to me about the wiles of the world. Only the Duchess of
Chevreuse was kind to me."

"Kind to you?"

"Oh yes. She understands and is my friend, our friend, but she counsels discretion. And now my mother is here. Louis, I can't bear it, the lectures, the gossip! I love you, but perhaps we're being foolish."

He felt stunned and held tight to her hands and didn't reply.

"Everyone is watching us now. And today, well, you made your regard so evident. Everyone saw it and is talking about it tonight, talking about me."

Louis pulled her to kneeling in front of him, gripped her shoulders. "It's a sin before God, but it doesn't feel a sin in my heart. I don't know if I can give you up!"

"Listen, my sweet Majesty, my dear love, I've had a thought. It came to me tonight when I was out on the balcony with Guiche. We could flirt with other people, particularly you, make the court, your mother, think you admire many."

Pride reared its head, under it hurt and confusion. "What are you saying? Is this a way to tell me you don't care for me anymore?"

"It's a way for us to have what we want. We'll see each other in secret just as we've been doing, and we'll remain great friends in public, but you'll notice others. Only you have to promise me you won't fall in love with any of them." And then she laughed that same arch laugh she'd made in the summer pavilion, and he felt himself grow a little remote from her, which was a good thing, because he needed his wits not to grovel at her feet and beg her not to break his heart. He kissed her hard again, put his hand under the bell of her gown, felt the softness of her leg above her gartered stocking, began to move his hand farther. A part of him felt as cold as ice. He almost wanted to hurt her.

"I have to tell you something," she said. "I'm with child."

His hand stopped where it was. When he could speak, he said, "I congratulate you."

"What is it? Are you jealous? It's wonderful, don't you see? We may—" she hesitated, then rushed on, "do as we please, and there will be no problems. And now we have another place to tryst. The Duchess of Chevreuse offers her château." She smiled brilliantly into the dark, but Louis didn't answer.

That old intriguer, he thought, puts her hands on our love?

"You're angry? Oh, tell me you're not angry! It's for the best, don't you see?"

Louis brought her hands to his mouth and covered them with kisses to disguise his feelings. He'd thought she'd let him finally take her tonight. He'd thought she was as anxious for their coupling as he. With child? He tried to wrap his mind around those words. And the Duchess de Chevreuse as friend? Too much was happening. It was like being swept along in a raging current. He was having trouble keeping his head above water. "Perhaps your idea is a good one."

She hugged him. "Oh, it's the only way, my love! I'm convinced of it!"

"You must tell me who to notice. For me, there is no one but you." He spoke slowly. Despondency made him thick-witted.

"Madame!" Candles showed Louise, a darker shadow in the shadows of the grotto's entrance.

Henriette kissed Louis boldly, her tongue flicking and daring. Her hands swept his thighs. "The viscount will help us," she said. "We have the use of his château at any time. Or the duchess. Good-bye, my darling." And then she touched him in a way she never had before, a way that left him gasping like a fish flung out of the pond.

"Where's the Princess de Monaco?" Henriette asked Louise, as they hurried toward the pond to join the others.

"I don't know, Madame."

❧

Catherine sighed and arched back into the tree while she ground herself into Nicolas. They were like two moths mating, their cloaks surrounding them like wings, their hoods covering their heads.

"Harder," she said into the well of darkness their hoods made.

Nicolas bit her neck, his hands under the skirts of her gown, on her naked hips, holding her in delicious balance for the pleasure they were enjoying.

"My breasts," she said, "touch them."

He couldn't do that; their intricate geometry would go awry and spoil everything, but the command made him feel as if he were cold steel and he would pierce her in half. The legs around his waist held him tighter, and she groaned and began to bite at his neck.

When she began to scream a little, he covered her mouth with his, and continued to move against her until she shivered and clawed him and said "oh" over and over again. A few final thrusts, and he was done himself. They dropped to the ground, still tangled, their cloaks belling around them, their hoods covering them. He put his hands to the wet all around her thighs. She held on to the edges of his jacket, as if she would drop somewhere if she let go.

"Did anyone see us?" she asked.

"Only those who passed."

"Lovely," she answered.

"You like the danger?"

"Don't you?"

He laughed. "I believe I do. But then again, perhaps not. Your cousin looks as if he'd like to run someone through these days."

"Péguilin? Don't worry about him. You're my secret."

"I love secrets. I love collecting them even more. Can you make a copy of His Majesty's love notes to Madame?"

"If I wished to."

His hand found a breast, pushed back the fabric, pinched it cruelly. "Can I make you wish to?"

She reached up and kissed him, then let her tongue lick all around his lips. Her hands were flying here and there, and the next thing he knew, she was standing, hood over her head, a specter, silent and unknown except to herself. More slowly, he stood, not bothering to arrange his clothing. No one could see under the cloak. "Someday, I'd really like to do this in a bed."

The specter laughed. "It isn't half as much fun."

And then she was gone, melting into the dark of the trees of the gardens, among the other courtiers farther away, who'd given them their distance, the courtesy of court, where lovers must take their chances as they could.

It was late. Cinq Mars stood before Queen Anne, wrapped in shawls like a mummy of that ancient land of Egypt. Outside opened windows, he could hear the sound of laughter and talk. The young court played in the gardens like children. The Queen Mother looked fatigued and haggard, the way he must look.

"I think he should be moved," Cinq Mars repeated.

"And my answer is always the same. Where might be safe? Right now, he's hidden in plain sight. I blame you. Don't allow him out."

Cinq Mars shivered. This was part of his duty, to take the criticism from her who never saw the boy. It had been the cardinal who carried a mother's love for the child, always. Cinq Mars had confessed the escape. And he'd just told her of the unexpected visitors, but not that the boy had been seen. He didn't know why—or he did. The ruthless cruelty of her. He didn't want to be ordered to kill the girl. "He mustn't be cooped up like—"

"Do as I say. He isn't to go out anymore."

He'll die, he wanted to shout, but he knew she really desired that. He despised her for it.

"Be gone."

Cinq Mars bowed and went into another chamber. Her lady-in-waiting, her faithful dog, his dear love, as old and tired now as he was, and for what, whispered to him. "Have you need of anything? More coins?"

"He has need of her seeing him. Do his needs count for anything?"

Madame de Motteville pressed her lips together, held out a bag of coins like a supplicant.

"He's growing," Cinq Mars said. "We need to move him, sooner rather than later."

"I'll come and see him, soon, I promise."

They looked at each other, their dramas, their passions, their mistakes all there. Now there were simply the embers of duty, not enough sometimes, but all there was. When did we become old? thought Cinq Mars. His love for her flickered and finally caught fire. He felt its light. He put out his hand to her cheek, and she turned her face into his palm and kissed it.

"Will you—" She didn't finish, but her eyes told him everything. Gently, carefully, as if she would break, he pulled her into him, breathed the fragrance of her hair, graying now, like his. "I must leave before dawn."

She took him by the hand and led him to her chamber. They undressed, held one another, no passion between them, not for a while. First, they had to become used to one another again. When they finally made love, it was without the unthinking ease of their younger days, but its slowness had a sweetness all its own.

"I'm too fat," she said, but he kissed her mouth closed, kissed her eyelids. How tender was the touch of a beloved's skin. How could he have forgotten this? How did he endure without?

Before dawn, he strode down the king's road, staying under the shadow of the row of trees that outlined one side. He had a horse tied to a tree far down past the landscape canal. To his right, across the road, a stray gondola or two floated aimlessly. He'd had a maid of honor more than once, in that other court, under that other king, the father of this one. He'd thought the queen the most beautiful woman in the world, fiery and Spanish and dark-eyed. Then he'd met Motteville, and she'd taken the whole of his heart. If it had been to seduce him into their scheme, she had been seduced, too, their love ebbing and flowing with their meetings. With what joy he had looked forward to their trysts, joy a fainter glow now but enough there to warm a man's heart. His chest felt warm. He had run his hands over her plump flesh this night and worshipped her as best he could. His beloved. What a web deceit made, its strands strangling the innocent and the guilty alike.

Chapter 21

From a second-floor colonnade, Olympe watched Madame hurry across paving stones toward the huge, arched opening that would lead her to another part of the palace. Gone to call on her mother. Rumors were flying about why the queen of England had come to Fontainebleau, rumors that made Olympe wild with jealousy and malice. The court had stayed out until nearly dawn, but not the queen's ladies, never the queen's ladies. Back in the long, ornately decorated gallery that was the queen's, she stalked like a tiger toward Maria Teresa, who sat quietly embroidering with her ladies; lawn gowns for the *dauphin* must have their embroidery by the highest ladies in the land.

"Did His Majesty come to your bed late, Majesty?" Olympe asked.

Maria Teresa looked up from her needle. "Yes."

"Madame kept everyone out until dawn, I hear," said Olympe. "She has no thought for anything but her own pleasure."

There was a stir. Olympe turned. Louis walked toward them without his usual retinue. Had he heard her words? Her face turned a little pale.

"Who thinks only of their own pleasure?" he asked Olympe, no customary smile for her. His face looked drawn.

"I asked who thinks only of their own pleasure," he repeated when no one answered.

Maria Teresa held her breath, not certain what to do. She had never seen him angry, wasn't certain he was angry now, but his expression was stern as he gazed at the Countess de Soissons. She could feel her dwarves gathering at her back, as if to protect her. "You were out very late, my husband," she said. Did he think she never noticed?

"I was. But no one bears responsibility for that save me. I dislike the bearers of gossip," he looked around, holding the eyes in turn of each woman in the chamber. "The innocent are always the most hurt."

No fools as to what he meant, the ladies around the queen quickly lowered those eyes, even Olympe.

"Come, dear heart," he said to Maria Teresa, presenting his hand to her, giving her his best smile, "walk with me up and down the gallery and tell me how my *dauphin* treats you this morning."

Maria Teresa dropped her embroidery. Louis paused long enough to give Olympe a significant look, his face hard, his eyes showing a warning that no one could mistake, and then he led his wife away. Her ladies watched them smiling and talking to one another as they moved down the long, long length of the gallery. They were like the best of friends, Maria Teresa chattering away in Spanish, and Louis listening with grave courtesy. In the morning light coming through the tall, opened windows, he looked like a prince out of a folk tale.

The women felt a little afraid of him, and somehow that increased their desire. He had not shown them sternness before. They were aware in a way they had taken for granted before this morning that he was king of them all and that he could banish them from court with a simple command. That he would. As easily as that he'd established their place and his. They were to say nothing to the queen of any rumors about him and another woman. Even Olympe understood.

❧

Henriette hurried to the set of buildings where her mother was lodged. She'd managed to keep the court up nearly all night. They'd walked on the rampart above the ballroom, where there was a cupola and two very small, open, temple-like structures that could have graced a Roman city once upon a time. Last night was the first time she'd seen her mother since her wedding. I can't command your love to continue, Louis had written in a note this morning, and I cannot command mine to disappear.

Her mother sat now surrounded by her ladies, the old faithfuls who had kept her company in all the dreadful years and who were now rewarded. Her mother's gown was new, as were her jewels—the others having been sold years earlier for her father's sake. There were young girls who were maids of honor to her mother, part of the largesse of having a king with a country again as a son. But her mother's face was as bitter, as discontent as ever.

She can't stay here in England, her brother had told Henriette last year. She'll drive me mad. Of course, their mother disapproved of Charles's liaison with the wild Barbara Palmer, who did exactly as she pleased and seemed none the worse for it. But then Barbara Palmer wasn't a princess, bound by duty and birth. They'll break you, the duchess's words echoed in her mind. Her mother's dogs ran to her, and she knelt to pet them, dear things, old friends.

"You're late," her mother said.

"Do forgive me, Mama, I overslept."

Henriette continued to play with the dogs, as if she didn't notice that the space around her and her mother was emptying of ladies. Avoiding what was coming next, she cooed and talked to the dogs, but her mother indicated that she was to follow her, and they went into a small chamber off the gallery.

"I'll come to the point," said her mother. "Your husband has gone to his mother to complain of your behavior. You haven't been married four months and yet you flirt disgracefully. What are you and His Majesty thinking of?"

"We're not thinking of anything. There's nothing between us, Mother, but admiration and friendship. I make him laugh."

"You make him sigh. Do you think I'm blind? I watched last night. He couldn't take his eyes from you."

It was difficult for Henriette not to smile. "Really, I didn't notice."

"Minette, listen to me. You are young and don't know the snares of the world. You are playing with fire."

"I am carrying Monsieur's child, Mother. Do you really think I would do something unworthy?"

Queen Henrietta's expression changed entirely. She kissed her daughter. "My darling! My dear one! Already? It's quite, quite wonderful!"

"Yes, I think so too, though it's too early to share the news with the court."

"Well, you must certainly end these late nights. The swimming in the river must stop, too."

Another bar in the cage they wished to build for her loomed. "Not yet."

"Oh, you must be careful. If you lost it, you might be blamed like Queen Anne." Her mother leaned forward, savoring old gossip, the opportunity to tell it. "She lost at least two little ones sliding in the halls of the Louvre like a hoyden with the Duchess de Chevreuse."

"When was this?"

"A very long time ago, long before His Majesty and your Monsieur were born, and so you must be careful with yourself. My brother was furious with her, didn't forgive her. So, it's good I've come for a visit. We'll begin work this night on a christening gown for your child."

"I'm going to dance tonight, Mother, and the night afterward, and the night after that."

"Minette!"

"I don't want to be wrapped in cotton wool like a delicate vase."

"Have you made love to him?"

"Of course I've made love to my husband. How else—" She stopped, realizing what her mother had implied. Her face went red. "How dare you ask such a thing of me?"

"You need to do as I say. You need to stay quietly in your chambers—"

"Like the queen? Why do you think His Majesty enjoys my company?"

"You don't need the approval of His Majesty—"

"Are you quite mad? We all need his approval."

"Henriette, Queen Anne sent a special messenger to me she was so concerned. If you aren't in love with him, then what does it matter whether you spend time in his company? You are one of the presences of this court, and you must set an example—"

"As she did, with her lover the cardinal?"

"It isn't your place to judge others—"

"Others judge me! I'm pregnant and that should please you and her. There will be an heir. Isn't that my most important duty? To provide an heir! Well, I've done it! Now leave me alone before I miscarry from your quarreling!" She could hear her voice becoming higher, could feel hysteria rising.

"My darling, I simply don't want there to be any kind of gossip about you. It does such harm, Minette. People like to believe the worst."

"Too bad for them." She walked to the door.

"Stop, Minette. You must listen. Go to Saint-Cloud for the rest of the summer. That will end the talk." Saint-Cloud was her husband's beautiful estate on the outskirts of Paris.

Henriette walked out into the gallery. Her mother's ladies, their needles paused, had their eyes on her. Defiant, she walked by. Louis must understand. She would go mad if she were going to be the focus of all eyes all the time. She wanted to love him, she did love him, but this was awful. You'll break, said the duchess in one of their wonderful discussions. She was right. The scandal of their love fell on her shoulders, rather than his. It wasn't fair.

Her mother didn't bother to follow, went instead to a window to look out at the spreading gardens of this ornate palace. She had begged Anne to match Henriette and Louis, but Anne and her cardinal wouldn't deign to consider it. Charles wasn't on his throne yet. Henriette was the nobody princess. And Anne must have a Spaniard. Anyone with one eye in his head could have seen that Louis would be stimulated by his very French cousin. Ha. She laughed to herself.

All last night she'd been thinking, what's happened to the court? There was something lighthearted about it, a spirit of adventure and secret excitement that had not been there even after His Majesty's marriage. And now she realized: it was her daughter. Her daughter brought an atmosphere of fun, which Louis's marriage to the infanta had not achieved. The new queen had instituted nothing original, been content to leave things as they were. Dutiful. Too dutiful. She remembered the stir she herself had caused at the English court in the other life she'd once possessed. She'd turned everything topsy-turvy, and even while quarreling with her, her husband had fallen in love. Yes, Henriette inherited her charm. Anne was dreary, out of touch, behind the times, the queen she'd chosen for Louis little better. The times were being redefined by her daughter. Like mother, like daughter. If she hadn't been so angry at Henriette's foolishness, so worried for her mortal soul, she'd have congratulated her. The apple, indeed, did not fall far from the tree.

Late that evening the court walked again along the ramparts of the ballroom roof. Musicians were stationed in the gatehouse gallery, and the soaring swell of violins spilled out over the courtyard and moat, over the chimneys and blue roof tiles, into hearts, the music piercing and sweet. Nicolas leaned against a balustrade of the roof, enjoying the high spirits and élan all around him. This was how life should be lived. Beautiful music. Interesting, cultivated people. A grand palace as backdrop. In a secret compartment in his chambers there was a note from Queen Anne's confessor. Madame and her mother had had a serious discussion this afternoon. There was also a note from Queen Anne, telling him again how much she depended upon him to talk sense into His Majesty, asking him to call upon her the next day. And he'd finally finished buying the command of the Mediterranean galleys for a friend's son-in-law. The son-in-law was commander in name only. The galleys were Nicolas's. The seas were his. Someone had said whoever is master of the seas has great power on land. He now owned the commanders of the Atlantic and Mediterranean fleets. He didn't know why he had to, but he did. It was another triumph, another safeguard, just in case. All was ready for a tête-à-tête later with Catherine. In his chambers, wine cooled, sheets were turned back. He'd show her what delight could be had in a bed.

Sometime after midnight, Louise and Fanny sat with their backs against the steep stone steps of an outside staircase. Fanny was crying. Her clever, never-at-a-loss-for-words Fanny. Too much wine. She'd had a little too much herself. All she could think about was the musketeer's threat and the urge within her to tell someone what she'd seen. But who? Everything

seemed more frantic since Madame's return, gaiety forced, stretched, con-
trived, Madame the same way.

A shout rose up from the courtyard. Courtiers were walking along the
balustrade of the suspended garden, seeing who could keep his balance.
Fanny stopped crying long enough to ask, "What is it?"

Louise stood up carefully. "I think the Count de Guiche just fell in the
pond." She laughed, but Fanny began to cry harder than ever.

"What is it?" asked Louise. "Are you so in love with him?"

"Of course I am!" Fanny was fierce, as if there could be no other way
to be in love.

"You didn't—you haven't—"

"I did and I have and I'm glad. The world's different after you've done
it, Louise."

Sweet Mary, thought Louise, digesting the fact that Fanny was no
longer a virgin. A year ago, watching an Orléans princess sully her reputation, they'd made a vow to stay pure no matter what temptation brought
them.

"He's cruel," said Fanny. "Do you know what he makes me do? Deliver
love letters that he writes after we're finished. While I'm still lying on his
bed. Love letters for Madame. And he makes me do other things, too."

Love letters from the count? But Madame loved the king, thought
Louise. She felt deeply shocked. "Tell him no."

"If I do, he won't see me anymore. And if I don't see him I'll die." She
held both hands against her breast, as if the heart underneath was breaking apart.

"Tell him it hurts you to see him write the letters."

"I can't. I can't lose him."

Fanny lay now with her head in Louise's lap, and Louise stroked her
hair, her puffy, tear-streaked face. She'd woken up gasping last night, certain the musketeer was in her chamber. In the lantern-lit courtyard to the
right of them, the laughing, crowing, cock-of-the-walk courtiers had more
than one man among them wet now, and the women clustered around
them. Above the stars sparkled, as beautiful as the diamonds Cardinal
Mazarin had bequeathed those he loved. Louise smelled the fresh, clean
forest. Did she dare go riding tomorrow? Would the musketeer somehow be
watching? So Fanny hadn't saved herself for her husband. Was it the wine
that made her feel less shocked than she supposed she should feel? Was
Fanny different, tainted now that she wasn't pure? That's what the nuns
taught. She was supposed to shun Fanny, to lecture her, to tell a priest, but
she wouldn't do any of those things. She didn't love her friend any less. It
was all very confusing. She'd need to ride out into the quiet of the forest to
sort it all out, only now she was afraid of riding out, afraid of encountering

the musketeer. It felt like the boy was doomed, that somehow she had failed him. She must break her invisible leash, tell someone. But who? She felt very wise and very stupid all at the same time. That was the lovely thing about wine. One didn't mind.

The next morning, Henriette stared at a towering vase of roses and lilies as she thought about her dilemma. She and Louis had come close to a serious quarrel during the night. Are you saying you want to end this? Then do it, he demanded. I'm saying it hurts me to be talked of, she'd wept. She drummed her fingers on the table at which she sat. So. Who should she suggest for him to flirt with? Definitely not the Countess de Soissons. Nor the queen's stunning maid of honor, though Athénaïs de Tonnay-Charente was very pleasant and certainly made Henriette laugh with her wit. But there was a single-mindedness about her that made Henriette wary. Two faces floated into her mind from among the young ladies all about. One was lovely but not lively, a Miss de Pon. The other was lively, but not lovely, a Miss de Chimerault. Yes, excellent, neither too sultry nor too beautiful. Now, who else? There ought to be one more. Everyone said good things came in threes.

There was a soft knock at the door, then Louise poked her head through the opening. "Shall I take the dogs?"

The dogs bounded out from under Henriette's feet, prancing and whimpering for Louise. So, thought Henriette. The decision was made. The third would be Louise. A perverse sense of mischief came up in her. This would raise Louise to a new level. She might even be able to get a decent husband from it, if her mother had any sense. She felt pleased with herself. It was her duty as a princess to see about her ladies, and she was doing just that.

"Wait a moment. I have something for you to deliver." She dipped the quill pen in ink and wrote the three names. She folded the letter and dropped sealing wax on it, using the ring Louis had given her to press into the wax. She smiled. Louis would just have to do his duty. Surely flirting with others wouldn't be too onerous. It wasn't for her.

Louis and Colbert met in the chamber of books.

"The taxes are coming in?" Dressed in a leather jacket and boots, a whip in his hand, Louis was going hunting as soon as his council meeting was finished. But more and more, he felt he must see Colbert, steady Colbert, secretive Colbert, stalwart Colbert. I depend on him, Louis thought, and he breathed a little more deeply at the thought of all that could go wrong if his dependence was ill chosen.

"Taxes dribble in slowly. About Her Majesty, the Queen Mother—" Colbert cleared his throat, then without a word gave the king a copy of a letter.

Louis read his mother's latest note to the Viscount Nicolas. There spilled out on the page were all her current frets, that Colbert might not be a friend to the viscount and to beware of him, that Henriette was with child, that there could be a terrible scandal, which must be avoided at all costs. On and on she went, writing of things Louis wished she had not.

"What is this reference to the Marquis de Créqui?" Louis asked. "Isn't he the new commander of my galleys in the Mediterranean?"

"He who is master of the seas has great power on land," answered Colbert.

"Who said that?"

"The late, great Cardinal Richelieu."

"Find out about this Créqui." Louis picked up one of Philippe's notes to the viscount, skimmed it. It was Philippe's usual, a demand to be on the council, but grateful for any scrap of regard from the viscount.

Face expressionless, Colbert handed over a note from Henriette in which she thanked the viscount for his kindness and understanding and little gifts. His pledge of loyalty to her meant so much, she wrote.

"How vital the viscount seems to be to my family," said Louis. "I hope they can survive without him. Give me the plan of arrest."

In September, in the heart of the province that was most loyal to the viscount, Louis would order him arrested. He and Colbert had begun to plan a coup; swift and paralyzing is what they hoped for. A mobilization of troops and intendants the day of the arrest, the troops to stay in provinces through October. All the viscount's houses and records sealed. Those who handled the kingdom's taxing to give over accounts and documents at once. Total abolition of the office of superintendent of finance. Louis to become superintendent of finance. With the viscount's arrest, money could disappear, trade wither. And there could be war.

Colbert struck a flint to some tinder to burn the latest detail of their plan, and once the sparks had taken hold, neither he nor Louis said a word until it was burned to ash.

"Majesty, if I might beg one more indulgence?"

"Anything."

Carefully, Colbert repeated the Latin phrase Nicolas had thrown at him. "*Contra felicem vix deus vires habet.* Would you translate that for me?"

"Against a lucky man, a god scarcely has power."

Colbert flushed.

"Is something wrong?" asked Louis.

"No, merely my own ignorance. I was told it meant evil to him who evil thinks."

Louis gathered up his gloves and riding crop.

"Good luck with the hunt, sire," Colbert said.

"*Alea iacta est,*" replied Louis, then, "The die has been cast. The Roman general Caesar said it as he crossed the Rubicon River. He won his battle. We'll win ours."

He was off to hunt; only riding, only hunting, the motion of the chase, the exhaustion of hours in the saddle, could soothe him and keep him in one piece for the charade of another evening ahead of him. He was riding the legs off his horses. How many evenings until September? How many evenings until he held Henriette naked? She'd sent him a list with three names, women he was to flirt with. Would that satisfy her? Or would there be yet another demand? There was no safety in this love of theirs, only risk. He'd thought she understood that.

Colbert sat where he was for a long time after the king was gone, not a muscle on his face displaying the fire that blazed inside. What a king he will make, Mazarin had prophesized. Let's pray we can grow him to manhood. The Queen Mother would have burst into fury to read the indiscretion of her family, yet His Majesty scarcely blinked. He had extraordinary command over himself. You have guided him to greatness, Colbert told the memory of the man who had been his own mentor. Was there a possibility the kingdom could be cleansed, the past overcome? The viscount's spies were better than theirs.

❧❧❧

In the next week, Louis flirted like mad with the first two names on Henriette's list. The court was abuzz, but Louis was bored. He met one of them now out on the private terrace above the golden gate, just off the ballroom. Fontainebleau's gardens spread out before him.

"What a lovely night," the young woman beside him, a Miss de Pon, trilled, excited beyond words to be singled out by him again.

"All nights at Fontainebleau are lovely. You're lovely, mademoiselle." I sound like a bad actor, thought Louis.

She lowered her eyes but not before he saw in the light of the burning torches on this balcony that he could kiss her if he wished. He leaned forward and quickly brushed her lips with his own. She caught his arm and leaned her mouth into his, and they kissed more deeply. It wasn't that it was distasteful. How could a lovely young woman's mouth be distasteful?

But there was some cool, aesthetic part of him offended. She opened like a flower because he was king.

"You'd better go in now," he told her.

He waited a while, then walked back into chambers lit by wall sconces and chandeliers, sat down by his wife, picked up her gloved hand and kissed it, and held it against his cheek while he talked to her.

"My dear Queen," he said, "we didn't find the stag the dogs scented today, though we rode for miles, all the way to Versailles and back. The beast had a rack of ten points, which would be a worthy addition to the gallery of stags, wouldn't it? I'm very tired tonight." He looked at her. "Take my *dauphin* to bed and I'll come soon to hold you both in my arms. I'll order my handsomest cavalier to escort you," he told her, pointing to Vardes, and the tall, rakish marquis was bowing to Maria Teresa in less than a moment. Proudly, she gave Vardes her hand. Proudly, she walked with him to the huge doors that would take them to the bedchambers. Proudly, she thought, I am the most fortunate woman in the world. Surely, her example was a light unto this vain court.

Henriette had been standing with Guy, engaging in a little flirtation of her own. As the queen's ladies disappeared from sight, she tapped Guy on the arm. "Go away."

"I don't wish to flirt with others," Louis told her when they stood together in one of the ballroom arches.

Henriette laughed, secretly delighted. "Walk me over to Monsieur. Now tell me why not? Miss de Pon is lovely."

"Yes."

"Did she let you kiss her?" She cut her eyes toward Louis and then away. "I can't stand it if you kiss them, Louis."

"I didn't want to, and it wasn't pleasant." A lie. It was pleasant, but it hadn't any meaning; didn't she understand his yearning for something deep, something splendid, something grand and significant? How long did she expect him to stay on the leash she'd created?

They walked to Philippe, standing with his friends. "Monsieur," Louis twirled Henriette toward her husband, "I reluctantly bring you your beautiful wife, as ordered by her."

Philippe was silent. He felt sometimes as if he were being pulled to pieces. Your wife is unfaithful, the Chevalier de Lorraine said. Guy swore she wasn't. Louis taunts you, he said. Don't allow it.

"Remind your friends," said Louis without looking at Guy, "that frowns are a discourtesy in this court." He walked away.

"That remark was for you." Henriette tapped Guy sharply again on the arm with her fan. He took the fan from her and cracked it in pieces. Lorraine laughed.

"How dare you! Monsieur, I command you to stop being friends with this boor who calls himself a gentleman!" She faced Lorraine, who looked quite beautiful tonight, an amethyst in one ear, a sapphire in the other. "And this wasp. I know what you say about me, wasp. It is ungallant and unkind." She turned to Choisy. "Take me for a walk."

Guy offered his arm.

"Not you. I think I may hate you." She looked again at Lorraine. "I know I hate you. Come, Choisy."

"Why do you do things like this?" Philippe took the broken fan from Guy. "Ivory and jade. What a waste."

"I do it because you don't."

"Bravo," said Lorraine. "He needs to be firm with her."

"Your presence and your inept advice are unnecessary." Guy took a step toward Lorraine, who, with a flutter of white hands, lost himself in the crowd.

"Don't allow the chevalier to insult Madame openly. It's degrading to you," Guy told Philippe.

"At least he comforts me in my dismay and confusion, which is more than I can say for you these days. You're sullen and gloomy again."

"I'll have the fan repaired tomorrow and send her four more."

"Walk with me out onto the terrace," Philippe said. And when they stood in the moonlight, staring out at the road that ran straight as an arrow beside the pond and led to stables and forest and heath beyond, he put his hand on Guy's. Guy leaned into the iron railings, holding on to them hard.

"Kiss me."

"No."

"For old time's sake?"

"No."

"Is the child mine?"

Guy turned and looked at his prince, his childhood companion, his sometimes lover, his beautiful and gifted and wounded friend.

"Tell me the truth."

Guy went down on one knee, the torchlight playing over the even angles of his face. "It is your child. They are not lovers." Yet, he kept himself from saying. Call Louis out, he wanted to shout. Demand honor. But he'd begun to despair that Philippe would never honor himself.

"Darling," said Philippe.

"Don't!"

"My wife is correct. You really are a boor." Philippe went back inside the ballroom to stand beside his mother, who stayed up these days, keeping an eye out, he knew, but perhaps it was too late. Madame de Choisy had everyone in gales of laughter with tales about one of her footmen.

Philippe's heart ached. Did Louis really love Henriette? Lorraine said no. Why did Louis not throw him some small bone, some scrap of responsibility that said, yes, you, flawed as you are, are worthy, too. All the Merciful Saints in heaven, if he had, Philippe would have fallen to his knees and worshipped him. Guy had his heart, the whole of it, except for Louis's portion. His big, brave, perfect older brother. His big, brave, perfect friend. Why didn't either of them appreciate his admiration? Was he so awful? So perverse? So beyond love? Was that why Henriette admired Louis? Hadn't he always known that he would lose her? He hadn't expected to care so much was all. The jest was on him.

As always.

He grabbed a goblet of wine from a passing servant, drained it, and immediately told a lightly risqué joke about a groom and the lady-in-waiting. His mother and Madame de Choisy laughed like witches at his expert mimic of both the groom and the lady, and he did, too, but only with his mouth.

Hours later, when he'd drunk so much that he was sober again, he stared at the door that opened to Henriette's chambers. In his mind, he saw himself walking through it, climbing into bed beside her, and pretending nothing had ever happened. If he pretended hard enough, wouldn't it all just go away? But in a few hours, she and Louis would look at one another, and it would be evident they were in love. He was the fool in this drama. Molière knew that: no one was more amusing in a play than the betrayed husband. And had he really been betrayed? Hadn't it always been a dream that he and Henriette would settle into their life like two doves and never stray? She'd simply strayed first, hadn't she? Perhaps, one day, he could forgive that.

His carriage was waiting below to take him to Paris, to another life he lived there, a life he'd ignored for a time, but it was his real life. Not this. Never this, except in daydreams and the hopes of others, including himself.

Chapter 22

There was a light knock on the door, and Louis's valet, La Porte, opened his eyes. He dozed in a chair, having learned to do so years ago, until His Majesty should be ready for him. But this wasn't His Majesty. Swaying slightly, Miss de la Baume le Blanc stood in the hall, along with La Grande Mademoiselle and Miss de Montalais. Tipsy, thought the valet, and sniffed.

"I—I know it's late, La Porte." Louise concentrated on not slurring her words.

"We come to see the dog," announced La Grande.

The valet bowed, precise in his movement. "Madame Belle will be delighted to receive you."

He led them to the huge cushion where Louis's favorite dog lay. Louise plopped down in a jumble of skirts and put her hand to Belle's nose. There was a large bandage on the dog's abdomen.

"Her nose still feels warm, La Porte. I don't think the new sticking plaster is working." Louise put her face close to Belle's. "How are you, my lady? May I pet you, your highness? I'll be gentle."

"What happened to the herb compress she made?" asked La Grande.

"His Majesty's physicians thought it unsuitable," answered La Porte. "They made their own"—he gestured toward the dog—"as you see."

Louise began to lightly stroke the dog's head, and after a time, with a groan, the dog shifted herself so that her head was in Louise's lap. "I don't think she's better," she said.

"I don't think so either." La Porte looked around him, suddenly aware he and Louise were alone. Where were the other two? He found them in His Majesty's bedchamber, La Grande rifling through a drawer and the other one dancing around chairs.

"Forgive me, Grande Mademoiselle, but what are you doing?"

"I'm writing His Majesty a note, or I will when I find paper...ah, here it is. Go away, little man. I don't take questions as to my behavior from valets."

"You shouldn't be in here," La Porte hissed, but he went back to the antechamber as ordered. The dog had gone back to sleep in Louise's lap, and she had her eyes closed and was stroking Belle's head. "They're in His Majesty's bedchamber. It isn't proper," he told her.

Carefully, Louise moved Belle's head, stood up. The dog had slobbered on the skirt of her gown, and she looked down at the stain.

"If you'll have your maid bring your gown tomorrow, we'll clean that," said La Porte.

"Does he know?"

There was only one "he" in La Porte's world. He pursed his lips, smoothed at the nonexistent wrinkles in his coat. The first thing His Majesty did when he entered his chambers was to come immediately here and visit Belle. If he didn't, she would limp to him, and neither La Porte nor His Majesty could bear that. "Who can say?"

"Don't you think he should know? There must be time for him to say good-bye, don't you think, La Porte?"

"It isn't my place to suggest such."

Louise blinked. La Porte felt as if he'd slapped her.

"Of course. Nor mine. The physicians know best. Fanny! Your highness! Where are you?"

The pair appeared framed in a doorway.

"I'm so drunk," Fanny said.

"Give this to His Majesty." La Grande held out a note.

La Porte opened the door. Louise was the last out.

"You'll come tomorrow?" he called to her retreating figure.

She turned, her skirts swirling. "Yes."

La Porte settled himself in his chair. Belle's eyes were open. A daughter had come to lie beside her. A son sat near her head. The other son La Porte could see standing at attention at a door. His Majesty was coming. La Porte stood up, walked toward the bedchamber.

"He'll be here soon," he said to Belle as he passed her. "Yes, my angel, I thought that would please you. He'll be here in just a moment. Just wait there."

But Belle was already straining to stand. Her tail had begun to wag, getting ready to greet her beloved master, as was La Porte.

CHAPTER 23

The next morning, feeling hemmed in and hungry for her wild forest rides, Louise tried to be content with a jaunt to the convent to visit Julie. She found the child in the garden that was part of the convent, Julie's task to find and discard snails that dared think tiny lettuces or beans might be shared. The garden here was famous. Those who had little or nothing might knock upon the door in one of its walls and be assured of departing with a basket filled to the brim with whatever was ripe for harvest.

She and Julie sat under the shade of one of the old apple trees that rimmed the garden, and Louise unfolded a handkerchief to reveal rich, flaky rolls she'd brought from the palace kitchens. As Julie crammed as much of one as she was able into her mouth—the nuns' fare here was plain—Louise talked to her of Madame's return, of the king's sick dog, of how she'd torn the lace collar of her favorite dress. She chatted idly, comforted a little by Julie's happiness with the rolls, by the spreading of the limbs of the tree against which they leaned, by the sight of nuns hoeing in the garden.

"I'll sew it for you," trilled Julie. "My stitches are more and more even, Mother Superior says."

"Well, wonderful. If you keep practicing your stitches, when I marry, you shall come with me and be my maidservant."

"And my brothers? And my mother?"

Oh dear, thought Louise, but she smiled. "Perhaps."

Julie beamed at her as if it were settled and reached for the last roll.

Louise pleated a piece of her gown, her mind gnawing again at the problem that was the boy. "If you had a terrible secret," she heard herself saying, "that you'd been warned not to tell, but you had to tell someone or die, what would you do?" How silly I am, thought Louise, to be talking to a child about this, but nonetheless she fastened anxious eyes on Julie's face.

"I'd tell Mama."

"What if you couldn't tell your mother?"

"I'd tell her." Julie pointed to the figure of the Mother Superior of the order, in the garden now counting baskets of picked beans.

Louise hadn't considered that. Her eyes on the Mother Superior, looking brisk and efficient among the baskets of beans, she asked, "What if you couldn't tell her either?"

Julie's brow furrowed in thought. After a moment, she said, "I'd have you take me to the palace and tell His Majesty."

Louise laughed. "How very grand you are. His Majesty, indeed." She stood up, shook out crumbs of roll from her gown. "Come with me, young lady, and we'll go for a nice ride on my horse before I return."

"The Chevalier de Choisy, you could always tell him," said Julie a little later when they were cantering along a lane near the convent. "He has a nice heart."

❧❧❧

That afternoon, Maria Teresa on his arm, Louis walked into Henriette's antechamber. Word was Philippe had left for Paris. He hadn't asked permission, which was disrespectful to Louis, but Louis knew where he went and to whom. Make certain someone is watching over him, he'd ordered D'Artagnan. Philippe chose rough companions when he was in certain moods. The least Louis could do was keep him from physical hurt. The other hurt, the internal hurt, well, it was too late for that, wasn't it? Another Mazarinade pinned to a pillow, but this time the writer was all but caught. Shall I bring her to you? asked D'Artagnan. Not yet. He wanted time to think about precisely what he was going to do.

Embroidering, Henriette's maids of honor were set out like so many charming porcelain shepherdesses. Henriette waved and came forward to take Maria Teresa over to her mother.

Louis looked around like a hunter choosing his prey—to know the originator of the Mazarinades for certain had eased something in him—and stopped before Miss de la Baume le Blanc, the third name on Henriette's list and perhaps an accomplice to the nasty little messages that had so unsettled him. If she is involved, she has no idea of what they say, argued D'Artagnan. I'm certain of that. I'd imagine La Grande Mademoiselle told her they were important to you and must be kept secret. It was interesting to Louis that D'Artagnan defended Miss de la Baume le Blanc.

Louise, sewing away, her mind playing over the choices Julie had given her, imagining conversations she might have, didn't even notice that he was standing before her. But the chattering of friends sitting near, like birds throwing out song, had stopped, and she lifted her head because of it, and there he was. His Majesty, the king.

"How do you do this evening, Miss de la Baume le Blanc?"

Louise gaped at Louis, unable to think. And then the blush began, a deep telltale stain that edged out at the shoulders and traveled up her neck and face, so that in seconds she was a perspiring and crimson wreck.

"The evening is warm," he said, watching the blush spread with what seemed to her were cold eyes. "Your visits to my Belle are much appreciated."

She swallowed, unable to force a word past her throat, and again the silence between them and around them seemed larger than life. What an absolute fool I am, she thought to the immense and loud pounding of her heart.

"Well, good evening to you," Louis said, surrendering to her inability to answer, and to her relief he moved on.

"You idiot," Fanny whispered the moment she thought he was far enough away.

"I—I couldn't think," said Louise.

"Obviously."

"Well, that seemed singularly unsuccessful," said Henriette to Louis.

"Yes, she rides beautifully, is kind to dogs, but apparently can't speak. I'll go sit by Miss de Chimerault again." Chimerault was another name on Henriette's list.

Louis sounded grim, and Henriette smiled to herself.

"Where's Monsieur?" Louis asked. I wonder if you even care. The sudden judgment behind that thought shocked him.

Henriette was blithe. "Probably still sleeping. He drank like a fish last night." She brushed at a thread on Louis's tight jacket. There was nothing there, but she couldn't help herself. It was a small, secret gesture of ownership.

Across the chamber, Maria Teresa's eyes focused on that gesture.

"He loves her," hissed a dwarf in Spanish.

Something like an explosion went off inside Maria Teresa's head. She stood, dropping her plate of light snacks. At once, she was surrounded.

"Are you well, Your Majesty?"

"Is there pain, Your Majesty?"

Louis was among them, her hands in his, and his expression concerned.

"I want to go to my chambers," she said.

He took her up in his arms, carrying her all the way, and once there shooed her ladies away and sat on her bed and held her hand.

"Women flirt with you!" Maria Teresa said.

"Of course they do. You mustn't mind it. There's nothing to it. It's our way here."

"I don't like it."

"Oh, my sweetheart, I can't be rude. It's a game, nothing more. No one is more precious to me than you. You are an infanta of Spain and the queen of France. There is no one higher in my regard. You carry my *dauphin*, the heir."

Maria Teresa shivered, unable to withstand his dark eyes, the slight monastic sadness in his face.

Louis kissed her tears, hand-fed her the Moroccan dates she so loved, the Spanish olives and flat bread. When finally he left her, he hated himself. His heart felt stony and empty.

"Never!" she screamed to the dwarves. "You are never to imply his lack of duty again!" They resorted to expert tumbles and chases to make her laugh, but she didn't.

"I'll say nothing more, no matter what you pay," one of them said to Olympe later. They met in secret on the servants' stairs.

"Of course." Olympe gave the bag of coins, her face somber, but inside her was triumph. It didn't matter now what was denied. The queen would be watching all the time.

❦

Late that night, his mouth still bruised from Henriette's kisses and several from the Pon flirt, Louis listened to Colbert.

"Créqui is son-in-law to the Marquise du Plessis-Bellièvre," Colbert said.

Louis closed his eyes. The marquise was high on the list of those firmly allied with the viscount.

"Therefore, in essence, the Viscount Nicolas controls the Mediterranean fleet." Colbert's voice was, as always, dispassionate, detached from the news he delivered.

Therefore, in essence, the viscount was the French navy. The flesh on the back of Louis's neck prickled. "I'll arrest him now."

"We haven't the funds for war, sire. He has."

It was like being dropped into the water of a winter river.

"Let him empty a bit of his money chests on this fête of his—he's invited everyone, six thousand at last count, I hear. Let the taxes refill our coffers even a trifle. Let him give you the million you asked for."

There was a sharp knock at the door, and it opened. Lieutenant D'Artagnan hesitated at the sight of Colbert, but Louis nodded his head for him to speak.

"Monsieur is in Paris at Madame Rouge's." Madame Rouge ran an expensive and exotic whorehouse for men and women and anyone with tastes in between. "There has been some"—D'Artagnan searched

for some word to cover the behavior of Philippe and his friends—
"awkward conduct."

"Is he hurt?"

"I'm afraid so. We've taken him to the Palais-Royal, and a physician is
attending him."

"Seriously hurt?"

D'Artagnan shook his head, thinking, there are levels of hurt, seen
and unseen.

"When he wakes up tomorrow, I want his confessor at his bedside."

"Yes, sir. Good night, sir."

When D'Artagnan was gone, Louis said, "The viscount's drawn a noose
around my neck. It lies loosely. He thinks it lies there without my knowledge, but all he has to do is tighten it, and I choke."

Colbert made no answer. It seemed wisest not to.

❧

The next afternoon Louis again greeted Louise, and again she was unable
to be anything but silent, gazing down at her sewing after one quick flick of
her eyes upward at him. He strode away, angry at being ignored, but something made him turn around and look back at her, and she was staring after
him, a strained expression on her face. He felt something he couldn't put
words to. Then Henriette was at his side, wanting to show him a new song
she'd learned, and the afternoon whiled away its hours in music, a whiling
away he loved, but every so often he would raise his eyes to Louise's, and
for just a second, perhaps less, they'd stare at each other and then drop
their eyes or look elsewhere.

"If he ever deigns to speak to you again, you have to say something,"
Fanny told her that evening, as they dressed in their best gowns and pearls
and pinched their cheeks since they couldn't put rouge upon them. "Come,
let's practice. Say, 'Good day to you, Your Majesty.' Go on. Say it."

And Louise did practice, imagining making him smile instead of frown.
She'd made an important decision. He was the one she was going to tell
about the boy.

But he didn't speak to her once during the whole evening. And where
was Choisy? Her champion, her companion, her adviser in these wars of ballroom flirting and maneuver had abandoned her. Off to Paris, I understand,
Madame de Choisy told her. He said he loved her, but where was he now
that she needed him? His Majesty was brave and gallant and wise for his
years and would know what to do about the boy. But he wasn't speaking to
her this night, and she hadn't the courage to initiate any conversation on her
own. Other ladies had his attention, but if he spoke to her again, she'd do it.

"I want her dismissed from court," Maria Teresa said. It had taken a day, but her mind was made up.

Anne, in the midst of details for the first small fête she'd given since the cardinal's death, drew in her breath sharply and put down the pen with which she had been busily matching presents to names. "That's impossible."

Maria Teresa began to cry. Anne moved from behind the table at which she sat, drew her daughter-in-law into her arms. "Hush now. What you ask simply isn't possible, nor is it necessary."

"He loves her! I know it!" Maria Teresa was shrill, and Anne could sense hysteria close.

"Nonsense! He loves you. Everyone knows that. It's all people talk of, his devotion to you." I'll say extra rosaries for this, thought Anne, dedicate a convent or something.

"Really?"

"Really. Come, help me with my fête tonight. I'm planning who is to get what prize. Which of your ladies do you want me to reward?" Spanish ricocheted between them, like balls from opponents on the tennis court.

"He's always talking with her."

"Of course he is. They grew up together. They're practically childhood friends, and don't forget, they're cousins."

"I'm his cousin," hissed Maria Teresa.

"Shall I choose the Countess de Soissons for an ivory fan or someone else? Miss de Chimerault? What have I said? Why are you weeping again, my dear? I must insist you stop. It's bad for the *dauphin*. Here, come kneel with me at my prayer stand, and we'll turn our thoughts and emotions in a more proper direction."

Both knelt, Anne pampering her creaking knees with pillows. The familiar murmur of prayers seemed to lull Maria Teresa for a time, but in the middle of them, she said, "You'll tell him not to talk to her so much? Tell him it isn't seemly."

Such has already been done, thought Anne, but there was a knock at the door, and Madame de Motteville glided in, leaned over to whisper in Anne's ear, but before she could finish, Henriette was there, her mother with her. Henriette seemed nonchalant and breezy, queen of this castle, thought Anne frostily. That must change. There was only one queen.

"I've brought my list of favorite ladies for you to reward, majesty—oh, good afternoon, Your Majesty." Henriette curtsied deeply to Maria Teresa.

"Tell her," Maria Teresa said to Anne.

"Tell me what?" asked Henriette, looking from one to the other.

"There's been talk," Anne said, "frivolous talk about you and His Majesty." Yet more frivolous talk, she managed, not without effort, to keep herself from saying.

Henriette gasped and stepped back.

"I was just telling our dear majesty," continued Anne, "that there was nothing to it but idle court gossip."

"My daughter is a princess of France and England," Henriette's mother sneered, "who knows her duty. There is nothing she would do that is dishonorable."

"And our queen," said Anne, iron in her voice, "is a princess of Spain as well as queen of us all, and she carries the *dauphin* of France under her heart, and I will not have her disturbed in the least way!"

"Disturbed!" cried Henriette. "I am disturbing? I, too, carry a child, a prince of the blood. What of my upset?"

And then she swooned to the ground, and the three queens stood staring at her for what seemed like a long moment before Maria Teresa staggered backward and fell into a heap of silk skirts herself.

Well, wonderful, thought Anne bitterly.

Bent over her daughter, chafing her hands, Henriette's mother said to Anne through gritted teeth, "If she loses this baby, I will never forgive you!"

Anne knelt over Maria Teresa. "If our *dauphin* is hurt in any way, His Majesty will never forgive you or her! Nor will I!"

Later, when both young women had been revived, and there had been more tears, but also a little sweet brandy swallowed by the expectant mothers, the three queens and Henriette sat alone again in Anne's closet. There had been a great deal of fussing and oh-noing over both young women by Anne's ladies-in-waiting, perhaps more than was good for them, and both were feeling fragile and righteous.

"I've sent for my confessor," said Anne. "He's going to pray with us."

Henriette stood up as if she'd just been pricked by a nettle. "I don't want your confessor. I have my own. I'm going to my chambers."

"I command you," said Anne in a voice that brooked no refusal, "to assure Her Majesty that what had been said is idle gossip and nothing more."

Without looking at Maria Teresa, Henriette jerked into a small curtsey, the gesture just on the edge of complete rudeness by court standards. "It's idle gossip, Your Majesty. I am your servant in all things, I'm sure."

And then she held out her hand for her mother, and the two of them left the chamber arm in arm.

"There." Anne leaned over and patted Maria Teresa's hand.

"She has no manners," said Maria Teresa.

But Anne's confessor was stepping into the closet, and Anne told him that there had been a small quarrel between the sisters-in-law and that they needed his guidance not to harbor hard hearts, yet didn't listen to a word of his slick homily about sins of pride and listening to gossip. All she could think about was that this affair between Louis and Henriette, whatever it was, was beginning to create just what she'd dreaded.

The confessor was gone; Maria Teresa seemed calmer.

Anne looked down at her hands, then said what she must, "You know you mustn't speak of this to His Majesty."

Looking very plain, very grumpy, and very stubborn, Maria Teresa made no reply.

Anne couldn't bring herself to tell her that it wasn't a good idea to point out a woman and then tell a man not to notice her, particularly a man as proud as her son. "He wouldn't be happy at this quarrel," she said instead. "He will think it beneath the dignity of a Spanish princess to think ill of anyone."

Maria Teresa blushed and then nodded her head; her years of isolation and ritual, her pride in her birth, gave her no choice but to believe.

Once alone, Anne went to her window and stared out at her gardens, at blossoming vines and lilies, at basil and carnations, without seeing any of them. What a ghastly little scene to have been party to, she thought. This was what she'd been trying to avoid, why she'd taken Madame away, so things might cool and Henriette might be brought to a sense of consequence. If Maria Teresa was suspicious, this little affair had already done enough damage. What else to do? She sent for the viscount, needing someone to talk to, someone to shoulder the responsibility of this not exploding in their faces and sending clouds of scandal all the way to Rome and the Vatican's practical, political heart.

"It's too funny." Athénaïs sat with Fanny and Louise the next afternoon, abandoning for the moment her own band of companions. In fact, she joined Fanny and Louise now whenever possible. I like you both so much, she told them, and both were flattered to have the approval and attention of a duke's daughter. They were all in the queen's gallery, maids of honor and ladies-in-waiting gathered yet again to sew like nuns on christening clothes for the *dauphin*. The combined presence of the two older queens was affecting the younger court, settling it down, dispersing heedless, heady vigor. One might say, it was becoming boring.

"Her father simply appeared this afternoon and ordered her trunk packed. He called upon the Countess of Soissons," Athénaïs continued, "and then left within the hour. Poor dear Pon was livid, weeping in our bedchamber in rage, but what could she do? Her father insisted she had to leave. I helped her to pack. Poor thing."

"So Pon is out of the game," said Fanny.

"Was she ever in?" Athénaïs laughed.

"His Majesty liked her," said Louise. She felt sorry for Miss de Pon.

"Well, it is true that His Majesty did seem to notice her," agreed Athénaïs, "but she has been saved by her father, as if dancing with His Majesty were fatal."

"Silly, isn't it?" agreed Fanny, and when Athénaïs went away to gleefully spread the gossip with another cluster of women, Fanny said to Louise, "I admire Athénaïs, I really do, but she would give her back teeth for an extra dance with His Majesty, and as for going out into the gardens with him, she'd lead the way and kiss him first, I bet."

"That's spiteful."

"Oh, open your eyes, and if he deigns to talk to you again, open your mouth."

Henriette and Catherine discussed the maid of honor's departure at one long end of the gallery under a tapestry of Ulysses' faithful wife, Penelope.

"I feel at fault. It's terrible that her father's taking her away," Henriette said.

"It will give the court something to chew on," said Catherine. "Better her than you. What an extreme reaction, though. Wouldn't that be awful, to be swept from court like that? And she must be devastated, particularly since she thinks she has His Majesty's interest."

Both shuddered. This was the center of the world, but a father or a brother or a husband could remove you from it if they so desired. It wasn't a question of fairness; it was life. Henriette thought about Philippe, thought about the fact that he hadn't ordered her away to one of his estates. I'm going to be kinder when he returns, she thought. She was on edge. Act the way you would if you were innocent, advised Catherine. She was innocent. Some kisses, some unwise words, that was all she'd done. This wasn't her fault, not all of it. Too many people wished to blame her, and her alone.

❧❧❧

Later, near to dusk, cloaked and masked, Catherine walked to Nicolas's house in the minister's courtyard of the palace.

"Can you imagine it?" she said, pacing up and down his chamber as she described the quarrel among the women of the royal family. "Queen Anne demanded that she apologize. Madame was beside herself, and as for her mother, well, she swears she will never speak to Queen Anne again. In fact, she's ordered her trunks packed and is leaving tomorrow morning early, which is, as Madame says, the one blessing out of all this. But the insult, the indignity is just too much! Madame says she will not talk to Queen Anne or Her Majesty willingly again."

"Has she spoken to His Majesty?"

"She sent a note."

"And his response?"

"He hasn't responded."

"If I may say so, Madame needs to tread lightly around this, Catherine."

Her expression was disdainful. Nicolas made a steeple with his fingers and regarded her over them. How strong-willed she is, he thought. She and her brother needed something large like a war to be happy. "When a man's mistress begins to make trouble, a man may choose to let her go," he said.

"She isn't his mistress yet."

"She'd have more power if she were. What is she waiting for?"

"What fools you all are. Ruled by that thing between your legs."

"We're only ruled by it until we get what we want. Then we can be remarkably cool-headed."

Catherine knelt before him in a rush of fabric and skirts. "What do you know? What has His Majesty said? Is he angry with Madame?"

"He hasn't done me the honor of sharing his state of mind." Queen Anne had, however, but that was not something Catherine or anyone needed to know. "I simply advise you and Madame to play this carefully." This was going to be a massive storm if the principals weren't more discreet, he thought. Queen Anne was furious, ready to do anything to see it ended.

"Tell Madame I have a shipment from Italy. In it are many beautiful things Her Majesty might admire, relics of saints' bones, rosaries, prayer books. A gift will make her apology seem more genuine. She must reassure the queen, Catherine. If she were wise, she'd throw herself at the queen's feet and beg forgiveness for being too flirtatious, or too flighty, or something. His Majesty is not going to be happy if his queen is not happy. Advise Madame to think about that. Advise Madame to take love to its next level. Now, that being said, put your arms around me and take our love there."

"Are you remarkably cool-headed?"

"Never when I am with you."

Later, when Catherine slipped back to Madame's part of the palace, she found Henriette crying.

"Look what he writes me," Henriette said.

Catherine read the words scrawled on the note.

It pains me that you have quarreled with my mother and Her Majesty, the queen. I don't want unhappiness among the women I hold dear to my heart.

"He blames me!" said Henriette. "I hate him!"

✵✵✵✵

Queen Anne held her fête, a lottery in her gallery, the next evening. Her chambers were soon crowded with courtiers come to enjoy the fun and largesse. Cardinal Mazarin had made lotteries all the fashion, and the gifts he'd given at his had been fantastic. One drew tickets to win anything from diamond earrings to painted fans, or rare crystal goblets or white wax candles or embroidered gloves. These lotteries were staged. Only select personages received the truly magnificent gifts, though Cardinal Mazarin had always insisted that one or two of the prizes go randomly. Let the fates decide, he'd say. The Queen Mother's tickets were as exquisite as some of the gifts, hand-painted, scenes of the gardens at Fontainebleau on one side, a large, inked number on the other.

Before the lottery began, everyone settled back to watch another snippet of the ballet Henriette would host in just two weeks. Half the court was dancing in it, and the other half was jealous not to be.

Guy and Henriette danced, wearing the costumes they would wear in the ballet, graceful together, Henriette as light on her feet as some wisp in the wind. All eyes were on her, admiring, and even Philippe, who showed up in the middle with his arm in a sling, applauded when the performance was finished.

Running over to Philippe when their dance had ended, Henriette said, "How was Paris?"

"It's done me a world of good."

"Did you miss me?"

"As much as you missed me, I'm certain."

She touched the sling. "What happened to you?"

"Exuberance unparalleled."

Henriette stepped back, the ironic tone in his voice unsettling, new between them. "Will you do me the honor to inform me the next time you're leaving?"

He didn't answer.

"I'm going to flirt only with you this evening," she cajoled.

"Every man here will hate me."

She smiled, tossing her head, but inside she was becoming upset. His words were playful, but his eyes weren't.

Choisy found a seat by Louise.

"Why didn't you tell me you were going to Paris? I'd have sent a note to my mother for you to deliver," she said.

"Hush, the chamberlain is beginning to call numbers. Look at your ticket."

"Ooh's" and "ah's" and other cries of astonishment filled the gallery as jewelry and wines and porcelain began to be distributed. Maria Teresa held up a large cross of rubies and gold she'd just won.

"What's the Chevalier de Lorraine won?" asked Choisy, craning his neck to see. They could hear his exclamation from where they sat. "I must see. Come with me?"

"No, I'll stay where I am."

Louis looked down at the pair of diamond bracelets his ticket number had won, and then his eyes went to Louise, as they'd done all this evening. Her neck is like a swan's, thought Louis, rising long and graceful from her shoulders—when she isn't blushing, that is. If she was an intriguer, she was the best he'd seen, but some instinct told him D'Artagnan was right. She was an innocent, rare at court, true innocence. Acting on impulse, he walked over and stood beside her, wondering if she'd rebuff him again. But she answered his greeting, though that vivid blush of hers began to slowly make its telltale mark. He suppressed a smile at the sight of it.

"Good evening, sire." Well, Louise thought, my voice is fairly steady.

Louis held out the bracelets.

Louise took them and examined them as gravely as he'd held them out, and then, bracelet in each outstretched hand, she said, "Thank you for allowing me to see them, Your Majesty. They're lovely."

Her lack of coquetry caught him. "Well then, they're in hands too lovely to return them."

Louise didn't answer. He watched a pulse beat in her temple. They continued to stare at each other.

"I can't accept these." Louise was unsmiling.

So was he. "You offend me if you don't."

"I have to tell you something."

Both their hearts raced.

"Speak."

"Not here, Your Majesty."

"Where?"

"I'll slip into the gardens in another few moments. I'll wait at the bench by the moat at the golden gate, sire."

"I'm yours to command, Miss de la Baume le Blanc." But under his politeness, he felt suddenly, wearily, disappointed. Either she was going to confess about the Mazarinades or she was just another flirt, using innocence as her first line of defense. Well, she had a full, ripe mouth. It would be pleasant to taste it because he had no doubt he'd obtain a kiss, and he found he wanted a kiss from her. It would be satisfying to upset that reserve of hers. Stepping away, he hunted down the other young lady from Henriette's list, Miss de Chimerault, and he sat down beside her and pretended interest in what she'd done that afternoon, but he couldn't help but search for Louise with his eyes as he talked. He saw that she was not wearing the bracelets, and he frowned, and Chimerault, who had been chattering, swallowed hard, and her eyes became big, and Louis saw that he'd frightened her. He smiled a quick, insincere slash of a smile, and she simpered and fanned herself and promised him things by batting her eyes, and it was all he could do to sit beside her. He preferred Louise's awkwardness to this smooth silliness. When he could stand it no more, he stood abruptly, made an excuse and found Henriette.

"Do you like my earrings?" Henriette tilted her head so that he could see them.

"Splendid."

"My kind husband just gave them to me. Now, I'm going to flirt with him tonight, and I don't want you jealous. He's been hurt."

She was both arch and demanding. Louis wanted to shake her. Yes, Philippe has been hurt and by them. Stop playacting, he wanted to say. Be my lover, or end this. Across his mother's chambers, he saw Philippe, and they looked each other in the eye for the first time this night. On Louis's desk, in a locked box, sat the report of Philippe's misadventures these past days. There were descriptions of sexual acts that made Louis close his eyes and stop reading. He didn't understand his brother, but there was a certain bruised darkness under Philippe's eyes that cut to the bone.

"I saw you give the bracelets to Miss de la Baume le Blanc. Very sweet," said Henriette.

"Yes, that's me." Louis saw that Louise and one of the maids of honor had slipped out. He excused himself to follow.

Outside, Louise sat on a bench with Fanny. When they heard footsteps on the gravel Fanny pulled her hand from Louise's tight grasp and walked away to stand under a tree some distance away. Louis sat down beside Louise on the cool of the marble bench.

"You don't wear the bracelets." It wasn't what he meant to say.

"I have to tell you something, Your Majesty, that is going to sound so mad." Pent-up words spilled out of Louise. "I've thought and thought about this, and I know nothing else to do but tell you. The day Cardinal Mazarin died, I was out riding, and a nearly grown boy came running out of the woods, and he wore this iron mask strapped onto his face, and he ran straight at me, and I thought I heard the word 'Mother' before my horse reared and I fell—" On and on she went, describing her adventure, her curiosity, her search.

"The musketeer came to the palace and told the Chevalier de Choisy he'd seen saw us out riding. I was not to say a word to anyone about that day I saw the boy, he reminded. Well, if he'd seen us, I thought, that meant I must somehow be close, and since something about the boy haunts me, I didn't stop searching, but I felt like I was turning in circles. A map, I thought. There must be a map of the area, and I found one in your chamber of books. I copied the map—by the way, I left an inky fingerprint on your leather blotter—I am so sorry, and I will pay for its removal, I promise. So with the map I began to explore the countryside any morning I could. I like to ride, and they all like to sleep late, Madame's household, I mean, and so no one paid attention to my getting up early. But one day, I found this monastery—"

And then she told him of that, of seeing the youth again, of the musketeer coming to Fontainebleau to accost her directly and demand her silence with threats that still frightened her when she thought of them. When she told Louis of hearing the musketeer call the boy "your highness," she could sense a sudden tensing in his body.

"Describe the musketeer."

Louise did so. "I still have the coins. I did spend one, but only one. All the others are still there, but the thing is, the Viscount Nicolas's men caught me on his property—it adjoins the monastery—and they took me to his house and he questioned me."

"What did you say to him?"

"Nothing I've told you, just that I was lost. He thought—" Louise stopped.

"What did he think?"

"That I was flirting, perhaps. That I'd come onto his property on purpose."

"Had you?"

"Of course not, Your Majesty."

"So he questioned you?"

"Yes, but I told him nothing. You're the only one I've told."

He took her hands. The way his heart leapt at his touching them shocked him, and he spoke over the shock. "I thank you for telling me this. And I thank you for your discretion."

She pulled her hands away.

"In a day or so, I'm going to ask you to lead me to the monastery. Will you do that?"

"Of course. Anything you request, Your Majesty. I'm your servant in all ways."

Before he could say another word, she had darted up from the bench and was running away. He could hear her steps in the gravel. He looked down at where she'd been sitting. There were the bracelets. He put them into his pocket and went back into the ballroom. He sat down by Maria Teresa, who clutched his hand in hers. She had been like a clinging vine all day.

Highness. That meant royal blood of some kind. What was a prince doing in an iron mask? Even your best friend may betray you, his beloved cardinal had explained. Maria Teresa chatted about the letter she'd received from her father, and Louis half-listened. He already knew its contents. There was nothing she received from Spain or anywhere else that he had not seen first. Nor would there ever be. He was very aware that Louise was not among the young women who managed to walk back and forth in front of where he sat so that he couldn't miss seeing them. He stood up in the middle of one of his wife's sentences, an expression on his face that sent D'Artagnan running to him.

Maria Teresa stopped speaking, stared up at him. "I've displeased?" Her mouth trembled.

Her love, her need, strangled. "No, little heart," he said in Spanish. "I just remembered something I must do." He turned to D'Artagnan, whispered an order. "From this moment on, I want to know precisely where Miss de la Baume le Blanc is."

That will be three of us, thought D'Artagnan.

And then Louis sat down again, hoping he hadn't revealed too much to the watching eyes, making his own eyes hooded and blank, like some fierce young bird of prey's.

CHAPTER 24

The household of Monsieur and Madame was in the big park. Philippe lay on the grass, his head on a cushion, a big hat over his eyes. Henriette and her ladies were practicing steps for the ballet with her dance master, a musician or two playing the music for them.

Pretending to be sewing, pretending her leg was hurt, Louise sat a little away from her friends, her back against a tree, her mind everywhere but on the tiny stitches her needle was taking. Someone dropped down to sit beside her. It was Choisy.

"I saw him give you bracelets last night."

"I gave them back." Plunk went her needle, in and out of the fabric.

"I came to lecture you. I was going to tell you it's dangerous to flirt with the king."

"I haven't flirted."

"Well, he's noticed you."

Louise raised her eyes. The iris around her pupils was as deep as a lake fed by ice and crystal snow. "It's all right if Viscount Nicolas or the Count de Guiche notice me, but not His Majesty? I must be very stupid. I don't understand."

"The viscount's regard, if handled judiciously, will attract a husband. Guiche, as you know, is untrustworthy and dangerous, but you don't like him, so I don't fret, and it gives you cachet to be noticed by him. His Majesty's regard will ruin you. Look how poor little Pon's father dragged her away."

"I'm ruined only if I take it seriously. And I have no intention of doing that, nor of flirting, even a little bit."

"You'd be the first. May one ask, why not?"

"I don't wish to be a whim, someone he smiles at until bored, and he moves on to someone else. Besides—" He's given his heart to Madame, she almost said but stopped herself. "Besides, I'm saving myself like a good girl should."

"Well, I came here with the set purpose to lecture you, and I find you know what you're about. This settles it. We have to marry as soon as possible, and then, my dear, you may flirt with anyone you please."

A tear fell silently onto the fabric. Choisy put his finger to the spot, touched the wet of it, made Louise raise her face so that their eyes met. "You're not in love with him?"

"Of course not," said Louise.

"Oh, darling, I hate that he's fooled with you even a little bit. You're too somber, you know." He took a fold of her gown and began to pleat it back and forth. "You could marry me."

"No."

"Oh, do." Looking very much the boy he still was but a little worn at the edges, Choisy made a face. "I misbehaved badly in Paris. Someone has gone to my brother and complained quite vociferously. It's twice too often. Marry me and make me respectable."

"No."

"I'll protect you."

"From what?"

"That heart of yours—"

They were interrupted. Guy sat down beside them. Louise picked up her sewing, but Guy grabbed it and put it behind his back. "A smile, and it's yours."

Louise stood and walked away.

Guy handed the sewing to Choisy. "Here, you finish it." He went to Philippe, kicked him hard on the sole of his boot. Philippe moved the hat from his face.

"I beg you to get up and accompany me. My notorious charm seems to have deserted me, and I must, I really must, tease Miss de la Baume le Blanc just a bit more, and you must guard me from her withering disdain."

❧❦❧

His council meeting over, Louis stood in his chamber of books, at the ornate cupboard. He had pulled down its front to look at the blotter. There, on the light-colored leather surrounding it, was a fingerprint, just as she'd said, except that it was faint enough to be almost unnoticeable. He put his finger atop it.

"Your Majesty."

He turned to face a footman.

"Monsieur Colbert wishes a moment."

Louis closed up the cupboard and waited.

Colbert brought in a stack of books, began to open each one, turning to the title pages, reading the dedications, all to the Viscount Nicolas.

"Fontaine, Corneille, Saint-Évremond," said Colbert. "Do you realize he's being called the superintendent of France's literature as well as of our finances? Our writers and poets give him accolades that belong to the crown!" He was as indignant as if he had found more evidence of treason.

It was among Colbert's many opinions that there ought to be a national academy, enfolding painters and craftsmen, writers and scientists, that the crown of France should support them for the greater glory of the nation. How determined and thorough Colbert was, like a mongrel that wouldn't give up a scrap of bone. But he is my mongrel, thought Louis, and he was suddenly grateful for this merchant's son who let no detail be too small, who seemed to encompass a kingdom in his head. There was nothing Louis wanted to do that Colbert did not embrace and have an idea for. He desired the same glory Louis reached for, and required that none of it must shine on him. That was one of the viscount's besetting sins, wasn't it?

Colbert hovered. Louis knew him well enough by now to know that there was news that neither of them would like. "Well?"

Colbert took a deep breath. "Miss de la Baume le Blanc. I've been watching her for some time."

"Because?"

"She was found in this chamber some time ago. It made me uneasy. The viscount is known to regard her highly, then she met with him at Vaux-le-Vicomte. It's possible she may be a spy for him." He continued over Louis's sudden scowl. "One can never be too careful. I have no proof that she is, sire. It's simply a possibility I beg you to consider."

He'd had no proof of the island, either; it had simply been a hunch he'd followed. Was Louis's own intuition about her wrong? "I'll consider what you say. Good day."

Louis went to a long window, stepped out into the morning sun, the sight of his palace and its spreading gardens. A mist hung in the distance, in the forests. The mist would clear by noon. When would the mists around him clear? She couldn't be a spy for the viscount; he could feel it in his bones, and yet, who knew? I have done many unworthy deeds, were his beloved cardinal's deathbed words. And so he had, as Louis now understood too fully. He had created the Viscount Nicolas and allowed him to flourish. If he were alive today, Louis would have no choice but to order his arrest along with the viscount's. The man he revered had played a part in the debauch of finance. Who then was truly trustworthy? Certainly not some young woman with eyes like lavender in the hills and a smile—which he had yet to earn—that was incandescent.

He leaned on the iron of the balcony, the muscles in his arms tense. He'd had this fleeting thought that he could lay his head upon Louise de la Baume le Blanc's sweet breast and be safe for a time. There'd been some sense that with her he didn't have to be forever the king, that he could be sometimes weary and yearning, and she would not mock, but would wrap her arms tight around him. So, did she, with her disarming innocence, lead him into a trap? Of what kind? He searched for a heart of gold, the way alchemists searched for the philosopher's stone. He began to believe neither existed.

Colbert summoned a horse. Within an hour, he was in the little village of Avon and at the door of the Carmelite convent. The Mother Superior listened to his request and then had the girl brought in. She was a wisp of a child, no more than five.

"Do you know who I am?" Colbert asked. And at a shake of her head, he continued. "I am a servant of His Majesty's, and I've come to ask you some questions. You know Miss de la Baume le Blanc?"

"Yes."

"Why does she come to see you?"

"I don't know."

"Why are you here?"

"She and the gentleman brought me here."

"Tell me of your home."

She described the farm, her family.

"When she came to us, there were bruises all over her body," the Mother Superior interrupted.

"Who struck you?" Colbert asked.

"It's my fault. He died, and I didn't, and I was first sick, and then he got sick, and we needed him so much to help," the child replied.

"I don't understand. Who died?"

"My brother. He helped Papa in the fields. It's hard now, without him. And one of our oxen died, too. Because of me, I made our ox sick, too, Papa said." She took a deep breath, and tears that had gathered in her eyes as she spoke dropped down her cheeks.

"Ah." Colbert took a moment. "I am filled with sorrow for your family's loss. But I must speak of Miss de la Baume le Blanc. Does she ask you to do things for her, like listen to the sisters' conversations here and tell her about them? It's all right. I am His Majesty's trusted servant, and you may tell me anything."

"Tell him," said the Mother Superior.

"She lets me ride her horse, and sometimes she takes me home to visit. She tells me I must come back here because my mother needs me to. She holds me when I cry. She gave me a blue ribbon and a comb for my hair. If

I learn to sew nicely, she says she will buy me a gown. She says if I learn to sew nicely, I may sew for coins and so help Papa. She says if I sew nicely, she will make me her maidservant."

"She asks you to do no listening for her?"

"She asks who to tell secrets to."

Aha, thought Colbert. "Yes?"

"We decided her mother, the Mother Superior, His Majesty, and the Chevalier de Choisy."

Colbert regarded the child standing before him. "And the secret?"

"We don't really have one."

He met the eyes of the Mother Superior. There was no more to be said. He took the child's hand, bowed over it as if she were a countess. "It is an honor to have met you."

He walked to his horse but stood beside the beast for a time to compose himself before pulling up into the saddle. He had come to find bad deeds by Miss de la Baume le Blanc and found instead France and its struggles. He considered himself a decent man. Not for him the gambling and drinking and love affairs of court. For him, there was his family, and there was this kingdom, which consisted of far more than those who peopled its court. There were also those who marched in its army, owned its shops, and tilled its soil. They, too, should have bread on their tables. A farmer should be prosperous, able to buy another ox should one die, able to sire another son should God take one. Little girls should be safe by the warm hearth of their homes. The despair. Ah, the despair that years of war left. Well, relief was in God's hands and in this king's. Back straight, he rode toward the palace, toward his immense task of bringing order to this kingdom, which he loved with all his precise, contained, and passionate heart.

Tomorrow he'd send one of his clerks to buy an ox.

❧❧❧

"You seem distracted," Henriette said.

"Do I? Forgive me." I do care for you, Louis thought. This is real, not that odd, flaring passion, like lightning on the horizon, for the quiet blue-eyed belle who, he noticed, was walking in the far park with Guy and Philippe as her escorts.

"The Count of Guiche admires Miss de la Baume le Blanc?" he asked. Guy had been rude to Philippe this day, he'd been told, kicking him on the sole of his shoe as if he were a minion and ordering him to follow, and follow Philippe had.

"As much as he admires anyone. How does your flirtation go?"

"Which one?"

"With Miss de la Baume le Blanc."

He found he was reluctant to speak of it. "She's shy."

"Be careful with her, won't you?"

"You act as if I am a heartbreaker."

"The king takes all hearts."

Her wide smile, the way she tossed her head, the smooth surety in her voice, annoyed him beyond bearing. He stood up abruptly. "I must pay some attention to the queen."

Maria Teresa sat in among the trees of the park with her ladies. As usual, she was embroidering on something small, something for their son. Walking toward her, he thought of her sincerity and trust, much like that of Miss de la Baume le Blanc's. Why was Miss de la Baume le Blanc so attractive to him and his wife so annoying? He was going to see the monastery tomorrow.

Quietly, furtively, trying to make no noise to wake, Louise slipped a note under Fanny's pillow. Lie for me, she wrote. Tell the gargoyle I had to go to Paris to see my mother. She sat in a silent stairway to put her boots on, walked to the gardens, no one in them at this hour. Lieutenant D'Artagnan stepped out so that she could see him.

"I'm not late, am I?" she cried.

"It's all right, miss. Follow me."

He led her to a stable she hadn't known existed, and in its yard were some twenty musketeers, most on their gray horses, and they nodded solemnly to her. But where was the king? thought Louise, and then she saw that he was dressed just as they were, blended in among them. He nodded his head abruptly at Louise, and then D'Artagnan handed her a tabard and a hat. How clever they are, she thought, and she went into a stall and took off her cloak and pulled on a tabard, which was a musketeer's short cloak, slit on the sides, an elaborately embroidered cross on its front, over her riding dress. She set the hat upon her head. Another musketeer helped her to mount, and then they were riding out toward the open heath behind this part of the palace. She felt disoriented, suddenly uncertain of herself, of finding the monastery, of knowing east from west and north from south, which was silly, one had only to find the sun and shadow and certain mosses.

"I'm accustomed to leaving from the common courtyard," she said to D'Artagnan nervously.

He pointed, and Louise saw the magnificent entrance gatehouse of the common courtyard rising in the sky and realized she was on one of the

village's back lanes, and she felt certain again. She snapped at her horse
with the riding crop, and the beast sprang forward. D'Artagnan allowed
her to lead.

There was only the sound of hooves on the floor of the forest.
D'Artagnan rode beside Louise, but Louis stayed back, surrounded on all
sides by his musketeers. They rode long and hard for several hours, Louise
never wavering, never asking to stop for rest. When the monastery was in
sight, the tower of its chapel rising up to the sky, she pulled her horse short.
She pointed toward the vineyards, the monks and boys working in them.

"What do we do?" she asked D'Artagnan.

"We go in," he said, and they rode right up to the gate.

"Open in the name of His Majesty," D'Artagnan called, pulling at the
rope of the bell on one side of the gate. After a time, the window cut into
the gate opened, and a monk peered out. Seeing musketeers, he pulled
his head back. When the gate didn't open, D'Artagnan nodded to two
young musketeers.

"Over and open it," he told them. One stood in his saddle while the
other held the reins of his horse tight, and in minutes the first was over the
wall. A bell began to peal, even as the gate was opening. The musketeers
rode into the enclosure, the chapel bell loud. Boys in the garden put down
their hoes at the sight of them, and Louise watched monks clap their hands
and point toward a side building on the chapel as boys lined up, and monks
began to shepherd them into the building.

Louis rode forward. "Where did you see him?"

She pointed with her riding crop. "I think he lives there." She was
pointing to the ornate stone house, its roses rambling over the columns of
the porch.

"Surround the house," D'Artagnan ordered.

Inside the house, Cinq Mars had been seated at a table sharpening the
blade of his sword. His precious charge sat in a corner, singing to himself.
At least that was what Cinq Mars called it, the singsong, sometimes endless murmur that would come out of the boy. He was rocking back and
forth, his arms around himself. Happy today, thought Cinq Mars.

I'll take him for a ride later, Cinq Mars was thinking when the chapel
bell began to peal. The boy put his hands to his ears, began to hit his head
against the wall. Pounding sounded at the front door, as several monks
rushed in from the back of the house. They made gestures with their hands.
Soldiers, that's what their hand gestures said. Had the Queen Mother
sent soldiers to take the boy? But even as that thought was forming, he

knew she wouldn't have sent them without a warning beforehand. It was something else.

"We have to get him away," he shouted to the monks, who surrounded the boy and jerked him to standing, no easy task with his rocking and size. They ran down the hall, half carrying, half dragging the boy. Cinq Mars maneuvered ahead and threw open the back door. Musketeers stood not a foot away.

He shut the door quickly, his mind going over every route. His orders were mortal sins: to kill the boy and then himself. Himself he could do, but not the boy, never the boy. It was a vow he couldn't keep, and he'd always known it.

"Make them stop pealing the bell!" he shouted. "Keep him here." He'd fight his way to the stables, take a horse, get the boy and himself on it, and be off. He opened the back door again, sword raised.

D'Artagnan now stood at the front of the other musketeers, his sword out of its scabbard.

"Cinq Mars!" D'Artagnan cried. Out of the corner of his eye, he saw monks pouring into the enclosure through the front gate.

"To my aid!" shouted Cinq Mars.

And D'Artagnan realized that the monks running toward them carried hoes and knives and rakes and seemed ready to use them. There were boys with them, boys whose faces were odd, and some of whom were wailing and jumping up and down.

"En garde," D'Artagnan shouted, and at once, he and the others made a tight square, their backs to one another, their swords pointed outward on the advancing monks, as Cinq Mars ran to the stable.

"Do I kill them?" one of the musketeers asked D'Artagnan.

"No! Aid! To our aid!" shouted D'Artagnan.

Hearing it, the musketeers in front of the house, ordered to stay with the king, looked at one another. On Louis's orders, they'd made no move to stop monks herding distraught boys into the side building of the chapel. Louis dismounted, took his sword from his scabbard, and ran around the side of the house with them, Louise behind.

The sight that met their eyes stopped them for a moment, monks surrounding musketeers, who valiantly deflected the wild downward thrust of rakes and hoes with their swords. Other monks grabbed at swords with bare hands and didn't seem to mind the gushing blood.

"Cease and desist," Louis shouted. Could they even hear him over the pealing of that chapel bell? He took his hat from his head so they could see his face plainly. "I order you in my name, Louis the Fourteenth, king and keeper of this kingdom! I order you in the name of all that is holy to desist!"

"It's the king!" shouted D'Artagnan.

Uncertain, monks stepped back, looked at one another. Hesitantly some began to bow, one or two fell to their knees.

Cinq Mars, who'd brought out saddled horses—he'd kept horses saddled ever since Louise had visited—began a wide run toward the front door of the house, but D'Artagnan moved from the square of musketeers.

"Stop in the name of the king!" he called. And then, "Old friend, it's me, Charles de Batz-Castelmore D'Artagnan. Stop! Don't make me kill you!"

"I order you to stop," Louis called. He had joined D'Artagnan.

Cinq Mars turned to Louis, brought his sword to his forehead in a salute. Then he lunged for D'Artagnan, cutting the musketeer in his side, but the loose tabard made the aim inaccurate, and D'Artagnan was quick enough to fall back so that the wound didn't disable him. Their swords met in that deadly clang of steel on steel that was serious battle. D'Artagnan inched Cinq Mars backward, the man fighting him like someone gone mad.

"Help him!" ordered Louis.

Other musketeers rushed forward, cutting Cinq Mars on each arm, and in spite of himself, Cinq Mars lowered his sword arm, just as D'Artagnan, his sword at point, pushed hard and deep through Cinq Mars's chest below his shoulder. Cinq Mars staggered back, and the other musketeers tackled him, dropping him to the ground.

A howl rang out through the chaos. A thin, nearly grown boy with a shocking iron mask upon his face ran into the melee, pulling musketeers off Cinq Mars as if they weighed nothing. D'Artagnan raised his sword, but before he could use it, Louise was there, hanging on his sword arm.

"Don't hurt him, please!" she cried.

"You mustn't touch him—" Cinq Mars shouted.

But D'Artagnan's blade grazed the boy, who gasped in shock and then to everyone's horror, grabbed the sword with his hands, his fingers quickly reddening. The boy sat down abruptly.

"Enough!" shouted Louis.

"Yes, it's enough!" cried the abbot of the monastery, who'd been herding the younger boys into the side building of the chapel but was now here, a sword in his hand. "Obey His Majesty!" he ordered.

So, thought Louis, he speaks, but the others remain silent. Louis knelt down to see this youth in an iron mask. Gasping, he lay on his side, but in a sudden, agile movement, the boy shoved Louis with his feet, knocking him backward. In another moment, the boy was surrounded by musketeers, swords all pointing downward, his abdomen their destination.

"Stop!" shouted Louis.

"He can't understand," panted Cinq Mars. And then he went silent. Better if they killed him, he thought.

The boy stood. It looked as if he was getting ready to charge, and one by one, musketeers gripped their swords in preparation. But he caught sight of Louise; she'd lost her hat and her hair was loose, out of its pins and on her shoulders. The boy tilted his head to one side. "Mama?" he said.

As if it were the most natural thing in the world, Louise replied, "Yes. Come with me like a good boy, won't you, my dear?" She stepped toward the boy, reached to touch him, but he stepped back, trembling.

"We'll go inside," Louise said, "where it's quiet. Come with me, dear boy."

D'Artagnan looked to Louis, who gave a sharp nod of agreement.

As if there weren't a dozen men and a king watching, half of them ready to pierce him if he made a single, wrong move, the boy followed Louise into the house, down the hall, into a chamber. Louis, his men, the abbot followed.

"Won't you sit down, my dear one," Louise said.

Hesitantly, the boy sat in a chair.

"What goes on here?" Louis demanded. No one answered him. "I want the mask taken off," he ordered.

"He'll become wild," said the abbot.

"Will you do the honors?" Louis said to Louise.

Carefully, talking to him all the while, explaining every move she made, Louise began to fumble with unfastening leather straps. Musketeers stood poised in a semicircle, swords drawn.

"Mama," the boy made the one word a song he repeated over and over. He had begun to rock back and forth so that Louise's task was difficult.

D'Artagnan walked outside the house to a prone Cinq Mars, surrounded by monks attempting to stanch his wound.

Cinq Mars opened his eyes. "Don't do this," he said, enough blood lost that words were difficult for him. "You mustn't, the cardinal's orders."

"The cardinal is dead, my friend."

"Queen's orders."

"I take orders from one man only. His orders stand above all others. So did you, once upon a time."

"You don't comprehend—" Cinq Mars stopped speaking, closed his eyes.

D'Artagnan leaned down, felt his chest. A rise and fall, but there was fresh blood on the bandage the monks had made.

"Will he die?" he asked them, but, of course, they didn't answer. D'Artagnan re-entered the house, walked down the long hall. He could hear the boy's tuneless, one-word song. How old is he? thought D'Artagnan, estimating ten and three or four years or so. Miss de la Baume le Blanc was still fumbling with the undoing of the mask. Thinking to help, D'Artagnan stepped behind her, but she had the final strap undone, and the mask clattered suddenly to the floor. The boy jerked his arms around his knees and leaned backward in the chair, howling as it fell over.

"Out! Everyone out!" shouted Louis.

D'Artagnan could see amazement and horror on the king's face.

"Now!" Louis pressed the heels of his hands to his eyes, and to D'Artagnan's horror, he bent over.

"Out! Out!" screamed Louise, fierce, suddenly as strong as any man around her, pushing at D'Artagnan, at any musketeer still in the chamber. Men obeyed, moving into the hall. She shoved at the lieutenant of the musketeers as if he didn't make two of her.

"I'm not leaving His Majesty!" D'Artagnan said.

Louise ran to Louis, in a crouched position now, hands to his face, weeping as if he'd seen his father fall in a battlefield, the child his wife carried die. And all the while the boy rocked back and forth in his curled position on the floor, rocked back and forth, howling.

D'Artagnan didn't know what to do. Louise stood before the king holding out her skirts the way a butterfly would its wings, hiding His Majesty with them, as if no one, not even his most trusted lieutenant, must see him weep.

"Hush," she said, but whether it was to the boy or His Majesty or to the world at large she spoke, D'Artagnan had no idea. D'Artagnan went to the boy, knelt so he could see the face of this child who had turned their world upside down. Even howling, even thin and half-grown, the boy looked so like the king that he might have been his brother, possibly his twin. The deep-socketed dark eyes, the shape of the proud nose, the full mouth, even the brown, thick hair, matted as it was. Shock filled D'Artagnan as too many possibilities, too many memories, spun themselves in his head.

"Who is this?" he asked the world in general and himself.

The question brought Louis to his senses. He stood, wiped his face. "D'Artagnan, put the mask back on," he ordered.

Louise made a sound, somewhere between a gasp and a cry.

"Leave, now!" Louis told her.

She ran from the chamber. Louis walked to the rocking boy and D'Artagnan.

"He has to be drugged with wine and chamomile and poppy dust," said a quiet voice.

Louis and D'Artagnan turned. There, against the wall, stood the abbot of the monastery. He hadn't obeyed Louis's command to leave the chamber.

"Order it," said Louis.

The abbot went down the hall, called a name, and after a time a monk appeared in the doorway like a dark shadow, his face strained and white.

"Give him the wine. Replace the mask. See to the cuts the sword made." Louis walked through the cluster of people knotted in the hall and ordered them all outside. Following, he walked to where Cinq Mars lay on the ground.

"Is he going to die?" Louis asked a monk attending him.

"Not today, majesty." Cinq Mars spoke in a whisper without opening his eyes. Then he said in a stronger tone, "Did you kill him?"

"No."

"Better that you had."

"You owe me some explanations."

"There is nothing to say, sire."

"There is everything, and you will begin now. Away with you," Louis ordered the hovering monk. He knelt down at Cinq Mars's side. "Open your eyes," he commanded, his own as hard as two stones. "Now. I command the truth even if you die saying it. My commands take precedence over any other, over my mother, over the cardinal. I am king. How old is he?"

Cinq Mars was silent.

"When did he become your charge?"

Again silence.

"Who are his parents?"

But there was no answer.

D'Artagnan stepped outside, wiping his hands on a huge handkerchief, his mind reeling, pushing far back into long-gone years, when rumors filled the court the way the boy's howls filled the chamber behind him. Louis turned as D'Artagnan walked to him, and D'Artagnan had never seen an expression like this one on His Majesty's face.

"Take the boy to Pignerol." It was a fortress across the mountains.

From the ground, Cinq Mars pleaded. "Let me go with him, I beg you, sire. He knows me. He feels safe with me."

"Certainly you go with him." Louis's words were clipped. "Who is the monk who attends him?"

"Father Gabriel," whispered Cinq Mars.

"The boy, Cinq Mars, Father Gabriel, the abbot, you're to take them all to Pignerol," he said to D'Artagnan.

"I can't leave you," D'Artagnan replied.

"You not only can, you will. Put your second best man in your place; take your best man and a small troop with you. Once there, lock them all in separate cells."

They walked back to the house, Louis talking as fast as he walked. "I don't want them hurt, but I also don't want them seen by anyone. I don't want that mask removed from the boy until I send an express order signed with my name and my name alone. I want this monastery disbanded now."

Only his holiness might order that, thought D'Artagnan, but he knew better than to voice those words.

"Herd all the monks and the boys into the chapel except the abbot. Tell them prayers are required for this day. Lock the doors behind them. Send someone immediately to Fontainebleau and bring back the rest of the Grays. Tell them to bring at least six wagons and three carriages and all the lantern oil and pitch they can put their hands to. They're to drive, no grooms. It's to be done quietly, in secret. Count the boys; see how many there are."

Inside the house, Louis strode to the abbot. "Take me to your chamber."

In the abbot's chamber, Louis was as clear and as cold as the chapel bell ringing earlier had been. "How long has he been here?"

The abbot rubbed his eyes tiredly. "Since he was a babe."

"Who knows he's here?"

"A great lady."

"What great lady?"

"She was always masked and cloaked. And his eminence, God rest his soul, sometimes he came."

"What monks attend him?"

The abbot measured Louis, the hooded eyes, the grim mouth, and said nothing.

"I can simply imprison them all or put them on my galleys in the Mediterranean, where they'll stay the rest of their lives, with their tongues cut out for safe measure." Louis's eyes never left the abbot's face. When the abbot didn't answer, Louis stood, slapped a riding glove against one hand with a sharp crack. "You are to remain here until I order differently."

"God is my commander, sire."

"I am God's first liege in this kingdom, and by God, you will do as I say, or you will be the first to row a galley, the first without a tongue! Paper and pen."

The abbot pointed, and Louis picked them up. Outside, he ordered a waiting musketeer to stand guard at the abbot's door. "He isn't to leave," he told him.

He saw that musketeers were guiding monks into the chapel, boys with them. He went to the house, passing Cinq Mars, who lay still. In the house, the monk called Father Gabriel knelt beside the boy, whose iron mask was strapped back in place. There was an empty cup on the floor, and the boy was still.

"Thank you, Father," Louis said. "If you'll go to the chapel now with the others." Louis said to a musketeer, "Follow him to the chapel. Keep sight of him at all times."

He found Louise in a nearby chamber, kneeling at a prayer stand, eyes closed. She didn't turn her head at the sound of his steps, but he'd deal with her later. Right now, he would gladly accept whatever prayers came his way.

"I've sent for the rest of the troop," D'Artagnan told him.

"I want the monks in the Bastille." Louis was at a table, scratching out words on a paper. "Here's a *lettre de cachet* for all of them. Have them taken into Paris as quietly as possible, at night. I want no crowds, no witnesses. The governor of the Bastille is to lock them up, no one else."

D'Artagnan blinked. A *lettre de cachet* meant the person jailed went inside without any record of the arrest. It was a way to lose people forever. "And the other children?"

"Give each of them this wine they make for the boy. Take them to the Carmelites in Paris and leave them in their courtyard. Once the rest of the musketeers have arrived, we'll disperse children and monks to wagons. You'll have the carriages. I don't want Cinq Mars and the abbot in the same carriage, nor the boy with either of them, so that means you'll guide three carriages. I want you in the one with the boy. We'll put a torch to this place. I don't want so much as a fence piling left standing, and I don't care what else burns down around this!"

"Yes, sire."

D'Artagnan's mind was reeling. Who was this young man with no hesitation in thought or deed? How many years had it been since there'd been a king with this kind of will, this kind of strength? D'Artagnan had seen the machinations of Richelieu, of Louis XIII, of Mazarin, not to mention the highest in the land, princes and princesses, noblemen and noblewomen in that cast of treacherous splendor that fought the power of the crown because they wished to wear it themselves. He thought he'd seen it all. There was a stirring in him, a militant respect. Here now was someone to serve. A young lion. A tiger whose claws were only now unfurling. A hawk who flew high above them all and called down orders from on high. Mary, Mother of God, the kingdom was in for the ride of its life. A sharp, soldier's pride filled him.

"I watched the monks. They communicate with their hands. Let everyone know. I want no escapes planned. Get a gag around Cinq Mars's mouth, and keep it there."

D'Artagnan walked outside to bind Cinq Mars's mouth himself. The monk attending Cinq Mars frowned, and D'Artagnan said, "He's committed high treason."

Back in the house, he walked down the hall toward the chamber that held the boy, but he stopped on the threshold because inside, Louis knelt on one knee before the youth, and it was clear he was praying. D'Artagnan stepped back quickly into the hall, crossed himself, and said his own quick prayer to send on high with His Majesty's, and then went back outside to see that everything was in order.

"Look sharp!" he snapped to anyone who crossed his path, his mind going over His Majesty's plan, adding his own improvements. In another few hours, there'd be plenty of loyal hands and keen minds. Before dawn tomorrow, the others would be in Paris. They should stop on the outskirts of Paris and send word to the governor of the Bastille to make ready for them. He'd have His Majesty write a letter to the governor now and send a musketeer on his way with it. The boys should be divided among monasteries in Paris, rather than going to one. He'd suggest that to His Majesty. Wagons would separate outside the Bastille, the boys in some, the monks in the rest. They would roll into a quiet, hidden courtyard in the bowels of the prison, and the monks would be dispersed like trapped mice. He shuddered. Poor men. The Bastille was a grim place. And there was brandy and wine to save. He recognized the mark on barrels in one of the buildings. It was a fine vintage they made here. That must be loaded onto wagons, too, and lumber back to Fontainebleau.

❧❦❧

Hours later, it was begun. Musketeers were everywhere. As the sun set, wagons stood ready to roll toward Paris. The carriages awaited only D'Artagnan's command to depart. And he would not give it until he saw the wagons on their way. Now, he waited for His Majesty to finish his private discussion with the young miss.

Inside the house, Louis questioned Louise, something he'd put off too long. "Have you ever delivered a sealed note to my chambers for someone?"

"Yes. For Madame."

"Someone other than Madame?"

"No."

"Has the viscount ever asked you to spy on me?"

"No."

"Why did you stand in front of me?"

"So that no one should see you weep."

Louis considered her. She stood with her back to a window. As the sun set, a last ray shone around her, highlighting the paleness of her hair. The eyes that met his were grave. She was blushing her vivid hue, but he didn't mind that. He said, his face hard, "This will make a good story when you tell it."

"I would never tell of it—"

"It's been suggested you place notes from someone to me when you go to visit my dog, put them on my pillow, other places, when La Porte isn't looking. Tell me the truth. I won't be angry."

"I don't. I haven't. I swear. I would never be disloyal to you! There's no one who could make me be." She straightened her shoulders as she spoke, a spark in her fine eyes.

"Do you know who the boy is?"

"No. Yes. I heard him called a royal highness. He's a cousin, isn't he?" She gazed at him solidly, truth in every angle of her face, line of her body.

God, thought Louis, when was the last time he'd seen anyone with eyes that showed all the way to the soul? "Yes, he is, but now I must ask you to do something for me and for your kingdom. You must never speak of this. On your deathbed, you must keep silence about this, about all of it, this day, what you saw, what you conjecture. Will you swear to me you will do that?"

She knelt and looked up at him with the earnestness of a knight pledging fidelity. "Yes."

Her terrible blush had receded. "No matter what, my death, yours, you are never to speak of this." Louis was grim.

She nodded, and he helped her to her feet. Frowning, considering, weighing one thing against another, he watched her exit. He'd meant to make her a bargain. Coins for silence. An excellent marriage. A place at court for her brother or mother. But none of those offers would go past his lips. Not when he looked in her eyes.

Outside, Louise walked forward to the musketeer holding her horse. He helped her seat herself in the saddle. The shock of everything that had happened was finally seeping out from her in tears.

"Escort her to Fontainebleau," Louis ordered from the doorway.

Later, when the wagons were on their way, he mounted his horse, nodded to D'Artagnan, who stood near the carriages.

"I hate to see that good wine go to the Bastille," D'Artagnan said. His Majesty had ordered that it be sent there instead. Someone might see the barrels at Fontainebleau, he'd said, and it was true, but it was a shame.

"I've ordered a cask put in your carriage. Drink my health when you arrive," Louis answered.

D'Artagnan saluted, stepped into a carriage, and they began their journey.

For the next few hours, Louis worked as hard as any musketeer with him, inspecting every inch of ground, moving hay and firewood into buildings, spilling lantern oil everywhere throughout the chapel, the house, the barns, the sheds, while other musketeers herded livestock—oxen, pigs, chickens, mules, horses, what dogs and cats they could—outside the gate and into the gathering night. He'd ordered the vineyard burned too, and musketeers moved among the trellised vines. Satisfied that everything that could be done had been, he gave the signal to light the fires.

They'd made a bonfire in the middle of the yard, and a musketeer holding a burning torch ran into each building. The barns and sheds burned fastest, and eventually flames were licking at the roof of the chapel and the house. And then a wind came up, lifting sparks, and the fire roared through opened doors and windows.

At his order, they quit the yard, went outside the wall because inside the fire had become a beast eating anything in sight with yowls of red flame and cinders swirling everywhere. The vineyards were burning, and the forest was aflame, but Louis didn't care. At last, after midnight, when all that remained was the rubble of brick and blackened stone, he signaled for them to leave, and they rode silently through the woods, away from the fire, away from what had been. It began to rain, but they rode on through it. When the lanterns of Fontainebleau could be seen in the distance, Louis shuddered, as if a ghost were walking over his grave. It was the ghost of his beloved cardinal.

CHAPTER 25

Somehow, he managed to catch an hour of sleep here and there the next day. No one seemed to find his absence or manner unusual, this when he felt disoriented, wild, and ill at ease inside himself every time he pictured the boy's face.

"We missed you last night," Henriette told him that evening as he stood by her and tried to pretend all was well.

"By the time I'd finished walking the grounds, it was easier to stay the night at Versailles." Louis spoke his lie absently. He couldn't take his eyes from his mother. The Viscount Nicolas was at her side, standing behind her right shoulder the way Mazarin always had. He was her new Mazarin, wasn't he? Louis closed his eyes at all that was in him. What have you done? he thought, staring at his mother. What is the truth? Am I not a king's son?

"Will you make improvements to it, do you think?"

Versailles was his father's hunting château. He wished to retire there to live once you became ten and five, Mazarin had once told him. He was going to turn the kingdom over to you. He was so tired, so ill that he couldn't conceive of ruling into old age, said Mazarin. Yet the king his father had been well enough to spawn a child?

Louis excused himself abruptly and walked over to Fanny, who was in the middle of a sentence and, at the sight of him, swallowed it whole. Athénaïs, to whom she'd been talking, backed away so that they might speak privately.

"Where is Miss de la Baume le Blanc?"

"Ill, sir."

"What's the matter?"

"Oh, as to that, I can't say, sir."

"Tell her I asked of her."

Fanny's eyes were as wide as tarts the cooks made. "I will, sir."

"Good. We hunt tomorrow. Tell her I expect her to join us. All of the maids of honor. Tell them it's my personal request to be there."

"Yes, sir. Of course, sir."

Louis narrowed his eyes, and Fanny's excitement became nervousness.

"I would prefer it if you did not speak to anyone of my interest in her. You do me and her no favor." He was stern.

"No, sir. I won't, sir. My lips are sealed, sir. Boiling oil couldn't get a word from me, except screams, perhaps. I'm sure I'd scream if I were boiled in oil."

He smiled suddenly, and Fanny felt like drooping and wished she hadn't chattered to Guy about Louise's absence yesterday.

"Thank you, Miss de Montalais. I hope you will become a friend to me. I have need of them."

"What did he say?" asked Athénaïs breathlessly the moment he was far enough away not to hear.

"He asked me to save a dance for him tonight," Fanny lied.

"Oh, Mother of Jesus," said Athénaïs. "Are you ready to die for joy? Here. Wear my pearl earrings. They're nicer than the ones you have. You have to tell me everything he says. Promise?"

"Promise."

❧❧❧

Louis went through the ceremony of being undressed for sleeping, put on his gown, climbed into his bed. His valet drew the curtains, and he listened to footsteps and murmurs as courtiers left the bedchamber. When his valet coughed three times, he was out of bed, and his valet had his riding boots and leather pantaloons and doublet ready. He knelt down and held Belle's face between his hands, fighting a panic that was like dark water rising over his head. Everything he had always believed in seemed slippery under his feet. Worlds were collapsing in him. What he thought he'd known, he did not know. What he thought he'd felt, he did not feel. There was no middle ground in this coming fight for supremacy. If there was the least shadow on his legitimacy, he was lost before he began, forever at the mercy of the cunning and discontented. He went to the wall and pressed the wooden carving of a dove that opened to a secret passage. The young musketeer who was assigned to him in D'Artagnan's absence waited at the other end, his face grave but excited. Louis didn't realize it, but all his musketeers were newly invigorated. Yesterday was already legend among them. Some spirit, some new sense that they were his elite corps and that he had secret and necessary tasks for them to perform on his behalf, had spread itself among them. There would be wars to fight, secret missions—were not half of them already upon one?—for the honor of this young king, who was the symbol of the kingdom, and, as they were coming more and more to see, a splendid, intriguing symbol.

Louis emerged near a garden wall where his horse was waiting. It was the grand Spanish stallion that he'd heard Miss de la Baume le Blanc had soothed. She soothed dogs and horses, it seemed, and wild, frightened boys. He would have to ride hard this night to be back at dawn, his second day and night of very little rest. Another man stood in the darkness, the snort of his horse alerting Louis to his presence. Colbert. He was entrusting Colbert with a portion, if not all, of this. He had to rely on someone. This was larger than he could carry alone.

Louis had sent a messenger ahead to expect him, and at the gate of the château's courtyard, a servant hurried forward at the sound of hooves, his lantern like a single eye in the dark.

"This way," he whispered, and Louis dismounted, Colbert following. The Duchess de Chevreuse waited in her chamber of books, a long, comfortable room with one wall of windows and one wall lined with shelves of books. It was rare to have so many books in one place. Louis looked around at the handsome leather bindings, the gold lettering, and thought, I'll have these if she denies me in any way. It will be the first thing I strip from her. Anger, which lay crouching in his heart, reared up on all four legs.

The duchess, Marie, remained silent, waiting for the king to speak. She'd missed nothing, his purposeful gait and tense expression as he entered the chamber, the musketeers who immediately paced the perimeter, checking for anyone else who might be hiding there, who nodded to him that all seemed well and took themselves away again, the silent, cloaked figure of Jean-Baptiste Colbert standing just at the door. What a handsome, vibrant man the king had become. All her intelligence, her interest in mankind and its innumerable permutations, all her sense for intrigue and the game of court, rose and spread in ever-expanding waves within her. This was a contest between them already. For what, she had no idea. But she knew its importance, which hovered over this young king like an unseen specter. Still he said nothing. Silence gathered and bunched and filled the distance between them.

"May I offer refreshment, Your Majesty?" She finally spoke, listening to the sound of her voice echo out into the room.

He scowled with a fierce, even baring of teeth, and her heart began to beat. For the first time, fear moved in her. What could this grim young man want with her, and she without a shred of beauty to protect herself? She rose, poured a goblet of wine for herself, drank several large swallows. Had he come to arrest her? For some old rebellion? Some old betrayal? To lock her up and throw away the key? His presence seemed enormous, dominating the chamber, dominating her.

"How may I be of service?" she asked. I'm an old woman now, she thought. Old women can do no harm.

"By telling me the truth."

An enormous demand. What, after all, was truth but one man's, one woman's version of a fleeting moment? "I am always truthful."

That lie hung for a time between them. He did nothing with it, which made her respect for him grow.

"Leave us," he said to Colbert, and when the man was gone, when it was only the two of them, "There was a quarrel between their majesties the year of my birth."

"Yes, a terrible one. Her Majesty's correspondence with the kingdom of Spain was found, and your father was furious."

"Yet they were on terms close enough to conceive a child?"

"A man needs to drop his guard only once."

"Twice. I have a brother."

"Twice," she agreed. She drank another deep, long, slow swallow of wine. His rage, contained though it was, radiated out from him in invisible waves.

"Did you ever perform a service for my mother that was of great delicacy, great danger?"

"Many times."

"Now would be the time to tell of them."

"I spied for her, wrote secret letters to Spain. And I plotted against Cardinal Mazarin, but not because she asked it. Surely you know all this."

"Nothing more?"

"I stood guard when she and the cardinal made love."

"Before I was born?"

Her mind went reeling. "No." She'd been in exile then. Would he banish her for this conversation?

"You didn't like the cardinal?"

"His influence was too pronounced."

"With my mother?"

"With your mother." She was too old to make a new place, as once she'd done, going off jauntily on a new adventure. She wanted to end her days here. It had always been rumored Queen Anne had married the cardinal. It must be so. What did he want of her? She could not verify the marriage. If anyone could, surely it was this king.

"Why did you intrigue against him?"

"It was what one did. Intrigue. It was my duty as a courtier, as a daughter of the Rohan-Montbazons."

There was a long silence between them.

"May I sit down, Your Majesty?" she asked. He didn't answer her, and the trembling in her voice moved to her body. She clasped her hands together in an attempt to control some of her shaking.

"At my command and under my direction, you will convince my mother that a certain friendship she treasures must be sundered, that my will is paramount."

"Yes. Your wish is my command."

His eyes bored into her, and she felt pinned to the ground by his fierceness. "I very much hope so. I very much hope you've told me everything. If I am betrayed, I'll destroy your husband, and then I will destroy your children, and then, and only then, I will destroy you."

With those words, he left the chamber. She could see and hear men moving outside, hear the jingle of harness. She slumped into a chair. She felt as if she'd been savagely beaten. A discreet knock came at the door, then Monsieur Colbert entered the chamber.

"You're to say nothing of this visit, this conversation, to anyone, not your husband, not even your confessor." The words were flat, said with no emotion.

She could see Colbert's immense intelligence shining in his eyes, his face. He works night and day, was the word, a drone. She had no sense of the dry emptiness of a drone. This man vibrated with will and determination and purpose, just as His Majesty did. "Am I to know the name of this friend I am to convince Her Majesty to renounce?"

"The Viscount Nicolas."

So, it is the viscount who is to fall, she thought. Will it bring war? She thought briefly of warning Nicolas, of playing both sides as once she'd done so well, but she lacked stamina. And Colbert would have her watched. From this moment on, her every move would be reported. She knew that as well as she knew her own name.

"His Majesty has asked that I tell you why the Viscount Nicolas has fallen from favor. It is a high honor and a responsibility to be taken into his confidence. He has a great regard for your friendship with the Queen Mother. Your influence with her is legend. I trust it will live up to its reputation."

In a few brief words, he told her about the lies and disarray in finance and about the island filled with weapons and soldiers. To behead the most powerful man in the kingdom was a brilliant stroke, she thought as she listened, the move of an intrepid warrior, worthy of a great king. It would awe the court. It was a perfect first move toward subduing the nobility. If she'd been younger, she'd have made this king adore her.

"What can I give His Majesty?" she asked. "Some gift that underscores my loyalty and devotion."

Colbert's eyes flicked to the wall of books, several lifetimes of acquisition, her father's, her first two husbands', both dukes', her own. The gesture did not go unnoticed.

Without hesitation she said, "Will you tell His Majesty that when I die, he would do me a great honor if he would accept these books that my family has assembled, as a sign of my loyalty to his reign and my honor at the trust bestowed?"

"I will tell him," said Colbert.

"Have you children?"

"I do."

"An alliance between our families is not inconceivable to me."

It was an extraordinary suggestion. Her family was one of the oldest, the proudest in France, and Colbert came from merchant stock. He was rich these days. No one who had worked for Mazarin went unrewarded. A brilliant tactician, he had managed the details of Mazarin's life—including the king's wedding—with verve and thoroughness, but still, he was a lackey. Nonetheless, she decided to gamble with the brashness that was her best, and worst, feature.

"I would never betray a member of my family," she said.

Colbert's dark eyes had become velvety soft. Either he was at his most truth-worthy or most dangerous. It didn't matter, really. She'd thrown her glove over his garden wall.

"I shall consider your husband's advancement a personal obligation," he said to her. And then he was gone, disappearing with his black clothes into the night like ink poured on dark stone.

She sat down very slowly, very carefully. It had been a long time since anyone had made her afraid, not since Cardinal Richelieu. She hadn't been afraid of Mazarin, who had believed that everyone had his price and had simply searched for that price. Mazarin hadn't had the sheer ruthlessness of his predecessor, Richelieu, but this one—well, he might be the child of Richelieu instead of him whom it was once whispered he was the child of. So long ago, those whispers. She had forgotten them. Life, wasn't it interesting, now? What excitement for her. And gray as she was, she was still necessary. Queen Anne was stubborn and ruthless when cornered. Even this young lion couldn't quite handle her. God, her Beloved, was good. The minion Colbert would rise. She could sense it, and her family would rise with him, if she behaved herself, for once. Perhaps she would. She was, after all, old.

At Fontainebleau, Louis allowed himself an hour or two of sleep at the side of his wife, woke, was dressed, and began his day, which included a hunt that took courtiers all the way to Versailles, where a picnic was set up, and the court gratefully descended from horseback to rest. Louis walked among them like a restless animal. He sat by his cousin, La Grande, who'd ridden as hard as he had and had mud on her skirts, tossed a note, its seal broken, in her lap. She read it and, shocked, raised her eyes to his.

"You're caught," he said.

"I don't understand."

"I know you've been writing these."

"I haven't—I wouldn't—"

Two musketeers had appeared.

"Go quietly with them, now," Louis said.

Tears rolled down his cousin's face. "I'm innocent, Majesty! You must believe me!"

"There's a carriage waiting. I'm sending you to your estate in the country."

Rain had begun to fall. The storm that had threatened all the morning broke. Courtiers, who'd been sitting on rugs and idly chatting, stood up and began to run for shelter. They were less than a mile from the old hunting château, in its overgrown park. The hunt had been long and particularly ferocious. It was as if the king had been determined to bring down the stag, no matter how long it took. Louis had taken the knife from the master of the hunt and cut the stag's throat himself, throwing down his blood-stained gloves as he strode past exhausted courtiers.

As the rain turned suddenly harder, Louise found shelter under a tree and put her back against its broad trunk. She felt strained to a breaking point. She'd barely been able to look His Majesty in the eye today and was scorched by what was in his expression when she did. She felt frightened and exhilarated, as scattered as these raindrops, which were now pelting down. The tree's thick branches and leaves provided a little shelter, but soon she'd be wet to the skin. It was all right.

Out from the sheets of pouring rain stepped Louis, his hat off his head. He held it over her. The chivalry, the foolishness, the courtesy of that gesture made her dig her hands into the tree's bark.

"You've captured me," he said.

She couldn't answer, even if she'd wanted to.

"I believe I'm in love with you."

She must have made some sound because he began speaking as fast as he could, as if he would outrun whatever her objections might be, objections he had to know himself.

"I'll be in the middle of a council meeting, or riding back from a long journey, and all I am thinking of is the exact shade of your eyes when you swore you'd keep my secret. The sky after a rain? At soft twilight? What is your birthdate? Who is your father? Why does your mother never come to court? All the things I don't know about you—I want to know them. I want to know you."

His eyes raked over her face, demanding, searching, appealing. This can't be happening, she thought. His hair was mussed, curling wildly. She could smell it. She could smell him. Exaltation and dread warred in her.

"Do I disgust you? Do you think me lighthearted, evil, going from one woman to the next, seeing who I can seduce? I'm not like that. I want to hold you like a talisman in my heart against all I must do." Now he looked at her directly. "It's as if I was blind, and now I see. I swear on all that's holy I don't trifle with you, Miss de la Baume le Blanc. Name of Jesus, I want permission to speak your given name. I was going to say nothing to you, to quell what's in me for both our sakes, but I can't keep myself from you. What is she thinking? I ask when I see you with your friends. What is she feeling? I wonder. Can she care for me even half as much as I find I suddenly care for her? Say you'll give me a chance to woo you, to show you that I would take the moon right out of the sky and hang it around your neck, if that's what you desired."

What his eyes promised—something true and sober and steadfast—went straight to her heart, and she felt like a newborn bird fallen from its high nest, turning in frenzied circles in the dust, struggling and afraid in its nakedness.

Louis smiled, joy blazing in his eyes. It was like the sun bursting out after a long night of dark. She felt dazzled. He was everything a man should be, strong and good and brave and gallant. He leaned in toward her, so that his great hat was covering them both, so that his hair was falling over his shoulders. They did not quite touch.

"Tell me I can hope."

His eyes were inches from her. She felt like fainting, like running away, like staying, like grabbing his mane of hair and pulling him to her and pressing her mouth to his.

"I think you care for me a little," he said, moving even closer.

She could see that the brown of his eyes had a tinge of green around the edges.

"I love you." He repeated it. Gently, he put his mouth on hers.

She couldn't move. Feelings tumbled like plates thrown off shelves. She felt soldered to him at the lips. He didn't move to touch her with his hands; his hands were in fact still holding the hat above them. The only place they touched one another was at the mouth, and even then not deeply, just a light kiss that was as sweet as any marzipan she'd ever tasted. One could die in this sweetness.

When he stepped back, it was all she could do to stay leaning against the tree. Her body wanted to follow his, felt bereft, abandoned, cold, and wet now with rain. The space between them literally hurt her. What's happening? she thought, and she felt as wild as the stag being brought to its knees by the maddened lunges of the dogs. The stag bled and lowered its antlers, as trumpets blew to announce its falling.

The downpour had lessened. Louis stepped back from her, said, "You hold my heart in your hands," and then he walked toward the chateau in the light drizzle. When he seemed far enough away, Louise followed.

"See that Miss de la Baume le Blanc has her horse immediately," Louis told a courtier.

The courtier found the horse as asked, took it to a wet and drooping young maid of honor who hadn't joined the melee of chattering, milling courtiers waiting for horses. Concerned, he said, "My dear miss, are you ill? Are you certain you can sit in the saddle?"

"Yes, ill." Ill with love, ill with dread, but alive from the top of her head to the toes curling with damp in her boots. She could hear the slightest rustle in the woods, could see the farthest bird flying, could smell the rain and earth and leaves and bark as if they were a bouquet at her nose.

"Wait here and I'll have a carriage sent for."

"No, just help me onto my horse." She was always more whole on horseback. She'd get some sense of herself as she rode back. She'd stay far back, not up front with the others where the king would be, His Majesty, the beautiful, sensual, aloof Louis whom they all secretly loved. Could she care for him? he asked. Such a question. He was the brightest star in their sky.

She settled herself in the sidesaddle. Already thoughts were clearer. She'd die if he ever tired of her. She felt a little stronger with the fatalism of that truth. This mustn't begin. She hadn't the heart for it. His Majesty had had a sudden fit—and like all fits, it would pass. She would ride this out, let it wither on its green, young vine.

CHAPTER 26

The woman began to weep, hard. Louis kept his face impassive. If the Duchess de Chevreuse knew nothing, this woman knew everything. In Madame de Motteville's hand was clasped a single piece of paper, a dreaded *lettre de cachet*, putting her in prison with no record of her arrest or whereabouts. Reading it, Madame de Motteville had burst into tears.

What an effective tool the letter was, Louis thought dispassionately as Motteville continued weeping, and his heart, which could never bear to hear a woman cry, remained as hard as the marble of the walls and floors around him.

"But why, sire? In God's name, how have I offended?"

He held out a second sheet of paper, which she took in trembling hands to read also, and then she made a sound deep in her throat, half growl, half moan, as she fell on her knees in supplication before him. It was another *lettre de cachet*, but this time the name was her daughter's.

"Two days ago I discovered a boy, half-grown, ten and five perhaps, in a monastery. He wore an iron mask so that his face couldn't be seen; however, I saw his face."

Motteville made another sound.

"The monks of that monastery are now in the Bastille," Louis continued, "and the boy has been taken to a safe place."

She brought one hand up to her heart, staring at him as if he were a ravening beast.

"When was the boy born?"

The question lay between them. Seated—which should have been Motteville's first understanding that something was wrong, for Louis invariably stood in the presence of women—Louis let the silence grow. It would take time to unlock these secrets, hidden for so long.

"In 1645," she finally said, her voice weak, strained, as if she brought the answer up from a place very far away.

He did a rapid calculation in his mind. Ten and six. Small for his age, but Philippe was small.

"How was this secret kept from court?"

"We—it was said Her Majesty was ill with dropsy. She received visitors in bed for the last months. He was taken away immediately. The cardinal saw to that."

"And when did you learn he was not as other children?"

"I no longer remember. He was but a baby."

"How often does Her Majesty visit him?" His eyes didn't leave her face. There wasn't a blink he missed, not even the tiniest movement of muscle.

"Never anymore." Motteville swallowed, looked away. "I go in her place."

"And why might that be, if you would be so kind as to conjecture?"

"He became distraught at her presence. Howled."

But that wasn't the whole truth. The whole truth was Her Majesty hated this child, and that Madame de Motteville would grieve but never tell. The boy's strangeness left her ill. It was the cardinal who would go to see him, twice a year, taking gifts of clothing and marzipan cakes and toys. At his command, Motteville would accompany him. So that you may tell Her Majesty of him, Cardinal Mazarin had said, his face sad, except that the queen never asked. It had been agreed that the queen and the cardinal never spoke between themselves of him. Such always led to dreadful quarrels, days of raging for her, of grief for him. She saw the boy as penance for her sins, Mazarin saw him as one of life's little tragedies, loved anyway.

"And the mask?"

"There was a certain family resemblance," whispered Motteville.

"When was it first fashioned for him?"

"When he was five," she said, her face a mix of sadness, distress, and memory. "A new one was made as he grew. It was ordered that no one see his face. Ever. It was clear—" She stopped, unable to utter the words.

How much he resembled me. "Yes," Louis finished for her. Whatever else was said between them at this moment, he did not want the word "brother" emerging from thought to tongue to the air between them. If he kept the spoken word at bay, he could do all he must do.

"Who else knew of this?"

"No one."

"Cinq Mars."

"He was the cardinal's most trusted musketeer. His orders were to care for and guard the boy as if he were his own." She knelt before him. "He's a good man, Your Majesty. Please don't—please be forbearing with him."

"Tell me about the abbot."

"He and the cardinal were old friends, from Italy, from the cardinal's days when he was a papal diplomat, before he came here to serve Richelieu."

"And the monks?"

"Assembled from Italy and Spain, Cistercians, who have taken a vow of silence and the mission of service to boys who are born idiots."

"Did the abbot know this boy's parentage?"

"No, sire."

A boy whom France's greatest minister deigned to visit, to bring treats for? The abbot would certainly have made conjectures if nothing else, thought Louis. "Does the Viscount Nicolas know?"

"No one knows."

"Return the *lettres*, please," Louis said.

Still kneeling, she crept forward with them. "Are you going to arrest me, majesty? Do so, if you must, but not my daughter, never my daughter. She has no part in this. The blame is mine alone."

"This interview between us remains a secret not even your priest must know. And I have a few new duties for you. You are to report every day about who calls upon Her Majesty and what is said."

Her loyalty had always been to his mother. Now she must redefine that loyalty.

"Any correspondence of Her Majesty's will be brought first to me. And I am most particularly interested in that between Her Majesty and the Viscount Nicolas."

He watched the struggle going on in Motteville's face. He let his hand touch the paper on which her daughter's name was written. Motteville met his eyes, odd, flickering lights in them, she thought, hard. She curtsied.

"Your every wish is my command," she whispered. "I will serve to the best of my ability."

She stood, backed from the chamber, bent forward submissively, her skirts held in each hand. Louis tapped restive thumbs on the stiff parchment of the *lettres*. There was no word yet from D'Artagnan, who had promised to send a musketeer straight back once the boy and Cinq Mars and the abbot were in the fortress. Louis walked to the cupboard, pulled down its massive front, unlocked a drawer, and dropped the letters in. These, with the monks', were the first he'd ever written, letters that erased a person from life, no record of arrest anywhere, so that he or she was essentially obliterated, until it should be the king's pleasure to make it otherwise. How many more will I write in this life of mine? thought Louis, and he stared at the shelves that held his curios without seeing them. Between his brows was the first line his face would imprint, a line of worry and sadness and absolute determination.

"They arrived quietly in Paris before dawn, went into the Bastille, and then word of them simply stops."

It was a Jesuit Nicolas knew, a highly placed priest with ties to the general of their order who resided in Rome, at the hand of the Holy Father.

"How extraordinary," said Nicolas. He was at Vaux-le-Vicomte, the estate to his mind still too unfinished in spite of the fact he was holding a grand fête with the king as a guest of honor in a few weeks. "You spoke to the governor of the Bastille yourself?"

"I sent my secretary, and the governor swore he has no knowledge of monks coming into the Bastille."

"And you're certain it was His Majesty's musketeers who took them in?"

"That's what was seen. Musketeers on gray horses."

"Odd indeed. You're right to bring it to me. I will find out what I can. But for now come and look at the drawings Le Brun has made for my rotunda dome. I'm satisfied with none of them."

He showed him the drawings, then the tapestries now in place in the king's bedchamber—it was the extravagant custom to have a bedchamber reserved strictly for majesty, and in it, Nicolas had already placed the richest fabrics and objects in the château.

The Jesuit fingered the thick fabric of the bed's long curtains. Nicolas told him how he'd established a workshop not far from the château whose sole purpose was to weave the tapestries that covered his walls and furniture.

"Everyone will be in ecstasies over them," said the Jesuit. "When you've done with your own, might I order some for my general in Rome?"

Nicolas bowed. There was a myth about a man named Midas whose every touch produced gold. He'd known courtiers would rush to copy what he'd done, and that eventually his tapestry mill would turn a profit. It already had its first commission, it seemed.

"You must see the gardens," he said.

"They cannot be more magnificent than your entrance court."

But they were. The stone château was surrounded by a square moat, and the water was like a necklace around the throat of a lovely woman. From the broad back terrace, a grand vista swept all the way to a hill on which stood a colossal statue of Hercules, uncrated and placed on its base just this month, Nicolas explained as they walked toward it. His brother, also a priest, sent him treasures and antiquities from Rome. When they walked to the hill and looked back, the château shimmering in the distance, Nicolas told him that they were standing at the end of an axis that stretched two miles from north to south, an axis with the house as its focal point.

"Breathtaking," said the priest.

Nicolas was gratified, told him of the men who had helped create this vision: a royal architect, painter, and gardener.

"Their genius will go down in history," said the Jesuit, bowing, "and so will yours for having the foresight to combine their talents."

Nicolas offered him dinner.

"I've heard from the general and council regarding your request," the Jesuit said, as he pondered whether to have foie gras or patties of braised tongue. "We would be most happy to accommodate."

Nicolas had gone to them to borrow a portion of the king's million. All his own funds were tied up here, in this. "If I may recommend the patties, they are my cook's specialty. And the interest for a loan would be?"

"Twenty-five percent."

When the man was back in his carriage, on the road to Paris, where, Nicolas knew, he would spread the word of the serene and orderly beauty of the house and gardens, Nicolas let himself feel the shock of the amount of interest the Jesuits would charge before calling for his secretary, telling him the story the Jesuit had brought.

"Circulate among the king's men," Nicolas ordered. "Find out what they have to say."

"They're remarkably tight-lipped these days."

Nicolas smiled. "Approach the one with the biggest debt."

One of the foremen who ran the building crews walked up the stairs of the château's broad back terrace. "There's been a fire, sir. A few acres burned, but rain stopped there from being much damage to your land. It was the monastery that caught fire," continued the foreman. "It burned to nothing but bare stone, its arbors too. No bodies found."

Monks again, thought Nicolas. "Were there any children found, any of the boys?" he asked.

The man shook his head and left Nicolas standing on his terrace, looking off into the distance, to the grand statue of Hercules upon its hill. His Majesty had stood in the rain yesterday with his hat over the blond head of lissome Miss de la Baume le Blanc, talking persuasively to her about something. Making love, Nicolas would imagine, though Catherine swore Madame had his full regard, that he flirted on her command. A young dog, thought Nicolas, not knowing in which kennel he wished to sleep. He could sleep in them all, as far as Nicolas was concerned. A distracted king allowed the leeway necessary to be all that he, Nicolas, must be, to have all that he must have, which was much.

Choisy found himself ushered into His Majesty's chamber of books on the ground floor of Fontainebleau. Three dogs rushed forward to sniff him as

Louis, looking out an open window, another dog lying on a cushion at his feet, turned to look at him.

"Thank you for coming."

"You have only to command, Majesty." Choisy was flattered. He circulated in the lesser circle that was Monsieur's.

Louis gestured toward chairs, and Choisy waited for him to sit down first. Dogs milled around them, finally settling at Louis's feet.

"You are acquainted with Miss de la Baume le Blanc," Louis said.

"She is one of my mother's favorites; mine, too."

"How long have you known her?"

"Since your uncle, the Duke d'Orléans, may he rest in peace, died."

"Tell me of her family."

"Her father was a soldier, long dead. There are a brother and mother, and half-sisters from her mother's second marriage. A small estate near Amboise, her brother's and her mother's, nothing there for her." He leaned forward, ready to gossip a little. "My dear cousin had to borrow in her own name to buy court clothes. Her family didn't give her so much as a extra coin."

"They quarrel?"

"Oh my goodness, no. I don't think my little cousin knows how to quarrel. She's an obedient girl."

"Has anyone her favor?"

"I'd like to think I do." And at Louis's expression of surprise, "I'm not as you imagine, sire."

"I imagine nothing."

What exquisite manners you possess, thought Choisy, and spoke quickly to cover pain at the king's unexpected kindness. "She's simple, really. Her idea of happiness is a hard gallop atop a horse twice a day. She loves the woods, the fields, the flowers. She adores all animals. I think she likes them more than people. She isn't of this world, sire." He stopped, aware he was talking too much, made a gesture that took in the many books, the engravings and paintings and sculpture, the elaborate embroidered draperies at the long windows, the world outside those windows with wide courtyards and plots and intrigues and betrayals. "She's pure of heart, and I don't say that lightly."

"You care for her, I see that clearly."

"With all my impure heart."

"Is it true that Monsieur dressed himself as a woman, called upon the Count de Guiche, and was not only slapped about, but pushed from the count's chamber?"

Taken completely off guard, Choisy gasped.

"Is it true he wept outside the door and begged to be allowed inside until you and the Chevalier de Lorraine came to his rescue and dragged him away? How often does the count strike my brother?"

"Sire...I have no— Who has told you such a thing?"

Olympe, but there was no reason to reveal that. Louis leaned forward in his chair. "Is it true?"

Courtier's charm deserting him, Choisy was silent, his mind working to find a way to answer.

"I'm going to take your silence to mean yes."

"No—"

"No, it did not happen as I've heard, or no, you don't wish to speak of this, even to me, because of your friendship with my brother?"

"I—I have nothing but admiration for Monsieur."

"I am so pleased to hear it. Did the Count de Guiche strike my brother and leave him weeping in a hall?"

Choisy closed his eyes. "Yes," he finally said.

Louis leaned back in his chair, and with a start, Choisy realized that their interview was over.

❧❧❧

"Her Majesty awaits you, sire."

Louis needed his keenest senses for this talk with his mother, but Olympe was on his mind. What had made her an enemy of not only Guiche, but even more so of Guiche's sister, Catherine? Catherine encourages him in his worst behavior, Olympe insisted as she told him of Guiche's behavior toward Philippe. Dismiss her if you dismiss him. He's seduced a maid of honor. His sister allows it. And Olympe was against the Viscount Nicolas now, dripping venom, telling Louis outright that the viscount had asked her to spy upon the queen.

He shook his head to clear it and stepped into his mother's closet, that most private of chambers—crammed and cramped with small tables and big, heavy chairs, crucifixes hanging between paintings, silver and gilt boxes holding relics, portraits of saints and her Spanish and Hapsburg relatives. He pulled the lace at his throat, his eyes drawn to an enormous portrait of the cardinal that faced him, the rich crimson pigment of a cardinal's robe filling the frame, the face, with its dark eyes and sensitive, smiling mouth, wonderfully alive, as if the cardinal would step down from the canvas and embrace him. God, how much he had loved this man. He began to perspire and was suddenly lightheaded. Would he faint? Crumble at his mother's feet like a child? Forgive her. Forgive me. The words rang in his ears as if someone spoke them, yet no one did. Had he heard a ghost? Rage evaporated inside him, and without it, he felt lost, no mooring to steady him through this.

His mother was finishing her breakfast, and she had looked up from her plate to send a chilly glance his way. Once he had begun each morning with a visit to her; all that had changed. He couldn't move his eyes from the portrait. The cardinal had stood before the altar as his godfather, this Italian who had never taken formal orders in the church, yet had been so wily and charming that the Mother Church had embraced him and given him title after title for his usefulness, this man who had thought all the world ought to possess at least one thing beautiful and that his godson must possess the most beautiful things of all.

"I'm surprised you deign to call on me. Am I not to be given a son's kiss of respect? Such manners," his mother said, glacial as last autumn's frost, patting her lips with her huge, white, embroidered napkin.

Louis sat down in a chair. "Tell me about my father," he heard himself say and was shocked that any words had formed at all.

Anne made a face. "A difficult man, even when I married him, and we were but children. Reared badly, savagely. A brave warrior, suspicious, untrusting, unkind, but brave." She cut up ham into small, precise pieces and speared one with a fork.

"Who of us is more like him, Monsieur or me?"

"Your father had a weakness for handsome favorites like Monsieur, which reminds me. We need to speak about the Count de Guiche and his conduct toward Monsieur lately. I've heard some things I refuse to believe."

"Amazing I was born if his taste ran to handsome favorites."

Her face softened at once. "My miracle, my God-given, what a darling boy you were." She smiled, temper dissolved in fond memory. "Come and give your mother a kiss and do stop all this sulking. It's for your own good that I chasten and lecture. Your conduct must be exemplary."

"What a miracle I am indeed, being born after years of barrenness."

"I wasn't barren. Your father—"

"Chose not to grace your bed. I made an interesting discovery a few days ago, Mother. I found a boy who wore an iron mask."

She dropped the fork and stared at him.

"More a youth than a boy, I would say. He would not speak except to howl. Imagine my surprise when I saw his face."

She closed her eyes.

"A face so like mine that I was without words but not without questions. Who is he, Mother?"

"Our beloved cardinal had a love child. We put him away in the monastery."

The words were out before Louis could blink. He watched her rally around the lie.

"It broke my heart, of course. You above all people know why."

"He resembles me."

"Nonsense. I'm sure he resembles the strumpet who was his mother. Oh, I thought I'd never get over it. Don't ask me to help, I told him. I won't lift a finger, I said, but I did. You know how I am, too giving of myself. I've always been that way."

"Your lady-in-waiting went to visit the boy. Why, Mother?"

She looked down at the plate, its breakfast in disarray. "She was the mother." She didn't raise her eyes. "I thought I would go mad when I discovered that she and Jules were lovers." She met Louis's eyes squarely with those words, resolute in the courage of her lie. "But I didn't go mad, and with time, I forgave. I also forgot. It's time to send the boy away, I think. Genoa, perhaps, or Spain. Perhaps a colony. Where is he now?"

Louis didn't answer. She licked her lips, pushed back from the table at which she sat, went to stand at the windows with her back to him. "I've quite lost my appetite over this."

"I desire a favor of you."

She didn't answer, and he waited, because he was so tired, so very tired. He felt like he could close his eyes and sleep for days. "I am going to arrest the viscount," he said.

She swung around, her face aghast.

"And I must know that you will support me."

"I thought you wished him to be chancellor! He would be a perfect chancellor! It's a mistake! There will be war! Oh, darling, you don't want war! Not yet. What's he done? Has it to do with this? He knows nothing of it. He's a good man, an excellent minister. You know how our beloved cardinal depended upon him. You must also. There is no other choice. You mustn't do this! It's dangerous beyond words!"

"On the contrary, I must—with you to help me, or at least, not to hinder."

She had her hands clasped together. Her voice rose. "I can't! I won't! It's a mistake I won't allow you to make!"

"This court is infested with his spies! If I wear a new coat, he knows it before the thing is placed on my shoulders. There isn't a coin in my treasury, yet he builds a temple to the god of his vanity a few miles from here. He has an island stockpiled with weapons and men. The commanders of the Atlantic and Mediterranean fleets reside in his pocket. He could isolate France by sea if he were so inclined! I won't have it. I won't have anyone that powerful among my ministers! I am going to arrest him and bring him to trial for his crimes against this kingdom. Speculation! False accounting! Thievery! But most of all, daring to plot against me!"

She was sobbing, and he was too tired to discern why. Was it rage that he didn't listen, rage that he'd found out about his brother and guessed the truth of his own birth, or rage simply because it distracted from the task at hand? He heard himself say, "Interesting that you call Madame de Motteville a strumpet, and yet she serves you on an intimate basis to this day. Interesting that the boy resembles me enough to be a brother. Interesting that you were estranged from my father for years, including the year I was born, a year in which you were caught sending treasonous letters to Spain, yet born I was. What a forgiving man my father was. Extraordinary when I think about it."

There was more to say but not today. None of the bitter accusations that had filled his thoughts for days would speak themselves. He rose from the chair, strode through her antechamber looking neither to the right nor to the left. Stairs took him to the fountain courtyard, and he was glad to be in the sun, glad to see it sparkle on the water of the pond, glad to see those few courtiers who liked morning strolling among the parterres of the suspended garden. The world went on the merry way it always had, never mind that his own was knocked askew.

She hadn't admitted the truth, and for that, he realized that he felt a deep and full respect. Courage in the face of adversity. Strength. Determination. She had been rock, and the cardinal had been water flowing around that which obstructed. Who was his father? Did it matter if no one guessed? She would never tell. He suddenly knew that to his bones. Not if she were tied to the rack and pulled to pieces. She would accuse Madame de Motteville of lies if Louis confronted them both, then likely have her poisoned.

But now the Mazarinades held new menace. They were blatant in their blare that the cardinal and his mother had been lovers. I didn't write them, La Grande had wept when D'Artagnan questioned her. I swear by all that's holy. Were they a threat, not about war as he had imagined, but about his birth? If his birth were questioned, the kingdom wouldn't hold together. I didn't write them, La Grande had pleaded. Who did, then? The viscount, as Colbert insisted? He stumbled on a paved stone of the courtyard.

"Sir!" barked the musketeer who followed him, catching him by the elbow.

He tried to control the shaking that had hold of him. "I think I have a headache," he said. He must lie in bed, close his eyes with Belle's dear head under his hand. She was a queen in all senses of the word, his mother, an infanta of Spain, the pride of the Hapsburgs. That blood ran through his veins. The other…well, he'd not think on that for a bit, rest, so that he could be king in all senses of the word, as he must be, as his beloved cardinal who might be so much more, had trained him to be.

"Don't touch me," he said to his musketeer when he stumbled again.

He'd make it to the bedchamber on will if nothing else. He was his mother's son. The world was fraught with missteps, wasn't it?

❦❦❦

The next day Anne dropped an invitation from the Duchess de Chevreuse to visit on a silver tray. "I don't wish to go."

Motteville continued her packing of what the Queen Mother would need, gowns for evening, favorite rosaries, brushes and combs, an embroidered bed jacket, shoes of all kinds. Haven't I always known this moment was coming? the lady-in-waiting thought, moving silently among the Queen Mother's litter of beautiful things: leather gloves, prayer books with ivory covers, silver hairpins, ribbons, gauze bows, great collars, and small caps of handmade lace.

"I'm not going," said Anne.

"His Majesty's command." The last was a whisper.

Anne stopped shredding to pieces the paper upon which the invitation was written and watched her lady-in-waiting. Motteville didn't speak, did not look in the Queen Mother's direction once.

"So," Anne finally said, "you've been ordered to spy on me, haven't you?"

Motteville continued her organized whirl from one thing to another.

Anne laughed, but there was no joy in the sound. "It's like old times." How they'd watched her, Cardinal Richelieu, her husband, but they hadn't been able to stop her. Spain was her first love then, not France. There was no survival for a queen without an heir, so she'd given the kingdom one and saved herself and then held as best she could the kingdom she'd once betrayed, because her son, Louis, was France.

There was another emotion underneath her rage: respect. He knew what he wanted, and he walked straightforwardly toward it, or as straightforwardly as a king was able. So, she'd done as queen. All right, she'd go and listen to what her old and dear friend had to say. If Louis had pulled the duchess over to his side, that was a triumph. How amazing, that Louis thought he could vanquish the viscount. Even Jules had been afraid to make the attempt.

CHAPTER 27

Belle's licking of his face woke him from his nap. He opened his eyes and saw that his valet was standing at his bedside.

"The Viscount Nicolas requests your presence in the courtyard, sire."

He dipped his hands in the cool water that was in a silver bowl, dried them. La Porte ran a comb through his tousled curls, straightened the lace at his neck and sleeves. He picked Belle up from the bed and carried her to her cushion in the antechamber at the window. Her daughter and sons swirling around his legs, he ran downstairs and out into his courtyard, crossed through the elaborate gatehouse that had been built to celebrate his father's birth, and walked across the bridge that overhung the moat into the common courtyard.

Men pulled hats off their heads. Women began to curtsy. His dogs started barking immediately at the cats sitting on the wall, but Phaedra, his female, ran straight to the horse the Viscount Nicolas sat upon and began to sniff the beast's legs. The viscount dismounted and made an elaborate bow. Louis noted the men with him, his private guard, gathered behind a coach. They wore matching tabards, like his musketeers, no cross emblazoned on them, but the color of the cloth all the same. The viscount's face was smiling, joyous almost. Louis realized his other ministers were there, standing at the coach. They, too, were smiling.

"I bring you your heart's desire, majesty," the viscount said, and he slapped the coach with one hand, then opened its door, and stepped back for Louis to see what was inside.

Chests, on the floor, on the seats, piled atop one another.

"Your million," whispered the viscount in his ear.

"Into my courtyard," ordered Louis, then, "Not your guard, Viscount. Leave them in the common courtyard."

"Of course."

"Wine for the viscount's guard," he called out, and he led the way across the bridge, through the gatehouse, into his private sanctum. The coach's wheels were loud on the paving stones.

People stood along the upper colonnade that mirrored part of the oval of his courtyard, a maid of honor or two, some of his gentlemen talking with them, his mother, dressed for travel, a Spanish shawl tied around her shoulders, her perennial lace widow's cap on her head. He met his mother's eyes, and they stared at each other unsmiling, each aware of the distance now between them.

"Wine for my ministers," called Louis, looking away from her. He felt fatalistic, what would be would be.

Soon the courtyard was filled with people, as many of them surrounding the viscount as surrounding him.

"A present for His Majesty, a token of my regard," the viscount said over and over when asked about the coach. Louis had ordered musketeers stationed at the two gatehouses that fed into this courtyard, and musketeers stood on either side of the carriage.

His mother came downstairs to mingle before her departure. He watched Nicolas take her a goblet of wine and present it on bended knee, watched her drain it as if it were ale and thank him. Will her friendship with him, her fear, win over her love for me? he wondered. It was possible. In statecraft, love was often trampled.

"Are you going on a journey?" Nicolas asked Anne.

"To visit my old friend again. As we age, we have such need of friends."

"I am always your friend."

If she answered, Louis didn't hear it.

"Monsieur, can you move everyone to the fountain courtyard?" Louis asked, and in no time, Philippe and his gentlemen had laughing courtiers and ministers following them through an arched entryway as if they were the pied pipers of the folk tale.

Silently, he walked his mother to her waiting carriage, which was just outside the golden gate. Madame de Motteville stood at the door, awaiting her queen. Once inside, Anne put a gloved hand on the ledge of one of the carriage's openings. Louis put his hand atop hers. "I have need of your loyalty," he said.

The sun was in his eyes; he couldn't read her face, but he thought he heard her say, "You've always had it," before the carriage lurched away.

Later, he ran upstairs to his chambers, thinking as his footsteps echoed on the stone of the staircases that he ought to have his entire army dress the way his musketeers did, the way the viscount's guard did, the same uniform for all, so that on a battlefield, one knew a Frenchman from a Spaniard or an Englishman. It was what the Roman legions had done, but somewhere in the following centuries, the practice had been lost.

As he passed through his antechamber, he saw a woman sitting with Belle and realized the woman was Miss de la Baume le Blanc. Joy blazed in him, for she had been avoiding him. "What a wonderful surprise!"

"I—we come to visit sometimes. I assumed you were—"

"In council? Does my presence distress you?"

Appearing from wherever he hid himself, La Porte suddenly joined them. "You know Miss de la Baume le Blanc, sir. Madame Belle likes it when Miss de la Baume le Blanc visits."

Yes, Louis could imagine laying his own head in Louise's lap and having her fingers stroke his forehead, and his eyes met Louise's. Love me, he told her silently.

"She's leaving us, Your Majesty."

La Porte grimaced at Louise's words, and she saw it and began that blush of hers. "I'm—I'm so sorry, Your Majesty. I shouldn't have spoken," she stammered.

Louis crouched down so that he was on their level. Louise's blush was growing. Belle made a soft whine, and he put his hand out, and she licked it. She was going to die, wasn't she? His physicians wouldn't say so, but it was true. A king wasn't allowed to stay in the presence of dying, but this was one death he had every intention of witnessing. How would he bear it when the most loyal being he knew no longer existed? He'd bear it like he bore everything else, wouldn't he, hiding its true depth from the world because there was no one who would not take advantage, except this lovely, blushing young woman who had come to visit his sick dog more than once and never bragged of it, never told others so that her kindness would be noticed, and now told him a truth few dared. She avoided him but not dying Belle. It had been a long while since he'd been around someone innately kind. Kindness had, in fact, left his life with the cardinal's death. He stood up, walked into his bedchamber, La Porte following.

"I won't allow her to visit again, sire," La Porte said to him.

"No, it's all right. It touches me that she sees after my dog, and someone has to tell me the truth." And I have to be man enough to bear it.

❦

That evening, he danced with Henriette, who was sparkling, really, full of the coming ballet she was hostessing for the court. She was arch and flirting, her fingers playing a sensuous little tapping against his wrist when they stood a moment together after the dance was ended, but for him, it was over. Now he must face the task of telling Henriette. He had loved her to madness, and now, he didn't. He understood none of it. He lifted her hand upward and made the motion of kissing it to stop her touching him.

"You must behave yourself," she said. "You're making my maid of honor sigh too much. Look at her." And she pointed in Louise's direction. "She's drooping, as am I." She met his eyes directly, no smile now upon her face.

"Who else shall I flirt with, my very dear sister? Your wish is my command."

"I can still command? I thought my power over you less."

He didn't answer. His silence was answer enough.

Henriette watched as he crossed the ballroom. I'm losing him, she thought. She felt like weeping, but one didn't weep in public. How delighted the Queen Mother must be. She must swallow tears for hours yet, and so she sashayed over to Guy and demanded that he dance with her. She knew she shouldn't encourage him, but what was in Guy's eyes was flattering. What was in Louis's these days was painful.

Louis went to Fanny, who rose up so abruptly that the chair she was sitting in fell over. He escorted her to one of the arches in the ballroom. "During supper I wish to speak with Miss de la Baume le Blanc. Will you escort her to the bench we met at last week?"

"Oh, yes, of course, whatever you ask—" Fanny babbled, still talking, even after he'd bowed and walked away. Holy Mother of God, thought Fanny, was he in love with Louise? A glimpse of the riches and regard that lay ahead showed itself in Fanny's mind. The world was about to be placed at Louise's feet.

Louis danced with others before, finally, he allowed himself to ask Louise to dance. She was very pale and didn't meet his eyes once. It was all he could do not to drag her out onto the balcony and kiss her until she begged him to stop. He felt so protective of her, of her nervousness, that he scowled, even though he knew he had caused her distress, and courtiers, watching, all felt sorry for Miss de la Baume le Blanc, who clearly had few social graces. As the dance ended, and the final notes of the violins spilled over the musicians' gallery, he and she faced each other in the final position of the dance.

"I must speak with you later," he said.

"Oh, no," she answered.

Crushed, for a moment he couldn't think. "It isn't a request," he said.

What happened next was a blur. He knew he was walking about the chamber, dancing with other women, with his wife again. He knew he was talking with this person and that, greeting the viscount and his wife, who was in from Paris. Everyone knew that the viscount had brought the king money that afternoon. He was like a blazing sun. All eyes followed him. Everyone wanted at least a word with him.

"The oddest thing, Your Majesty," said Nicolas, "there's a mysterious tale circulating through Paris that your Grays took monks to the Bastille."

Gone was dismay about Louise. Louis was instantly alert. Was the viscount on the scent already?

"That monastery near Vaux-le-Vicomte burned down. Surely you didn't have the monks there arrested for accidentally destroying good wine?" Nicolas continued. People standing with them laughed.

"One of them came to the palace begging aid, and I sent my men to put out the fire, but they were too late. The Grays were in Paris to take the unfortunate boys to convents. The monks are on their way, at my expense, to Rome."

"Bravo, Your Majesty," cried Nicolas's wife. "How generous of you. I'll be the first to give something toward the reestablishment of their monastery."

"I knew there was a good explanation," said Nicolas.

"You must allow me the honor of dancing with your charming wife," Louis said. He heard himself make polite conversation with the viscountess, who wanted to talk all about the monks and must compliment him again and again on his kindness to them. He returned her to Nicolas, standing now with Catherine, who wore bold, scarlet feathers in her hair.

"My dear," said Nicolas to his wife, "I believe you know the Princess de Monaco."

Louis went to his friends, Vivonne and Péguilin and Vardes. "Make certain the viscountess has partners for every dance until the dancing ends," he told them. "See that she has an escort for supper."

Later, as people crowded toward a table where food was piled in high pyramids and the amount of silver serving pieces was dazzling, one of Nicolas's most reliant spies bustled forward, a certain Madame du Plessis-Bellièvre, plump and gray, her manner so innocuous, so kindly, that people were always telling her things they shouldn't. She sat down by Nicolas. "His lieutenant of the musketeers hasn't been seen."

"Where is he?"

"No one knows. There was some kind of special mission, just a few days ago. The whole company left the palace in the evening and didn't return until the following day. Our loyal lieutenant never returned at all."

Monks and musketeers yet again, thought Nicolas. Now why would Lieutenant D'Artagnan not return from the fire? She left him, and here now was Catherine, those crimson head feathers furling against one silky cheek.

"And who was that?" she asked.

"Someone from my home province, an old friend. Surely you've met her. Her son-in-law is His Majesty's commander in the Mediterranean."

"Your wife is charming," Catherine said, glancing back toward the dancing, where Nicolas's wife moved and swayed, jewels as glittering as the crystal drops of two chandeliers.

"She will be gratified to hear so."

"There's dismay in paradise. Madame cried half the day yesterday, and she hasn't been alone with him for days. You men really are too cruel to us poor creatures who adore you so."

"I hear Lieutenant D'Artagnan is missing from action."

"Visiting his wife in Paris, no doubt."

"No doubt. But if you should hear otherwise, you will let me know?"

He watched Madame, surrounded by admirers, His Majesty among them. Had their affair died already? Words from a song he'd heard the king sing only a few days earlier came into his head. His Majesty had played the guitar and sung the words in a low, sweet tenor. No one watching could conceive the young king capable of guile. Perfidiousness underlay the heights he and the king operated from. Could it be that His Majesty already understood that? Meet me by moonlight alone, he'd sung in his tender voice, I would show to the night flowers their queen, nay, turn not aside that sweet head—'tis the fairest that ever was seen, then meet me by moonlight alone.

❧❧❧

Finally, it was time for supper, and courtiers crowded around the tables set in chambers down the hall from the ballroom. Food spilled over silver trays, pigeon and braised quail, turkey served with partridges, ham, tarts, truffles. Louis saw that Maria Teresa, her plate full to brimming, was talking to someone with her mouth half-full as she fed her dwarves, as usual, with her own fingers, dropping food into their open mouths as if they were dogs.

He shut his eyes to the sight and half ran down servants' steps into his gatehouse, his special entrance to his courtyard, stepping out the door cut into the wooden gates, and there Louise was, sitting on a bench with Fanny, who immediately flitted somewhere out of sight. Louise stood up at the sight of him.

"See that we're not disturbed," he told his musketeer.

He felt uncertain. Did she find him distasteful? Boorish? Wasn't that what Madame called Guy? A boor? He searched for something to say. His mind was empty. Boldness deserted him. Cure me, he thought, as you do my animals. Be my darling, my beloved. Take my heart in your tender hands and cherish it. Heal it.

She peered at him, not smiling. Her face was mainly shadow, but there was enough light from a nearby torch to see some expression. My flirting hurts her, he thought. And then words just fell from his mouth. "Tell me how to talk to you. I so want to talk to you, and it seems that all I do is make mistakes."

"Why would you want to talk to me?"

"I love you."

"Don't say that!" Before she could run, he grabbed her by the wrist. "I'm not pretty enough! I'm not clever enough! You'll tire of me in a fortnight, and it will break my heart!" she said.

"Why will it break your heart?" He didn't let go. His eyes didn't leave her face, the shadows and light playing over it. "Do you—could you care for me?"

Her expression became disbelieving, almost disdainful. She has feelings for me, he thought. "Sit down." He was urgent, at his most coaxing. "Hear me. Trust me, please. I would never hurt you, never."

Louise sat down, on the very edge of the bench, and he let go of her wrist.

"What do you want?"

Her voice sounded despairing. How serious her expression was. No flirtation, not the least flutter. No guile, as Choisy had warned. To love you, to worship you, to adore you, to take care of you. The words were there on his lips, but he couldn't say them. The truth was if he truly wished to protect her, he wouldn't ask her to be his mistress. There was pride, precedent, history, in being the king's mistress. It was a position of power, but she was too gentle. The sudden conflict between desire and chivalry silenced him. He didn't want to hurt her, but, oh Merciful God in heaven, he wanted her, so he sat silent, knowing he should be saying loving words; he knew the lines of a hundred ballads, poems he could recite to her, but at this moment, not a one came to mind.

He heard the rustle of her gown as she made a movement, felt her hand touch his, gently, delicately, a thing of beauty, that simple touch, and again, such a turmoil of feeling was in him that he could not speak. Her kind gesture moved him. All his life he had used silence to escape, to buy time, and later, after he had learned how his lack of words affected people, to intimidate when often it was he himself who was intimidated. But there was no motive to his lack of words now. His quiet came from an impulse to love so immeasurable he couldn't express it. He was nothing at this moment but a young man in the presence of someone he was growing to adore, and behind the adoration was the amazed certainty that he could lay his beating, desirous, tumultuous human heart in her hands, and she would not drop it. His throat hurt from all that he wasn't saying, but her silence was easy to bear, unquestioning. No performance was required from him. He shut his eyes to that gift. Had there ever been a moment in his life when he had not had to perform?

"I can't love lightly."

She whispered the words. She's warning me, he thought. Protectiveness rose, the lion in him coming to attention. All his instincts were to shelter, to aid, to spread his cloak before her so that her shoes should never touch dirt. He would keep the world at bay. She was not a brittle court creature, able to survive the envy and hatred, to thrive on it, as others did—not Henriette, of course. Here his thoughts stumbled, fell over themselves like buffoons in a play. He would deal with Henriette later. He brought Louise's hand to his lips. The moment his lips touched her, desire took him. He saw himself biting the flesh his lips touched, turning her palm over and licking it, but he stopped himself. "Will you at least consider my regard? I know that to return it means much sacrifice for you, but I swear I would guard you from any harm. My love for you is not light, not facile."

He thought she nodded her head before she rose and walked away, her tread light upon the gravel of the road to the stables. He remained where he was. If he should be so fortunate as to win her love, there must be a way love might be consummated without hurt to her. As it was, she was now under his protection. Should she reject him—anger rose here, fiery, a panther's night scream—should she reject him, he would see that anything she desired was hers, that she had a position at court beyond maid of honor, that offices and salaries of some kind were hers, that her husband— Merciful God, the thought of that word made his jaw clench—was a good man, worthy of her.

Worthy of her.

Pray God he could be that himself.

❧✿❧

The carriages had been rolled out of the stables and lurched now to the landscape canal for a night's drive. The Queen Mother hadn't managed to squelch the nightly trysts. Henriette sat in hers with only Catherine across from her. She sat near the window opening, waiting.

And then there Louis was, his horse seeming to dance up beside the carriage. In another moment, he'd dismounted and was inside, his horse trotting obediently alongside.

"I've missed you so." Henriette grabbed his hands. "It's wrong of me, but I hate that which takes you away, your kingdom, your duties. There, I've said it. Punish me with twenty kisses."

"I'm wrong to love you."

Frozen, Henriette didn't reply.

He rushed on. "It's weighing on my conscience and oppressing me. You are my sister in the eyes of the church. My confessor tells me so, all the holy men I consult. You are my brother's wife, and I must love you as a sister."

"You don't love me anymore?"

Louis took her hands and kissed them front and back. "I am in agony over this, over the hurt I've brought. I wouldn't blame you if you never forgave me, but I do beg forgiveness most humbly. I am king of France, and so I must set an example to my people, to my court. There is no one like you. You're the brightest ornament here. I adore you. I always will, but I may love you only as a sister. Forgive me!"

And somehow he opened the carriage door and bounded out of it, was atop his horse, and had galloped away before she could speak. Catherine and Henriette listened to the fading sound of his horse's hooves on the gravel.

"The Queen Mother," Catherine said. "This is her work."

Henriette crumpled into a little heap, and Catherine moved across the space between them so that Henriette's head could lie in her lap.

"He still loves you," she said, stroking curls. "How could he not? It's his conscience. Let him lie with his worthiness for a while. It's a lonely bed. He'll be back."

This hurts, thought Henriette. This hurts so much.

❧✦❧

Louis tossed the reins of his horse to a servant and walked through the dark gardens until he had reached the grotto.

"Leave me," he told his musketeer. He went into the grotto, and finding a corner, he sat down on the floor and leaned his head against the cool tile and stone walls. The only sounds were of the trickling water nearby, of the wind sighing in the trees. He closed his eyes, and guilt came with its hammer and tongs. He let it say every ugly word. He was a boor; a flirt; an unfaithful, lying, sneaking bastard—that last, perhaps, in more ways than one. She was lovely and kind and dear, and he did love her, just not the way he'd thought, and he'd really hurt her in not knowing sooner. His confessor said that God had transmuted lust into purity, that now he loved in the way a brother should, that he had been tempted and tested, and that he had triumphed, but he hadn't asked for his love to change. It simply had.

And he'd hurt his brother, been happy to do so. God, he thought, when some of the pummeling had slowed, and he could wearily crack open his eyes. He stared out into the dark. How did one live life without hurting others? That's what the saints, the church, preached over and over again. How did one do it?

He left the grotto, stole into his palace like a thief, and walked down silent hallways. In the chamber of books, he stood motionless, his thoughts stalking ahead of him to the viscount. He sold one of his offices to give you the million. He is no longer attorney general of the Paris Parlement, so Colbert had whispered at some point during this long night. In the web and tangle that was precedent and right, it meant trying Nicolas in court would be easier. Now the viscount no longer had the right to be tried by his peers, members of a parlement that had rebelled into open warfare only a few years ago. Was the viscount so arrogant that he threw away his best safeguards? Was he so certain of his place, his weapons on his island? Was one of the cards in his deck the knowledge that Louis might not be the son of a king? The confidence selling the office showed made Louis shudder. He went to his cabinet, pulled down its heavy square, found the *lettres de cachet* against Madame de Motteville and her daughter, brought them to a candle, and lit each, holding the paper carefully until it had charred enough to burn his fingers. He wouldn't arrest Madame de Motteville or her daughter. It had been a hollow threat. Did that make him a hollow king?

The boy was out of sight, but not out of mind. He knew who the boy's father had been, but who was his own? And when would D'Artagnan return?

CHAPTER 28

T he Marshall de Gramont is here," one of his secretaries told Louis.
Louis took a deep breath. He wasn't looking forward to this
interview. "Send him in."

He stood out of respect for the man entering this chamber, a marshall
of France, one of the kingdom's officers of the crown, serving at the king's
discretion. Sons did not inherit this honor. It was singular and usually
lifelong. The marshall, lean and commanding, bowed. His loyalty to the
crown had never wavered. He'd commanded armies and given funds. He
was an intrepid warrior.

"Thank you for coming so promptly. I'm afraid that today I give with
one hand and take with the other, sir." Louis handed the marshall a letter
closed with heavy wax seals. "I have an important favor to ask of your son-
in-law and his father, the Prince de Monaco, a favor no one, not even you,
must know of."

"I will send my son with this at once."

Louis cleared his throat. "That is not possible. I must deliver news
unworthy of the love and respect I bear your family. Your son has
insulted Monsieur."

The marshall's head jerked back a moment, and Louis watched him
summon his resources to hear what Louis would say. This was a man of
enormous pride and honor. It was one of the reasons Louis trusted him, his
fidelity to conducting his life in an honorable way. He handed the man
a paper describing Guy's conduct and waited as the older man read the
words there.

The marshall refolded the rectangle of paper when he'd finished reading. There was only the sound the paper made as its stiff edges met one
another, then he said, "I am desolate that a member of my family should
behave so."

"As am I."

"An apology will be forthcoming, Your Majesty."

"I am not owed an apology. My brother, a child of France, is."

The marshall held both letters out to Louis, who took only the one describing Guy's conduct.

"I will resign from my office this afternoon—" the marshall began.

"Never," said Louis. "I depend on you. I always will. For your son—perhaps an absence from court for a time?"

The marshall looked down at the sealed letter in his hand, the red of the wax dried out solidly where the heavy metal of the seal had pushed melted wax upward. "Since you allow me the honor of continuing to serve you, I would deliver this to the Prince de Monaco myself."

"That would please me. It is of vital importance to me."

The Marshall de Gramont bowed himself from the chamber, his face stiff, his eyes lowered.

"Father!"

Guy stood up and at once bowed, and Catherine dropped into a deep curtsy.

The marshall stepped forward and slapped Guy across the face as Catherine gasped.

"You were unspeakably disrespectful to Monsieur!"

His father's hand a red imprint on his face, Guy replied, "It is impossible to disrespect Monsieur, sir. There is nothing to respect."

"He is a child of France, and you are to accord him the courtesy that goes with that position, which will begin with an immediate apology to him. It is not a request."

Guy looked around the park in which he and his sister stood, a desperate expression crossing his face as bonds of duty tightened themselves. He was his own man in all ways but this. "I will apologize, to please you."

"Your reasons for doing what is honorable impress me not at all. You are to leave Fontainebleau and go to Paris and remain there until I say otherwise. Today."

Catherine and Guy stared at their father with dismay. It was as if he had banished Guy to a remote island where there was no food and water or people. They revered their father as the head of their family; both were slightly afraid of him, yet both loved him as they did no one else in the world.

"What your mother and I have heard even in Paris about your conduct toward the maids of honor is scandalous. You dishonor them also. I send you away for your own sake," the marshall said. "In spite of the fact I see

nothing of myself in you, you are my son, and I won't have you ruined."
He regarded this child of his, passionate, handsome, proud, whom life had
graced with all things.

Guy held out his hand. "Father—"

The marshall turned, didn't look back as he walked away. His authority was such that Guy would obey. He knew it, and Guy knew it, but
Catherine ran after her father.

"Father, please," she begged. "Wait, listen to me—"

The marshall didn't pause, so she was forced to trot beside him.
Without looking at her, he said, "In my pocket is a letter from His Majesty
to your father-in-law and to your husband. I can only trust that your conduct is not described, Catherine. There would be nothing you've done that
would make His Majesty ask for your removal from court, is there?"

Catherine stopped where she was, pressed her hands to her mouth,
didn't answer.

The marshall saw her involuntary gestures. "I am singularly blessed in
my children. I have risked my honor to tell you this, to prepare you if you
need to make amends with your husband." He put out his hand, as if he
would touch her face, but he stopped himself. "Ah, Catherine," he said,
"you were always my heart, a wild and foolish heart. I pray you haven't
made too much inconvenience for yourself."

She knelt before him, and he gave her his hand, and she kissed its
knuckles before he resumed his march toward the palace.

His Majesty had written a letter to the Prince de Monaco, thought
Catherine, her mind flying in every direction to remember if her conduct
had been that indiscreet. Would her husband recall her? She'd die if he
did, absolutely die.

※

Philippe ran through antechambers, never minding the curious looks sent
in his direction. He threw open a door without knocking, and Guy, standing at a window in his chamber, a fully packed trunk at his feet, glanced
at him.

"I was waiting for you." Guy turned back to the view out the window.

"You don't have to leave! I'm not angry. I never was."

"My father commands it."

"I'm overriding his command!"

"You may not do that."

"But I can! I am!" Philippe fell to his knees, held out his arms. "Don't
leave. I'll go to your father; I'll change his mind."

"His mind doesn't change, my prince."

Philippe grabbed one of Guy's hands. "Stay for one more day. I'll go this afternoon to your father. I'll explain—"

"What? That it is permissible to treat a child of France the way I treated you? Even I am disgusted by what I did."

"Whatever I allow is permissible. You are my dearest confidant, and I would be lost without you. I would be—"

"And will you change your brother's mind, too?"

"My brother's?"

"It was he who summoned my father, who pointed out—quite rightly, I suppose—that my most recent behavior was disrespectful to a prince."

"But I don't care! It's over and done with. What we do between ourselves is our affair. His Majesty knows that."

And when Guy didn't respond, Philippe began to plead, "Don't go!"

"Get up off your knees. You know I hate it when you beg."

Philippe stood, tears rolling down his face. "I feel like I am holding on to my wits with my bare hands, that any moment I am going to explode and there would be nothing left of me. You mustn't leave me!"

"I have to. I'm in love with your wife, you know. That makes me dangerous."

"I don't care. Take her! Just don't leave me!"

"At this moment," Guy said, "I despise you. A proper man would call me out!"

"But I'm not a proper man." Philippe had begun to sob. "I never have been, have I? I'm just silly, useless Prince Philippe who loves you with all his heart. Don't leave—I don't mind if you love her. Everyone else loves her, too. I've married a little paragon. Isn't that hilarious, Guy? Philippe the sissy, Philippe the queen, Philippe the half man, is married to the most desirable woman at court! A waste for both of us—"

Guy had stepped back against the window. His face looked wild, as if he would have jumped out the window, if he could.

Philippe threw his arms around Guy. "We'll go have a bottle or two of wine and laugh at this. I'm over her. I thought I loved her, but I don't! Let me have an heir, and she's yours. I give her to you. Just don't desert me, my friend, my beloved, don't leave me here among the jackals—"

Guy slapped him across the face. "How dare you speak so about the woman I love? You aren't worth the lace on one of her sleeves. You're nothing! A worm! A coward! A despicable creature that we all laugh at among ourselves."

"Don't—"

"Don't what? Speak the truth? Are you not even man enough to hear truth?"

"You're saying this because you're angry. You're always cruel to me when you're angry—"

"And sometimes when I'm not, yes? And you always take it! Have you ever thought about killing me for my conduct?"

"I never think about hurting you."

Some of his despair conveyed itself to Guy, who took a moment to find command over all that was in him, a mixture of anger, sadness, reproach, and disgust. "Don't love me," he said, his hard, handsome eyes staring past Philippe at some distant speck, some future in which Philippe played no part.

"One doesn't choose whom one loves, does one?"

Guy laughed, the sound was bitter. "Apparently not, since I'm in love with your wife."

"It's because I'm not on the council, isn't it? I'll demand he give me a place, and you'll be by my side—"

"You never made him afraid of you. He doesn't respect you. He made a fool of you with his flirtation with your wife. Now, no one respects you!"

Words were in Philippe's throat, begging words. I know you loved me once upon a time, he wanted to say. I can wait until you do so again. "I love you so," he whispered and could only watch as his friend, his beloved, his true heart shook his head in contempt and walked past him out the door, out into the hall, and even though Philippe knew he shouldn't, knew it would only bring more harshness, he ran after him. He threw himself on Guy's back. "Stay!"

Guy unclasped Philippe's clinging hands and let him drop with a thud.

"Oh my darling, don't leave like this—"

But Guy walked on down the hall. My heart is breaking, Philippe thought. It is splintering into pieces right here inside of me, and I shall die with the pain of it. He put one hand to his chest and leaned against the wall, breath jagged and cruel. I am a despicable thing, he thought, a thing nobody can love.

Footmen gathered around him, none of them daring to touch him, and one of them ran to find the Chevalier de Lorraine.

Philippe gasped like a fish thrown on shore. Prince, heir, child of France. None of that matters, he thought, because I am despised, a faggot in the eyes of the people I love most in the world.

"Go! Leave him to me. Be gone. All of you!" The Chevalier de Lorraine waved a handkerchief at the footmen. Carefully, as if Philippe were ancient porcelain that would shatter at the least touch, he took him by the hand.

"Come, my darling," he said, as soft, as kind, as honey-voiced as any mother soothing a distraught, grieving child. "Come with old friend Lorraine now. There's a good boy, a good prince." And he led him away—Philippe stumbling and sobbing—away from eyes and ears to someplace quiet, and he stayed with him while Philippe wept, and held the chamber pot for Philippe to spit his guts into afterward, and when that was done, he dipped his handkerchief in scented water and wiped Philippe's mouth with it.

"That's a good boy," he repeated to Philippe's white, desolate face. "The best boy in the world."

He found Louis in one of his chambers in the midst of a meeting of the ministers, as well as Colbert. Papers were spread over a table, and they were absorbed in their task. Collection of taxes, thought Philippe.

Louis looked up and saw his brother's face. A miscarriage, he thought, Henriette's had a miscarriage. He stood and reached out his hand.

"How dare you send one of my household from court!"

Louis flinched. Philippe was shrill. He was going to throw one of his tantrums. The men in the chamber hurriedly gathered papers, bowed themselves out as quickly as possible.

"It wasn't your place to do so! He's my dearest friend!"

"You let him treat you like a lackey!"

"It's my place to decide how I'm treated!" I sound like a screaming Paris street queen, thought Philippe. It was as if he stood above himself and watched the creature below who shouted.

"It's my place to decide, as king of this realm," said Louis. "It's my court. Everyone here is here because I wish it! And I no longer wish the presence of the Count de Guiche!"

"But I do!"

Louis went to a drawer, wrenched it open, brought back a piece of paper, began to read the words on it. "The count then demanded that the prince lick his boots, and the prince crawled to him on hands and knees and did so. 'The bottoms, too, said the count.'" Louis stopped, looked at his brother. "Must I read more? Because there is more if you wish to hear it."

Philippe didn't answer, and Louis noticed the bruise forming on his face. "What's that?" he demanded. "Did he hit you? By God, I'll have him thrown in the Bastille if he so much as laid a finger on you!"

"He didn't like my sobbing. I sobbed like a girl. I begged and wept and went on my knees." Relishing the fact that he was repelling his brother, Philippe knelt the way he had before Guy. "That's the child of France I am. I would lick his boots and more any day of the week. I have!" He smiled.

Louis held up a hand to blot out the sight of Philippe's face. He could find no love for his brother in this moment.

"Bring him back. I am begging you!"

"No."

Philippe put fists to his eyes and began to moan. The sight of it was so like the boy that for a moment Louis couldn't move. Doors swung open, and a musketeer, one hand on his sword, ran forward, but Louis stopped him with a gesture. He knelt down. Philippe sounded like some wounded beast for which there was no respite. In desperation, Louis put his arms around his brother, and in the surprise of that, Philippe became silent.

Louis stroked his brother's hair, curlier, thicker than his, always. There were so many ways that Philippe was more beautiful than he was. His heart was kinder; he was the first to see a jest, the first to sense another's sadness. He loved Philippe, and yet he always hurt him. Some of it was intentional, some not. The weight of that behavior felt crushing. He kissed Philippe's forehead, held him tight. "Don't weep, my brother, my dear one. Don't weep. It breaks my heart. I love you. Don't weep." He said the words over the pain in his chest, the constriction in his throat.

"You took my wife from me."

Guilt pummeled. "I didn't! I haven't! There is nothing between us that shouldn't be. I'm guilty only of admiring her too much. I apologize for that."

"You lie."

"I don't. I swear it on my unborn son's heart."

"Bring him back!"

"No."

"I beg you!"

"It isn't fitting. He may not act the way he does."

"That's why you hate him, isn't it? Not because he sometimes treats me badly. You hate him because he doesn't bow to you."

Louis dropped his hold, stood. "Leave my presence."

Slowly, as if it were a very difficult thing to do, as if he had to think about each gesture the way an old man would, Philippe stood. "He won't bow deeply enough for you, will he?" His voice was hoarse. "You won't rest until you've broken us all, will you? Well, congratulate yourself, brother. I am broken."

"Get out! Now!"

When the door shut, Louis sat down in a chair. God forgive him because he didn't know when he was going to be able to forgive himself. God forgive him, he had loved Henriette. It was only by the mercy of God that they hadn't taken it farther than they had. How much the boy resembled Philippe, as much as the boy resembled him. Another brother whom he sent away, the boy who must disappear so that his presence couldn't threaten Louis's throne. Tangled webs. A phrase from an English play that his cousin, Charles of England, had spoken of to him was in his mind: what a tangled web we weave when we practice to deceive. The web just kept growing larger.

It always would, wouldn't it?

❧❧❧

Completely alone, Louise still sat in the stall of a confessional in the chapel of the palace. Above the altar, marble angels were trapped in flight. Figures of saints stood majestic and silent and grand in their alcoves. The ceiling vaulted to a crescendo of oval paintings each adorned in gilt, interlocking frames; it was beautiful and cold, as cold as the stone and marble that made it glorious. Louise had just been able to make out the shadow of the priest to whom she'd confessed on the other side of the grate. Forgive me, Father, for I have sinned in thought if not in deed, she'd told the priest. I am thinking of surrendering my virginity.

His words had been small, hard pebbles. Fornication is a sin in the eyes of God. Your virginity is your crown, the crown you bring to your husband, the honor you owe as a daughter of God. Let not silken, lustful, deceitful words and admiration lead you astray. You would become a Magdalene, a whore not worthy to kiss the hem of the garment of Christ.

A fit of lust, she thought, blinking when she finally stepped into the bright sunshine of a courtyard. A whore? Is that what I am? The words didn't seem right, though of course they must be. Would she become a whore for His Majesty? When he touched her, the touch didn't seem sinful. Is that what they were, filled with sin when what she experienced was a radiance that he should love her, he who was so gallant and noble and lonely, the sun of the court, whose sadness she sensed when he stood near enough? To the prince, like an altar fire. The motto of her house singing in her blood. She was so drawn to him that she could not have backed away to save her life. Within were deep, wordless shifts moving her forever and irrevocably out of girlhood and into destiny, where one day her name would be written in books of history. Young and lithe and troubled, she ran across the empty courtyard to the buildings beyond.

On her bed lay a small object wrapped in silk. When she opened it, she found the diamond bracelets. *Wear them so I see that you care for me, I beg*, said the note, and it was signed "L." She traced the loop of the L with her finger but didn't place the bracelets upon her wrists. What was going to occur was inevitable, but she had to wait just a bit longer because it was large, the largest thing that had ever happened to her, and on some incoherent, wordless level, she knew it and must give herself time to catch up with it.

CHAPTER 29

D'Artagnan was back. He waited in the garden grotto, and Louis almost embraced him he was so glad to see him.

"Separate cells, the mask still on, as you ordered," D'Artagnan reported. "I regret to inform you that the abbot died on the journey. We found him on the floor of his carriage and buried him as best we could on the side of the road."

Louis's mind flew to the Holy Father in Rome. Already he had much to account for. What concessions would the Pope demand?

"Go to Paris and visit your wife, Lieutenant, for in three days I send you back. Here are your orders." Louis held out a paper. "This is in my own hand. No one else has seen it. Burn it after you've read it. I want a messenger sent on each step of the way to inform me of your progress. You understand me, Lieutenant?"

Fatigued beyond words, D'Artagnan slapped his gloved fist to his chest and bowed. There wasn't a shred of the boy in the countenance of the young man standing before him. Long live the king.

Louis remained in the grotto. One more meeting, and then he was free to return to the long canal where his court was gathered in the moonlight. He heard steps, and one of his musketeers held up a lantern so that the Chevalier de Lorraine could find his way in the dark.

"You were very kind to my brother in his distress today," Louis said.

"Your brother has my deepest regard." Lorraine was like a hornet with its stinger at the ready, and Louis could hear in his voice that he would do combat for Philippe with words, if not swords, and he was glad that Philippe had some champion. "I thank you for your kindness to him, and I give you my blessing."

Eyes narrowed, Lorraine stared hard in his direction, attempting to see his face better in the darkness, to sense his meaning, but Louis didn't want his face seen. "I give you both my blessing," Louis said.

Lorraine could digest those words to whatever meaning he wished. "Good night."

"Sire, your generosity in this—"

"Good night, Chevalier."

Louis stepped so far back that he was hidden completely by the shadows, and then he watched his brother's friend, very likely one of his brother's lovers, bow formally and follow a musketeer out into the garden, into the pines an ancestor had planted to cool the grounds and delight the eye and gladden the heart. Louis walked the long way around the pond, past the stables, to reach the landscape canal. He wanted night air on his face. Ahead, Henriette had ordered servants to place lanterns along the banks of the canal, and the lanterns twinkled into the dark, and his courtiers were gathered in small clusters among the lights. Lully played the violin, as only he could—Henriette was one of his favorite people—and the notes hung sweet and long, like the sounds newborn stars would make. He saw his fair-haired talisman sitting with Choisy. Over the sudden, rapid beating of his heart, he could feel something inside himself ease. Here was home.

He sat down beside her, and Choisy moved away. They were collecting the lanterns, making a wide circle with them, and Lully had moved close to the circle, and people were dancing in it, the women with their skirts like gauzy, night moths' wings. He saw she didn't wear the bracelets, and he felt awkward and thick-tongued; he could sense her nervousness and knew she was going to speak about what he'd asked of her. He tried to steel himself for any answer.

"You do me such an honor to say you love me," she began.

What did this mean? Was this a gentle no? Why didn't she wear the bracelets?

"I think I have always loved you. I will—I will do whatever you wish of me."

He put his hand on her arm, and she stopped speaking. "Go to our bench by the golden gate as soon as you can," he told her.

He went to the circle, watched the dancing for a while, stepped in the circle, and danced a measure with Henriette. They were like tense strangers to each other.

"You desert me all evening, sir," she said. "I see that is my fate."

Louis looked for but didn't see his brother. "Monsieur is not here?"

"He is not in the best of moods." Henriette met his eyes. "I am so unhappy."

"Will you talk with my confessor?" She frowned, but he plunged on. "He is helping me with my despair; perhaps he might help with yours." How awkward and stiff I am, thought Louis, like some scripture-quoting fool, some *dévot*. She was staring at him as if she no longer knew him, and he motioned for someone to take his place in the dance. It was true. She didn't know him. He was someone else now. Catherine loomed before him as he made an attempt to escape into darkness, to go to Louise.

"My brother is most distraught."

"I am desolate."

"He means no harm. His temper is too hot. I would be so grateful if you would welcome him again."

"Your father must make that judgment, not I."

"A word from you to our father would facilitate all."

"Am I so powerful?"

"Of course you are. Everyone is talking about La Grande Mademoiselle's absence, wondering what she did to offend you. No one wants to offend you."

"He was rude to Monsieur." Something in his eyes made her drop her own, fall into a curtsy, and allow him to pass. Later, she would think about it and wonder what it was. And in a few years, as the court grew accustomed to his courteous but absolute will, she would find it alluring.

"See that no one follows me," he told his musketeer.

There she was.

"Go away, but not too far," he ordered the musketeer. He offered his hand to Louise, led her inside his gatehouse to a door that was his own special entrance to the palace. He shut that door, and they were in near total darkness, except that upon a landing above them torches flamed to light his way. He could hear Louise's quick breaths. "I'm going to kiss you."

He meant to be gentle, to be tender, and he began that way, but then passion pushed him harder. He didn't want to stop, but he had to make her a promise, he had to say what was in his heart. Almost drunk with the taste of her, he lifted his head. "I vow I will always be true to you. I vow you will always be in my heart."

He meant it. He couldn't yet know the difference ten years would make, even five, couldn't yet know the temptations that would be thrown at him—temptations no man would be able to resist. He still thought a man's heart retained its boyish essence. He didn't realize that power and adulation and self-will hardened hearts in ways that he could not—at twenty and two—imagine. All he knew was that he adored her, the way she tasted, the way she smelled. He kissed her long throat, her hands. He knelt in front of her in the dark and lay his head at the stomach of her gown.

"No one must know," she whispered. "I couldn't bear it if people knew. Promise me that."

He opened the door and drew her back out into the gatehouse, where there was some light. His musketeer disappeared into a shadow. He led her under a torch, so that its light showed every angle of her face. "You're certain—"

"Yes."

She trembled, but she met his eyes straight on. There was no artifice about her, no flirting shake of the head, just shaking breaths and an oddly direct stare out of those half-lavender eyes. "Trust me. Will you trust me?" he asked her.

"Yes."

And then he led her back into his entrance, only left the door open so that better light might spill in, and they sat down together on the first step of the staircase, arms intertwined. They had agreed to love one another. Each was filled to the brim with words and feelings, but both were too shy, too inexperienced, to say what was in their throats, and gradually a peace came over them so that no words were necessary. It was enough to sit with arms around the other and know that love was alive, acknowledged, amazingly returned, and that this was just its beginning.

"I rode in the woods yesterday," she said. "I felt that joy was coming to me, that your love was true."

He had no words to answer that.

"I must leave now."

He helped her to her feet, nodded his head to his musketeer to escort her back to the canal. He wanted to sit alone for a time. She placed her honor in his hands, promised herself with no bargains about jewels or gifts or what might be hers in return. Her lack of artifice dazzled him. She put no impediments before him, save those of secrecy. No one must know, she said. And no one would. She would be his treasured secret, the holy relic to which he would go for the love his soul so craved. When he had been crowned at fifteen, there had been hours of ceremony and prayer to prepare him for what lay ahead. Battles. War. Peace. Work. Negotiation. Duty. Unworthiness everywhere. Every man and every woman's heart stained by ambition promising fealty with lips but without intent.

Not hers. She promised nothing she would not do.

Suddenly, his practical mind threw out something that made him jerk as if he had been kicked by a horse. I don't have a place to make love to her, he thought. I am the king of France, and I have nowhere to take her, for his own bedchamber could not be used, nor hers. How would he arrange that? Who would he trust? God, he wished he were older, more worldly, but he wasn't, and neither was she. And that, for a very long time, would be the most beautiful part of their love, its tender, young, loving kindness binding them together like tendrils of ivy, lithe and nimble and so very greenly strong.

Louise walked with Fanny back toward the landscape canal.

"Did you ask him to allow the count back at court?" Fanny had been weeping on and off since Guiche had gone away.

"I can't quite yet, Fanny. It—it isn't the right moment."

"But you'll ask him?"

Louise took her hand. "When the time is right."

Just ahead of them were the others, laughing and dancing. Louise stood at the edge of the group. There were always going to be other people's desires, needs, upsets hovering on the edges of their love, weren't there?

❧❧❧

Catherine had slipped away from the others for a time.

Nicolas watched her dress, shadow playing over her as she moved about his bedchamber. The light from the candles caressed her creamy flesh in precisely the places he so enjoyed caressing. "How long do you expect to be gone?" he asked her.

"As long as it takes to convince my husband I am a loyal wife."

Nicolas smiled that she found no irony or shame in the statement. She was, in fact, frowning as she concentrated on tying garters that held up the stockings that encased her fine legs.

"How does your brother do?" The news that the Count de Guiche left the court had swept through it like a raging fire early in the day, had sent one of Madame's maids of honor weeping on Nicolas's doorstep to beg his help.

Catherine made a face, and Nicolas was reminded again of the coolness of the younger courtiers, whose hearts were so bloodless. Catherine was concentrated now on her life. Her brother was on his own. "You'll write?" he asked.

"If I can." She walked to the bed, turned her back, and he pulled tight the laces that would tie her top in place. He could see that in her mind she was already miles away, already at the seacoast court of Monaco charming her husband. Her cousin, a wild young captain in the king's guard, was escorting her. "Is it wise to travel with Péguilin as escort?"

She turned around to smile at him. "He insisted I not travel alone. Are you jealous?"

"Always."

She looked over her shoulder as she opened the door. "Good."

Putting on a robe, Nicolas poured himself some wine, opened letters, his mind idly running over the fact of the Count de Guiche's exit from court, over Louis's ruthlessness in that. La Grande Mademoiselle was now absent from court. No one knew why, but he intended to find out. Words scrawled on the page before him suddenly caught his attention. The letter was from his Jesuit friend.

My dear Viscount,

I thought you would want to know monks from the burned monas-
tery were ordered to colonies across the sea, have already departed on
their journey. The archbishop who arranged it happens to be a friend
to me. It's said they engaged in treason. And I thought they made only
wine. There is word, unverified, that the abbot and other prisoners are
in the fortress of Pignerol. I thought this would be of interest to you...

Was he in danger? Could it be possible? He blew out candles and lay in
bed, no longer soothed by the aftermath of lovemaking. His mind was restless, probing, keen. And the next day, when he learned D'Artagnan had
met with the king, then disappeared again, he knew without a doubt that
someone was maneuvering like a rat behind the walls.

He was thinking on that when his secretary told him he had a visitor. It was Fanny de Montalais again, as drooping and red-eyed as she'd
been yesterday.

He settled her in a chair, offered her a small goblet of wine, watched
her swallow it back. His instinct about people told him this one missed
little; she was too bright and observant.

She held out a letter. "Will you, can you, see that this gets to the Count
de Guiche?"

"Of course." He poured more wine into her goblet. "I do have a small
price for my help, however. Tell me what it is you're keeping secret."

Her eyes became big. He sat back quietly, at his ease, waiting.

"The king and Madame are no more," she whispered.

Yes, he knew, but he acted surprised. "Is there someone else?"

She stood up and bolted out the door.

So, thought Nicolas, there is. He'd find out who. A steely wariness grew
in him. What else was His Majesty hiding? And why?

❧❧❧

He waited several days before he traveled into Paris. Word from his
sources at the Bastille said there was no record of a group of monks having been brought in or dispersed as prisoners. A call upon the governor of
the Bastille produced the same answer. None of Nicolas's persuasion or
threats changed the governor's response. He stood in the dirt of the street
and stared for a time at his carriage horses before continuing on the tasks
he'd set himself this day. There was a beseeching letter from La Grande
Mademoiselle asking him to intercede with His Majesty. Tell him I never
wrote them, she begged. Wrote what, precisely?

It was easy enough to find Guy, killing time, brooding and dangerous, in rooms at his father's townhouse. The chamber in which he received Nicolas was littered with sheets of paper. Nicolas moved several from the cushion of the chair. It looked like poetry, love poetry—quite bad.

"Wine for you? No? Well, forgive me if I drink yours for you." Guy poured himself a goblet of wine, drank it down, turned to face Nicolas. "To what do I owe the honor of this visit?"

"The court is dull without you. I came to see how you do."

"I am dull without court." Guy poured more wine.

"Ladies are drooping and bereft everywhere. I bring greetings from a full half-dozen." He began to reel off names, and Guy laughed. He gave Guy the letters from little Fanny de Montalais and watched Guy drop them on a table, uninterested. "I might, if it pleased you, speak with His Majesty in another few weeks or so on your behalf." Nicolas made certain his tone was offhand.

"I'm not sure it pleases me. I'm not made to be his lapdog, gelded and safe."

"The commander of the Mediterranean is a good friend of mine. What about a command there if court has lost its luster? The coast is beautiful, the women even more so. The sea swarms with pirates from the Barbary Coast. It's said they wear an earring in one ear and bow to Allah before they slit your throat."

Guy's eyes gleamed for a moment. Nicolas could see he was stirred by the idea, but he said, "So I would be your lapdog, rather than His Majesty's?"

It was close enough to the truth to make Nicolas smile. "Impossible. You are no man's lackey. You are the son of a marshall of France, a born warrior like your father."

"Correct, Viscount, I am bred for war, not acting someone's toady."

Your insolence is invigorating, thought Nicolas. Everyone was too cautious these days, His Majesty's warrior cousins quiet on their estates, La Grande sobbing about her exile like an actress on the stage. It was good to see some of the old civil war insolence. Nicolas could feel his own rise. "Monsieur sends his greetings."

Guy didn't answer, and Nicolas looked around at the litter of papers on the floor, on chairs. "You write the story of your life? Or moral maxims for us to live by, like the Duke de La Rochefoucauld? Let me see if I can quote my favorite correctly." He paused. "'We are never so happy nor so unhappy as we imagine.'"

"I write love letters."

"Ah, so your heart ties you to court."

"Yes."

"May I be of service and take one back with me?"

"Would you? How kind." Guy scribbled something across the top of a paper already dark with inky words, folded the paper, lit a taper to melt a stick of wax. It dropped onto the last fold, and Guy pressed a seal in the wax. He repeated the actions with yet another paper.

"Come to my estate and stay a while," Nicolas suggested, taking the letters from Guy. "The countryside is magnificent, my horses are the finest in France, as is my cook. I am there but only to oversee workmen and the details for my fête. I seldom stay the night and would welcome your presence. I took the liberty of glancing at one of your love poems before I sat down. They might improve in Vaux-le-Vicomte's air."

Guy laughed.

Nicolas's finger caressed the name written across the front of one of the letters. "Your sister isn't at Fontainebleau, unfortunately."

"Oh? Where is she?"

"Gone to Monaco."

"As is my father."

The marshall was in Monaco? Whatever for? thought Nicolas.

Looking Nicolas straight in the eyes, Guy said, "It would be a service to me if you delivered the letter addressed to my sister to Madame instead. It goes without saying that I wish no one to know."

"Of course."

So, thought Nicolas, stepping into his carriage a few moments later, the wind blows that direction, does it? Who had His Majesty's eyes these days? The other letter was for Fanny de Montalais. How opportune. She'd have to answer some questions in return for Nicolas delivering it. He smiled to himself at the way fate played to his advantage. He must make time to visit La Grande Mademoiselle personally and hear her sad tale and so learn more of this young majesty's machinations.

He had one more stop to make before heading south to Vaux-le-Vicomte. He stood in a dark hallway idly slapping his gloves in one hand as he waited for a servant to tell the mistress of the house that he had arrived, then he followed the servant to a back parlor, where Madame D'Artagnan, proper young wife that she was, had just risen from an embroidery stand near a sunny window and was falling into a curtsy.

She was surprised, flustered, and impressed, all of which he never minded seeing. "Forgive my intrusion," he said to her, at his silky best. "Will you tell your husband I've come to see him as he asked."

"But he isn't here, Viscount. Did my servant tell you he was?"

"There must be some mistake. He wrote me to meet him today. He's still on his journey, is he? Now where was it he went? Pignerol?"

"You know, then? No, he's been there but is gone again. I just had a letter from him." Her eyes moved to a paper on the mantel near the embroidery stand. "I am so distressed. He mentioned nothing of your calling on him in the letter. It isn't like him to forget such a thing. Won't you let me offer you wine? Please."

Nicolas allowed himself to be persuaded to sit down, allowed himself to accept a goblet of wine, allowed himself to sip it and enjoy the sun in this parlor and the company of a young woman very impressed that he had come to visit her husband personally, very upset that her husband was not home, and very anxious that this oversight would not hurt her husband's standing. With just a little prod here and there, she showed him the letter, and Nicolas was able to run his own eyes over it. It told him nothing, but then, D'Artagnan's wife had told enough.

Nicolas chatted with her a while longer, admired the cushion cover she was embroidering, invited her to tour the tapestry works at Vaux-le-Vicomte, asked a discreet question here and there, and finally took his leave. She had no idea where her husband's final destination was nor did she know anything about his mission.

In his carriage, he pondered what he'd just learned. What did it mean, D'Artagnan and Pignerol? What mission was he upon? Why had the king not shared it with council or at the very least with Nicolas himself?

"Are we going to Vaux-le-Vicomte, sir?" It was his secretary.

He nodded his head and closed his eyes. Some intrigue was in motion. Did he question His Majesty directly? He had such an interesting new piece of information to consider. That bad poetry he'd picked up from Guiche's chair wasn't all poetry. On one sheet was a bit of an old Mazarinade. Nicolas certainly remembered the originals, filthy songs, pamphlets, treatises, all against Cardinal Mazarin and, often, the Queen Mother. Why would a wild young courtier write out a few lines from a decade-old Mazarinade? What did he do with such? Interesting.

"I'm going to Vaux-le-Vicomte. You're not. I want you to leave for the fortress of Pignerol in all haste," he told his secretary. "I want to know about the latest prisoners who graced its portals. Pay whatever you must to obtain the information."

CHAPTER 30

I n the queen's gardens, La Porte bowed very low to present a key and a
letter. Henriette's dogs barked at him, and Louise knelt to pull them by
their leashes and hush them.

"From His Majesty," La Porte said.

Louise couldn't look at him. Harsh red stained her neck and her averted
cheek. When she didn't speak, he left the letter on the ground, the key
atop it.

Louise tore open the letter once she was certain she was alone. This
afternoon—they were to meet this afternoon.

She sat with the others in the afternoon watching the royal family dine.
Then she told Fanny that she had a headache and ran down steps and
across courtyards. There was a musketeer waiting for her where Louis's
note said he'd be, by the door of the clock tower in the queen's gardens,
and he escorted her up the stairs of the tower and through empty vesti-
bules and up more stairs before coming to a halt before a door.

The musketeer stood to one side as she unlocked the door. He allowed
himself one sidelong glance at her face, which was pale. She was very
pretty, had a startling sweetness about her mouth. He could love a girl like
her. Fortunate Majesty, he thought.

Louise stood with her back against the closed door behind her.
Draperies were drawn, so the chamber was dim, but she could see flowers
and candles, already lighted, placed here and there. There was wine and a
covered tray at a table. And then she saw La Porte running his hand across
an embroidered coverlet as if he had just taken every wrinkle from it. She
put her hands up to her face, her instinct to hide. She hadn't expected
anyone to be here.

La Porte made a small, neat, brisk bow. "I'll be just outside should you require anything. Your maid?" He raised an eyebrow expectantly.

"I didn't bring her." She felt stupid. She hadn't thought about undressing, hadn't even brought a nightgown. Women who knew brought their maids with them, of course. She looked down at her feet, the tips of her shoes just jutting out from the hem of her gown. Tears were very near. Already there were four who knew, and that was three too many: Fanny; the courtier who'd given this chamber; the musketeer; La Porte, who was now leaving.

Alone, she sat down in one of the big armchairs pulled up to the table, afraid to move, afraid to touch anything, uncertain of what to do. Before she could decide, the door opened, and she started and stood up, her awkward movement making the chair push back with a grating sound against the floor.

"You're here," Louis said. "I wasn't certain—" He stopped. Shyness was suddenly so great that he couldn't cross the space between them and take her in his arms the way he'd pictured himself doing. His being king didn't matter at this moment.

But his hesitation, his uncertainty made Louise smile, and her smile, because she was relieved to see him awkward and fumbling too, was its incandescent best. She felt bold suddenly, teasing, full of life. The handsome young king of France was hesitant before her. The handsome young king of France desired her. The handsome young king of France loved her. It was as if bubbles were twisting into invisible, effervescent ribbons inside her. She curtsied, pert and quite charming. "Will Your Majesty eat?"

"No."

She curtsied again, even more pert. "Will he have a goblet of wine?"

"If you will."

She poured them both wine and pulled out the armchair for him. He sat down in it, raised the goblet, and she did likewise.

"To us," he said, and some spark from his dark eyes caused such a swell of love in her that she thought she'd die from it right then and there. How happy she felt. How free. There was no one else in the world but them. She would be his mate, his plaything, his lover, his friend, whatever he desired. There's nothing I wouldn't do for you, she thought, and the thought was on her face, unspoken, but read by the other heart in the chamber.

"I was afraid you might change your mind."

"I did, a thousand times. You ask much from me."

"I know I do." He put down his wine, pushed back his chair, knelt before her.

Her heart had begun to beat hard. To have him so close was wonderful. She could feel heat between her legs, in her breasts, as they kissed and twisted their hands in each other's hair. How were we able to stop before? she wondered.

Her hand in his, she followed him to the bed, where he sat down and turned her so her back was to him. The handsome king of France is unlacing my gown, she thought. When it was open, and her back was almost bare to him, she felt his kisses on the thin fabric of her chemise. He unfastened the hook that held her skirt together. The material made a sighing sound as it fell to the floor. Now she wore only her opened top, her chemise, and her hose, and his hands were gone from her. What was he doing? She turned around.

He was unfastening the ribbons and buttons of his tight doublet, pulling at them like an impatient boy. "I seldom undress myself," he said.

"Shall I call your valet?"

"No!"

The blaze in his eyes was enough. She let go the top and stood before him in her thin chemise, helping him to undo buttons and ribbons. He shrugged out of his doublet, its intricate cut satin and leather; he pulled his voluminous shirt over his head. So, she thought, he has a mole on the right shoulder. He moved himself back on the bed, not yet taking off breeches or hose, and she was glad of that. She wasn't quite ready for that.

He had hold of her wrist, and she joined him in the bed. They sat a moment gazing at each other, and then she reached out to trace the fullness of his mouth, and he made a sound as she did so, and she suddenly felt incredibly provocative and seductive. It was exhilarating. She ran her hand down the curve of his neck, leaned forward, and kissed the mole on his shoulder.

"I don't want to hurt you," he said. "I think it will likely hurt you because it is the first time."

She didn't answer; she was too absorbed in touching his bare chest with her hands. He began to kiss her hard. The chemise was gone; she had no idea how, and he touched her breasts, and she closed her eyes. No one had ever touched her like this before. He ran his hands up and down the sides of her body, and she tried to kiss his mouth whenever it came close enough. He was kissing her everywhere, places she'd never imagined being kissed, and finally his breeches were off and she saw what a handsome young king looked like naked, and it was very beautiful. She lay back, and it did hurt when he entered her, but it didn't matter. He was whispering a hundred wonderful things to her, that she was so soft, that he adored her, that this was so good, that she was his sweetest heart. When he made a sound as if he'd been stabbed and fell against her, she just lay there under him, content.

They stayed intertwined. She lifted her leg to run her toes along the long line of his thigh, his buttock, up as high as her leg would reach. She felt adored and safe to do whatever she wished.

"I love you." He kissed her face, repeating the words, "I love you, I love you, I love you." It was as if he poured shiny light into her heart.

At a soft knock on the door, Louis raised his head. "I must leave soon." He nuzzled his head into her neck and held her so tightly she could hardly breathe. Then he sat up, began to dress himself, but gave up and went to the door, and La Porte entered, his face empty of expression. He did up all the ribbons and bows, tied the garters of the stockings, brushed Louis's hair into its curling abundance.

I want to do that, thought Louise, but she didn't dare come out from under the covers. When Louis was dressed, looking as splendid and beribboned as he had when he'd entered, the valet disappeared.

Louis sat down on the bed, pulled Louise out of the covers. He kissed the delicious part in her hair, and his hands moved up and down her back. "I don't wish to leave you. There's dinner for you. Eat it. You have to keep up your strength because it's all I can do not to throw you back in bed and make love to you again, so you'd better be ready for the next time." He laughed, his expression teasing.

She smiled into the fabric of his jacket. The next time.

"I have to go." With a last kiss on the part of her hair, he walked to the door. "Knock on the door, and my valet will help you dress. My musketeer will see you to the gardens, and you can go back to Madame's from there. I love you with all my heart. Don't doubt it. Wear the bracelets tonight, as a token of what is now between us. You are my heart, Louise."

And then she was alone. She sat among the mussed sheets, this or that detail of their lovemaking coming to mind. She felt as if she had a million bee stings all over her body, each one a place where he'd kissed or touched her.

She got up from the bed, washed herself with water in a bowl. She was sore, but it wasn't a terrible thing. She was very curious about what they'd just done. She'd have to think about it more. She found her chemise, put it back on, stepped into her skirt, began to hook its waist. There was a polite knock on the door, and she hurriedly found her top on the floor and thrust her arms into the big, full sleeves.

La Porte stepped in, not looking her way. "May I assist?"

She didn't want him to, but she couldn't lace this top herself. The shoulders hung too low; the sleeves were too heavy. It was cut to embrace a woman just at her shoulders, to graze across the top of her breasts. She turned her back to him, and he began to tie the cords so that she was encased, a slim reed rising out of the bell of her skirt. She stayed where she was when he was finished, willing him to leave, ashamed before him, ashamed of her presence here, of the mussed bed, of the blood there, of what he had to be thinking of her, no longer a virgin now, but the fallen woman, the Magdalene.

"If I may," he said quite gently, "I will do miss's hair."

"No! Yes! I don't know." She felt inarticulate, uncertain.

"If you prefer, I can send for your maid."

"Oh, would you?" She felt stupid that she hadn't thought to keep her maidservant near. But she hadn't thought any of this out.

He was at the door, speaking to someone. How many more people know? she thought wildly, and when he turned back to her, everything must have been written on her face because he crossed the chamber, picked up a brush that Louise had not even noticed, stood behind her and began to brush her hair, her shining, thick, silver moon hair, into the required fashionable curls about her ears and neck.

"It's only the musketeer I talked to. He'll find your maid."

She remembered something. "The bracelets—"

"Here." The brush came around in front of her to point. "Miss de Montalais found them and gave them to us."

She had to sit still a moment at the power and might that Louis could summon, which he had summoned for her. She swelled with the knowledge of his love, opened to it like a flower unable to withstand the power of the sun's light. Violet, people would say of her later, a year from now, when her relationship to the king of France could no longer be kept a secret. A beautiful shy wood violet is how she would be described.

La Porte's hands were certain. Her hair was pulled back into the requisite bun, ringlets pinned to cascade over her ears. He brought a mirror and held it for her. She looked lovely. He'd done her hair perfectly. She blushed at the sight of herself. She put a finger to the glass, to the wide, not quite smiling mouth, swollen with a king's kisses. Without realizing it, she straightened her back pridefully.

"Miss's earrings?"

She reached for the pearls that he must have collected from who knew where, the bed likely. They'd been in her ears when this began. Her maid was here now, entering timidly, half running toward Louise when she saw her, a shawl and Louise's brushes in her hands.

La Porte bowed very low before Louise. "I am your humble servant in all things," he said. "It is my honor to serve my master and now you."

"You-you won't say anything. Please don't say anything." She knew her maid hadn't thought to bring some coins because she hadn't told her to. "I'll send coins to you—"

Lifting up out of his bow like a martinet whose strings had been jerked, La Porte's small, neat nostrils pinched together. "I require no payment.

Your secrets are safe with me because His Majesty's secrets are safe with me. They always have been."

He was gone from the chamber before Louise could respond. The maid just stood where she was, looking from Louise to the bed and back again.

"I've taken a lover," Louise heard herself say. "You must tell no one."

The servant nodded her head.

"It's imperative," Louise heard herself say, wondering who was saying it, perhaps the happy, prideful young woman emerging from within her. "No one must know."

Louise went to the box on the table and slipped an exquisite bracelet onto each wrist. She'd wear them with pride. Her beloved was the handsomest, bravest man in France. He was a demigod, not only to her, but to all the kingdom, and she had just been graced by his kisses and act of love. If this was the only thing that ever happened between them, she would leave the court, and all her life she would treasure this moment, when the king of France knelt naked before her in a bed and bent to kiss the soft inside of her elbow. Sealed by his mouth now. She was his forever.

❦

Late that night, Louise sat in a carriage with Fanny as it swayed around the landscape pool, her face and shoulders out the window to feel the night's breeze, to see the stars, to try and quiet this flaming in her body that the very thought of Louis brought into being. She didn't notice a horseman's quiet approach. But suddenly there he was, bending down and planting one quick, killingly sweet kiss on her lips. Before she could even move he was riding on. This was how it would be, wouldn't it? Always too quick, too often unspoken, always a good-bye implicit, but always thrilling.

"Have you made love?" Fanny demanded.

She didn't want to talk about it just yet. "Hush."

"You have. I'm glad. Now you understand my despair."

But she didn't. "Come sit beside me." She held Fanny's hand as Fanny's tears began. She hadn't been able to save a moth from dying in a candle's flame earlier this night. The image stayed in her mind.

Did the moth know the alluring flame would singe its wings and that it would die?

Or did it just bless the heat of the flame?

And did it die happy?

CHAPTER 31

Back again at the fortress of Pignerol, D'Artagnan shook off weariness with a short nap—any musketeer worth his musket could nap while still in the saddle, if need be—and then went to survey the state of his prisoners. It didn't take long before he found himself watching Cinq Mars's face carefully. It was nothing more than instinct, nothing more than the faintest movement of eyelids in the gaunt angles of Cinq Mars's face, but D'Artagnan thought, he's going to attempt something.

"How is the boy?" Cinq Mars asked.

Not well. He ate little or nothing, made continual clicking sounds when he was not howling, and he defecated in corners. He tried to tear the bandage from his cuts, pulled all bandages off his fingers. Under no circumstances must he die, D'Artagnan had shouted to the musketeers, the priest in charge of his care. But how did one force an insane boy to obey? He made no answer to Cinq Mars's question. What was there to say?

"I must see him." Cinq Mars was forceful. "He doesn't do well without me. Let me see him. His Majesty doesn't wish him to die, does he?" The musketeer caught the shadow that moved across D'Artagnan's face and repeated, "Let me see the boy."

Cinq Mars had to be carried in on a litter. He couldn't stand for long yet, though his own wound had stopped bleeding. Outside the boy's cell, D'Artagnan motioned for his musketeers to set down the litter, for one to unlock the door. He leaned down and with a grunt picked Cinq Mars up into his own strong arms, walking through the door and kicking it closed again with his heel. The boy sat in a corner rhythmically hitting his head against the wall. The contents of food bowls were everywhere. A flask of watered wine stood on its side, a slow drip falling into a puddle of wet. The boy's hands had dried blood on them.

"Put me down near him," Cinq Mars said. He groaned as D'Artagnan propped him against the wall, and the sound set off a howl from the boy.

The sound harsh in his ears, disturbing enough to make his flesh crawl, D'Artagnan brought a pillow for Cinq Mars's back and then stepped to one side. This boy was little more than an animal, a maddened, crazed beast. How could he be cared for?

"Hush, now, hush," Cinq Mars crooned, the tenderness of his voice at odds with his harsh face, his perennial grimace. "Hush, my prince, my handsome one. It's all right. It's fine. I'm here now. Old Cinq Mars is here. Hush, my boy, hush."

It might have been a lullaby.

The boy never looked at him, never acknowledged he was near, but the howling gradually stopped under the drone of Cinq Mars's words, though not the rocking back and forth. D'Artagnan moved his jaw a little to take tension from it when the boy finally became silent.

"Get fresh food for him," Cinq Mars said in the same tone as his lullaby. "We're going to eat now, aren't we, my prince? We're going to feed this strong, handsome boy. Yes, we are. Cinq Mars's good boy. Cinq Mars's handsome prince."

Outside the cell, D'Artagnan gave the order, then took the tray to Cinq Mars himself.

"Sit in that chair there," Cinq Mars ordered. With slow and careful effort, he cut meat from a fat, roasted pullet and divided bread, eating some of both as he did so. He poured a bit of ale into a cup. Carefully, clearly hurting, he placed the plate of meat and chunks of bread and the ale in front of the boy, sat down on the floor, to one side of the boy.

"Good," he said, "so good. They've outdone themselves in the kitchen for you. Eat for your servant, Cinq Mars, my prince. Eat the food in front of you. Go on." He began to eat, making smacking sounds.

The boy rocked back and forth. An arm darted to the meat. The boy never stopped moving but began to eat what was before him. The mask stopped at the mouth, so that its wearer could eat with ease.

"Something to clean him with. Don't step in front of him or too near," Cinq Mars ordered. When he had what he needed, he wiped the boy's hands, wiped as much of his face as showed under the iron mask.

"You miss your Cinq Mars, don't you?" Cinq Mars said. "Of course you do. That's a good boy. You're a good, fine boy. Your mother would be proud. Why does he still wear that cursed mask? What can it matter here? Take it off, and let me stay in here with him. He's accustomed to me."

"No," said D'Artagnan.

"He won't eat unless I'm here."

D'Artagnan leaned down and picked Cinq Mars up again, walked with him to the door and kicked it, and one of his men opened it. Howling filled the cell, whitened the face of the musketeer who'd opened the door, made

Cinq Mars curse. He cursed D'Artagnan all the way back to his own cell, and when D'Artagnan laid Cinq Mars back in his bed, Cinq Mars told him exactly what he thought of him and the Queen Mother and the cardinal and His Majesty, cursing them all with a string of snarling oaths.

"Bastard," he finally said, out of breath. "You're a bastard, and the Queen Mother is a cunt I curse to my dying day who hasn't the compassion of the lowest whore on the streets, and His Majesty is a bastard, lower than the cunt who bore him."

"You took an oath to serve him."

"The king I took an oath to serve is long dead."

"The king never dies. Long live the king."

Later D'Artagnan sat on a terrace with the governor of the fortress. He placed a bag of gold on the stones at the governor's feet.

"That's for your trouble and your loyalty. His Majesty expects complete obedience from you, and I tell you from first-hand experience, this isn't a king to trifle with. What has Captain Cinq Mars said to you? Don't lie. If you do, it will be you locked behind in a dungeon, the darkest one at the Bastille, while we pry it out of you."

"He offered coin to allow him and the boy to go. He said he could write one letter, and in three days I'd have a thousand gold *louis* and the blessings of the Queen Mother herself."

"There aren't a thousand *louis* in that bag, but a sum to make up the difference will come to you in a month, I swear it on the soul of my wife. Forget you ever heard the Queen Mother's name in this." D'Artagnan's voice was so grim the governor blinked. "Who else has talked to him?" D'Artagnan asked.

"No one."

"A servant?"

"Your men have been there whenever a servant has entered."

They were silent, drinking wine the governor's wife served them.

"Is the boy completely mad?" ventured the governor.

"I can tell you nothing about him."

"His howling frightens the guards."

"It would frighten anyone, wouldn't it?"

D'Artagnan sat up until late going over details of the next step of his mission in his mind. A letter to His Majesty lay written and sealed, would be given to the governor to deliver with all haste the next day. Keep me informed, His Majesty had ordered. I want to see it as if I were standing there beside you.

CHAPTER 32

Paul Pellison, the Viscount Nicolas's personal secretary, sat on the edge of the public fountain staring up at a fortress built into the side of a mountain in a little village called Pignerol. Bleak and forbidding, the façade of the fortress told him nothing. Its governor had been equally stoic. No promise of any amount of coin moved his lips nor did a letter with the viscount's seal. But guards were lesser mortals. They usually liked to drink at a tavern somewhere before they went home to plump wives and too many children and even more wine. They liked to talk among themselves about their work, as any man did. He went into the tavern around the corner from the fountain, ordered wine.

"Do the guards from the fortress ever come here?" he asked the woman who brought his goblet. She had the hard-eyed squint of a woman who might own the place.

"They live here. I have to send them home to their wives like bad boys." She looked Pellison up and down. "You from Paris, too?"

"Too? You've been entertaining visitors from Paris?"

"Musketeers, big ones, handsome things, cheeky, pinched me more than once where they shouldn't have, they were from Paris, I could tell." And she mimicked his accent with a quick change of expression and emphasis. "You all talk like sissies," she said, then sighed. "But these boys weren't sissies, I can tell you."

"Many of them?" asked Pellison.

"Fifteen, twenty. They bought up our wine and all the food we could cook."

"Going on a journey, it seems."

"To Monaco," said the woman. "At least that's what the stable boy heard. I hear the view of the sea is pretty there."

"I hear that, too," said Pellison.

"So you're Sandrine."

Louise's maid stood perfectly still and hoped against hope that stillness would suffice. A musketeer had appeared out of nowhere, and now here she was, standing before the king of France, as La Porte pulled hunting boots off his feet.

Louis cocked his head to one side, puzzled. "Are you or are you not Sandrine? Not that shirt, and I want a brocade jacket."

Sandrine nodded her head, the best she could do.

"You serve Miss de la Baume le Blanc. Yes?"

Again, Sandrine managed a movement with her head. Her eyes met his, but she had to look away. She saw him around the palace. Everyone did; it was the custom of French kings to live in public, but to be this close, all by herself, in his most private chamber, well, it was too overwhelming.

"Sandrine, I am going to need your complete loyalty. You will be the holder of a secret, the secret of my love for your mistress. Have you the strength to hold that secret?"

Her nod was a jerk.

He stood, still in his hunting clothes, his hair wild and unkempt, planted himself inches from her. It was as if she could feel some holy warmth radiating out from him—so she'd tell her children one day.

"Will you play messenger between your mistress and me? La Porte will bring you notes which you must see her receive. Request your mistress to be in the chamber where we meet after dinner. Will you deliver that message for me?"

She dropped into a curtsy, nodding like a maniac at the floor. To her shock, he reached out and brought her up out of the curtsy. He bowed over her hand.

"I am your servant if you help me. You will never regret earning my trust." He turned away, went over to a chair where his valet had laid out clothing for him.

"You may leave now, Sandrine," La Porte said.

She turned in a circle, not remembering which door she'd entered.

"That one." The valet pointed. In his hand was a small bag. "From His Majesty," he told her.

She was in the maid of honors' bedchamber before she had the wits to see what was in the bag. She took a peek. There were coins. She swallowed. More coins than she had seen in her lifetime. She sat down on the little cot in a back attic that was hers. Merciful Mother of Heaven, they were rich, and the king himself had bowed over her hand. The world as she knew it had just tipped over.

This time Louise felt less shy and more impatient. She was in the chamber again, sitting in a chair, hands clasped in her lap. When the door opened, and he entered the chamber, she jumped up from where she was sitting and smiled. She even forgot to curtsy. "I thought you might not send for me again—"

"You're all I can think about."

She sank down on her heel to curtsy to him, but he pulled her close. Her ear was against his chest, and through the sumptuous fabric she could hear his heart beating hard. For her.

"My ministers think me solemn as they talk about this and that, but all I am thinking of is you. I was half-afraid you wouldn't be here—" he said between the kisses he was now placing on her face.

"I will always be here."

Louis put his mouth on the bare flesh that began a sweet swell of breast. His hands explored the soft part of her upper arms hidden by the lace of her full sleeves. She stood with eyes half-closed, trembling a little, which touched Louis. She was no court diamond, polished to hardness and facile in feeling. He wanted to obliterate for a time all else in his life. He led her to the bed, pulled at her laces and ties, at his laces and ties, and then they were mostly naked, and he kissed her like a soldier on pillage, entangling his hands in her hair. Lovemaking was easier this time, wetter, fuller, sweeter, and he could not have imagined that it would be more overpowering than the first time, but it was.

Even when it was over, he couldn't stop kissing her. He kissed down one side of her and then the other, and she shivered and sighed, but was silent. Tell me you love me, he willed her to say, but she was silent, closing those hypnotic eyes and covering her face with one arm. The arc of her arm, the hollow of its pit, were beautiful. And now he wanted to make love again, and this time he was slower, more curious, more focused on her. He wanted to bring her to the passionate cries his wife made, but soon he was kissing her like a wild man, and his release was close to pain it was so good. He pulled her tight against him. "Every night, we must send one another a note. Will you do that? I won't rest until I've had a note from you," he said.

"What shall I say in the note?" Though Louise didn't know it, her voice carried happiness like a silver bell in its tones.

"That you love me. That you miss me."

"Every second I'm not with you, I miss you."

He ran his hands down her body, fierce and possessive and as happy as she was. "Tell me that. Tell me of your day. Wish me good night. There will be no secrets between us, yes?"

"Yes."

"Are you always so obedient?"

The happiness in her face dimmed. "I told you I wasn't clever—"

He stopped the rest of her words with a kiss. He traced the achingly fine planes of her face. "I don't want clever. I want true-heartedness."

"To the prince, like an altar fire."

"What is that?"

"The motto of my house. Appropriate, yes?"

She made him laugh. "Come hunting with me tomorrow," he demanded. He loved the way she looked on horseback.

"If Madame goes, certainly I will."

That's right; he forgot. He couldn't command her at will. She was not the *maîtresse en titre* with her own household and lodging. She belonged to Henriette's household. Well, so be it. They'd maneuver around it for now. She was *maîtresse en titre* of his heart.

"Have you any other orders for me, Your Majesty?"

She teased him, smiling at him in a way that he could not resist. "Wear a blue ribbon here," he touched above one ear, "for love of me tomorrow. And when you write to me, tell me what you've fretted over in the day. I would rid your life of any worries. Now, get out of bed, you lazy wench. Go over there and then walk toward me."

She did as she was told, naked to the afternoon light coming through the windows and naked to his eyes. Her face was somber as she walked toward the bed.

Yes, he thought, I didn't imagine it. There is a slight limp.

"Do you hate it?" she asked when she was at the bedside.

"Back into bed, my beauty." He leaned over to examine her leg, stroking it. "How did you come to hurt it?"

"I fell off a horse when I was little. And it never healed properly."

"How old were you?"

"Three."

"You were riding at three?"

"Even before. I rode wedged between my father and the neck of his horse. It's one of my first memories, being lifted atop his horse, looking at the world from there."

The urge to talk about the viscount was in his throat, to tell her his fears and his ambitions, but he stopped the words and allowed himself to be sidetracked by the way her waist moved so beautifully into the swell of her hip, and then he had to turn her over to look at her buttocks, and caressing those led to other things, and before either of them knew it, they were entangled and straining against one another again in that age-old joining of a man and a woman, and the feel of her was so supple in his arms, the knowledge that he could love with complete safety was so alluring, that he cried out like someone killed, surprising himself and her.

"Do I displease?" she said into his mouth, knowing she didn't.

And all he could do was kiss her into silence and follow along like flotsam on the huge wave this pleasure made. He insisted on taking her down to the bath chambers with him. He'd had to plan for it as if he were invading a country, and he'd lain awake in bed envisioning their route. They crept down secret corridors and halls, finally down a secret staircase, he in his breeches, she in nothing but the sheet he'd grabbed from the bed, a musketeer ahead of them, both of them collapsing now and then with laughter at the chance they took. Once there, Louis sent his musketeer away and insisted on bathing her in the great marble tub cut into the floor.

She was upset. "It isn't seemly. You are the king."

"I want to know every inch of you."

He was determined in his washing, thorough, stopping to kiss her in places that called to him—the blade of a shoulder, the soft middle of the back of the neck, the space between thumb and forefinger. He saw that she was looking at one of the portraits on the wall. An ancestor of his had been quite a collector of paintings, and the bath chambers were a private gallery that only kings might admire.

"Do you like her?" The portrait was of a woman, a hint of a smile on her face. "She's called the Mona Lisa, and a man named Da Vinci painted her. If he were alive today, I'd have him paint you. Yes, that's what I'll do. I'll have a portrait made of you and put it in my closet."

He'd cover it with drapery, so that no eyes should see it. He wanted one of her dressed in her finest and one of her naked in this marble bath. He stepped into the bath with her and one look at her slitted eyes led to kissing, but he was too aware of passing time, of obligation. Half-naked but sure-footed, he rewrapped her in the sheet and led her back up the secret stairs. They surprised his valet fussing with the covers on the bed.

"We'll hunt tomorrow before noon," Louis said to her. "Do you have a proper horse? And I'll see you tonight. I'll ignore you except for one dance, but only because I don't want anyone remarking on my attention to you. My every thought will be of you." He talked on as his valet dressed him.

La Porte tied the ribbons of the tight, red leather doublet Louis wore and allowed himself one glance at his master's face. There was something radiating from the king's eyes, happiness, some new self-possession and assurance. He looked the young god. This one gives him the passion he craves, the valet thought, and the passion lights an indomitable flame. He smiled a little smile to himself that only the pillows saw.

Dressed beautifully, Louis pulled Louise forward. The sheet fell from her breasts, and he touched one as he set the sheet about her shoulders again and held her face in his hands. "I love you," he said. "A note every night, beginning tonight."

Once he was gone, La Porte went to another door and allowed Sandrine inside. He ignored them as they began to dress Louise, his eyes on the chamber, checking it over. There must be no sign that His Majesty had ever been here. He began to unfold clean linens across the bed.

When Louise was at the door, one hand on its latch, La Porte pointed to a box on the table, near the meal neither His Majesty nor she had touched.

"For me?"

Her artlessness touched him. La Porte sniffed, to cover his growing softness for her.

Louise picked up the velvet box. In it were earrings, diamond earrings in a cluster shape long enough to reach her shoulders. They were beautiful, absolutely beautiful, but it was too much. She shut the box abruptly. She could never wear these. She already had bracelets. Everyone would notice. Questions would be asked. Whispers begun. Who courted le Blanc? Who gave her diamonds? And even more to the point, what had she given to obtain such jewels? "I can't accept these," she said to La Porte.

He was frost itself. "That, my lady, you must take up personally with the generous giver of such largess. You there—"

Sandrine froze where she was.

"Stay a moment, if you please. I have instructions from His Majesty."

When Louise was gone from the chamber, the valet pointed to a neat pile of soft linen chemises, handmade lace at the sleeves and throat. "These are for her. The lace, you see it? It was woven by nuns in Spain."

❧❧❧

In her bedchamber, Louise opened her trunk, put the velvet box in the toe of a shoe. There under a shawl was the gold Choisy had given her and the ring from Madame. How long ago that seemed, but it wasn't. The boy was in His Majesty's hands. All would be well, and all would be well, and all manner of things would be well. It was a prayer the nuns had taught her. She said it quickly for the boy, then she had a happy thought. She'd sew a coat for His Majesty. She was an excellent seamstress. She'd have La Porte take one of his jackets for a pattern. She'd use the gold to purchase the handsomest, softest velvet from Venice or Genoa and she'd stitch fur on the end of the sleeves and along the opening and perhaps she'd line the inside with fur, too. It would be very expensive. It would likely use up many of these coins, and that would be a good thing. Something in her wanted them gone.

On her bed lay three roses and a nearly ripened orange, jasmine tying the roses together. She hadn't seen them when she first walked in. Suddenly she wanted to dance, to cry out to the world her incredible good fortune, that the most wonderful man alive loved her, sent her roses, and gave her diamond earrings. She grabbed the roses and crushed them to her as if they were Louis himself. That he should love her was a gift from God. It was worth the guilt that seeped in at night. It was worth the penances her confessor would give when she finally confessed, though she was avoiding that task for as long as she could. It was worth the knowledge that if the world knew, she'd be labeled dishonorable and disgraceful. I can bear anything, she thought, for the sake of his love.

❦

In another hour, she was in Madame's bedchamber arranging the princess's curls, her happiness locked tight inside so that she shouldn't betray herself. She could see that the princess was fretful and heavy-eyed again. Guilt pinched, but she willed it to disappear. And then, as if sensing something, Henriette slapped at her hands as she worked to make a curl lie in perfect grace on Henriette's shoulders, and, startled, Louise stepped back.

"I don't like my hair that way! That's not the way you did it last time. If the Princess de Monaco were here, she'd tell you. I look like a hag." And as Louise, eyes downcast, curtsied to leave, "No. Don't go."

Henriette rubbed her forehead. "Forgive me, Le Blanc, I just don't feel myself anymore." But as Louise's hands touched her hair again, she grabbed a wrist, held it. "The bracelets again today?"

"I'll take them off. You have only to say so."

Their eyes met.

"Please, Madame, let go," Louise whispered, and Henriette released her wrist and waited until she was out of the chamber before bursting into tears. Louis didn't love her, and Philippe was acting so awful these days. He didn't love her either anymore. Everything was spoiled, everything.

❦

"Oh, do stop!"

Catherine pushed her cousin away, and before he could protest or fall to his knees and ask her forgiveness again, she opened the door and was out in a broad hallway of the palace of this seacoast kingdom that was hers by marriage. Silly to have started anything with him, Catherine thought, standing before a pier glass in the hallway and repinning a curl his groping had loosed. That's what came of a halting, lurching journey in a carriage to visit a husband one didn't truly wish to see. She missed Nicolas, she really did. Insouciance was so much more beguiling than begging. Climbing stairs that would take her to a tower with a favorite balcony looking out on the sea, she thought of her husband's ill-disguised dismay at her appearance, his clumsy lovemaking when she'd all but demanded that he bed her. He had a mistress. Her cousin had learned that for her, a little countess in this tiny dot of a kingdom who was on another balcony somewhere doubtless pining for the Prince de Monaco, who was doubtless counting the days until Catherine would be on her way back to Fontainebleau. She and her father had been ships passing in the night, he leaving the day she arrived, giving her little more than a nod when she'd come all this way to please him, to quiet his fears. Well, her fears.

She walked out onto the stone balcony, the wind from the sea whipping those curls she'd just so carefully arranged, but she didn't care. If this little kingdom had nothing else, it had its splendid sweep of mountain and rock right to the sea, quite spectacular, this mountainous curve on the edge of the Mediterranean. Hard to believe dreadful pirates were just out of sight, beyond the waves lapping against rock and here and there at a bit of beach as silvery as the strands in Nicolas's hair. Nicolas said every time a French galley sailed from Marseilles it was a gamble as to whether it, and its goods, would make port.

She really hadn't needed to come. Her husband was perfectly satisfied with their arrangement and his no-doubt-plump mistress. What a bore. Now she would have to be rattled in every tooth and bone to return to court, and there was her cousin Péguilin to deal with, all heavy hands and even heavier sighs.

Something below caught her eye. A small troop of horsemen were gathered in a side courtyard, and to her surprise, they were king's musketeers. The color on their tunics was unmistakable. She leaned over the thick stone edge of the balcony. There was Lieutenant D'Artagnan himself, talking with her father-in-law and her husband. She'd have him take a secret letter back to Fontainebleau to Nicolas.

Running downstairs, composing the letter in her mind with every step, she flew into the courtyard, but no one was there. The broad gates were closed, as if they had never been opened. She ran up outside stairs, to a rampart at the top of the wall, and there they were, riding away. She stamped her foot. Damn it all. Well, she was sending a letter to Nicolas if some messenger had to ride the legs off his horse to catch up with them. Inside she flung an order at a servant and ran up to her chamber, sitting at a table, pulling paper and ink and a quilled pen forward, dashing off words about her boredom and her desire to see him again.

At a knock, her husband, rather than the servant she'd expected, entered, and she pulled a piece of paper over the one upon which she'd been writing. "I'm almost done," she said. "I'm writing an important letter to Madame. May I send her your regards, my dear?"

Her husband sat down in a chair without answering as she folded the letter, melted wax, pressed a seal into its softness. "I would have liked to have placed it in Lieutenant D'Artagnan's hands myself," she complained. "I ran as fast as I could, but they were already gone. Riding away as if their lives depended upon it."

"Lieutenant D'Artagnan wasn't here, Catherine."

"Nonsense. I saw him with my own eyes. Don't you think I know His Majesty's lieutenant?"

"He wasn't here, and you didn't see him."

Something in his voice caught her attention, and she turned around in her chair so that she could see his face.

He held out his hand for the letter. "I will, of course, have your letter delivered, and by special messenger if it's that important to you."

"Is it a secret? Some sort of state secret?" She began to laugh. "Oh, I must know."

"No, you mustn't."

He wasn't going to tell her. Intrigued, she knelt in front of him, wedging her body between his legs, leaning her elbows on each of his thighs, tilting her head to one side, looking at him through her lashes. "I can keep a secret."

"No."

She moved closer, put each hand at the groove where his clothed thigh met hip. "I'll tell you a secret if you'll tell me a secret." She batted her eyes at him. "A group of us went to see Ninon de Lenclos. It wasn't my idea. The Countess de Soissons invited me, and I couldn't say no to her, as you well know. Ninon told us the most interesting things, showed us a way she'd kept her many lovers satisfied. I was shocked, of course." Ninon de Lenclos was a famous courtesan who'd been lovers and then friends with most of the men of the king's father's court.

"It was naughty of me, I know," Catherine continued, "but I thought perhaps I'd learn something that would be of interest to my husband. Is it of interest?" Catherine unbuttoned him, enjoying the power that was hers at this moment. She put her mouth on him, a trick Nicolas assured her that every man adored, and her husband gasped and held tightly to the arms of the chair. After a while, she grew bored, stood, lifted her belling skirts, and, naked underneath, sat down on him. He grabbed her, and they ended on the floor, tangled together like rutting beasts, she beginning to enjoy herself, biting and gasping, until, too suddenly, he was done. She lay with her skirts bunched and gathered at her waist, showing everything a woman was never supposed to show. "Did you like my secret?"

He smiled, and she snuggled against him.

"Give me your letter, Catherine, and I'll see it reaches court," he said, patting her bare rump.

He wasn't going to tell her. Catherine clenched her fists. "It doesn't seem so important now," she said.

He laughed a little.

Fool, she thought, sitting up and pulling down her skirts. He hadn't even waited to see if she was satisfied, and she wasn't—on any number of counts. He kissed at whatever was nearest him. "You're pleased with me, with us, with my position at court?" she asked. She was a fool, too, believing her father's frets that her husband might be unhappy.

"Oh yes," he said. "Not that I want you visiting courtesans, but still… May I visit you tonight, my dear?"

She forced a smile. Doubtless, he'd want this little variation repeated. That settles it, she thought. I am leaving here as soon as I can arrange it. She found Péguilin later, dragged him to a bed, and bucked against him until she began to weep, and her own release was there. He was all loving and sweet strokes with his strong hands, but she moved away from him, sat on the edge of the bed. It was all of it too boring. Her cousin was useful but clumsy. If he said he loved her one more time, she'd scream. "I saw Lieutenant D'Artagnan today," she said to the wall, more to distract him from his lovemaking than anything else.

He grabbed her shoulders, forced her to look at him. "He was here on the king's behalf, Catherine, and you didn't see him."

"You know about it?" she exclaimed. "Tell me!"

"There's nothing to tell, except that his mission is a secret one."

"What is the secret?"

"I don't know."

"You didn't ask?"

"When I heard it was on behalf of the king, that was enough for me."

"Get out of my bed!"

"Catherine—"

"Get out!"

That night, the Prince de Monaco, her father-in-law, got drunk at supper, and she moved to sit next to him and asked in a low voice, "Why was the lieutenant of the king's musketeers here today?"

"Prisoners," he slurred. "Secret prisoners." He put his finger to his lips. "Hush. Mustn't tell."

And then her husband was behind her, and a servant was helping her father-in-law to stand up, and she was on her husband's arm, going into one of the palace's galleries, where the nobility of Monaco had gathered for dancing because of the honor and excitement of her visit. One of the locals leered at her, and she noted that all the women's fashions were at least two years old. She managed to elude both her husband and Péguilin and locked her bedchamber door hours later, shaking her head at the excitement over their lodging of criminals, as well as at the lack of finesse here, never mind that the furniture came from Italy and that the galleries had been built in the last reign and that her father-in-law had an excellent collection of art.

She slept with the letter to Nicolas under her pillow, and the next morning, she walked to a cliff overhanging the sea and tore the letter to shreds and threw the shreds into the wind. Now here was a secret. The most powerful man in the kingdom was her lover. He'd toss a necklace of emeralds at her as if it were a mere bauble when next he saw her, and there'd be a private feast with rare wines and oysters and other delicacies that he'd hand-feed her, both of them naked. He was giving a fête in a few weeks that would be talked about for years. She'd been there as he planned the fireworks, the fountains' spray, the playlet by Molière, the fold of every drape, the placement of every vase in His Majesty's magnificent bedchamber. The grounds of his new country château were splendid, an order and unfolding presence about them that was extraordinary. More than five thousand people were invited to his fête. His chef was going to feed them two suppers. Even her father-in-law and husband were invited. Should we go? they'd asked her. It's such a journey. Bumpkins. Anyone who was anyone would be there. How could they even ask? Well, tomorrow she'd be on her way back to Fontainebleau. The day couldn't get here fast enough.

❧❦❧

The ink on the letter was dry now. Cinq Mars folded the paper into a small square. He wrote the Viscount Nicolas's name across the square's front and waved the paper back and forth to dry those words. Then he tucked the square into his sleeve and began the business of stoppering the ink and drying the tip of the quill. He put the ink and pen back into the drawer in which he'd found them, looked down at his hands. Ink stained a finger. He looked around the chamber. There was nothing with which to wash his hands. He licked the ink with his tongue, but he couldn't remove all of it. They'd bring him food soon. He'd pray they didn't notice anything. He went to the window, looked out into the courtyard, down upon the musketeers standing in groups talking. Where was he exactly? He had been blindfolded when he was put into a carriage at Pignerol, but now he was sure he smelled the sea. What was happening?

CHAPTER 33

A nd then my dwarf began to chase the parrot, and where would he go but to Monsieur's shoulder, and Monsieur would have laughed, but the parrot chose that moment to defecate, and Monsieur was unhappy, but Madame laughed," Maria Teresa chatted in Spanish about her day.

Where is she? Louis thought, looking among the courtiers gathered for an evening of gambling, but then he saw Louise, his secret in the bower, his heart of the rose. He placed his wife at a table to play cards. D'Artagnan's last message said they were in Monaco. They were having to keep the boy drugged much of the time, and he was ill with it. D'Artagnan was worried for him.

"I tell about bird," Maria Teresa said to the ladies at the table.

"Oh, it was too funny, Your Majesty," said Athénaïs, all bright vivaciousness. "When it landed on Monsieur's shoulder, he screamed, 'Shit,' and at first we thought it was his irritation with the bird. Little did we know he was being, in truth, literal."

Louis walked to Louise, who was playing hazard with several of her friends. He wasn't going to rest well until he knew the boy had reached his final destination, a small island off Monaco, little on it but an old fortified monastery. He glanced toward his brother, but Philippe didn't look at him. They hadn't spoken to each other since their quarrel. Too many quarrels in the family. I didn't write the Mazarinades, his cousin La Grande insisted in letter after letter. She was ready to swear any number of holy oaths upon her innocence. If not she, then who?

"Does it please you to gamble, Miss de la Baume le Blanc?" he asked. He just wanted to hear her voice.

"I always lose, Your Majesty."

He held out a coin. "Here. Perhaps this will bring you luck."

She took it, and their eyes met for a quick moment, then Louis walked around the room to give coins to all the maids of honor. He wanted to stay near her, but of course he couldn't. When she began to draw a crowd because she was winning, he was unable to resist standing by her again.

"What is the fuss all about?" he asked.

"She can't lose," said Choisy.

"I'm so happy. It's unusual for me to win," Louise said.

Choisy watched as she pushed the pile of coins before her toward Louis, then, a sudden instinct rising in him, looked from her face to the king's.

"Take my pile of coins, sire. They're yours. They began with your coin," said Louise.

"A gallant gesture," said Nicolas, who was one of those watching the game.

"If only all my court were so generous," Louis said. "No thank you, ma'am. Have a pink gown made. I'd like to see you in pink, as pale as the roses—" he stopped, aware suddenly that he was likely betraying too much. "Enjoy your play," and in another moment he was at his wife's side. "Let me take you outside to see the stars."

"Like the summer roses in the queen's garden," finished Nicolas smoothly, his eyes moving from a retreating Louis to Louise and back again.

Louise laughed, her laughter was so clear, so joyous, so heartfelt, that nearly everyone nearby found himself smiling.

"Miss de la Baume le Blanc," said Nicolas, moving to sit down right beside her, determined to follow this hunch that had taken hold of him. "Take my coin and make my fortune."

But Louise was already pushing back her chair, raking the coins into a napkin. "Play in my place, if you would, sir. I have good fortune enough."

❦

Outside on the balcony, Louis stared at the sky for a long time without speaking, all the things he wished to accomplish there before him like the twinkling stars in the sky above, all the reasons why he might fail also there. Where was D'Artagnan? How was the Duchess Marie faring with his mother? Was the writer of the Mazarinades aware of the question of his birth? Or were the notes simply taunts that had a deeper meaning than the taunter realized? A small sniffle made him look down at his wife. "Dear one, why do you weep?"

"Too many women."

His heart began to beat very fast.

"Too many women, they flirt with you, always."

"Yes, women do flirt with me. I am, after all, king of France. But their flirtations don't touch my heart. If I seem to flirt back, it's because it's fun. Nothing more. No one can take your place in my affections."

"I don't flirt."

"Yes, but you're very devout and serious, and I am frivolous and only a man, a man who has had the good fortune to be wedded to a saint. Dear saint, don't despair of me."

"I am not a saint."

But he saw his words pleased her. He could see that she loved that he had compared her to one. "You are."

"Saints don't feel jealousy."

"Then pray to have it removed for your sake and mine, my dear." He walked her back inside and gestured to several of his friends to take her off his hands. Vivonne, who spoke Spanish well enough, came forward and smiled down like a lean wolf at Maria Teresa.

"Tell me the story of your parrot today," Vivonne said. "My sister said it's a wonderful story, but no one tells it as well as you."

Louis leaned against the ornate woodwork of one of the walls and saw the Marshall de Gramont had returned. Thank God. He straightened, and Gramont made his way to him.

"Your journey went well?" Louis asked him.

"Just as you would desire, Your Majesty."

"You'll come and tell me of it later tonight."

❦❧❦

Nicolas placed another coin on the toss of the die, several piles of coins already before him. He was winning. Without seeming to, he watched the swirl of courtiers spin around Louis. So, the Marshall de Gramont was back from Monaco, was he? As he walked by, Nicolas called to him. "I'm winning, Marshall. Come and sit beside me." He pushed a neat column of coins he had won in the marshall's direction. "I saw your son in Paris not long ago."

The marshall made a snorting, derisive sound. "My caged tiger."

"An apt description, sir. I invited him to Vaux-le-Vicomte. There's plenty of forest where he may ride himself to exhaustion."

The marshall raised a goblet of wine in Nicolas's direction. "If you can provide any means of exhaustion, you have my gratitude."

"I offered him a position in the Mediterranean fleet. I know the commander well. He could have a galley if he so wished."

"And his answer?"

"He wasn't interested. The offer remains open. To be of service to your family would honor me. How was your visit to Monaco?"

"There must be some mistake. I've made no visit to Monaco. Look, Viscount, you've won." Gramont changed the subject smoothly. "My wife is beside herself about your fête."

"New gown?"

"Three. She can't decide which to wear."

"My humble apologies, sir. Shall I rescind the invitation?"

"She'll never speak to me again, and, alas, I am fond of her."

Louise walked by, arm in arm with Choisy. Was His Majesty interested in this little meadow flower? wondered Nicolas. Where were all these people he paid to spy on the king, on his every word, on his every change of expression? His orders had been explicit. He'd put his best spy to turning over rocks about Louise de la Baume le Blanc. And his secretary wrote that there had been an unusual prisoner in the Pignerol fortress, one who screamed and cried and whom no one was allowed to see. It had frightened the guards, who claimed they'd heard the prisoner was so deformed he was a monster. And a small, select troop of musketeers led by the inestimable Lieutenant D'Artagnan had taken that prisoner and two others, a musketeer and a priest, away. And now the Marshall de Gramont lied about going to Monaco. Why? What game did His Majesty play? What secret was so secret it could not be shared with his most important minister? Nicolas looked around the gallery. Moody faces, happy faces. Court was a wheel that kept turning, and those at the top balanced like acrobats to stay there, their drop depending on a king's whim. He'd climbed high. He didn't intend to drop.

❧❀❧

"My brother tells me yet again I'm a disgrace to the family honor," Choisy said to Louise.

"How upsetting for you. He doesn't understand you. Perhaps you ought to leave court for a while, go live in the country, or go to England. Madame always speaks of her visit there with such joy. What's the old saying: out of sight, out of mind?"

"Speaking of family honor, what's the state of yours these days? God, you're blushing. Come with me." He pulled her into a huge vestibule, tugged her toward a door, and, Louise protesting, pushed her into a chapel.

"We shouldn't be here," she said. They were on the king's balcony, where the royal family sat. Below them, on another floor, the chapel spread itself to the altar and back.

"The last place anyone is going to be tonight is here. Sit down."

She was glad there was only dim light around them because she knew her blush had deepened. Her face felt like it was on fire. They sat in silence for a time.

"Do you have a lover?"

"No!"

"Is your lover His Majesty?"

She strained her eyes at him, horror, upset, fear all playing at different moments across her face. "No! No! No!"

"I knew it."

"You don't know anything!"

"Precisely how long do you think you may keep this a secret?"

"Forever!" She threw the word at him. How dare he put his hands on this most precious part of herself?

"Oh, so the relationship is chaste, is it?"

She made a sound.

"Can you keep carrying his child a secret?"

Louise's hands began to twist in her lap. These were not matters she wished to think about.

"How long?" he demanded.

For some reason, she didn't lie. "A week."

"You think he loves you?"

"Yes."

Dear God, she was in over her head, thought Choisy, and she had no idea how much so. "You have to be cunning about this, my so very dear cousin."

"Oh, I am. No one knows. We're going to keep it a secret."

"What if you become pregnant?"

She looked away to the altar, whose beautiful soaring angels made her writhe with guilt inside. "I'll hide it."

"How?"

"I'll go away and then come back."

"Marry me, and I'll take you to England."

"It's the attention of men you want. How could I be happy in that?"

"I can make love. I like making love to women—"

She reached out and put her hand over his mouth to stop his words.

"I offer you honor," he said, pushing her hand away. "There's no honor in what you do."

She stood up. "I'm going back." She opened one of the huge chapel doors, and light from the chandelier in the vestibule framing her, said, "I'm honored that he has even looked at me."

How sweetly foolish you are, Choisy thought. They'll hate you when they know. They'll compliment you, but for something in return. One had to be a horse trader to be a good royal mistress. She handled horses like no one he knew, but he had few illusions about her ability to handle people. A myth was in his mind, a story from the ancient Romans and the Greeks before them, the story of Icarus who had longed to fly, whose loving father to please him had built wings; and Icarus had flown like a bird but too close to the sun so that the wax holding the wings together melted, and he had fallen from the sky. Choisy went to the railing and knelt, his eyes on the glorious altar below, and said a prayer for her.

❧❧❧

I won't go back inside, Louise thought. She'd go outside, to the queen's garden, and reach her chambers that way. Thinking about Louis, she walked across the gravel paths. Light showed from the gallery where everyone was gathered. The light, tingling smell of oranges seemed to be everywhere; she was approaching the orangery. It took a while before she realized she was being followed. She moved through an arch of the open-air gallery and stepped back against deep shadows made by one of the statues there. Between every arch leading outside and on the wall behind her were stags' heads. This chamber was a monument to the love of the hunt. A musketeer, a young man, rushed through an arch. She could see him more clearly as he stepped into the pools of light the torches made.

"Miss," he called.

She moved out of the shadows.

"I escort you," he said. "His Majesty's orders. My humble apologies if I frightened you."

She smiled then, her smile as wide, as beautiful as the quarter moon. Her beloved reached out to protect her. "Thank you. I welcome that. I'm going to my chamber," and as they began to walk toward the oval court and the queen's staircase, "I imagine you ought to tell me your name."

❧❧❧

Anne sighed and drank her wine, staring up at the same stars that her son and daughter-in-law had stood under earlier in the evening. The Duchess Marie wore one down by simple graciousness. Anne felt exhausted from it all, no longer completely clear in her mind as to why it was foolhardy, except that it so clearly was. To take on the most powerful man in France, whose financial tentacles were wrapped around the foundation of the kingdom, was a fool's errand.

"So, you'll fight against your son?" asked Marie, picking up the thread of an earlier conversation.

"No."

"You'll betray your son to the viscount and prevent the arrest? Doubtless, he'll forgive you in time. Perhaps an exile for you, like your royal husband's mother, but I do assure you exiles can be most wonderful. I do believe my best lover was a Dutchman, of all things."

"He's wrong," answered Anne.

"He's the king," replied Marie, and once more she mentioned the island stockpiled with weapons and soldiers.

"There's been some misunderstanding," said Anne. "He is going to tell my son about it all."

"And when might that be? When the king does as the viscount dislikes or offends him? People hold secrets because the conduct behind them is shameful."

Yes, thought Anne, thinking of her own secrets. I'd thought to be done with intrigues, and here I am in another one. If he fails...If he failed, she'd go on her hands and knees to the viscount for him or she'd sit atop a warhorse and lead a charge in Louis's name. "My son has my loyalty, but surely there is a better way."

"And what might that be?"

"Go to the viscount, speak with him, take away his island."

"And the viscount would walk away from his riches and power without a struggle?" asked Marie.

"He would be allowed to keep something."

"Who decides how much? The viscount or His Majesty?"

"Oh, you tire me!"

"Let's go for a walk in my garden. One of my sons has sent a basket of plums that are crying to be tasted. There's nothing better than plums ripened by sun, yes?"

CHAPTER 34

Throwing off covers, standing naked before a long window, watching the rise of the sun touch the cupola above the chapel, he knew what he was going to do. I'm going to Monaco, he thought. Henriette's ballet was tonight. He'd leave as soon after that as possible. He'd make Colbert provide an excuse for his absence.

Later, standing in one of his costumes for the ballet, Louis explained what he wished. "What reason for my absence? I can think of nothing."

Colbert pursed his lips. "A pilgrimage?" he suggested after a long pause. "For?"

"Ah…the well-being of the *dauphin* and the queen." Colbert continued slowly as he built the edifice of the story in his mind. "And the only person you will tell is Monsieur. You will go to him today and inform him you're worried about the queen, that you've had a vision—no, a dream—that this is what you must do, that you must go as a simple traveler, in disguise, and pray before—"

Colbert paused, his mind obviously rustling through its bins of random knowledge. Louis watched him in the pier glass, interested, eager even, to hear what he would say next. Philippe would be intrigued with the idea of a secret pilgrimage and touched that Louis trusted him. It might begin to heal the breach between them. And Philippe couldn't keep a secret. He would tell someone, who would tell someone else, and by the time Louis returned, the story would be out.

"You must go to Sainte-Baume, which is the cave where Mary Magdalene is said to have lived the last years of her life."

How fitting that he should mention the Magdalene. Louis turned so that he faced this man who had become so necessary to him.

Colbert continued. "It is quite near Marseilles, which is quite near—"

"Monaco," finished Louis. He called out for the tailor, shrugged out of the costume, and sent the man away with it. "I know nothing of the Magdalene coming to France," he said. "Tell me about this cave."

"'It is claimed by some that she became a great advocate for the Christ after the resurrection and that because of her preaching, the king of Palestine had her banished by placing her in a boat and putting it out to sea. A boat, I might add, without sails or oars. It's said she reached the shore of southern France. A favorite servant of my wife is from Provence and is a follower of the cult of the Magdalene there. The Magdalene is the patron saint of Provence. It's said she preached and performed good works and converted the barbaric Gauls, which is what we were, sire, before we were Christians. The last years of her life she lived alone in a cave, and there is a shrine and a basilica built to hold her bones."

The Magdalene he'd created, whom he loved with all his heart, was in his mind. "There's someone I want you to protect while I'm gone, someone so dear to me that—" he stopped because it did not do to reveal so much to another man, even one you trusted. One of Belle's sons walked forward and laid his head against Louis's leg, and Louis stroked the dog. "I have sworn to protect her from the eyes of the world, and while I'm gone, you must see that she has all she needs. Her name is Miss Louise de la Baume le Blanc."

He was alert for the least sign of judgment in Colbert's face; this was, after all, one of the most devout men of court, but Colbert's face remained impassive.

"Of course, sire."

"I want a saddle made for her, with interlocking L's in gold thread all about the edge."

"It will be done, sire."

"What word from the duchess?" His mother had returned late in the evening, gone straight to her chambers without a word to anyone.

"I received a letter from the Duchess de Chevreuse this morning, sire. Here it is."

Louis ran his eyes over the words the duchess had scrawled. She is not satisfied, but she is loyal. He closed his eyes. Pray God that was true. "La Grande Mademoiselle will be among the audience tonight."

"Yes."

Another Mazarinade had surfaced. Neither of them now thought her the instigator. It would be a most unwise instigator who ordered another sent while under suspicion herself. Perhaps, as Colbert had always maintained, the author was indeed the viscount.

The ballet was held in the ballroom. The audience, glorious in jewels and lace and high heels, walked to the rows of chairs set among the arches.

The actor and troupe manager, Molière, moved from one member of his troupe to another. His actresses were in the ballet itself, as chorus for songs and as dancers in the interludes. The principal parts went to courtiers, except for the soprano brought in from Paris, who more or less sang the loose threads of the story that framed the interludes of dancing. It was a frail frame, thought Molière, who found the fashionable long ballets with no cohesive story line tedious, but no one had asked him.

Courtiers settled into chairs to watch a bevy of women dance out as shepherdesses, followed by men as shepherds and children costumed as fauns. At the last moment, Monsieur had suggested the queen's dwarves join the cast of the fauns. They'd bring laughter from the audience, Madame and Molière had decided, which was never a bad thing in a long production. Maria Teresa clapped wildly at the sight of them.

Costumed as the goddess Diana, Henriette carried a bow and quiver and wore a silver crescent as her crown. She was still slim enough to dance, and rumor was she and Maria Teresa had had words in the queen's gallery this morning, Maria Teresa insisting that dancing would endanger Henriette's child. If I were more cow-like, I might worry, Henriette snapped back, and since the queen was as wide as she was tall these days, neither lady was now speaking to the other.

One eye on the performance, the audience leafed through their book of verses. It was the custom for the court poet to create verses about each courtier who danced in the court ballets, verses that used the theme of the ballet to compliment, and in some cases lightly mock, the courtier in question.

Henriette's nymphs had been picked from among the prettiest young women at court. Choisy couldn't take his eyes from Louise. Her hair loose on her shoulders, she wore a shorter, shimmering green skirt that showed her slim legs and ankles, and she was radiant, happiness spilling from her like light from a lantern.

"My word," said the Chevalier de Lorraine, "La Baume le Blanc looks positively glorious." He peered down at the verses in the leather book. "This beauty, recently risen, in color fresh and clear, is springtime with her flowers," he read, not caring that he talked aloud. "Our court poet is a prophet. She's growing more beautiful right under our eyes. I wonder if she has a magic potion. Soissons was telling me about a witch in Paris—oh, here's Monsieur. Hush, now, Choisy, don't distract me."

And then, after Philippe had danced his solo and been roundly applauded, Lorraine continued talking. "You know, His Majesty called on Monsieur today. I have no idea what they spoke of, but Monsieur was thoughtful afterward."

Applause interrupted him. His Majesty had just danced onto the stage with more vigor and style than any dancer there.

Nicolas led the applause and murmured the word "magnificent" to

Madame de Motteville, as all watched Louis leap in and among lithe girls in silvery green skirts and then dance with Henriette as his partner.

"Always," answered Anne's lady-in-waiting.

"How was Her Majesty's visit with the duchess?" Nicolas asked. "You'll come to see me later with all the details, I know. I hear there's an old secret, a love child or something."

Motteville's gasp made him turn his head to her.

"Ask me no questions, so that I may tell you no lies," she said, and before Nicolas could respond, she'd stood up and moved to stand by Queen Anne.

The audience sat through summer with its gardeners and dancing flowers, the dwarves again creating laughter, and now it was winter's turn. Louis danced on, in full costume, skirts, headdress, and bosom, of the goddess Ceres. He played the part with a deadpan seriousness and gigantic leaps that delighted the audience. Molière, whose idea it had been, smiled.

Everything after that was anticlimactic, never mind that the musicians played like a heavenly chorus, never mind that all the cast gathered on stage for the finale, dancing and singing, and finally falling into stylized poses as various attributes: love, abundance, joy, prosperity, the kind of heavy symbolism loved by this century. Among the melee of congratulations and compliments and preening about in costume afterward, Louis managed to pull Louise behind the large cutout of the sun for one quick moment.

"I'm leaving for a week. If you need anything, go to Colbert," he told her.

She couldn't answer because he was already walking away. She stared sightlessly at the glitter and paint on the cutout. Now Mister Colbert knew? Who else had to be swept into their secret to preserve it, and how long would it be preserved if more and more people were told? How would she look Mister Colbert in the face and not blush?

Colbert, however, was concentrated on Madame de Motteville, and he ran her to ground the way a dog would a fox. "I saw you speak with the viscount."

"He knows," said Motteville.

Colbert spoke sharply, for once displaying emotion. "He knows what?"

"He knows about the child."

Within moments, she found herself in a tiny antechamber, standing before Louis. Once the intrigue of living in court, disloyalty like rotting apples forever tumbling from their basket, had enlivened her, made her bold and daring, given the days a sense of adventure, but at this moment, she felt old and used and pulled too many ways by too many competing loyalties. The expression on Louis's face frightened her.

"What did he say?"

"Very little. He asked about the visit to the duchess, said he'd heard there was a secret, a love child, nothing more." She didn't dare raise her eyes to meet Louis's.

"Look at me," he said, and when she could make herself do so, "Find out what he knows, but tell him nothing, not so much as a hint, a breath of the truth. Tell him you would dishonor Her Majesty to speak of such things. Weep, have a tantrum, seduce him, but find out how he knows this and tell him nothing in return. Do you understand me, Madame de Motteville?"

She nodded her head.

Louise stood behind Henriette, who was receiving courtier after courtier, each of whom must tell her how gracefully she'd danced, how beautiful she looked, how wonderful the ballet had been.

"—and I think it's disgraceful the way Madame encourages the king's regard. Our poor queen—"

Both Louise and Henriette turned their heads to see who spoke. It was Athénaïs, standing with Olympe, and when she saw that they'd heard her, she clapped her hands over her mouth and backed away into the crowd. But Olympe, head held high, met Henriette's questioning gaze, a malicious half smile on her face, as direct as a slap.

"I feel ill," Henriette said. How dare she look at me so, she thought.

Louise helped her to one of the benches near the opened windows, sent Fanny running for wine.

"Make them go away," Henriette said, as courtiers began to cluster to see what was the matter. The look on Soissons's face implied triumph, malice, happiness that she was sad. Did the countess relish her distress? What others around her did so also?

"Shoo! Leave her alone! She just needs some air." Louise pushed at courtiers, forcing them back away, but the Chevalier de Lorraine moved around Louise as if she didn't exist.

"Monsieur sends me to see how you do. Remember, you're carrying his heir."

Henriette didn't answer.

"I'll tell him you're irritable, as usual," said Lorraine and left her.

Louise knelt in front of Henriette. "You look so pale. What is it? What can I do?"

"I don't have his regard, but he looks happy," Henriette whispered, "not sad, like me."

"No, no, not really. We all know he loves to dance, and I heard he so liked your ballet." Louise picked up Henriette's fan, began to wave it back and forth at Henriette's face.

"You're so kind, La Baume le Blanc."

Louise saw that her eyes had fastened again on the bracelets. How could she ignore them with Louise fanning her? Please, precious Mother of God, prayed Louise, please.

"I'm glad you wear those. His Majesty asked about them, now that I think on it, several weeks ago. It doesn't do to offend, you know. Just—just don't take any of it too seriously. I won't have one of my household hurt because of his flirting."

"No, no, I don't take it too seriously. I'm grateful to have some jewelry, actually."

Henriette laughed. She wiped at her eyes, stood, and shook out the skirts of her wonderful costume, in a color Louis himself had picked for her, once upon a time when they'd been in love, a kind of sage-green silk taffeta decorated with arabesques of pearls.

"Thank God there's at least one person around me without guile. Thank you, my dear," she said to Louise and marched out into the milling courtiers, her back straight, her earrings dancing.

Hours later, her head hurting from wine and self-reproach, Louise stumbled into her bedchamber with her friends. Everyone took off jewels and stockings and gowns and climbed into their beds, yawning and tired and more than a little drunk.

That Louis would be gone a week filled her with longing. How pliable my conscience is becoming, Louise thought, and as she remembered her lies to Madame this night, remembered Madame's sad and bewildered expression, she moved restlessly in the bed until Fanny told her in a hissing whisper to be still.

His court settling into their beds, but he himself dressed for travel, Louis knelt beside his dog. Maria Teresa had cried when he'd told her he was going on a secret pilgrimage for their child's sake. She'd dropped to her knees. Forgive me, she'd said, her eyes shining, her arms outstretched. My jealousy has been a canker in my heart. Guilt had filled him, but also right beside it, a slithering snake in the garden, was relief. La Grande had knelt before him like a supplicant tonight. Her abrupt dismissal and her abrupt readmission to court had her all but groveling.

"Belle," he said, stroking the dog's head, remembering when he'd been a boy, when he'd been so certain he'd break no sacred vows, when he'd been so certain hearts remained pure, "I shall be gone a while. Wait for me, my sweet. Promise you'll do that."

❧✦❧

"So what did you think of the ballet?" asked Catherine. She sat in Nicolas's bed, a shawl and nothing more on her body as he fed her slices of melon.

"Quaintly sweet."

"That's damning praise. Did you think I danced clumsily?"

Nicolas leaned over and kissed the swell of a breast. "Nothing you do is clumsy. Dare I hope that the enthusiasm you've just displayed is because I was missed? And yet I see Captain Péguilin following you with his eyes like a loyal spaniel."

She leaned back on her elbows, the shawl opening, her hips and breasts white and inviting, her legs long and tempting. "It was boring in Monaco. Captain Péguilin was boring. The gentlemen were without finesse. Why was Lieutenant D'Artagnan there? I've been meaning to ask."

"What? You spoke with him?"

"I most certainly did not. I was informed by my father-in-law and my husband in no uncertain terms that it was a great secret and I wasn't to tell a soul, but of course, you know. Tell me. I promise I won't breathe a word about what is obviously king's business— What have I said? Why are you leaving the bed?"

Abruptly pulling a loose nightgown on, Nicolas walked into another chamber, sat down at a table upon which lay papers and books, love letters and pleas for help. One of the royal tailors brought the news that His Majesty made a secret pilgrimage. Trouble was brewing. Best to prepare.

❧✦❧

It was raining when Louis arrived in Monaco, his destination a private château belonging to Catherine's father-in-law, prince of this kingdom, who waited for him.

The prince rose from his chair when Louis stepped into the salon, cloak dripping with rain. "Let me offer you dry clothing at once, sir, and food."

This was an ally, a man old enough to be his father, who had signed treaties with Louis's father. He'd expelled the Spanish from the garrisons they'd once occupied here, giving France a secure friend on her southeastern coast, and in reward, his sons had played in the gardens at

Saint-Germain as Louis's companions when he'd been a boy. Let them see the grandeur of this court, his beloved cardinal had said. Then no other will be able to seduce them completely.

"Lieutenant D'Artagnan?" asked Louis.

"Upstairs, sir."

"Who is it?" D'Artagnan's voice asked when Louis knocked on the door.

"The king." Once inside, he saw that the boy sat at a window, the iron mask upon his face. Louis took in the sight of a monk and said to him, "Out. Cinq Mars?"

"In another chamber."

Your Majesty, D'Artagnan wanted to say to Louis, I'm afraid for the boy. There were tales to tell, of having to knock the boy down, of the priest and D'Artagnan having to straddle the youth to pour even a bit of the wine down his throat, of him tearing off bandages, of the howling as they rode through the night, of his incessant rocking back and forth before the wine took effect. The boy was drugged now, but the expression on Louis's face told D'Artagnan this clearly wasn't the time to express concerns.

"You also," said Louis.

Perhaps it would never be the time, thought D'Artagnan. He walked out behind the priest.

Alone with the boy, who did not move, Louis said, "I don't know what else to do. It's for the sake of the kingdom. It's possible I share your father, and no one must know. Our cousins, the Condés, they're great warriors, proud of their bloodline, their closeness to the throne. They'll fight me for the crown if they think their blood more worthy than mine. You'll have the freedom to take off your mask once I have you settled. I'll send furniture and hangings worthy of a prince, I promise."

There was no indication from the boy that he'd understood or even heard.

"You'll be treated with the honor you deserve," Louis continued, going over in his mind all that must be accomplished in a few short hours. "I wish I might have known you," he said. Perhaps one day, God willing, he would.

❧✿❧

The old Prince de Monaco was silent, his eyes on Louis, who was walking the outside perimeter of a fortified monastery, vacant except for a handful of monks. It was an old medieval keep, a solid three-story square of stone, with small windows on its second floor and towers in its corners. It sat on the literal edge of the sea, a jut of dangerous rocks on its seaward side. Atop its ramparts, one could see the forest that covered the remainder of the island. Saints of the church had lived in it once upon a time, converted pagans, and been massacred by the Saracens. It had never revived after that, was a tiny outpost forgotten by the Vatican and by the prince himself most of the time, simply one of four islands on his coast, all small, all mostly uninhabited except by fishermen who made their living bringing their catch into the harbor to sell.

Dozens of questions had been flung at him by the young king of France on their short sail over: how bad were storms, when was the last time pirates had attacked, did the Pope show any hint of interest in the monastery, were the pirates in the Mediterranean as fierce as he'd been told? Now this king was looking at him with flickering eyes, eyes that bored into him, measured him, set him down again with a certain weight assigned to him, and the prince realized with a start that he'd been asked another question, a question he hadn't even heard in his abstraction at the rapid, unexpected sequence of events that had begun with the secret visit of the Marshall de Gramont.

"Are you a man of honor?" Louis repeated the question.

"I am."

"On your honor, no one must know you've done this for me. No one must know that I visited you. No one must know the importance I place upon this child. The boy is dear to me, more than that I cannot say, but I will tell you this, he has the beginnings of leprosy—"

The prince drew back in horror. No one knew how this frightful scourge spread, but everyone was certain of its contagion. He'd order every stick of furniture in the small château in which the youth had stayed burned. The carriages conveying the boy would be burned, too.

"—and his only servants will be the monk and the musketeer, though I will send others, but they will never see the child. He is to live on the top floor of the keep." He can walk the rampart of the roof, thought Louis, take off the mask, turn his face to the sun and sky there, become brown and whole. "If you keep my secret, I will honor you. You and your son will become my greatest friends."

The prince bowed. "I was yours before your words." Curiosity as to the identity of the boy had died with the word leprosy. He followed Louis upstairs, up long flights inside a square tower, until they stood on the roof. The view was magnificent, great blue sea to three sides, the green of an island forest on the other.

Louis walked the length and breadth of the roof. His brother could be free here, could be treated as the beloved son of a queen.

In a bedchamber of the prince's château in Monaco, Cinq Mars held his breath at what he was witnessing. The king of France had gently unfastened the mask from the boy's face, removed it, and was looking down at this half-grown, drugged, sleeping child. Cinq Mars watched as Louis smoothed the boy's hair, his forehead. He watched in amazement as Louis gave the boy a quick kiss on the lips, then knelt beside him to pray.

What have I done? thought Cinq Mars. He had given the letter to the château's stable boy, told him to take it to a merchant's house, any merchant, and pulled the gold saint's medal on its necklace at his neck as payment.

Louis held tight to his brother's hand. Pray God this prince would be as happy and free as he could be. Pray God he would never wear the iron mask again. Pray God he, Louis, find the compassion to forgive his mother. Pray God his enemies did not learn of this child and use the scandal to wrest the throne from him. Pray God his own son did not suffer the affliction of this boy. Pray God forgive him for keeping it all secret still.

He stayed long on his knees, the prayers inarticulate after a time, more feeling than thought. When he was finished, he opened his eyes to find Cinq Mars watching him. "I don't even know his name. What's his name?"

"Prince Jules."

Prince de Mazarin, he would have made him, had circumstances been different. Perhaps, when his mother died, he'd do so. Louis pointed to a leather portfolio. "In there, you will find papers making you guardian for this child. You are made a count, Count de Cinq Mars, for your services, and more than enough for a fine life will be yours, if you continue to care for him as you have in the past. I'll want you to come to court once a year to report on him. Who in your family do you wish rewarded?"

Cinq Mars named his sister.

"I'll see she has everything she needs and more. I'll see her children are brought to court. Have you funds?"

There had been a chest of coins, but who knew where it was now. "No," he answered.

Louis almost smiled. "Yes. A chest of coins was found among your belongings and saved. We are nothing if not thorough. My treasury is empty, and I never overlook an opportunity to fill it. It remains yours. He'll have every luxury but that of company. You're to live with him on the top floors of an old monastery nearby. I've told the Prince de Monaco that he has leprosy. The few monks who continue to live there will be terrified, and it will keep the curious too afraid to satisfy their curiosity. There's a rampart roof where he may walk free and see the sun and rain. I don't want the mask on his face again unless you deem it necessary."

Louis took a ring from his finger; it was set with emeralds. "Send me this ring should there be trouble. If I receive this, I'll come to you myself." He turned to Father Gabriel, who was standing near the sleeping boy. "Can you write?"

The priest nodded.

"Write down the names of those in your family whom you would wish rewarded, and I shall do it."

How determined he is, how thorough, thought Cinq Mars. Do I tell him about the letter?

"Father," said Louis to the priest. "Now will you hear my confession?"

The shock on Father Gabriel's face was mirrored on Cinq Mars's.

"Leave us," Louis ordered Cinq Mars, then he knelt before the priest.

"Bless me, Father, for I have sinned—" and Louis recited the litany that had begun weeks ago with his toying with the affections of a dear princess and thus hurting both her and his brother, that moved on to falling in love with and seducing an honorable girl, and that ended with exiling another brother to a nearly deserted island to live in obscurity. His spirit felt lighter as he confessed. Thank God for that; there was still so much to do.

Nicolas reread the letter that had arrived from his secretary. The trail of the wandering D'Artagnan and the mysterious prisoners led to Monaco. His Majesty, so Monsieur told the Chevalier de Lorraine, who told Nicolas, went on a secret pilgrimage to the Magdalene's cave, which, if Nicolas was not mistaken, was close to Monaco. Do I really believe in coincidence? he thought. He considered the sloping, inked letters of the words, spread on the page before him. What do I do with this? He was ordering his secretary off this quest and to Belle Isle. He wanted the latest word on the state of its fortifications, a recount of men and weapons, of ships. He did not wish to pick up a saber and wave it at His Majesty, but he would. But perhaps his fête, its magnificence, its abundance, its wealth of guests, would be saber-rattling enough. Shining little Louise de la Baume le Blanc was His Majesty's new lover. An interesting choice, the choice of a man with a tender heart, but he possessed a lion's heart, too. Nicolas could hear its faint roar. La Grande Mademoiselle had returned to court. He sent me away because he thought I wrote disgusting old Mazarinades to him, La Grande whispered. As if I would.

Louise saw her musketeer standing in an arch of the open-air gallery and excused herself from her circle of friends.

"And where are you off to?" asked La Grande, shading her eyes and looking at Louise.

They were embroidering, but at least Madame had declared the queen's gallery too stuffy and marched her ladies outside to the garden, and other courtiers were there, young men, drawn to the sight of the ladies, holding long skeins of thread for them or making suggestions about color, all the while winking promises with their bold eyes. Madame's charming laugh kept ringing out at frequent intervals, and Catherine made no pretense of embroidering at all, but walked arm in arm in the distance with her cousin.

"To the nearest close stool, Highness."

"Oh, very well."

Louise walked past garden statues and into the cool shade of the garden's open-air gallery. Her musketeer waited. Had he a letter from His Majesty?

"It's the dog, miss," he said. "La Porte sent me to find you."

Skirts in her hands, she followed him up twisting stairs. La Porte's face told her everything.

"Is she—"

"Very nearly."

Inside the king's closet, Belle lay in a nest of fine linen. Louise settled herself on the floor, put her hand on Belle's nose. Her children were there, all lying close, their noses pressed into their mother's side.

"I don't know what else to do," said La Porte.

Louise could see how upset he was. She kept her hand on Belle, began to repeat the rosary, and La Porte and the musketeer knelt, their voices joining hers. After a time, Belle's legs jerked and she made a whiffling sound, and her children lifted their heads, rose, and began to circle her, sniffing every inch of her.

"I think it's over." Louise bent forward and put her head against Belle's. "He's going to miss you very much," she whispered. "You were a fine dog."

La Porte had to sit down he had begun to cry so hard.

Louise made her way back toward the garden. When would His Majesty be back? She longed to see him, to lie with him in bed again. The pretense at embroidery had ended, and everyone was playing a game of blindman's bluff. There were giggles and shouts of laughter, and La Grande was the blindfolded pursuer, and her laughter was loudest of all.

"Come and join us." One of the king's gentlemen whirled her into La Grande.

"You're it! You're it!"

She let them tie the handkerchief around her eyes. She would have to pretend to enjoy this, when all she wished was to sit quietly by herself for a time. So, she thought, this is what it is like for him.

CHAPTER 35

Louis rode back into Fontainebleau at dawn, having woken in the dark and summoned those musketeers with him out of sleep. The blue tiles of the roofs and the chimneys loomed in the distance, and in a short time he rode past palace walls. He slipped off his horse, glad to have arrived. The surface of the carp pond was still. His fish slept. The row of long windows in the ballroom blinked at him as sunlight touched their panes. He'd gone to the cave of Mary Magdalene. Pulling the hood of his cloak over his head, he had joined the other penitents standing in line to light a candle, to leave prayers and supplications with her. He'd prayed on his knees for himself, for all the women he'd loved, his mother and his wife and Louise and Henriette, he'd prayed that she should forgive him, that he had not harmed her too deeply, and finally, for her for whom he had been reared, whose glory and honor he must sustain and increase, France, his kingdom. He'd prayed that he should rule wisely.

The leagues he'd traveled in the last days fell away from him as he dismounted in his private courtyard. He had been unflinching, riding longer and harder than any of his musketeers, rolling up in his cloak and sleeping on the ground when he became too tired. His endurance and strength of will as well as his visit to the shrine were already adding to his growing legend among his men.

"A council meeting this morning," he informed his master of the household, as he sat in a bath, "and a hunt afterward. Inform the queen and Madame that I'd like their ladies to join me." He waved the man away. "Tell me how she died," he said to La Porte.

"Quietly, her children with her and Miss de la Baume le Blanc. I hope I did not displease by doing so."

"No."

Belle lay wrapped in finest linen, waiting for him in a basement. La Porte brought him notes from Louise, one for every night he'd been gone.

He read through them hungrily, kissing the signature of each one, especially the one in which she described Belle's death.

"And this," said La Porte.

And there it was, another Mazarinade. He didn't even read it all the way through.

"It was lying near Madame Belle in the basement."

Louis folded Louise's notes and put them inside his shirt next to the flesh of his heart. The Mazarinade he put in a pocket in his doublet. Hold your friends close and your enemies closer, said his beloved cardinal. If not La Grande, then who? The viscount. It must be.

His gentlemen shared the gossip of the last few days.

"Where's Monsieur?" he asked. No one seemed to know. He stopped by his wife's chambers to greet her and give her a quick kiss. He could see from her face, from her ladies' faces, that everyone thought they knew where he'd been. He led Maria Teresa to a window and told her about the cave and shrine. Her eyes glowed so sweetly that he had to drop his.

"My dog Belle died," he said.

"Your valet sent me word. I'll have my father send you a dog from Spain."

I don't want a dog from Spain, he thought, but he kissed her hand and thanked her.

❧❧❧

"Your Majesty's journey went well?" asked Nicolas when the council assembled.

Louis surveyed the three men with him, the men the cardinal had bequeathed him to run this kingdom, men who had served for years, who knew its every secret, one of whom was the lynchpin. When he fell, what would the others do? One Louis was certain would stay by his side, but the other?

"I made a pilgrimage," he said, deciding that a portion of the truth was the best lie, "to the grotto at Saint-Baume to pray for the queen and the *dauphin*. I had a dream to do so, and the affection I bear the queen and my unborn son made obeying the dream imperative, but I don't wish this spoken of. I went as a private man, not as sovereign."

"Did you go to Monaco, sire?" asked Nicolas. "Being so close…"

"Yes, I did stop to see the prince, but only to rest my head on a soft pillow for a night." Nicolas knew something, he thought. How much?

Nicolas pushed forward a paper that showed taxes collected thus far. "From the reports I'm receiving," said Nicolas, "the harvest will not be a plentiful one."

Yes. Many of those at the shrine had been there to pray because they feared the scarcity in their fields, feared surviving the winter. His hood drawn over his face, he'd moved among them and listened. The ribs of my cow show through her skin. My one good pig died. There is nothing for fodder. What will we do?

"Perhaps we need to purchase wheat and corn for the winter," said Louis. "Will you request the intendants of each province to send a report about their best estimate as to the harvest and those most in need? And will you obtain prices from the Dutch and the English and Swedes as to what they'd charge us for grain?"

Nicolas wrote down the instructions.

"We'll take the funds necessary from the *dauphin*'s birth celebration." Louis smiled one of his rare smiles. "I'll make it up to my son later. I've been thinking, what is the state of fortification on our coasts? Being upon it, if only for a night, has put concerns in my mind. How many of our galleys are attacked by pirates? Will you have the new commander of my Mediterranean fleet come to court? I'd like to question him. Who was the old commander?"

"The Marquis de Richelieu," answered Nicolas.

"Summon him to court, also," said Louis.

"They'll be here for my fête," said Nicolas.

Louis nodded his head. "Excellent. Inform them I wish them to call upon me. Mister Le Tellier, I understand you have the ordinance prepared that will make certain there is regular payment of my troops. All of you have a copy. Please read it and report any discrepancies you see before I sign it. If I may, Le Tellier, have you the breakdown of troops once we cut back?"

"Household troops, ten thousand; infantry, thirty-five thousand; cavalry, ten thousand."

"Fifty-five thousand," said Nicolas. "Still extraordinary when compared to other kingdoms."

"And you, my superintendent of finance," Louis faced Nicolas, "you must give me a report of your trade armada soon and that island to the west—what is its name, now—"

"Belle Isle, sire, which is the base of my whaling company, such as it is. I regret to report that we have as yet to kill a single one."

"You must capture one before your fête and bring it to swim in your landscape canal." To general laughter, Louis pushed away the papers before him. "That's all for now. Viscount, will you give me the pleasure of your company just a while longer?" As the two others left the antechamber, Louis said, "Monsieur was not at my rising from bed this morning."

"Perhaps he was unaware that you had returned."

"There has been quarreling between us. I think you must know that."

All his courtier's instincts up, Nicolas spoke carefully. "I am fortunate to be counted among Monsieur's friends."

"Will you tell him for me that I wish to settle the quarrel between us?"

Nicolas bowed. "I will do what little I can."

"As always, I thank you. What service you are to my family."

At the door of the antechamber, Nicolas turned. "I've heard you lost your favorite hunting dog. When you visit Vaux-le-Vicomte, let me show you the pups in my hunting stable. Perhaps one may take your eye."

"How kind of you."

Nicolas walked through antechambers, looking out windows to see who was in the king's courtyard. He should have been reassured by His Majesty's flattery, but he felt more wary than ever.

❧❦❧

Louis, surrounded by dogs, stood in the dim of the basement staring down at the linen-wrapped sweetheart that had been his favorite. La Porte had uncovered her head, and Louis touched it once before motioning for the valet to re-cover her.

"We'll bury her this evening, after I return from the hunt."

The hunt, the kill, would be in her honor. He'd bring the stag's heart and bury it with her. He'd send notes to Maria Teresa, to Henriette so that they might join him when he had her buried. Henriette's presence would ensure Louise's. They'd bury her near the spring that was the source of Fontainebleau's name, the spring that had been found by an ancestor's favorite hunting dog, Bleau. He was burying his boyhood when he buried this dog.

"You have much to live up to," he told the dogs swirling around his legs as he left the basement. They barked and ran toward a figure in the distance. Colbert waited near the orangery.

"I have some bad news, Your Majesty," he said.

Was there any other kind? "Tell me now."

"I've unearthed the existence of another of his spies."

"Well?"

"It's your mother's confessor."

❧❦❧

It was all over Fontainebleau that the king had returned and wished to go hunting. Those who'd seen him go to Mass this morning with the queen spread the word. Maids of honor and ladies-in-waiting went scattering to dress. Louise felt almost ill with impatience and excitement. She had dragged out the trunk from under her bed and was rummaging through it wildly to find something special, something unique, anything that would catch his eye.

Fanny sat on the bed.

"Aren't you going to dress?" Louise asked her.

"You must ask him!"

Louise stood, grabbed Fanny by the wrist, pulled her out into the hallway.

"Quarreling," sang Claude to Madeleine, and they laughed.

"Have you lost your mind?" Louise demanded. "You act as if no one is listening."

"You have to ask him to forgive the Count de Guiche."

"What if my doing that makes him angry? Have you thought of that, Fanny, that everyone asks favors of him? I can't join the rest. I don't wish to."

"You of all people can. You of all people can have your heart's desire with him. Do it for me, Louise. Can't you see how unhappy I am?"

Fanny's last words were said with tears in her eyes, but Louise didn't stay to comfort her. Back in the bedchamber, she continued to pull items out of her trunk, but she had to stop. Her hands were trembling. She felt like crying herself. She was afraid to ask him, afraid to bring the least ripple to their love's perfection. She didn't want to be a supplicant like everyone else.

❧❦❧

Later she stood in a mix with the other maids of honor, just outside the king's gatehouse, as grooms walked horses up the road from the stables. Louis remained in the gatehouse with Henriette and Maria Teresa, neither of whom were joining the hunt, and every now and again his eyes went to the maids of honor, who stood together like bunched and fragrant lilies. Louise met his eyes just once, and that was enough. His desire was clear, and his love.

Louis's master of the household brought a dashing filly forward. "It's my privilege to offer you a better mount as a special gift from someone who cares for you," he said to Louise.

All around women were being aided in settling themselves into the sidesaddles that were the proper and fashionable seat for a woman on horseback. The courtier put his hands together so that Louise might place her foot into them.

"The saddle has been specially made for you," he said quietly, as she gracefully, lightly vaulted herself up. He touched a design of gold stitching, and Louise saw the design was intertwining L's. "He asks that you stay in his sight."

She should have been unhappy that yet another person knew, but she wasn't. What about your honor? Choisy had questioned. Today, she went hunting with the king of France. That was her honor. With a light touch of the whip, she was off, trotting the filly into the center of the milling, talking, mounted group.

At the sound of the trumpet, the hounds, down the road near the stables, snarling and growling and pulling at their leashes, were let go. Barking and some of them beginning to bay, they ran out into open ground, and runners followed them. The court began to ride down the road, past manicured gardens surrounding the palace, toward open country, toward forest.

Once the stag was killed, they stopped at Versailles. Blue slates on its steep roofs, it was pleasant enough, two wings extended from each side of a center pavilion, three floors to each building, one of them attics, but it was small and simple, little ornamentation on its exterior, a few busts on the corners of the roofs but no grand marble statues and columns and wreathing. It had been a place for his father to rest overnight should his hunts run long. There were grounds at the rear, very large parterres for courtiers to walk in, a lovely oval pool with handsome wrought-iron railings, vast spaces beyond for riding to nearby hills. There was no room to chamber households or the servants to manage them. Compared to the Louvre or Saint-Germain or Fontainebleau or his cousin's Luxembourg in Paris or his brother's Saint-Cloud, it was nothing.

Louis walked into the king's bedchamber, the heart of the château, the center of the U made by the adjoining buildings. She wasn't there. Surprised, he took off his gloves, walked to the window and looked out. No one was in the front courtyard. They were still in the gardens, lingering over the remains of a fine picnic and the wine he'd ordered served. He leaned out those windows, trying to observe her from among the others. Where was she? His desire to be with her after an absence of a week was almost more than he could bear. When too much time had passed, he stopped pacing and decided to leave, was pulling on his gloves as the door opened, and she ran in.

"Where were you? How dare you keep me waiting?" he flashed.

"I couldn't get away. I was sitting by Monsieur, and he wanted to talk—oh, don't be angry with me. I'm so sorry! I would never offend you, Your Majesty."

She's afraid of me, thought Louis, and that was not what he wished from her, not after being away from her for days, but it was what came with his power. With her, he didn't wish to display power, and yet hadn't it been the imperious king in him that was offended at being kept waiting, a king who kicked more and more at the traces of any restraint?

He pulled her into his arms, and she broke down and cried. He could just make out some of her words: "so sorry," "there was no way I could get away," "missed you so much." Her time didn't belong to her or, for that matter, to him. It belonged to those whom she served, to Henriette and to Philippe. He had to remember that. He began to kiss the part in her hair. "We don't have time for this. Come and lie with me."

It felt like he couldn't breathe until he made love to her. She's becoming necessary to me, he thought. Their lovemaking was hurried and rushed; they didn't even undress. Then she was up and straightening her gown, and he lay on the bed and watched, his heart hurting because this wasn't what he'd envisioned. He didn't want her to leave yet, and he could see how distressed she still was.

"I am so sorry I displeased—" she said.

"It is I who am displeasing. It was unworthy of me to be angry. If you must be late, perhaps next time you might send me a message."

"I could think of no way—"

"My master of the household. He's down below among the courtiers with orders to keep his eyes on you. He would have been happy to bring a message."

"Of course. I'm so stupid."

He rose from the bed, took her face between his hands. "Don't say those words. I am not angry." He felt better to see some of the worry leave her face, to see her incandescent smile, which he had to kiss. "I love you."

Then she was gone, leaving him alone with his thoughts, which spun and sparked and ran into each other. They must return to Fontainebleau, must bury Belle. How short his time with Louise had been today. His mother's confessor was a spy to the viscount. Dear God. When was the last time his mother had confessed? What had she said about her visit to the Duchess Marie? Had she ever spoken of the boy? Was he setting a trap that the viscount already knew of? Was it all for nothing? Would he end up having to pretend that he'd never meant arrest, bowing and scraping to stay in the viscount's good graces? If the viscount knew the possibility of his birth not being what it seemed, the man already possessed a larger weapon than his fleet. How gentle Louise was. He must remember that with her, there would never be deliberate hurt. He must bring her brother to court. He must win the confidence of her mother. He must surround her with some allies.

❧❦❧

A crowd assembled for the burial of Belle. Maria Teresa sat in a chair surrounded by her ladies. Henriette did not come, yet allowed her ladies' presence.

"Madame is not feeling well," said his brother. Philippe's face was closed, unreadable.

"Thank you for being here." Philippe of all people knew how much Belle meant, had grown up with her, too. "My brother." Louis pulled Philippe close, fiercely kissed each of his cheeks. "You are always my brother. Forgive me any action that has hurt you. I do only what I think best," he said in his ear. Over Philippe's shoulders he made certain he knew where Louise was.

D'Artagnan dug the grave. Louis's confessor said prayers. All the women present dropped flowers into the grave. Last of all, Louis placed the wrapped stag's heart on the body, and then musketeers began to throw dirt in the grave. Belle's sons and daughter milled around, pawed at the dirt. Louis whistled and knelt to pull the ears of Phaedra. He thought of the Mazarinade that had been left near Belle. Any one of the people here might have put it there.

"You have to take your mother's place. Can you do that?" he asked the dog to cover his thoughts.

He stood, saw Nicolas standing some distance away, talking with D'Artagnan. Louis gave his hand to Maria Teresa, who was crying, to lead her back into the palace. D'Artagnan would never betray, of that he was certain, but he didn't like it that Nicolas talked with him. Did the fox sense the hounds gaining? What if he bolted, holed himself up on that island of his, but he wouldn't do so before his fête, would he? His pride, for all its cloak of charm, was too great.

"Come to my chambers this evening," Nicolas said to D'Artagnan. "We'll drink a glass of wine and talk about your travels."

"I'm to Paris. I've a young wife I haven't seen in days, Viscount," answered D'Artagnan.

"Fortunate man. Well, come and call on me when you return. I hear Monaco is beautiful this time of year. I want to know whether I should visit."

Colbert opened the door and ushered Anne's confessor inside. Unsmiling, Louis remained where he was. The priest padded calmly forward, his face pale and pleasant, his robes dark and severe, a creature of court as well as of Rome.

"Your Majesty." He smiled. He and Louis had known one another for a long time. "To what do I owe the honor of this summons?"

"To the fact that you share with the Viscount Nicolas everything my mother confesses to you. To the fact that I am not pleased that you do so." Louis leaned forward, his arms braced on the table that separated them, the angles of his face hard. "Not only do you betray the most sacred of vows, you betray the Queen Mother of this kingdom and her son, the king, as well as soil the robes you wear. I can only imagine the Holy Father in Rome will agree."

He would use this confessor's breach of trust to bolster his explanations to the Pope about scattering monks to the far corners. Now, what did the viscount know?

AUGUST 1661

CHAPTER 36

Cinq Mars watched the boy carefully. The young prince sat in the
middle of the rooftop, rocking back and forth. The mask was on his
face. Whenever they attempted to take it from him, he defecated
on himself.

"Make the wine," he said to Father Gabriel.

The priest shook his head. Like Cinq Mars, he was concerned about the
amount the boy had swallowed these last weeks.

"Do it," said Cinq Mars, "not enough to make him sleep, only enough
to quiet him a bit."

How much he wanted the mask off. As much as His Majesty did. How
much he wanted to see this young prince raise his bare face and receive
the kisses of the sun. He wanted the boy brown from the sun, toasted and
golden. Could he teach him to swim? Likely not, but there was a narrow
spit of sand not far from this place, and he wanted to take him there, let
him enjoy the waves.

"It's old Cinq Mars," he called out when the wine was ready. He set
the goblet near the boy, sat down himself, not too close but near enough
for the young prince to see him. He raised his own goblet high. "To you,
your highness, to your health, to your long life. Are you thirsty? Drink with
Cinq Mars now."

He sipped his wine. He'd stopped thinking about the letter. It would
find its destination or not. Something would happen or not. He had always
scorned the politics of court, hated its practical cruelty, which in his mind
culminated in the Queen Mother's behavior. But for the moment, he was
content to be sitting in the sun with this boy he loved. With time, with
steadiness, with routine, the boy would thrive again. He was too thin, had
stopped eating in the confusion and upset that had been theirs for too
many weeks.

The roar of the sea on the rocks below them filled his ears. The warmth of the sun actually began to penetrate his clothing. It felt like it was seeping through to his bones. He drank down the rest of his wine, stretched out, folded his arms behind his head. To nap in the sun, what luxury.

He heard the boy pick up the goblet, so he opened his eyes, but didn't turn abruptly or make any other movement. He listened to the boy drink a little. Imp, he thought, not eating enough to keep a bird alive much less a long-legged, growing young man. He moved to kneel beside his young prince, cautious, waiting for the signs that showed the boy was disturbed, but other than a rapid blinking of the eyes, which he could see through the slits of that cursed mask, the boy was still.

Cinq Mars unfastened strap after strap and waited. There was no outburst. Ingenious, the man who made this. Fiendish. He waited a moment. The boy was breathing more rapidly. What would he do? Watching anxiously, Father Gabriel squatted a foot or so away. After a while, the mask was in Cinq Mars's hands, its intricate straps dangling like the arms of a sea animal.

The boy remained still. Cinq Mars and Father Gabriel smiled at each other. Cinq Mars walked to the roof's thick ledge, threw the mask over the side, watching in angry glee as its leather girders streamed upward like arms begging for help. A shout made him turn, but not quickly enough to stop the boy, who apparently had run across the roof, was standing even now on the thick perimeter of the rampart ledge, and before Cinq Mars could open his mouth or make a move, leapt over the side. Cinq Mars shouted to every god in the world, closed his eyes to not see the boy's body hit the jagged rocks. He would have climbed over, would have joined the boy, but Father Gabriel held him back.

It was dangerous and difficult to clamber over the rocks, slick with sea and moss, his wound gasping like a mouth between his heart and shoulder, but he did it anyway. The sea mustn't have his dear prince, but the body was so broken, was partially wedged in an impossible crevice of rock. He would break his child to further pieces bringing him home. The tide was coming in. When it reached his neck, he abandoned his task, half swam, half fell back to dry land. The mask lay there. One of its straps had caught on a shard of rock, and it bobbed up and down, waiting for him. He tore it from the rock that had captured it, somehow made it to shore, bruised, cut, bleeding again. Then he sat on the sand, as the sea licked his boots and tears seeped out of his eyes, his body aching, his wound screaming from the sea's salt, before his heart finally grasped its loss, and he began to howl, just as the boy had so often done, and Father Gabriel, standing in the shadow of the fortress monastery, left him alone.

CHAPTER 37

Today the court traveled to Vaux-le-Vicomte to the fête the Viscount Nicolas was holding. The road from Paris was clogged with carriages driving along at a snail's pace one after another, people hanging out windows to call greetings to passersby on horseback. All roads in the region were solid with carriages and riders. Some of the court had left at dawn. The public courtyard of Fontainebleau and the stables were in an uproar. Coachmen, grooms, postilions, stable hands, and link boys had several hundred courtiers to place in carriages or on horseback.

For a month or more, there had had been talk of nothing else but this party and the beauty of Vaux-le-Vicomte. Those who had visited during its construction repeated what they'd observed: it had more fountains than any palace or château in France; the viscount had diverted a river to create its water beauties; a major poet was in the midst of writing a long poem about the beauty of the place; a royal painter, gardener, and architect had combined to create what was a miracle of composition, this last from Monsieur, who had visited the château recently and who had been talking about its charms ever since.

Louis paced as he waited for his wife. Maria Teresa was late, as she was more and more often, making him wait, an unbearable habit of his mother's that his wife seemed to have adopted. Philippe and Henriette had already set off with all their friends and household, and so he wouldn't see Louise until he arrived at Vaux-le-Vicomte. He was irritable. For his court to have been talking about the viscount the way it had for weeks, to see the way the courtiers fawned and simpered, set his teeth on edge. Now his mother's confessor was silenced, telling the viscount what Louis wished. What he didn't know was if the viscount realized that he and Philippe might not be the sons of Louis XIII. The Mazarinades seemed to hint at such knowledge, and what a weapon that was against his reign. The man had uncanny luck; even the weather bowed to his will. The skies were clear and blue, and there was enough of a breeze to cool off afternoon heat.

Suddenly, he saw his mother's ladies appear like a cloud of beautiful butterflies and walk toward carriages. Someone called to him to say that the Queen Mother had ordered them to go on to Vaux-le-Vicomte without her, and then D'Artagnan approached him, his face somber in a way that alarmed Louis, and for a moment the thought crossed his mind that Maria Teresa had gone into labor, that his *dauphin* might be born too early, but he saw that D'Artagnan held out something in his hand. It was the ring he'd given Cinq Mars.

"If Your Majesty might come with me?" D'Artagnan said, and they walked into the dim cool of a vestibule where Louis saw ten or more of his best musketeers gathered.

"It's dangerous, Your Majesty," D'Artagnan said, as he hurried Louis through the labyrinth of chambers that would place them in the Queen Mother's part of the palace. "Cinq Mars is with Her Majesty and Madame de Motteville, and he demands to see you."

They walked into his mother's antechamber, filled with her guards, their faces taut. D'Artagnan knocked upon the door of Anne's most private room. "His Majesty is here," he called. Just before the door opened, he said to Louis, "You don't have to go inside, sir—"

But the door was opening a crack, and Louis stepped through it, with D'Artagnan right behind him. His mother sat upright in a chair. She was fully dressed, but Louis saw at once something was wrong. Hovering beside her, her eyes like dark holes in her face, was Madame de Motteville.

"I never meant—" she said at the sight of Louis, but Cinq Mars's words cut over hers.

"Silence, woman! Get out, Lieutenant!" From behind them, from his position against a wall, Cinq Mars pointed the dueling pistol he carried at Louis.

"I remain with His Majesty," said D'Artagnan.

Every sense suddenly on alert, Louis turned so that he could see Cinq Mars completely. The man looked as if he'd just stumbled out of the forest, his clothing dirty, his hair in knots, his face a grimace in stone. There was fresh blood on his shirt. His wound is open, thought Louis, his mind moving rapidly, and he can make only one shot with that pistol. It held only one shot.

"What is it, Captain? What is this about?" Louis said.

"He's dead."

As the words were said, Louis realized what lay in his mother's lap: the iron mask, its straps hanging down her skirts like flaccid arms. "How? When?"

"He jumped from the roof into the sea. He died on the rocks."

In his mind's eye, Louis could see the lonely old monastery, the sea practically crashing against one side, the roof, the sun, the jagged rocks, the body hurtling toward them.

"Lock the doors," Cinq Mars ordered D'Artagnan, "now."

"Put down the pistol," said Louis. "You've traveled a long way to bring me sad news. Let me order food and wine for you, and we'll speak of this—"

"Will that be before or after I kill your mother?"

Madame de Motteville screamed and threw herself on Anne as Louis took yet another step toward Cinq Mars.

"Back! Now!" Cinq Mars aimed the pistol at him, and Louis met the man's eyes, read the determination in them, and stepped back. Someone will die today, he thought over all rushing through his head, how to disarm him, how to persuade him to put down the pistol, how to attack him if necessary.

"Get it over with, you coward," Anne hissed. "Do you think I care whether I live or die? Shoot me and have done with it!"

Cinq Mars shouted for Madame de Motteville to move, and she did, running straight at him as Louis ran forward, too, and they collided into each other and Cinq Mars, knocking him backward, into the wall, as the pistol discharged, and they all fell and Anne shrieked and covered her face with her hands.

D'Artagnan ran to the tangle on the floor, Cinq Mars, Madame de Motteville, the king of France.

Louis was the first to move. "She's bleeding." He jerked off his doublet, wadded the cloth into the wound at Motteville's breast.

Cinq Mars grabbed her from Louis. "My God, my God, my darling girl, my sweet, oh no," he said, pulling her into his arms, beginning to weep like a man whose heart can bear no more.

Pounding and thudding and shouts sounded on the other side of the door, and D'Artagnan unlocked it, rapped out orders, and five of Louis's best men ran into the chamber. Cinq Mars stood, made a lunge for the table where Anne sat, and seized a letter opener, its blade as sharp as any knife.

Anne pulled down the edge of her black gown, so that one milk-white breast was almost completely bared. "Do your worst," she spat at him.

Every man in the chamber ran toward Cinq Mars, who took the blade in both hands, raised it high, and plunged it into his chest, near the reopened wound, falling against one of the younger musketeers who tried to stop him. Both of them crashed to the floor. The musketeer pushed at Cinq Mars and scrambled to stand, but Cinq Mars was unmoving.

"Clear my mother's guard out of the antechamber, get Madame de Motteville in bed, and find my physician," said Louis. There was blood on the snow-white shirt he wore.

Anne knelt beside her lady-in-waiting now, cradling her head in her lap, holding the wad of Louis's doublet against the wound. "Place her in my bed," she ordered the musketeers.

"If he's alive, take the captain to Paris, to the Bastille," said Louis.

D'Artagnan got down on his knees to examine Cinq Mars.

"He was my child, too, more mine than hers," breathed Cinq Mars. "The child of my heart." He closed his eyes.

D'Artagnan pulled a handkerchief from his pocket and laid it over Cinq Mars's face. "Dead, sire."

Louis went into his mother's bedchamber. His mother had begun to clean Madame de Motteville's wound with water.

"Will she die?" Louis asked.

"Hard to say. There's cloth in the wound, which could mean infection. I saw it all the time on the battlefield," Anne answered.

A physician was in the chamber now, and Anne handed him the bloody cloth.

"It's my fault. I let him in. I'm sorry," murmured Madame de Motteville.

Louis led his mother to the window, away from listening ears. Anne looked dazed, frail in a way he'd never seen before. "I must be leaving." He spoke to her gently. He felt as if he'd been thrown from off a horse and hit the ground hard. He couldn't imagine how she felt.

"I'll follow you shortly."

"It isn't necessary that you go, Mother. We've lost a member of our family."

She looked from him to the window, to the trees and lawn. He wondered if that was what she was really seeing. "It's better he's dead. He should have died years ago."

Anger and grief surged through Louis. "Aren't you even going to weep?"

"My tears dried up long ago. Don't look at me like that. You don't know what it's like to give birth to a child you can't acknowledge, and you never will. Men receive the pleasure of the act. Women receive the burden and the shame."

"You possess a heart of stone."

"Queens don't survive without growing hearts of stone. What of you, off to a fête at which you are guest of honor given by a man who has served this kingdom for years, a man you intend to arrest? We do what we must to protect the throne," she said. "Our hearts grow cold."

"Who is my father?"

She closed her eyes. "I will not dignify that question with an answer."

She walked away from him, back toward her closet with its saints' portraits, crosses, relics under glass, its too many chairs and tables, its portrait of the cardinal. She pulled the bell cord to summon a servant as she passed it.

Louis followed. He wanted to strike her, wanted to shake her until she begged for mercy, but a servant appeared and stood in the frame of the door, big-eyed at the sight of overturned chairs and blood on the floor of this chamber.

"Clean this up," Anne said, "and send for my dresser and my confessor."

"I wouldn't advise that. Your confessor is a conduit to the viscount. He's been telling him what you confess for years."

She gave what he thought was a bark of laughter, but in the middle of the guffaw, he realized the laughter was a wail. She sank to the floor, huddled into herself the way he had seen innumerable wives and mothers and daughters grieve their dead soldiers on a battlefield. Her dresser appeared in the middle of her ragged sobbing, and Louis waved her away to wait, and the woman leaned against a wall, her hand on her mouth at the sight of the blood and disarray everywhere, at the sight of the most regal woman at court wailing like a peasant. Louis couldn't force himself to go and comfort her. Finally, Anne lay on her back and stared up at a ceiling that was painted in expensive gilt, each honeycomb with a crown and her initial in it.

"I'll make your excuses to the viscount," Louis told his mother.

"Change your shirt. There's blood on it."

"Mother—"

"You'll need a tale to satisfy people's curiosity about this, because they are already talking, I do assure you. You," she said to the dresser, "wine for me, right now, and my hair, I think we'll just redo my hair. And some rouge perhaps." And to Louis, she continued, "Treachery always comes from the place you least expect it. Remember that. At least my beloved didn't have to hear of this. It would have broken his heart. He always hoped he could bring the child to live in one of his houses. Fool. His heart was always softer than mine. I loved him for that. Mother of God, I feel a hundred years old."

He helped her up, grasped the iron mask, and carried it to his own bedchamber, set it on an ornate table, waving away his master of the household, who'd come to find out what the delay was. As La Porte pulled a fresh shirt over his head, Louis began to shake. "Leave me," he ordered.

He sat down in a chair to get some kind of command of himself. He could reach out and touch the mask, a contraption of iron and leather that someone had fashioned to hide a boy who hadn't asked to be born. Bands of iron tightened around his heart, and it felt, for a moment, as if they would kill him. He sat until his breath began to even. He must live until his or her death in a marriage with a woman he did not love and did not desire. He must outwit those who raped his kingdom, and there would always be someone else once the viscount was vanquished. He must leave the question of his father unanswered, must bury the very fact of the question the way he'd buried his best dog so that it might not be used against him. He must forever and a day distrust his only brother because the power that came with the throne seduced the best of men.

He stood.

La Porte appeared as if by magic. They continued his dressing without either of them saying a word. He would ride miles today as if nothing had happened, smile, dance, be able to do no more than speak a few words to the woman he loved, whose kindness and sincerity were a solace he had not known he so craved. The boy was dead. All his years of sacrifice and, because he'd killed himself, Cinq Mars could not be buried in hallowed ground. It was too much, and yet he must continue on with this day. That was his iron mask, strapped to the face of his soul, and only death would ever undo its grip.

"I think there is someone," said Catherine.

Louise's hand tightened on Fanny's. They rode inside the carriage with Madame and the Princess de Monaco, and though the maids of honor were dressed in their finest, and Louise wore her diamond bracelets, they were overawed at the finery of the princesses riding with them, their gowns crusted to stiffness with embroidery and ribbons. Even their leather shoes were embroidered, and they wore jewels in their hair and at their ears and necks and on their arms and on the fingers of their long gloves, magnificent jewels, splendid and sparkling.

Catherine turned imperious eyes on the two sitting opposite. "What have you noticed?"

"I think he fancies the Countess de Soissons," said Fanny without missing a beat.

Catherine's eyes narrowed on Louise. "You see more than you say. What do you think?"

"I don't know, Princess. He seems kind to everyone."

"You wear his bracelets all the time. Perhaps it's you." Catherine let out a peal of laughter, cold and mocking. "That would really be too funny."

"I believed it for a moment because of the bracelets," said Henriette.

There was a silence. Both princesses stared across the carriage at Louise, who shrank back against the leather seat, feeling impaled by what was in their faces.

"Or Miss de Chimerault," said Fanny. "It could be her."

Catherine removed her gaze from Louise. "I thought you were convinced it was Soissons. You two watch him tonight, and we'll compare notes later."

Henriette put her hands over her ears. "I don't want to know who he flirts with. Lord, this is taking forever. How much longer?"

But they were just one carriage in a sea of carriages all moving slowly toward the biggest fête in the kingdom.

❦

By afternoon, throngs of carriages jockeyed for space in the viscount's entrance courtyard. Only certain carriages were actually being allowed in; the rest were stopping long enough to let down their passengers, then being directed to stables somewhere in the outbuildings. Courtyards and front lawns were a melee of people walking about under the noses of horses that coachmen were trying to control, while grooms and servants milled around to help people from their carriages and lead them across the château's entrance bridge and toward its front terrace and magnificent porch, where the viscount stood with his wife and family receiving guests.

Linked by iron railings to form a fence, towering pillars the height of three men were the first barrier visitors met. Beyond, past lawns cut by gravel paths and sitting in the circle of a moat more decorative than practical, was the château. It rose grand, serene, and secure, with a vast central dome, nothing rambling or awkward or simple about its stately demeanor. It was a splendid triumph celebrating the concept of order and harmony on a great scale, celebrating the way a house might be enhanced by its landscape. Everywhere the eye fell, there was something to admire, from the grace of stone figures, which adorned the house, to the breadth of the entrance terrace, accented by its narrow stone bridge across the moat. People milled about everywhere, on its terraces and in the courtyards and leaning out the windows and over the stone balustrades of the moat. A long line of humanity waited to greet the viscount.

When Henriette's carriage lumbered up to the moat, servants surrounded it and directed the coachman to bring it forward, and one went running toward the château to inform the viscount and Philippe, who had traveled in a separate carriage.

"Make way for the princess," shouted one of Nicolas's footmen, and Henriette walked across a handsome bridge toward the château.

"Isn't this magnificent?" exclaimed Fanny to Louise. "Look at the people."

Henriette, her household fanning out behind her, stopped just on the other side of the bridge, waiting for the viscount and for Philippe to come to her. Nicolas bowed low. Philippe nodded coolly in the direction of his wife.

He'll never be mine again, will he? thought Henriette.

"I am so delighted you've arrived. Now the fête may be said to have truly begun. If you will step this way and allow me to present again my wife, and this is my brother and my sister…" said Nicolas, beginning to introduce his family.

All around them people nudged one another for space and tried not to miss a word. Until Louis arrived, Henriette and Philippe were queen and king and would be treated so. The viscountess led Henriette and her ladies to her own bedchamber and left them there to refresh themselves. Someone ran up to Fanny as they climbed the stairs to the viscountess's chambers and said something to her and then was gone again.

"Guiche is here," Fanny whispered to Louise. "Promise me you'll ask the king to allow him back."

"No."

Fanny stopped where she was on the staircase. She looked down at one of her gloves. "I can't lie for you forever."

"Is that a threat?" asked Louise.

"I don't know," said Fanny.

In the bedchamber, once the viscountess left them, women ran to the walls, which were lined in pier glass from wainscoting to ceiling and reflected to infinity everything. Each woman stood in front of silvered glass admiring herself or adjusting her ribbons or neckline. Against one wall was a huge cabinet of solid silver. All the candlesticks and wall sconces and chimney dogs were solid silver, too. There was a small bed, with just the slightest headboard, as well as a huge bed with hangings. Genoa velvet, the most expensive of fabrics, covered all the furniture.

"Well," said Henriette, turning around in a circle, "I must have pier glass on all my walls, too. My bedchamber at Fontainebleau feels positively paltry."

Catherine sat on the small bed, her skirts spreading around her in a beautiful arc. "Isn't this wonderful? It's a daybed for naps."

"There is no time for naps. Let me see you all," Henriette commanded.

Maids of honor lined up obediently, and Henriette walked in front of them, considering what each of them had worn.

"We don't have anything matching," whined Madeleine.

Their old trick of wearing some little adornment to mark them hadn't been of interest to Henriette lately, but she could feel she was the center of what was clearly going to be a magnificent party. She'd sensed it as she walked across the moat. Maria Teresa would be no competition in either wit, conversation, or style. She, Henriette, would be the one all eyes followed. Was she going to give the Countess de Soissons or the Queen Mother the pleasure of seeing her despairing and drooping at the best party in years? Oh, they'd love that, wouldn't they? Was Philippe going to continue to ignore her? How did she bear that, particularly knowing it was all her fault? What a mess she'd made for the sake of Louis, who somehow triumphed over his guilty love and left her wallowing behind in the murk. It was over with Louis, wasn't it? How could that be?

She swallowed past the lump that seemed to be permanently in her throat these days. Everywhere she looked she was reflected, her gown as deep a green as the emeralds she wore. It made her pale skin look almost bleached, which was the shade this century preferred its women to be. She looked wonderful, and she carried a child. She'd give Philippe his son, and then he'd forgive her a little. Her mother had warned that the undercurrents of court were treacherous. There were those who were hoping tonight to see her misstep, to see her sad. I am Madame, she thought, the fairy queen of court. Let me act it even if I don't feel it. Philippe liked it best when she was buoyant and lively. She tossed her head and lifted her chin and determined to make five men quarrel over dancing with her by midnight. No one was going to know how weary and small her heart felt.

"Your roses," said Fanny.

The Viscountess Nicolas had given Henriette a huge bunch of pale lavender roses. Fanny rummaged through drawers in the big silver cupboard, giving a little yelp of triumph when she found hairpins and a small pair of gold scissors. In no time at all, she had a cluster of roses made for them all. She pinned one at the corner of the low neck of Louise's gown. "I didn't mean it, what I said on the stairs," she whispered. "I'm not myself anymore." And then, louder, "What do you think, Madame?"

"Perfect. I, for one, think I am going to have to flirt quite outrageously tonight. I trust you'll support me in my efforts." For a moment, she almost wept at the memory those words stirred, but she managed not to.

Giggling laughter rose in quite its old way. Henriette led her ladies out of the bedchamber, pausing at the top of the stairs until she was seen by the viscountess, who hurried toward her as the whirl of people in the huge vestibule below turned to watch her descend the stairs.

※

As he rode through the woods beside the carriages, his despair quieted a bit. It was a beautiful afternoon. The forest smelled green and moist. He filled his lungs with cool, clean air. If only half his blood were royal, did that make him any less equal to the task ahead? He could feel the sense of destiny that had always driven him. You were born for this, his beloved cardinal had told him. A piece of the past was gone, as dead as Cinq Mars, as the boy. Any question of his birth would be a sometimes faint rumor, as old as the Mazarinades, until the question faded to a whisper that no one could hear. He was king, he, Louis the fourteenth of that name, he and no one else, and he would make a mark in this time and space of his so large that all else was forgotten.

Their caravan of coaches and riders and musketeers and household troops stopped so that Maria Teresa might stretch her legs. He left his wife and her ladies fluttering around the carriages and walked to his mother, who had abandoned her carriage to stand alone, under a magnificent oak whose thick arms grew low to the ground and spread their length out as if they would amble on forever. He saw that she had been weeping.

"Are you well?" he asked.

"I have a pain. It's nothing." Her eyes met his. "I am going to say this once more, for both our sakes, then you are never to ask me again for I will never answer again. Your father was Louis XIII of that name. He sired you. No other."

They stared at each other, the will of each enormous, emotion between them flickering the way Louis's eyes did when he was at his most dangerous. He bowed and turned away. So be it. Her words would be the truth he held to his heart. Her truth would be the strength from which he struck. As he returned to his wife, Olympe sauntered up, Athénaïs a little distance away.

"Is it true," Olympe whispered, "that a musketeer attacked the Queen Mother?"

"It's true that there was a lover's quarrel between a musketeer and Madame de Motteville in the Queen Mother's presence," said Louis.

"I heard someone was shot with a pistol."

"Someone was hurt and may die," said Louis. He spoke very gently, and Athénaïs, seeing the expression on his face, lowered her eyes and cursed herself for being anywhere near Olympe. "I tell you this as a friend. I would ask your discretion and kindness in seeing that gossip about this goes no farther."

"Of course. I'm yours to command."

But he knew she'd talk. He depended on it, and thus truth would become intermingled with lie, and in time, no one would know the difference.

❧❧❧

They were quite late, but carriages were still arriving, and people were everywhere. The last time Louis had seen this many people in one place had been on a battlefield. He'd visited Vaux-le-Vicomte on his return from his wedding. There had been crowds of workmen and piles of building debris, and so he wasn't prepared for the breathtaking, completed beauty of the place, beginning with the row of towering pillars, their double-sided heads gazing with stone eyes far over the head of any visitor. Philippe had told him—he'd said, you're going to be amazed at what's been created—but he'd believed his brother exaggerated, the way Philippe was prone to, loving or hating with equal intensity. Riding down the château's long entrance lane had been like approaching a shrine to beauty; the château was a jewel sitting high in its jewel box of garden, terrace, and woods.

He dismounted at the edge of the moat, went to help his wife and mother from their carriages. God, the number of people, everywhere he looked, all along the lawns of the neat outbuildings, everywhere on the entrance terraces, at every window of the château. How could the viscount accommodate this many? It was more splendid than any entertainment he or his mother before him had ever given, and that was enough to spark anger. The viscount flaunted his spoils for all the world to admire. And they did.

Nicolas walked forward, his wife beside him. Behind him Louis saw his brother, Henriette, his cousins, among them the formidable Condé, with his prince's blood and warrior's heart, who'd made war on the kingdom for years, fleeing to Spain and fighting on its side, until Louis's marriage had sealed a peace, healed a war. Condé was a great general brought to heel, allowed back to France, among his beloved cardinal's last frenzied acts, to patch up the breaks in the kingdom, trying to give his precious young king something united over which to rule.

All the great families were represented, clustered in the huge entrance courtyard or on the terrace steps, waiting to bow to him and Maria Teresa, but were their hearts vanquished? He very much doubted it. Where was Louise? Ah, there she was. He felt more in command at the sight of her. She wore a new gown of a soft summer green because he'd given it, telling her it was the color of true love and that she must wear it for his sake. He took a deep breath and smiled at the viscount when what he really wished to do was order his immediate arrest. There were two kings at this fête, and they met each other in the entrance courtyard. The viscount's motto was cut into stone on the porch above him. What heights might he not reach, so the words said. Or fall from, thought Louis.

All through the rest of the afternoon and into the long night, through all the pomp and ceremony and walking in the garden and having supper served to him on bended knee and admiring one thing after another because everywhere the eye looked there was something to admire and making his way among courtiers, financiers, judges, lawyers, priests, nuns, bishops, archbishops, governors of provinces, he couldn't stop the sense that Nicolas challenged him directly with this fête, saying, see, boy, my power, my prestige, are enormous. You tread dangerously, boy, to threaten me in any way at all.

CHAPTER 38

He fell in love with the fountains, as did all the court. Never had so
many been assembled in one place, dancing points of water in the
long and magnificent gardens that framed this exquisite château.
They spewed their drops upward in a continuous symphony of water and
sunlight, and he was dazzled. He fell in love with the visual trick of the
long landscape canal, set lower than the plane of the gardens, so that one
walked toward a gushing set of water spouts and their grottoes, unknowingly for a time, and then there was the unforeseen edge, and below one
was a long, long canal of water, fed by water that played over the most
magnificent collection of stone statues he'd seen in an age, each set back
in a private grotto behind the million droplets of water that sprayed everywhere, and above them rose a hill, higher than the château, and atop
the hill stood an enormous statue of the ancient hero Hercules, and from
this Hercules, one looked back to a vista of garden and château that was
breathtaking in its beauty and orderliness. He listened with real interest
to Nicolas's brother, who told of searching artists' studios and collectors'
private galleries and even the Vatican in Rome for the statues displayed in
and around the château.

He fell in love with the grand salon, an oval eighteen meters long and
eighteen meters high that was the center of the château and rose two stories above one's head. Its arched openings were closed by no doors but led
directly onto a terrace and the sweeping gardens beyond, so that one felt
every breeze from the outside. There wasn't another house in France with
this feature, Nicolas told him. Late-evening light was pouring through the
arches and upper-story windows, playing on the white and black marble
of the floor with its center medallion reflecting the center of the salon's
dome above.

He fell in love with the artistry of the tapestries on every wall, tapestries
woven right here in a workshop the viscount had created. He fell in love

with the bedchamber created specifically for him—no one else had slept in it, no one would, not even the viscount—the most expensive velvet attainable on the bed covers, the bed curtains, and the walls, wood gilded everywhere, twin crystal chandeliers hanging down from a coved ceiling.

He's a thief, pure and simple, Colbert had said earlier, in a moment when he and Louis gazed at the vista of the château and gardens from the statue of Hercules. Your architect, your painter, your gardener created this. Your workers worked upon it. Yes, so they had, but what splendor had been created, thought Louis, his heart soothed by the beauty everywhere. What profusion. What hospitality.

"Here she is," D'Artagnan called out, and his girl in summer green, only the bracelets on her wrists and the pearls in her ears and the lavender roses near her breasts for ornament, walked into the bedchamber and into his arms. He buried his face into her neck, breathing in the smell of the roses and her. He wanted to tell her about the boy he would never know, about Cinq Mars's death, about his rage at the viscount, but all he said was, "Tell me that you love me. Tell me that you always will."

"I love you more than my own life. I always will."

D'Artagnan coughed.

Yes, she must go. "Stay where I can see you," Louis told her.

"If I can, you know I will, Majesty."

He must keep Henriette near to see his beloved, and if he kept Henriette near, Maria Teresa became fretful and irritable. He hadn't meant to create these quarrels among the women he loved, and yet he had, and he didn't know how to mend them. A performance in the gardens was planned. He must rise and walk back into the gardens with Nicolas, make certain the swallowed fury in him didn't show.

❧❧❧

"He's here. I've seen him," Fanny whispered excitedly to Louise as they settled themselves for the performance. "He says he is staying out of sight of His Majesty, and that he has a treat planned. Oh, I'm so happy."

"I'm glad he was kind."

"May I sit by you? I can't find my friends." The woman who spoke looked both motherly and anxious. It was Madame du Plessis-Bellièvre, Nicolas's best spy, but Louise had no idea of that, and she nodded in answer as courtiers rustled and whispered and looked expectantly toward the sets of stone steps. Musicians were assembled, violins in hand. On the lawn, set close to a tier of steps, was an enormous shell.

As everyone watched, the actor Molière appeared at the top of the steps. He was dressed not in costume, but as he dressed every day, as if he were in the common courtyard of Fontainebleau. He ran down the steps and walked straight up to Louis, sitting in the first row. Molière made a huge, sweeping burlesque of a bow that made his audience laugh out loud.

"Alas, I'm all alone. Alas, there wasn't time to prepare. Alas, I am desolate. Alas, I am abandoned. Alas, I must have aid." Molière declaimed like a tragic actor would, pronouncing each word in a loud, slow tongue-roll of syllables. He held a dramatic pause long enough to give the most restless courtier a chance to still, and then he said, "Most august Majesty, will you aid me?"

"What can I do?"

"Snap your fingers. For you, the gods will obey." Molière leaned forward and whispered loudly, playing every action to exaggeration, "Stand, sire, and say, 'Let the play begin.'"

Obediently Louis stood and, understanding the value of drama himself, turned to face his courtiers. Every face was expectant. Every face was smiling. It was theater at its best.

"Let the play begin." To the audience's delight, he declaimed the way Molière had, that long, loud rolling out of syllables that was the standard for a tragedy.

Fanny grabbed Louise's arm. "Look at the shell."

The shell at the top of the tier of steps was opening, and a woman unfolded from its depths, shells in her hair and hanging at the hem of her diaphanous gown.

"Mortals, I visit you," she began to sing, walking slowly and gracefully down the steps, singing that for the king, nothing could be difficult, and so nature was obeying his command.

"Sage, young, victorious, valiant, and august, mild as severe, and powerful as he's just," she sang. "Nothing will be refused him. Trees will talk; nymphs and demigods will come forth."

To the audience's delight, trees behind the top tier of steps began to sway as actors dressed as fawns and satyrs danced into sight. The premise of the play was slight, nothing more than simple scenes that then led to dancing, which was what the court was most interested in. The premise was that of a man attempting to meet his lady love interrupted by bores, a musician who insists on singing his tune, a card player who must describe in detail his latest game, and lastly, the one that had both Louis and his brother laughing out loud, a man determined to reform the signs of all Paris inns. When it was over, Louis stood to lead the applause.

"Did you like it?" he asked his brother. He was doing everything in his power to charm Philippe back. He owed him that courtesy.

"Wonderful," said Philippe. "What wit Molière possesses."

While they had been watching the play, which ended as dusk began, servants had lit hundreds of lanterns to outline garden paths, to outline the house itself. The many statues in the garden, the dome of the house, its cupola, stood out in bold relief. It was like standing in a fairy world. Courtiers stood in clusters discussing all that surrounded them.

"Well, it makes Fontainebleau seem positively rustic, doesn't it?" said the Chevalier de Lorraine to Philippe.

"He's here," Philippe answered.

"He doesn't dare!"

"He dares anything." Philippe smiled, his face so happy that Lorraine stepped backward into Fanny.

"Clumsy troll," he said to her.

"Someone wishes to see you," Fanny said to Philippe.

"Where is he?"

"Follow me." Fanny was merry, almost dancing in place.

"Such a play, so fanciful, the music so splendid," Madame du Plessis-Bellièvre held Louise in a conversation as if they were old friends. "Are not these lanterns entrancing? My dear girl, walk a moment with me? I have a message from your mother."

Louise walked with her toward the grand central garden path that led to the château's big salon.

"I told a small lie," said Madame du Plessis-Bellièvre. She smiled kindly to assure Louise. "I have no acquaintance of your mother, though it would be an honor to meet her. Perhaps someday you'll introduce me? Ah, did my lie disappoint you? Little dear. Do you miss your mother? Doubtless her duties keep her engaged. We're going to be fast friends, I can feel it. There are some people I meet, and I just know that I will adore them. I enjoyed the performance, didn't you? That Molière is quite droll."

"My sides hurt from laughing. And the dancing was beautiful."

"You yourself are a lovely dancer. I've often noted it at court."

"Thank you." Louise glanced back toward her friends, clustered with Madame, who was walking with the king and queen toward the house. It was easy to walk in the garden with lanterns everywhere, not quite day, but certainly not dark night either, but rather something enchanting, the soft light glimmering everywhere. She had promised Louis she would stay near, and yet she strayed.

"I can see you wish to join your friends," said Madame du Plessis-Bellièvre. "I'll take but a moment more. I asked you to walk with me because there's someone here who very much wants your favor, and I am, oh, what shall we call me? An ambassador of sorts."

"My favor?"

"Someone very high." She waved her fan back and forth. "He owns all this."

"The vi—"

"Hush," she interrupted with a kind smile. "Don't say his name. Just know he wishes your regard and congratulates you on your standing with His Majesty."

Louise felt rooted to the ground with shock. The viscount knew of her and the king? "There's some mistake."

"How discreet you are. He will like that, as it would be his honor to make you a quiet gift to show his admiration. No one need know." Madame du Plessis-Bellièvre's smile grew wider. "Say, perhaps twenty thousand." She waited, quite certain of the effect the sum she'd just named would have. It could buy most anything.

"You've made a mistake. You must excuse me." Louise gathered the wide skirts of her gown in each hand, trying not to look as if she was running for her life as she walked away, but all the same, she half ran, half walked back toward her friends, toward their laughter and pointless chatter and the place she had among them, simple Louise de la Baume le Blanc, no more, no less than they.

Philippe stopped. They were on the edge of the gardens before a long arbor hidden deep in one of the side gardens. "Where is he?" he asked Fanny.

"Go in if you would, Monsieur."

Philippe walked under the vines. He could see a figure sitting before a small table covered with candles, and as he walked toward their light, he saw it was an old woman, covered in shawls, a great feathered hat on her head.

"Tell your fortune, my lord?" she asked.

"Where is he?" Philippe demanded.

The woman grinned at him.

"Is that you?" Philippe began to laugh.

"None other," said Guy. "Molière spent all afternoon on this. I intend to amuse myself telling fortunes to a very select crowd tonight."

"You're mad."

"Very likely. How are you?"

"I miss you. Come back to court."

"I'm banished from court, and it seems you've forgiven His Majesty."

"No."

"I saw you together tonight. You're friends again. You've forgiven him."

"He's asked my pardon. Belle died, and we both cried, and he told me he would always love me. He has sent to Spain for a horse for me like his—"

"My kingdom for a horse."

"What?"

"Nothing, a play an Englishman and I once talked about. So you forgive that he gave the governorship of a province that was yours by inheritance to someone else. You've let that go completely, haven't you? And there's no place on his council yet, is there?"

"The viscount has my best interests at heart—" Philippe began.

"The viscount has his own best interests at heart. I just wished to see if anything had changed. I'd heard you threw quite a tantrum. I'd heard you weren't going to his risings or going-to-bed ceremony, but I would imagine you are now."

Philippe was silent. All the joy he'd felt at the sight of this man was destroyed, and in its place, anguish and the old sense of failure.

"Go away," said Guy. "You bore me, little man, little prince. That's all you'll ever be. Go away."

CHAPTER 39

Louis and his family sat at a table draped in expensive cloth. Kneeling to present trays of pheasants and quails roasted and tied with strips of ham, tiny baked apples and potatoes set around them, the viscount and his wife served them. It was their gesture to honor royalty and their right since royalty dined in their house. It would be the first of several courses. The plates they ate from were solid gold. Behind them, a long table held gold trays and urns filled with roses, lilies, and trailing vines. Louis ate calmly, as if gold plates and trays and urns were common, when they were the height of extravagance; not even the royal family possessed this much.

In other chambers of the château and out in the gardens, the court sat on chairs or atop cushions eating from silver plates and drinking from silver goblets. In the outbuildings, the fireplaces roared as cooks and servants stood before them tending pots and sweating like fiends in hell. Small boys turned the spits that held rows of chicken and quail. There were almost as many servants as there were guests. Spoons frothed cream, cups ladled expensive sugar from faraway islands, knives folded butter. Profusion. There must be more than enough. All of it must be delicious. Not a single guest should leave unsated. Those had been the orders from the viscount himself.

Supper finished, Nicolas led the royal party back into the gardens again, cooled and changed by night. Lanterns rimmed the edges of every fountain, and in their light, the water jetted high, caught gleams of lantern light, and disappeared into the dark.

"This is so much fun." Henriette turned around, spinning like a top. She'd had a little too much to drink. Several of the young men she'd flirted with during the festivities waited like bees for another sip.

Fanny approached. "If you would follow me, Madame, there is a surprise for you. And both of you." Fanny pointed at Louise and Lorraine. "There's a fortune teller, but she'll only see a select few." It was a fashion of the times, to consult fortune tellers and have horoscopes drawn. Everyone did it.

"Not Monsieur?" asked Lorraine in surprise, but Philippe was already walking away.

They followed Fanny until they were standing before the arbor in the side gardens. Louise narrowed her eyes. She could just make out a figure sitting before a table upon which candles blazed at the end of the arbor.

"First, Madame," announced Fanny.

It was difficult to see much once Henriette stepped inside. Candles glimmered at the arbor's end, where an old woman waited. Henriette sat down where the woman indicated.

"A large smile, but a sad heart." The woman's voice was gruff, raspy. The sounds of laughter, music, conversations were faint, in the distance, as if they were in a secret, leafed world and somewhere near was a party, but it didn't extend to here. "His Majesty doesn't love you anymore."

Shocked, then furious, stung to the heart to hear the truth so boldly, Henriette stood.

"Are you going to run away from me after I've gone to all this trouble and been so patient?" Guy's voice said from under the hat. "Sit down and talk with me a while."

"I think I've had too much wine," Henriette said, peering at him, trying to ascertain it was truly him inside the disguise.

"Aren't you glad to see me? Here is your fortune. There is a man who loves you with all his black heart. You're a fool to turn your back on him. Answer his love letters. Allow him a secret tryst. Come to this bower at midnight and be kissed."

"What if I don't wish to be kissed?"

"Oh, but you do."

In spite of herself, Henriette laughed. "I am glad to see you again."

"You'll be more glad at midnight. Don't make me find you, because I will."

Henriette tilted her head to one side, bit her lip. How soothing it was to be admired. How much Louis would dislike this if he knew. And Philippe, too. She didn't wish to hurt Philippe, but he was ignoring her.

"Yes," said Guy. "It's going to be fun to love me. Now go away before I tear off this disguise and begin my kissing lessons now. Send in Miss de Montalais."

"Well?" said Lorraine when Henriette appeared at the arbor's entrance.

Henriette ignored him. "Your turn," she told Fanny.

At the other end of the arbor, Guy opened his arms, and Fanny whirled past the table and sat in his lap, covering his face with kisses.

"You'll ruin my makeup," he told her, "and Molière was hours on it.

You've been a good girl tonight. You've been my sweet messenger more than once, and I thank you for that." He kissed her again. "My little trick has begun to bore me, so send in my last two victims, then meet me in an hour by the circle pool."

Louise walked slowly toward the figure at the end of the arbor. Madame and Fanny had both worn smiles from their fortunes. What was hers? She crossed her fingers for luck.

"I know your secret." Guy spoke in his own voice.

It took a moment for Louise to fully recognize him under the hat and wig and face paint.

"You're a whore," Guy said, "and it doesn't matter that the one you bed is a king."

Louise ran out of the arbor, past the Chevalier de Lorraine, who stared after her, an eyebrow raised, and then, intrigued, entered for his fortune. Guy lounged back in his chair, not even pretending anymore.

"Well?" Lorraine said, impatient, not yet realizing who was in front of him.

"You possess a malicious heart and the sting of a scorpion, and you won't be good for him, but he's yours. I won't take him away."

Lorraine recognized Guy and challenged, "Do you think you can?"

"I know I can. Lucky for you, I have no interest. Go away and play nicely with your little prince, whose heart I broke tonight. Again. I'm good at that." Guy stood, dropped the hat on the candles, half of which guttered out and began to smoke. The hat's feather disappeared in a blaze, and while Lorraine was still gaping at that, Guy walked away, out into the dark.

After midnight, anger having made an ache in the center of his forehead, Louis excused himself and went to the bedchamber that was his. He motioned for his gentlemen to stay where they were, walked into the bedchamber, and stopped at the sight of two of his mother's ladies sitting in chairs.

"The Queen Mother," said one, as they rose quickly to curtsy. "She wanted to rest and felt she couldn't climb the stairs to the viscountess's chamber, sire."

"Leave us, please." Louis opened the gate of the *ruelle*, walked to the bed, and looked down.

Anne opened her eyes. "I'm very tired," she said.

"I'm going to arrest him tonight."

She struggled to sit up. "No!"

"Yes, right this moment. I'm going to call for D'Artagnan and arrest him for crimes against the kingdom. Gold plates! Silver cups! Two hundred fountains! A hundred orange trees in silver tubs! A thousand servants! A château my workers have built! Not to mention massing men and arms without my knowledge and commandeering admirals of my fleet!"

"You cannot arrest him at his own party! It isn't worthy of you. Let him have his moment in the sun."

"Whose side will you take if there is war?"

"You hurt me. Yours, darling, always yours. I have a pain, right here." And she put her hand atop a breast. "It won't stop. It's the boy. He's inside me, calling, the way he sometimes did in life."

Louis sat down on the bed, took her hand.

She leaned against his shoulder. "Will you have my carriage fetched? I think I must leave this party. Promise me you won't arrest him tonight. I couldn't bear it, not tonight. People will say you did it out of jealousy. It will look petty. Those were the only gestures your father was capable of making, petty ones. Be a grander king than your father was. The viscount is at the crest of his power. Let it settle. Let everyone assume you cannot do without him, the kingdom can't, this night having proved it. And then, when you do arrest him, it will be all the more terrifying."

"Are you always so eloquent?"

She didn't answer. He stayed with her until she was in her carriage, her ladies with her, some of them almost in tears at having to leave. Nicolas at his side, Louis watched the carriage roll through the iron gates.

"I would have given her my bedchamber," Nicolas said. He and Louis stood in the torchlight of the porch. "One hears Madame de Motteville has been injured."

"Yes," said Louis. "It was shocking. It would spoil your fête to speak of it. I'll tell you of it tomorrow."

"Will you do me the honor of following me, sire? I have a small token of regard to give you."

They went into a chamber on the other end of the salon. Nicolas walked to a cupboard, took a key from a pocket, unlocked a door, found what he was looking for, held it out to Louis. "For you, Your Majesty, with my kindest and most humble and most loyal regard. I am your servant in all things."

Nicolas's name was written on the outside of a note. Louis turned the paper over and over, not wanting to read it in front of the viscount. "Thank you, Viscount. Your kindness, like your hospitality, overwhelms. Please, return to your many guests."

Nicolas bowed.

Louis walked to a branch of candles and opened the note.

I'm being held captive by order of the king. I beg your aid and tell
you I have in my hands a secret which their majesties will do all in
their power to hide. There is another child, another prince. I beg you,
for the sake of this royal prince, come to our aid. I write this from
Monaco and am your most humble servant. Cinq Mars, captain in
the cardinal's musketeers.

Louis crumbled the note. Nicolas handed this over as if it were little or
nothing. Had he no idea of what he gave back? Or did he toy with Louis,
the way a cat did a mouse? Louis held the note to a candle and watched it
take fire. Inside him was a fire, white-hot and unspoken. He didn't move
until bits of ash fell onto the viscount's polished floor, some of the ash
wafting out the window into the lanterned night.

❧❧❧

A clock had tolled three of the morning. Louise and Choisy walked
toward the hill that held the great statue of Hercules. The farther they
were from the house the more magical the night. Soon, the music playing in the salon was as faint as an echo, and there was only the sound of
water from the fountains, the sound of their shoes on the gravel. Most of
the guests were near the house, seated at one of the many tables set in the
gardens or ranged upon the terraces or inside dancing. It was even quieter
once they reached the mound that held the Hercules.

"Who is that following us?" asked Choisy.

"My musketeer."

They sat down against the enormous base of the statue.

"I hear there are to be fireworks. We'll watch them from here,"
Choisy said.

"I can't. I have to be where His Majesty can see me."

Choisy took her hand, kissed it twice before settling it in his own. "I am
leaving court for a time. I'm not certain how long I'll be gone. I behaved
badly the last time we were together, and I didn't want that to be your last
memory of me. You have been a dear friend, and I love you. That statement
requires no answer. Your welfare will be foremost in my prayers. If ever you
need me, you are to send for me. My mother will know where I am."

He moved closer, pulling her against his side. "Take Julie for your
servant once she's old enough. You'll have such need of loyal servants."
There was so much more he wanted to say, various warnings and advice,
but he knew she wouldn't listen. If she was still in power when he returned,
he'd become her counselor. She was going to need one. She was about to
become a real player in the treacherous shoals of court. Would she stay

upright? Could she? Well, at least he wouldn't be here to witness either her joy or her sorrow.

"Write me," he said, "care of my mother. Write me and tell me how you are. His Majesty needn't know."

"There are no secrets between us."

Love and pride were in her voice. No secrets, thought Choisy. Was she such a fool?

"We must go back."

He didn't argue. "There's your musketeer. Wave to show him you haven't been ravished." And when she stood up, he said, "Look at the château from here. Is this not the most beautiful sight you've ever seen in your life?"

Everywhere lanterns outlined beauty, the straightness of the paths, the many fountains, the château itself rising up into night. "The viscount is indeed an impressive man," said Choisy.

They walked hand in hand for a time, until they were close to the house, then Choisy bowed to her and left. She walked toward Madame, the others with her. People were pouring out of the house, into the gardens. There was a collective gasp from those around her as rockets shot up into the air.

"Oh, look!" cried Henriette.

The rockets' flames made fleurs-de-lis. On the Grand Canal, a whale of fire appeared. Now from behind every statue in the garden, a rocket was released. It was as if they were standing in a fantastic day made by the light of the rockets, their patterns, L's for Louis, M's for the queen, lighting this world of the viscount. Everyone stood still, not wanting to move. Maria Teresa, seated in a chair with wheels, clapped her hands.

"I'm so glad I stayed awake for this," she said to Louis.

When the last light died in the sky, there was a collective sigh.

"How beautiful," said Henriette.

But now, from the cupola that crowned the viscount's wondrous salon dome, more fireworks were set off. They sailed into the sky, dropping at the far end of the garden, making an arch of jeweled light falling to the ground in a shower of splendid sparks, showing off his house and gardens for one last time. On and on they went, and when the last one faded to nothing, people blinked, not wanting to speak.

Louise shivered. Sometime during the magical display, Louis had come to stand behind her, kissed the back of her neck, just under where her hair was swept up in its fashionable bun, a quick kiss, like the touch of moth's wings. Whore, said Guy. Others would say it, too, but not to her face. She'd have to learn to pretend they weren't thinking it. She put her hand to the place he'd kissed. How odd that she didn't feel like a whore at all.

Guy's words scalded. She could feel something in her moving a little into shadow. It was something carefree and innocent.

It was over. Other courtiers would stay until dawn, when the viscount would feed them a breakfast, but Louis was escorting his sleeping queen home. She was even now in a special bed they'd created in her carriage. He walked up the broad stairs of the terrace that faced the gardens. Nicolas stood in the central doorway of his grand salon rotunda. "Thank you for such exquisite splendor, viscount."

"All inspired by you. The honor of your regard outshines everything."

"And thank you for your gift."

Their eyes met and held until Nicolas said, "You have my every loyalty."

"That gladdens me. I'm told Le Nôtre designed your gardens."

"Yes. He's somewhere about working with a fountain that hasn't spewed to his satisfaction."

"Give him my compliments, and my compliments to you. The house is magnificent, the fête was even more so." He stepped up onto his saddle. He'd ride back, let the late-night dark receive his thoughts, and there were many of them. Henriette and Philippe were staying, so he could not say good-bye to Louise or hold her a final time. Out of the corner of his eye, he saw Fanny flit by, and then someone was at his boot. He looked down. A groom held up a note. From Louise, thought Louis joyfully, and he spurred his horse toward a burning torch and opened it.

It was a Mazarinade. Words spewed at him.

> *The Cardinal is at a loss about*
> *How he should f--- the Queen*
> *Never having f----- any c---*

He crumpled the paper without finishing it and stood in his stirrups and held the crushed note to the torch and let the fire devour it. The second betrayal burned to ash this night, and now he knew who sent the Mazarinades. How simple it was. How much less frightening than he had imagined. The next time he came to this chateau, it would be to choose what would be his.

"There," Nicolas said to his wife, as they watched the king's entourage weave its way though their gates, "he enjoyed himself."

"Really?" she replied. She had a clear-headed sense that Nicolas respected. "And I've had two different people tell me tonight that there's talk that you're going to be arrested."

Later, he asked Catherine.

"Impossible!" she exclaimed. She rubbed against him like a cat. "You've just summoned all France to eat from your dish. He wouldn't dare."

SEPTEMBER 1661

CHAPTER 40

The Marshall de Gramont rode through the gates of Vaux-le-Vicomte. The viscount wasn't there; he was in the province of Brittany with the king, who was presiding over a meeting of the provincial assembly, but the château was bustling with people—workmen, servants, family, and visitors—for stories about the magnificence of the fête and the château's beauty were already spreading throughout France and beyond its borders, and people came daily to see it.

The marshall tossed the reins of his horse to a stable boy and walked toward one of the sets of handsome outbuildings. They flanked the front courtyards of the château and made their own world. He walked upstairs, waving away Guy's servant, and opened the door to the chambers in which Guy was staying. His son was bent over a table, writing. The marshall watched him for a long moment until, finally aware that he was being watched, Guy raised his head and, startled to see who stood there, jumped to his feet, dropping his pen. "Sir! I thought you were in Brittany."

"So I was."

"How is the viscount?"

But his father didn't answer, instead walked forward to the table strewn with papers and rummaged through them. Guy put out his hand as if to stop him.

"He told me it was so," said the marshall, "but I wanted to see for myself." He held up a paper, Guy's handwriting scrawled across it.

"Buggerer of goats, buggerer of boys, buggerer in all ways," he read, his voice indifferent, as if the words weren't slurs of the worst kind. He let go the paper and, slowly, it drifted to the floor.

"How you shame me," he said. His hands moved through other papers on the table until he was holding up a pamphlet, the one from which the damning words came, its type tiny and curving and difficult to read. "How came you by this?"

Guy closed his eyes a moment. "At the Palais-Royal shops, I saw an old wooden chest, curious carving on it, which amused me, and so I bought it. Inside were a hundred or more of these old Mazarinades." He smiled so that his father wouldn't see the pain he felt at his father's contempt. "They made interesting reading for someone who was a boy in the civil wars. A crime to let them be forgotten, I thought." He shrugged, insouciance covering mortification.

"Where is this chest?"

Guy pointed.

"You will burn its contents and these papers upon the table, now, in my presence, please."

He stood in silence as Guy lit a fire, brought paper after paper to it, and burned them.

When the last pamphlet was curling in the flames, Guy said, "Have you come to arrest me or to banish me?"

"I would have done either, most gladly, but His Majesty was kinder than I am."

"His Majesty?" Guy cut in. "Did not the viscount tell you of this?"

"I've had little conversation with the viscount, who busies himself receiving relatives and friends and those who come to worship at the shrine of his importance. His Majesty requests your presence in a regiment. He reads you well. War will cool your fire or kill you, one or the other. He has the grace not to be angry with you for my sake, for the sake of your growing up together, for the sake of his brother's affection for you, but I am angry for him. Why did you do this?"

For old time's sake, thought Guy, because they were there, because I wanted to make him tremble, because it amused me, because I could, because I'm bored, because I'm bad.

When there was no answer, his father said, "You are to leave this place today and go to your mother in Paris and take your leave of her. The orders for your military service are with my chamberlain." He held out his hand. "Farewell."

Just like that, they were finished. Guy knew better than to argue or cajole. He knelt to kiss his father's hand, looked into his father's face, and saw there was no softness there, for his father's code of conduct was rigid and unchanging. He listened to his father's retreating footsteps on the stairs as outside the window he heard servants calling to one another. Before the viscount had left for Brittany, he and Guy and a visitor had sat drinking and talking in the château's glorious salon, the gardens visible everywhere their eyes fell. The visitor was an English count, who had traveled across the channel specifically to see Vaux-le-Vicomte, to meet the viscount. Talk had drifted, as talk will when the wine is good and the afternoon better, to the vagaries of life, and the Englishman had quoted to them from his book of prayer, translating the words slowly, and sometimes badly, into French. The race is not to the swift, he'd said, nor the battle to the strong, nor riches to men of understanding nor favor to men of skill, but time and chance happen to them all. Guy didn't know why he thought of those words, but they remained in his head all the way to Paris.

⚶

Nicolas stepped into the sedan chair that would take him back to the house of a cousin where he slept during this sojourn in Brittany. The king had kept him after this morning's council meeting to talk about the gift of money which the provincial assembly had presented the crown, and the conversation, easy, complimentary, had lifted Nicolas's mood. He'd had a fever, then chills, since the fête, disturbing dreams and images playing in his mind. Those around him were in a kind of fever themselves, his wife and certain of his friends convinced he was to be arrested, urging him to retreat to Belle Isle and remain there. Yet there was no warning from Her Majesty; from her confessor; from poor, ill Madame de Motteville. To go to Belle Isle would be such an open move, such a direct hit. It would splinter to pieces his summer of soothing the king, would stir up the hornet's nest he very much imagined His Majesty's temper when crossed might be.

"There's people who want to talk to you, your greatness," one of the sedan-chair bearers told him. "Shall we stop?"

A crowd was gathered before the town's cathedral, petitioners with requests for who knew what—Brittany was after all the seat of his power, where he'd begun as a local official—and Nicolas felt both ennui at the obligations of his position and satisfaction at this evidence of his importance. The king simply needed time to accept Nicolas's importance, that was all. "Yes," he said.

It was a mistake he would mull over for the rest of his life.

⚶

Sacred fingers of the Christ, thought D'Artagnan, breaking into a sweat, have I missed him? The viscount wasn't in the courtyard. He put his fingers to his mouth and whistled, and some fifteen musketeers were immediately at his side.

"Follow me," he ordered, and he ran out of the courtyard, through the castle's gate, but there, in the distance, in front of the town cathedral, was the viscount's sedan chair, its bearers having set it to the ground, because people had crowded to present the viscount with petitions. "Surround the chair," D'Artagnan told his men.

"A message for the viscount!" he said loudly as he pushed through the crowd.

Nicolas pulled himself up and out of the chair and took off his hat in a gesture of courtesy, smiling his charming smile. "Lieutenant D'Artagnan, what have you for me?"

D'Artagnan was curt. "I arrest you by the king's orders."

People stepped back. The chair bearers looked at one another. Nicolas's hat dropped out of his hands and into the dirt. "May I see the warrant?"

D'Artagnan gave it to him. He stared down at the words for a long time, and when he raised his eyes again, his face was white, the way it had been when his fever first began.

"Let's affect this without a fuss," he said, and he sat back down in the sedan chair, his hands gripped tight on its arms as he stared straight ahead.

❧❀❧

Waiting, Louis stood at a window in the castle of the Duke of Brittany. In the courtyard below were musketeers. He'd told everyone he was going hunting as an excuse for their presence, but they were assembled to chase down the viscount, if need be. Behind him, now that his council meeting was over, mingled courtiers and friends, various ministers and local officials and members of the prominent Breton families.

Have we spun the game too long? thought Louis. Was it a mistake to come to Brittany? Regiments stood ready to land on the viscount's island. A messenger from its governor had been captured in the early hours of this morning with a message for the viscount. The note, hidden in the heel of the messenger's boot, warned the viscount of the presence of the king's troops. Am I too late? thought Louis. Colbert was convinced the viscount would bolt, would commence a war from his island. Had D'Artagnan failed? Had the viscount eluded him?

A musketeer came running through the castle's gate. He saw Louis at the window and waved his hat back and forth. Louis closed his eyes, then he turned around to face the men assembled here, not a woman among them. He'd left his love, his wife, the ladies who graced his mettlesome, proud, self-seeking court, as well as his brother, at Fontainebleau, where they would be safest. Under his shirt, in a pocket sewn in his doublet, was one of Louise's gloves. He moved his hand to it, touching it for good luck.

The chamber was gradually silencing as men realized the king was watching them. One conversation after another ended, and they waited.

Everyone who was important was here, several officers of the crown, his royal cousins.

"I've arrested the Viscount Nicolas," Louis said.

There was a shocked silence, a moment of absolute quiet in the chamber. What he announced was a thunderclap over their heads. A million thoughts flew through Louis's mind. It seemed to him that he saw every face and read the feelings behind the masks of flesh. His minister of war, one of his inner three and an ally of the viscount, wiped perspiration from his upper lip. Still no one spoke. A ballad Louis had heard a few nights earlier, a local ballad of this province with its treacherous seacoast, went dancing through his head along with thoughts of all that might happen now. Would credit hold? Would there be war?

The sea has donned her robe of green, went the ballad, her robe of green, 'tis hope they say, evening has come, gone is the day, the sea has donned her robe of green with all about the skirt a screen of the ocean's fairest flowers. Lilting had been the voices singing the ballad. His thoughts had been of Louise. The sea has donned her robe of green, let love be ours. How could the viscount have had the audacity to attempt to bribe her?

Paris would be in an uproar once the news reached them in a week or so. Who here would be disloyal? Which of his provinces would revolt first? Colbert's bet was this one. The musketeers in the courtyard waited. If he wasn't downstairs among them in half an hour's time, they would storm this castle.

"I thought it necessary," he began the speech he'd delivered a thousand times in his mind, "and now I shall explain why…"

He didn't know it would be the first sentence of an absolute monarchy that would become the envy of Europe and the triumph of his life's work, that only the incompetence of great-great-grandsons and the marching forward of time—the birth of the ideas of independence espoused in the new world across the sea—would unravel what he set into motion with this moment.

"Long live the king," someone shouted when he was done, and others took up the cry, and he walked to the window and showed himself to his troop below, his heart pounding, because he could not yet know there would be no war; just as he could not yet know that his will, and his alone, would become the crux of a kingdom and the backbone of two hundred years of power and the last thing he would regret before he died.

READING GROUP GUIDE

1. Louis is twenty-two when the novel opens in 1661. What do you remember about being twenty-two? Did you have to make a difficult decision at twenty-two or face difficult circumstances?

2. What obligations is Louis born into? How might they be difficult?

3. In the seventeenth century, there was no concept of adolescence. Young people were pitched into life, ready or not. Did you have to grow up too soon? How has that impacted your life today?

4. Louis is unable to bring himself to love his wife. Is this her fault or his?

5. How might arranged marriages be difficult? What is the seventeenth century's concept of marriage?

6. The young queen of France has grown up in a Spanish convent; the only man she'd ever met was her father. Is she prepared for the court she marries into? Should she have changed?

7. What is the role of a princess and/or a queen? What is their primary responsibility?

8. The real life story of Princess Henriette is a riveting one. What fairy tale does her story remind you of?

9. Should Princess Henriette have refused the king's admiration? Would you have done so?

10. Louis has a complicated relationship with his brother, very much impacted by the nature of power and the nobility around him. Do you think he could have been kinder to Philippe? Why or why not?

11. The brothers are rivals in many ways. Is "all fair in love and war"?

12. Louis's brother Philippe is gay. How does this impact his presence at court? Do you know someone who is gay in your family, among your friends, or at work? What have you witnessed about how he or she is perceived?

13. Would Louise de la Baume le Blanc have behaved differently if her mother had been at court? What kind of influence does Choisy have over her?

14. Louise de la Baume le Blanc seems to bring out a special quality in Louis. How would you describe it? Why would she be attractive to him?

15. In France, there is great controversy over Louis XIV's arrest of Nicolas Fouquet. Is the Viscount Nicolas simply doing as has always been done as far as filling his coffers?

16. The boy in the iron mask seems to be Louis's brother. Why is this dangerous?

17. Loyalty is one of the themes of the book. How do these different characters display loyalty:

    a. Viscount Nicolas
    b. Colbert
    c. D'Artagnon
    d. Henriette
    e. Philippe
    f. Maria Teresa
    g. Louise
    h. Guy
    i. Olympe
    j. Catherine
    k. Duchess de Chevreuse

18. Have you ever been disloyal? Is loyalty easy or difficult?

AUTHOR'S NOTE

These four months in the life of Louis XIV when he was twenty-two capture a moment in history when he showed all that was the best in him: ardor, passion, gallantry, courage, and resourcefulness. I couldn't resist him. Much of what I've written in this novel is true. What fun to guess the rest. Here is a glimpse of the history I based the story upon:

The iron mask: This is one of the enduring legends of French history and fiction. There is no definite proof of a man or boy in an iron mask. There was, however, a man who wore a mask of black silk, who was treated with utmost respect, kept isolated from all other prisoners, and who died without a name on record. No one knows who he was.

The arrest: When he was twenty-two, Louis had his powerful superintendent of finance arrested in September 1661 to the astonishment and shock of all around him. It was an earthquake in the terrain of court and finances. Financiers and tax farmers were brought to trial and fined. Colbert reorganized France's system of finance and its system of governance. The superintendent, named Nicolas Fouquet, remained in prison at Pignerol for the rest of his life.

Nicolas Fouquet: He was witty, polished, cultured, the unnamed superintendent of art and literature as well as the named superintendent of finance. He patronized many writers and artists. Controversy still thrives in France about whether his arrest was deserved or not.

Vaux-le-Vicomte: Fouquet's estate exists to this day and has been lovingly restored. Louis claimed the three artisans Fouquet had summoned to work together—Le Vau, Le Brun, and Le Nôtre—and put them to recreating Versailles, which was transformed from a hunting lodge and tryst for love to the most famous palace in Europe.

Love: Louis XIV was faithful for the first year of his marriage, but by the summer of 1661 was paying enough attention to his sister-in-law to make scandal bubble. Then talk died back, but until late autumn only Louis knew why: someone unexpected had captured his heart.

A blue jacket: In a romantic, tender, secret gesture, Louis XIV wore a blue jacket, likely sewn by Louise, for fourteen days straight in the fall of 1661.

Louise: She is known in history as Louise de la Vallière. She never stopped loving the king but became a nun of the Carmelites in 1674. Queen Maria Teresa was among the huge crowd to witness the ceremony of her taking the veil, but Louis XIV was not.

Athénaïs: Ah, readers, that is indeed another story...

ACKNOWLEDGMENTS

For help in research: the late Nancyhelen Fischer of The French Connection; Henri Leers, translator; Count Patrice de Vogüé, owner of Vaux-le-Vicomte; Sophie Hubert of the Fontainebleau Museum Château; Nick Poyntz of the blog mercuriuspoliticus.wordpress.com; Professor Jeffrey Merrick of the University of Wisconsin-Milwaukee. For serving as first readers and/or proofreading eyes: Joan Boote, Ann Bradford, Alice Lemos, Chris Ritter, Sandi Stromberg, Tammie Thomas. For manuscript cleanup: Kristin Kearns, Burning Designer Studios. For support: Joyce Boatright, Sandi Stromberg, Jean Naggar, my longtime and very dear agent, and Jennifer Weltz of the Jean Naggar Literary Agency. For revision suggestions and seeing the book to completion: Heather Lazare of the Crown Publishing Group. For providing a quiet place to finish last revisions: the Helene Wurlitzer Foundation. For continued belief in my work: Dominique Raccah of Sourcebooks.

ABOUT THE AUTHOR

K arleen Koen is the *New York Times* best-
selling author of *Through a Glass Darkly*,
as well as *Now Face to Face* and *Dark
Angels*, an Indie Next bestseller. *Before Versailles*
has been included among the year's best historical
fiction by the *Library Journal*, *Pittsburgh Historical
Fiction Examiner*, and *RT Book Reviews*. Koen is an
experienced freelance writer, magazine editor, and
writing workshop instructor. Visit her online at
karleenkoen.net and karleenkoen.wordpress.com.

Through a Glass Darkly

Karleen Koen

*Sparkles with all of the passion, extravagance,
and scandal of a grand and glorious era*

As opulent and passionate as the eighteenth century it celebrates, *Through a Glass Darkly* will sweep you away to the splendors of a lost era. From aristocrats to scoundrels, its rich, vivid characters create their own immortality. Here is the story of a great family ruled by a dowager of extraordinary power, of a young woman seeking love in a world of English luxury and French intrigue, and of a man haunted by a secret that could turn all their dreams to ashes…

Praise for **Through a Glass Darkly**:

"A brilliant historical novel. A lovely romance, a gripping
character study…There's something for everyone in *Through
a Glass Darkly.*" —*Richmond Times-Dispatch*

"A heady mixture of sophistication and melodrama, elegance,
decadence and homely virtues…stylishly wicked, smartly
written, and unabashedly bold." —*Detroit Free Press*

"Koen is a graceful, natural writer, and *Through a Glass
Darkly* is a notable accomplishment." —*Kirkus Reviews*

For more Karleen Koen books, visit:

www.sourcebooks.com